Book 3
of
The Dimension Guardian Series

Dimension Guardian
The Realm of Humans
Fate

K.J. Amidon

www.the-amiverse.com

Website: www.kjamidon.com

Published by K.J. Amidon

ISBN: 978-0-9832280-4-2

Cover art by K.J. Amidon

Printed in the United States of America

Dedicated to:

My family and friends who inspire me every day.

My 13-year-old self who thought that the original write of this series was good enough to publish—you sweet, naïve child.

Table of Contents

Chapter One

Yokouro DeVastes strode confidently through the crowded halls of the main establishment of the Trade. Employees were occupied helping demon lords as they shopped through the workers the Trade offered, getting ready for the harvest season. Yokouro had already sent Kakuri through the halls to handle the needs of the DeVastes palace while he went into the back portion of the Trade to Juki and Rutu's office.

There were many familiar faces among the patrons of the Trade, and lower-level lords that had not been present during the most recent DeVastes Territory Lord's Meeting rushed to greet Yokouro, bowing their heads and greeting him emphatically. He smiled politely, but made it clear that he was not interested in a lengthy interaction.

As the main Trade establishment was a collection of large canvas tents, Yokouro had to walk through many different sections to get to Juki and Rutu's office at the back. It was far quieter than anywhere else in the Trade, which made him feel as though he could finally catch his breath from the forced social niceties.

Yokouro did not bother to announce himself before walking into the office. Juki was sitting at his desk, engrossed in work, while Rutu's desk on the other side of the office was unoccupied, cluttered with paperwork and parchments.

"Yokouro," Juki greeted without lifting his head. "What brings you here today?"

"Kakuri is looking for some more workers. Your employees said you were back here, so I thought it was a good time to meet up and discuss a few other things that he doesn't need to know about."

"This is not a good time, Yokouro," Juki said. "This is our busiest time of year."

"I know, but your employees have everything under control. Otherwise, you wouldn't be hiding back here."

"I'm not hiding. I'm working," Juki corrected, lifting the parchment he was reading over.

Yokouro glanced at Rutu's desk, pointing.

"Where's Rutu?"

"At home sick," the older lord answered, tossing the parchment atop the others on his desk and leaning back in his chair, rubbing his temple with a heavy sigh. Yokouro looked over his drawn expression, taking note of the bandages around his right hand and the bruise forming at the base of Juki's jaw.

"Really?" he asked skeptically.

Juki opened his eyes just long enough to give Yokouro a warning glare.

"I'm just saying," Yokouro said, raising his hands peacefully, "there have been a lot of rumors."

"I am aware…"

"If it's going to be such an issue between you two, why don't you just let him help you kill Kawakara?" Yokouro asked.

"It's complicated, Yokouro."

"So you keep saying," he said. "But I need my allies strong moving forward. And with you getting beaten every other day and Rutu also tearing you a new one every time he sees you, I have to insist that you deal with the issue as quickly as possible. I can't have my best man so distracted."

"Yokouro, if you do not want me to lose my temper, drop the subject and tell me why you came all the way back here to talk to me," Juki warned, his hand falling back to the arm of his chair as he turned his cold eyes on the younger demon lord.

Yokouro contemplated how much he could push Juki, but he could tell from the darkness in his eyes that Juki was too tired to placate Yokouro for long, and the younger demon knew better than to truly upset Juki Kage.

"Have you been paying attention to the dealings within the Middle Dimension?"

"No more than usual, why?"

"Then I guess you have heard that my name was leaked to the public in relation to the attack on the school in the Darkness Realm," Yokouro said with a triumphant smile. "My *full* name."

Juki sighed. "Why would you do that?"

"Because it will stoke the fire," Yokouro said, placing his hands over the parchments on Juki's desk and leaning toward him. "This is a good thing. Slowly, I'll release information about some of my more nefarious accomplishments, and the humans will soon be hunting down anyone they suspect of being a demon as they become more filled with fear. And the lynchings will bring more demons to my side."

"Yokouro…" Juki groaned, rubbing his face roughly.

"You know, you and Rutu have both been doing a lot of that annoyed-tone and rubbing-your-face thing lately."

"Because we're frustrated," Juki said. "We've already told you that sparking a war between demons and humans is a bad idea."

"Why? Demons can overpower humans easily. It will hardly be a drawn-out war."

"When you scare humans enough to start killing anyone they think is different from them, you cause more destruction than cohesion. You think the demons will start rallying together? You're an Old Blood Lord, you know that they're going to turn to *us* for guidance on how to handle it. Without a leader, demons are just as disorganized as humans."

"Well, that is what I'm hoping for," Yokouro said with a strong nod. "And in the chaos of trying to hunt down demons, humans will start killing one another. You know how easily fear can turn humans on each other. And their panicked crimes will only strengthen me for my fight with Dalton."

Juki closed his eyes and leaned back in his chair again, looking as though he could not muster the strength to argue with Yokouro further.

"I told you that I've thought this through."

"Yes, you have," Juki said quietly.

"But you don't approve?"

"I'm trying to think of how to best serve my subjects through this plan of yours," Juki corrected.

"This will serve *all* demons," Yokouro declared. "This is a good thing, Juki. And as soon as I can get Dalton and his dragon magic fully integrated, the faster we can move forward putting demons in their rightful place at the top of the food chain."

"If you push things too fast, Yokouro, you are going to break him," Juki warned. "Dalton has barely cracked that wall between him and his power. Give him time to chip away at it. Don't stress him to the point where it shatters. It could kill him."

"I don't have the luxury of waiting," Yokouro growled, leaning even closer to Juki, his fingers flexing over the parchments, causing his nails to tear into the papers. "I need to end this. You have no idea what it feels like to have this clawing away at you every waking moment. I have conflicting destinies, Juki. I'm trapped like this until I can defeat that damn dragon spirit inside Dalton, and I feel like it's going to tear me apart. Do you have any idea what that's like?"

"No," Juki said honestly.

"It's like having a constant ache in your muscles. Like you're straining to hold your arms and legs in their sockets and keep your eyes from collapsing under the pressure. Over nine thousand years I have dealt with this pain. I have had to deal with hopping back and forth between the Demon Realm that wanted me dead, and bowing to that idiot Antiquan the Third all the while having this power radiating through me. I cannot wait any longer. I need this to *end*."

"I understand that you're in pain, Yokouro," Juki said. "But being reckless with Dalton makes it more likely you'll have to endure the pain longer. You've been lucky so far and everything has worked in your favor, but your luck might not hold. You must remember that it's not only Dalton you're facing. There are four other very powerful Guardians at his side."

"What, the two baby humans with their wolf and that mutt Keito?" Yokouro scoffed. "I'm keeping my eye on Eclipse and Mitoki. I've already got them well confined. And with our new ally," he said with a devious smile, "Dalton will be just as penned."

"If you keep spreading yourself thin, you're going to start letting things slip," Juki said. "Just like your control of the Elders."

Yokouro groaned, standing straight with a roll of his eyes. "The Elders. They're just morons. They can't even properly handle the information I've given them."

"You've got a far more extensive set up in the DPC than the Elders. Use them instead if you think the Elders are being ineffective," Juki suggested.

"Half of the contacts I have in the council are Kage intelligence agents. It's *your* set-up in the DPC, not mine." He let out a soft snicker. "Makes me wonder where else your spies are lurking."

Juki's face broke into a cold smile. "It's best you don't know."

Yokouro grinned as well to mask his curiosity. He had tried not to think about the extensive network of connections Juki and Rutu had at their disposal, but occasionally, he had wondered how many Kage spies were watching him during his endeavors.

"Speaking of intelligence," Yokouro said, "there is another reason I came to see you."

"Oh?"

Yokouro crossed his arms. "You never informed me that Dalton had an apprentice."

Juki was stoic, staring at the younger demon lord with a carefully-schooled expression. The silence and impassive face caused Yokouro's grin to widen.

"Now, if I didn't know you better, I would be worried about what other information you've been keeping from me," he said. "Why keep silent about the boy?"

"There is no reason to involve him," Juki said, his tone even and controlled.

"There certainly is," Yokouro disagreed. "He is the easiest way for me to get Dalton to incorporate his dragon energy. And I think I know how I'm going to do it."

Juki heaved a sigh and stood, grabbing his outer robe from the back of his chair and adjusting it over his shoulders.

"We should talk to Rutu about this," he declared. "He figured you would start scheming ways to use the boy, so he's made some preparations."

"Already?" Yokouro asked, surprised. He followed Juki out of the office through the back door, trailing him to the small barn where Juki's horse was penned. "Does it ever frighten you just how much Rutu knows in advance?"

Juki chuckled, shaking his head. "Every damn day."

Chapter Two

The parts Dalton liked least about his job as top-ranked Guardian were press conferences and paperwork, and since the news had gotten out that Yokouro DeVastes was one of the two demons that attacked the school three weeks previous, Dalton had been swamped with nothing but press conferences and paperwork.

Trying to keep everyone calm, the only thing he could think to say was that an investigation was being launched to determine the accuracy of the claim that Lord Yokouro DeVastes was, indeed, a threat once again.

He hated pretending that he did not already know the truth.

Dalton walked back to his office from his fourth press conference that day, head hanging in exhaustion. He was tired, and more than slightly annoyed that he had been sleeping in his office for the past three nights rather than returning home to his family.

Overwhelmed anew by the stacks of files heaped on his desk, he groaned as he closed his office door. He allowed himself a few moments to privately rant about how much Yokouro had taken over his life before he forced himself to sit and work.

Not even two weeks had passed since leaving the Darkness Realm and he was already more exhausted from paperwork than from the Guardian Tournament.

Near the end of the day, just when Dalton was giving himself some hope that he could return home that night, there was a knock at his door.

"Come in," he called, setting aside the file he had been reading and closing his eyes tight as he leaned back in his chair.

A man slowly opened the door, taking in Dalton's oddly-disheveled state worriedly.

"Forgive me, Guardian Teban," he said, stepping into the office with a stack of papers in the crook of his arm. "Do you have a moment?"

"Of course," Dalton said in reflex, standing to offer a handshake to the other Guardian. "And please, call me Dalton. I'm terribly sorry, I'm sure we've met before, but I cannot remember your name."

"Maneth," he answered, taking Dalton's hand. The longer, sharper nails told Dalton that the average-looking man in front of him was a demon Guardian.

"What can I help you with, Maneth?"

"I was told to bring these to you. They need your signature," he explained, passing the stack of papers across the desk.

"What are they?"

"Investigation propositions for the demon Guardians," Maneth answered, lowering his head as he spoke. Dalton's eyes shot back to Maneth's face.

"We're investigating demon Guardians?" he asked.

"The Elders have asked that demons within the council branches be investigated to be certain no one allies with Yokouro," Maneth explained.

"And Sanyai agreed to this?"

"They did this while she was away," the demon said vaguely. "She's in the Human Realm trying to bring some demon refugees to the Middle Dimension."

"Why doesn't she set them up with a safe house in the Human Realm?"

"No other realm offers refugee status to demons," Maneth said. "If a demon is discovered in any other realm, and is not a part of Council, they are turned over to the demon Guardians and, eventually, returned to their lord back home."

"You mean their Old Blood Lord?" Dalton asked. Maneth blinked, surprised that Dalton had knowledge of the Old Blood Lords.

"If the refugee has some social status, maybe," he answered once he shook off his shock. "The Old Blood Lords are busy enough without dealing with every defecting demon."

"Were you raised in the Demon Realm?" Dalton asked, motioning for Maneth to sit in one of the chairs at the front of his desk.

"No. I was born there, but my family sought refuge when I was about two," he explained.

"Why did they leave the realm?"

"My family lost their title," he said. "We weren't being hunted down or anything, but my family lost face. And my parents felt it was important for us to leave entirely to avoid the shame."

"Who was your Old Blood Lord?"

"We run Kage."

"Do you still claim loyalty to them?"

"Absolutely," Maneth said. "Demons are very loyal to their Old Blood Lords. It's a point of pride for us to defend our lords."

Dalton drummed his fingers over the stack of papers Maneth had brought.

"May I ask you something?" he asked. "Surely demon Guardians knew who Yokouro was long before this information leak. Why didn't they speak up?"

"We were ordered not to."

"But this demon is a mass-murderer, and you are *Guardians*."

Maneth sighed heavily. "You have no idea how difficult it is to be a demon Guardian," he said. "When we're sworn in, one of the things we must vow is to keep quiet about the Old Blood Lords. But in vowing to do that, we put ourselves at risk for claims that we withheld information, as was the case with Yokouro."

Dalton took a moment to think over what Maneth had said. He had been extremely frustrated with the way Keito withheld information from him, but he had never thought about how difficult it was for the demons to walk the line between breaking their vows as a Guardian and upholding the oath.

"Do you happen to know what Old Blood Lord Keito pledges to?" Dalton asked.

"I'm fairly certain he claims loyalty to Vestera."

"Is that why demons under the DeVastes name hate him so much?"

Maneth laughed lightly. "Demons are very divided when it comes to Keito DeVero. Across all lands, demons either worship Keito or despise him. He's not someone demons want to get involved with unless they're in his good graces. He is extremely powerful."

"But he's not as powerful as the Old Blood Lords," Dalton said.

"No, no, of course not," Maneth agreed. "I meant politically. Keito is the Wandering Child. That affords him an enormous amount of political power."

"What does that name mean? The Wandering Child?" Dalton pressed. "I've heard a lot of demons call him that."

Maneth hesitated. Dalton's heart sank, certain Maneth was going to pull the same trick as other demons and claim that it was not his place to say.

"I really shouldn't tell you," he said slowly. Dalton felt his tired eyes begin to roll. "But with everything going on with the Old Blood Lords, it would be wrong to keep you in the dark."

Dalton was unsuccessful at stopping his jaw from dropping. Maneth laughed.

"I know, I'm actually going to tell you something most demons wouldn't," he said knowingly. "And I hope it doesn't get you into any trouble. Wandering Child is the nickname Keito was given as a kid, long before he joined the Guardians. He's actually quite notorious in the realm. Even without a title, there are very few demons who do not know his name. There are things about his past that you could not even begin to imagine."

"Like how he was a thief as a teenager?"

"I'm fairly certain he was younger when he was a bandit," Maneth corrected. "But Keito's done even worse things. A lot of people have tried to attack him and found themselves dead as a result."

"People like who?"

"All kinds," Maneth said with a shrug. "First it was because Keito was a mixed breed. Since he was born on the DeVastes land, and they can be purist to a fault, there were many who sought to eliminate him. And when he lived with the Kages, he—"

"Wait, *what*?" Dalton interrupted. "He lived with the Kages? Like on the Kage Territory?"

"No, in the Kage Palace with Lord Juki," Maneth corrected. "He lived there for quite some time, I believe. After that, he was brought under Vestera's protection. That's why he's called the Wandering Child. He's been a big part of all the lands in the Demon Realm. Lords Juki and Rutu have been known to favor Keito and protect him at all costs. Vestera has almost started wars with the Kage Territory to get Keito away from them. And, technically, the DeVastes Territory is Keito's home, and he's been fighting against Yokouro for decades. He holds an enormous amount of political power because the Old Blood Lords are so invested in him."

"How did he get into such a high social circle? I thought you said he didn't have a title."

"He doesn't," the demon said. "As for why all the Old Bloods took such an interest in him…" He shrugged. "You're going to have to ask Keito for that answer."

"Keito doesn't ally at all with the DeVastes Territory though, right?" Dalton asked nervously.

"Definitely not with Yokouro. But he probably has some respect for Kakuri."

"The one who was Old Blood Lord when Yokouro was…well, dead, I guess," Dalton added, getting the confirmation from the nodding demon Guardian.

"I wouldn't worry about Keito's loyalty to you," Maneth assured. "If anything, Keito's connections right now are invaluable."

Dalton's eyes dropped back to the investigation proposals.

"But doesn't that mean he'll also be investigated?" he asked.

"Possibly," Maneth said. "And any demon that claims DeVastes or Kage loyalty will be scrutinized closely."

"Including you."

"And Sanyai. She's also loyal to the Kages."

Dalton sighed, putting his head in one hand. "What a mess." He continued to drum his fingers over the stacks of papers. "If I sign off on these, who will conduct the investigations?"

"The Elders want to put together a committee. I did hear a rumor about Keito being on that committee, since he is the Wandering Child and can spot followers faster than any other demon. But I don't know how true that is." Maneth dropped his gaze, pursing his lips as he debated what to say. "If these investigations *do* happen, it would be very important to have Keito on the committee. The council is getting into dangerous waters with the demons."

"What do you mean?"

"Demons are already limited in their privileges within Council. Demons in the realm are getting nervous about how far the DPC will go. They're thinking this is just the start and that soon humans will be hunting and slaughtering all demons. Keito has some political weight he can use if things get out of hand. It's best to keep him as close to this as possible. He's more connected than any other demon in Council. He'll know what to do to keep this from turning into an all-out war between the humans and demons."

~/\~

Hanyi's head was low as he stepped through the open doors into the Guardian Building. His shoulders were slumped from finishing a difficult case, the late hour, and the worry at being seen by other Guardians. He had forced himself into the habit of visiting the Guardian Building only during hours where the halls were mostly-empty. He had been stopped far too often by younger Guardians. At first, he was flattered, but the meetings and questions became tedious when he was trying to do his job.

He had started to appreciate why Keito always kept such an unapproachable demeanor.

Hanyi turned the corner to go to the Records office, eager to file his final reports and go home, when he nearly collided with a familiar Guardian.

"Dalton!" he exclaimed, a surprised smile taking over his features. "Working late, I see."

"You, too," Dalton said, pressing his hand to his chest. "You startled me. Not many come to the back offices this late."

"Why haven't you gone home to your wife and daughter, yet?" Hanyi asked, teasingly placing his hands on his hips in scolding.

Dalton groaned.

"I've been here for a few days, actually. All the press conferences and meetings about Yokouro have taken over my life."

Hanyi's shoulders dropped.

"You need to go home and be with your family," he said. "I know you have work, but honestly, you can't be going after Yokouro completely drained."

"Tell that to the rest of Council," Dalton grumbled. "I was starting to get all the statements finalized about Yokouro, and then yesterday, I had a stack of papers dumped on my desk demanding that the Guardian Branch conduct internal investigations on all the demon Guardians."

"What kind of investigations?"

"To see if they ally with Yokouro DeVastes or any of his allies."

Hanyi's eyes went wide, his mouth dropping open.

"You know you can't approve that plan, right?" he said strongly. "That's an open invitation for demon Guardians to turn against the Guardian Branch."

"One of the demon Guardians explained to me how bad that could get. And I may not know much about the Old Blood Lords, but even I know that most demons in the branch would be seen as a danger to Council if we conducted those investigations."

"What are you going to do?" Hanyi asked.

Dalton raised his shoulders in a defeated shrug.

"I have no idea," he said honestly. "I tried to meet with the Elders, but they wouldn't see me. I called my grandfather and he said that I was not an authority on demons and had no reason to question their decision."

Hanyi let out a heavy sigh.

"Time to call in Keito."

"I tried to call him, too. He didn't answer his phone," Dalton said. "I even tried Sanyai, but it's like the demons have all disappeared."

"Probably sensing what's coming," Hanyi said with a slow nod. "Hopefully Keito's already heard about it. He and Sanyai might be able to keep the demons calm. And hopefully they don't actually conduct the investigations. That will really hinder *us* finding Yokouro's informants."

Dalton let out a long sigh, leaning against the wall, his eyes dropping to the floor.

"What is it?" Hanyi asked, seeing his torn expression.

"Can I ask you something, Hanyi?"

"Of course."

"Did you ever have moments where you questioned Keito's loyalty to your team?"

Hanyi remained eerily still, studying Dalton as the question hung in the air between them.

"What have you heard?" was his response.

"I heard that he *lived* with Juki," Dalton whispered. "And thinking about what happened last round—"

"Oh, *that*," Hanyi said. "I guess it was only a matter of time until you heard. I understand the concern, Dalton. I remember when we first heard that, everyone on our old team wasn't sure how to react. But you're looking at it from the wrong angle."

"How so?"

"Keito and Juki are actually something resembling friends, as bizarre as that sounds," the wolf explained. "But Keito is very loyal to the Guardians. Keito's friendship with Juki is actually very beneficial to *you*. Think of how you can use Juki's loyalty to Keito to your benefit."

"Something tells me that Juki wouldn't do something just because Keito asks."

"You would be surprised," Hanyi said, his eyebrows high.

"Why was he living with Juki?" Dalton asked. "I got an explanation of why he was called the Wandering Child. But I..." He trailed off as Hanyi turned over his shoulder, hearing something that Dalton could not. "What is it?"

"I swear I just heard Keito," Hanyi said, turning around the corner once more and smiling broadly. "I found him!"

Dalton quickly went to Hanyi's side, seeing Keito walking with Sanyai, both of them locked in deep conversation.

"Keito!" Dalton called.

Both demons turned quickly, startled. After a split-second's hesitation, they approached Dalton and Hanyi, Keito casting a quick glance over his shoulder as they came to a stop.

"Dalton, you're working late," Sanyai said with a smile.

"No rest for the wicked," he tried to joke. He turned to Keito. "I tried to call you a few times, but you didn't answer."

"Sorry about that," Keito said. "I've been busy."

"I wanted to ask the both of you if you've heard about the investigations of demon Guardians."

"Unfortunately," Keito said.

"That would make things very dangerous," Sanyai added. "Any demon that hasn't already declared a side is starting to take an interest in what Yokouro's saying."

"Declared a side?" Dalton repeated. "You mean for or against Yokouro? Or with their Old Blood Lords?"

"For or against Yokouro," Sanyai clarified. "And word has already reached home. The nobility of the Demon Realm is getting worried. This is a slippery slope and many are already contacting the DeVastes Territory, asking what Yokouro plans to do if the demons are removed from the DPC."

"Everything the council does seems to be helping Yokouro start his war," Dalton groaned. "Are there a lot of demon Guardians defecting to the DeVastes Territory? Is Yokouro gaining more supporters?"

"Not necessarily," Keito said. "There are now two active lords on the DeVastes Territory. Most demons are approaching Kakuri before they talk to Yokouro. They're being cautious."

"But I'm assuming that Kakuri is quite loyal to Yokouro," Dalton mused.

"Of course Kakuri is loyal, Yokouro is his father," Sanyai said. "But he's—"

"Yokouro has children?!" Dalton gasped, interrupting her.

"You didn't know that?" she asked with a soft laugh. "Kakuri is Yokouro's oldest. He also has a daughter, Lady Elora. And he has grandchildren now, too, right?" she turned to Keito, who nodded.

"Kakuri has children," he said. "Kakuri took over for Yokouro when he was first killed. But once Yokouro got his physical form again, he went through the process to be reinstated. He and Kakuri are running the DeVastes Territory together."

"And does Kakuri want to see all humans subjugated to demons?" Dalton asked, worry causing his voice to quake.

"I don't think so," Sanyai said. "But it's difficult for him to go against his own father."

Keito turned to look behind him.

"They're here," he said.

"Oh, excuse me," Sanyai said quickly, taking a half-step to the side before disappearing as she ran further into the building.

"Who's here?" Dalton asked.

"We have a meeting with the Elders," Keito said, turning back to Dalton. "As for the investigations on the demon Guardians, let me see what I can do. I'm trying to get them called off."

"Can you do that?" Dalton asked.

"I'm going to try."

With a gust of wind, Sanyai reappeared, holding a small book and two files in one hand.

"Got it."

13

"Try not to stay too late, Dalton," Keito said with a forced smile. "Be sure you spend time with your family."

"I will." Dalton knew it was a pathetic response, but he could not think of anything to ask Keito that would keep the demon from turning around with Sanyai and leaving the Guardian Building.

"Do you think I should be worried?" Dalton muttered when Keito and Sanyai had disappeared from sight.

"About what?" Hanyi asked.

"Whatever Keito's clearly planning," Dalton said. "He's meeting with the Elders? When I called today for an audience, they said there were no openings. But clearly they made time to meet with Keito and Sanyai."

"I don't know that you need to be *worried*," Hanyi said. "Sounds to me like Keito is trying to handle this investigation thing. Which will take it off your shoulders. And now you're walking away…"

Hanyi hastened to catch up with Dalton as the human went to the main entrance of the Guardian Building, stopping on the top step and looking over the main courtyard. He could see Keito and Sanyai standing side-by-side, watching as a group of black-clad security officials entered the Dimension Protection Council compound. In the center of the security detail walked two familiar figures.

Dalton's heart plummeted and his blood ran cold at seeing the Kage Lords casually approaching the two demon Guardians. Sanyai dropped to one knee and bowed her head while Keito bowed at the waist, waiting for the Kage guards to stop in front of them. Dalton saw Juki's lips move, though he could not hear what the demon lord said from his distance, and the two demon Guardians straightened. After a brief conversation, Sanyai motioned in one direction, leading the entourage toward the central building, likely to the Elders' Chambers. Keito trailed behind Juki and Rutu, his head down as he walked.

"He's taking the Kage Lords to the Elders?" Dalton whispered. "He might as well be flaunting that he's blackmailing the Elders."

"You don't know that, Dalton," Hanyi said, placing a hand on the human's shoulder to break his stare. "If you think about it, Juki and Rutu are the highest authority from the Demon Realm that can call off these investigations."

"But they're working for Yokouro."

"Not necessarily," Hanyi said. "Remember? They've got their own agenda. They *helped* us escape that building."

Dalton let out a heavy sigh, shaking his head.

"I don't like how complex this is getting."

"I understand the frustration well," the wolf grumbled.

"I feel helpless," Dalton continued. "Like I should be part of that meeting, but that I'm not allowed to be, despite the fact that everything they're likely going to talk about concerns me in some way."

Hanyi lightly pat Dalton's shoulder.

"I wish there was something I could do to help," he said. "But unfortunately, the only thing I can suggest is that you go home and spend time with your family. Walk away for the rest of the evening. You need to rest, Dalton."

"What if the Elders are in danger? It *is* the Kage Lords."

"Juki and Rutu are way too smart to attack the Elders," Hanyi said. "Also, you can incessantly call Keito later tonight and tomorrow and ask what happened if you're really worried." When Dalton turned to the older Guardian, confused, the wolf laughed, his grin turning devious. "If he ever doesn't answer your call again, keep calling him until he picks up. Trust me, it works if you annoy him enough."

~/\~

The sun had long since descended in the Middle Dimension, and everything in Eclipse's body was screaming to go home and sleep. It had been a struggle to complete cases around the grueling training Master Genbuki was putting him through. Even though he complained about how difficult his master was being, he had to admit that he was feeling much stronger—perhaps even stronger than he had been before his injury in the tournament.

But he did not want to be in the Guardian Building that night. As he walked to his office through the mostly-deserted halls, he cursed himself for forgetting his investigation paperwork on his desk two days previous.

His head was slumped as he pushed open the door to his office and began rifling through the papers. It took him a few minutes to find the correct paperwork amid the mess of files, but he had no such luck finding the blue Guardian Code book he had pulled out for reference. After searching his office twice, he groaned and rolled his eyes, deciding he would just take the file home and fill in the proper codes later. Tucking the file under his arm, he turned off the lights in his office and began closing his door.

He stopped when he saw the door next to his office ajar with the light spilling into the dim hallway.

"Mitoki?"

The youngest of Team Dalton whirled around, seeing Eclipse peering into this office.

"Oh, Eclipse. You're here late."

"So are you," he noted. "Why are you here so late?"

"I had a meeting with a few other Light Realm Guardians and then I ended up losing track of time," he said, motioning over his own cluttered desk. "What about you?"

"Forgot some files for the case I'm working," he sighed, flicking the file under his arm. "While I'm here, do you have a copy of the Guardian Code book for misconduct pertaining to inter-realmal permit use?"

Mitoki smiled. "Ooh, someone's in trouble," he sang, turning in his chair to roll closer to his bookshelf.

"Damn newbies," Eclipse groaned. "Sadly, the tensions between new Guardians and demons seem to be higher than with seasoned Guardians. All these new kids go running after any hint of demon activity."

"I'm noticing that, too. Though, there isn't much activity in the Realm of Light, so I've been lucky," Mitoki said, sliding one of the books off the shelf and standing. "Getting crazy in the Darkness Realm?"

"Seems like it's getting crazy everywhere. There was at least twice the amount of security around the compound tonight than usual."

"I've been in the building all day. I haven't noticed," Mitoki said with a soft laugh, extending the book to Eclipse. The older Guardian was about to grab it when he noticed the bandages around Mitoki's right hand.

"What happened there?"

"Nothing," Mitoki said, extending the book further so Eclipse would take it. "Sprained it on a case."

Eclipse tried not to let his training as a Guardian note how fast Mitoki had explained the injury, or the way he had immediately hid his arm behind his back after Eclipse had taken the book.

"I'm sorry," Mitoki said with a nervous laugh. "I'm tired. I should ask how you're doing. How's training going?"

"Fine," Eclipse said simply. "I think I have most of my strength back. My evaluation is next week. But I think I'll do just fine."

"That's good to hear," Mitoki said. "I was worried."

"Me, too." Eclipse cast a worried glance over Mitoki's face. Even though Mitoki always looked pale and more fragile than the average Guardian, Eclipse could not help but notice the dark bags under his eyes and the way his shoulders slumped. "Are you alright? You look tired."

"Just…a lot going on right now," he said, forcing a smile.

"And don't you have a wedding coming up soon?" Eclipse asked.

Mitoki seemed surprised that the older Guardian remembered his engagement. "We decided to push it back a bit. We'll probably set a date in the next week or so." He shrugged, turning back to his desk and motioning briefly over the papers. "I've been so busy I haven't been able to help Rebecca with any of the planning."

"Then you should spend more time at home," Eclipse said, adjusting the book and files in his arms to avoid eye contact with the younger Guardian. "Not much longer now until we're back in the tournament. You should spend as much time with her as possible before we meet up for the next round."

Mitoki let out a sigh, his face showing his conflict as he drummed his fingers over his desk.

"Yes, I guess you're right."

"Come on," Eclipse groaned, jerking his head back into the hallway. "Let's get the hell out of here. It's late enough. Thanks for lending me this, by the way." He motioned to the book as Mitoki turned off his computer and grabbed his jacket from the back of his chair.

"Are you going to bring it back?" he teased.

"Of course."

"Where is your copy?"

"I don't know," Eclipse said with a shrug, stepping into the hallway before Mitoki, allowing the younger man to turn off the light in his office. "My shit goes missing all the time."

"Do you think that has anything to do with the disaster-zone that is your desk?" Mitoki quipped as they started down the hallway.

"What the hell are you doing creeping on my office?"

"I'm not," Mitoki said. "But maybe I'm the one taking your things and seeing how long it takes you to realize they're gone. You know, call attention to how disorganized you are."

"You seem sadistic enough to do that," Eclipse agreed with a nod. "But that does mean I can cite you for misconduct because you're obstructing my work."

"Hopefully you'd be able to find the correct code book for that report," Mitoki laughed.

"I could just steal it from you."

"Guess I better start locking my office."

When they stepped out of the Guardian Building, Mitoki paused to take in the amount of guards standing in the courtyard.

"You're right, there are a lot of guards tonight."

"That's even more than when I got here," Eclipse noted, pausing as he was descending the stairs. His eyes scanned the figures lining the courtyard, following them toward the central building, where he saw several people walking through the courtyard. In the dim lights of the lampposts around the compound, it was difficult to distinguish features, but the way the robes billowed on two of the figures had Eclipse and Mitoki both staring, not sure if they could believe what they were seeing.

"Is that..." Eclipse started.

"That's the Kage Lords," Mitoki completed, stepping to Eclipse's side. "What the hell are they doing here?"

The two froze in place, watching as Juki and Rutu continued toward the exit of the compound. As the group drew closer, they could see Keito and Sanyai walking with the two Old Blood Lords, locked in deep discussion. Upon reaching the center of the courtyard, the entourage stopped. Sanyai fell to one knee before Juki and Rutu while Keito bowed his head deeply to them. After a few final words, Juki and Rutu turned, their guards following as they left the compound. Sanyai and Keito looked to one another, whispering something as they started toward the Guardian Building.

Keito stopped in his tracks. Eclipse and Mitoki knew he had spotted them, despite how still they were being and their distance from the demons. They could feel his eyes scanning them, trying to read their reaction to what they had seen.

Before Eclipse or Mitoki could shake themselves out of their stupor and go to Keito to demand an explanation, Keito turned and rapidly left the compound, not once looking back at his teammates.

Chapter Three

Dalton was surprised to find himself nervous the day he was to evaluate Eclipse. He tried to blame his uneasiness on the constant stress of the previous month, but he knew that he was fighting the anxiety about possibly having to force his teammate to retire after losing sight in his eye.

Even though both Dalton and Eclipse were visibly nervous at the start of the test, the committee evaluating the injured Guardian did not allow the two any time to discuss things beforehand. Eclipse performed the tasks asked of him as if he was going through Annual Guardian Testing, his anxiety fading when he realized how well he was handling the examination.

Not only did Eclipse pass the evaluation, he showed marked improvement from his previous Annual Testing numbers.

Dalton was grinning broadly as he approached Eclipse after the test, shaking his head.

"I think only you could obtain such a devastating injury and rally back even stronger than before."

"You can thank Master Genbuki for that," Eclipse groaned. "He kicked my ass harder each day to get me to this point."

"I'll be sure to thank him when I see him next," Dalton said, clapping Eclipse on the shoulder. "Let's get some lunch."

"Aren't you busy with everything else you're supposed to be doing?" Eclipse asked, raising a quizzical eyebrow. Dalton whined, his head falling back as he lamented his workload.

"Please, save me from my job."

"We're meeting up in just a few days," Eclipse laughed, walking with Dalton out of the cavernous testing room and following his lead toward the mess hall of the Dimension Protection Council Compound. "Surely you have a lot to do before you're tied down by the tournament."

"I don't care," Dalton said. "I'm ready for the break at the lake."

The compound mess hall was half-filled, making it easy for Eclipse and Dalton to find a table further away from the other employees of Council.

"How's everything else been treating you?" Eclipse asked as they sat with their trays. "I know you've been busy with the information about Yokouro leaking, but you found some time to train, too, right?"

"No," Dalton groaned, poking at the dry chicken on his plate. "I know I should be training, considering the weird power spike last round, but I just haven't found time."

"That's not something you want to leave to chance, Dalton," Eclipse said. "Look at what happened to me."

"I know, I know…"

"Must've really freaked you out when you had that power spike…"

"It did," Dalton agreed. "But honestly, everything else has taken over my life. The information leak with Yokouro. And then the demon investigations. And then Keito—"

"Demon investigations? Keito?" Eclipse repeated, raising a hand to stop Dalton. "Sounds like I missed something."

Dalton dropped his fork to his tray and leaned forward.

"I've been trying not to think about it too much, but I need to talk to someone about it. It's driving me crazy," he started. "The Elders wanted to investigate the demon Guardians. See if anyone is allied with Yokouro."

"That's stupid. Any demon would know not to let their allegiance to Yokouro show after everything that's been going on lately."

"Very true. But they were set on it. I tried to contact the Elders and tell them that their internal investigation would hinder *our* investigation into Yokouro, but they wouldn't hear of it. I managed to ask one of the demon Guardians some questions and we ended up talking a bit about Keito, and what that nickname, the Wandering Child, means."

"What does it mean?"

"That Keito has lived under control of all three Old Blood territories. But even more than that, Maneth told me that Keito lived with Juki. As in he lived *in* Juki's house."

"*What?*"

"That was my reaction, too."

"Why?" Eclipse demanded.

"I don't know. Something about the politics with the DeVastes land, and then after a while living with Juki, Vestera pulled Keito into some kind of protective custody. I have no idea what to do with that information. It's more troubling when I think about how quickly Keito was ready to believe whatever Juki said, and that Juki and Rutu were somehow helping us."

"I thought they did help you," Eclipse said.

"They did, but…it's all so confusing." Dalton rubbed his face roughly. "I tried to ask Hanyi about it, and he told me that Juki would be willing to do things for Keito because they were *friends*, whatever that means. And then, next thing I know, Keito has brought the Kage Lords to a meeting with the Elders. The next day? The investigations were called off."

"*That's* why they were in the compound?" Eclipse asked.

"You saw them?"

"Yeah, I was here late and they were leaving the central building. Keito and Sanyai were with them." Eclipse's eyes went distant on his own untouched food. "And then Keito left before I could ask him what was going on."

Dalton leaned back in his chair. "Now you see my concern."

"But it was a good thing that the investigations were called off," Eclipse said.

"Yes, but something tells me that Juki's interference comes at a cost. And I have to wonder if Keito is striking some kind of deal with the Kage Lords, or if Juki is going to ask Keito to repay the favor by inhibiting our investigation into Yokouro. It just seems too risky to be placing so much trust in the Kage Lords."

"I can't argue with that," Eclipse said with a strong nod. "Why the hell would he live with Juki? And what does that mean for Keito's previous interactions with Yokouro? If the Kages and Yokouro are allies..." He trailed off, his mind beginning to buzz with the sheer number of possibilities.

"Also, Keito told us that he wanted us to stay away from the Kage Lords if at all possible. I don't like to think it, but I wonder if it's because he's got some sort of loyalty to them."

"That is troubling," the younger man murmured. "And, even if Yokouro is eliminated from the equation..."

"We still have two ridiculously powerful demons that could cause a lot of damage," Dalton concluded, understanding Eclipse's train of thought.

"After they met with the Elders, did you ask your grandfather if he had been blackmailed or pressured into calling off the investigations?"

"I tried. But he didn't tell me anything. I tried to sidestep the question a little and ask him how often he had interacted with the Kage Lords, and he just snapped at me and told me that it was his job to handle the politics and my job to handle the investigation into Yokouro. Beyond that, he didn't really tell me anything."

"That's suspicious." Eclipse said. "This is starting to feel more and more like a trap, but not even a trap for Yokouro. A trap for *us*. Like all of this is some sort of game everyone is playing at our expense. You told me a little about what Yokouro said when you saw him, but—"

"Guardian Teban!" a voice called from the door. The mess hall fell silent for a few moments as everyone turned to Dalton, who had jumped and whirled to look the messenger running to his table. "Good, you're both here," the messenger said as he approached.

"Is something wrong?"

"Your office received a call from the Jacobsen Guardian Hospital. Guardian Ecaep is being transferred from his hospital in the Realm of Light. They need you to fill out his paperwork."

"Transferred to the Guardian hospital?" Dalton repeated, standing quickly.

"What happened?" Eclipse demanded.

"They didn't give details about the nature of his injuries. He's being transferred because he needs the healers. The medications aren't working," the messenger elaborated as the two Guardians began hurrying toward the door. "I've called Guardians Treneke and DeVero as well. Should I tell them not to worry?"

"No, they should know. We'll meet them at the hospital once they get the message," Dalton said, breaking into a jog once he was out of the mess hall, trying not to appear frantic as he and Eclipse rushed toward the hospital.

~∧~

Dalton called Jikia and Tarrena when they reached the hospital to tell them what he knew about Mitoki's condition. But even after filling out all the necessary paperwork, Dalton did not see Mitoki's family in the hospital waiting room. Dalton had been able to distract himself from the unsettling realization of their absence by writing in the provided blanks, but Eclipse had spent the time watching every face entering the waiting room, becoming more suspicious the longer he did not hear someone ask for information on Mitoki Ecaep.

Dalton and Eclipse were sitting in the uncomfortable chairs when Jikia and Tarrena entered the waiting room.

"Are you boys okay?" Jikia asked, hugging them in greeting.

"We're fine," Dalton said. "We just got the message that Mitoki was being transferred here. They won't tell us why he was admitted at all. We don't know anything else, yet."

"I'm sure he'll be fine," Tarrena said, breaking her hug with Dalton to hug Eclipse tightly. "Have you told Keito and Hanyi?"

"They've been called," Dalton said.

"Are you alright?" Tarrena asked, backing away from the hug when Eclipse did not return the embrace.

"I'm fine," he whispered. "I just need some air."

Eclipse hastened out of the waiting room, leaving the others nervously waiting in the semi-crowded area.

When he returned, they had found seats in one corner, trying not to draw attention to themselves. Dalton always hated the Guardian hospital. If a Guardian found themselves in the Jacobsen Guardian Hospital in the Middle Dimension, the outcome was not often pleasant. That hospital was a last-resort for horrifically injured Guardians, and it was sometimes a matter of luck whether a Guardian would leave the building alive, despite the healers' best efforts.

Two hours of nervous fidgeting later, Hanyi walked through the waiting room doors.

"Hey, what's the word?" Hanyi asked, hugging Jikia and Tarrena as everyone stood to greet him.

"We don't know. They haven't told us anything," Dalton answered. "They won't even tell us why he was admitted in the Realm of Light."

"They might not know, yet," Hanyi said. "Information takes a long time to trickle down to the front desk."

"Have you seen Keito?" Tarrena asked.

"No. Did you call him?"

"The branch called him," Dalton said. "I don't know if they got through."

"He'll show up. He's been busy lately. Might take him some time to check his messages."

"Of course he's been busy..." Eclipse growled under his breath, sitting once more.

Hanyi hesitated, confused by the dark tone.

"What do you mean?"

"Nothing."

Tarrena sat next to Eclipse, her expression worried as she gently rubbed his shoulder, trying to comfort him without asking why he seemed so unsettled.

Hanyi looked between Eclipse and Dalton.

"...did something happen?"

"We're just worried." Dalton waved the question away, though he was also wondering why Eclipse seemed so on-edge.

The hours passed slowly. Other groups of friends and families were approached as Dalton, Eclipse, Hanyi, and the two dragons waited for news. Dalton felt his heart fall and his stomach turn when bad news was given that a Guardian had passed away. Of the six groups approached by doctors and nurses, five of them were asked to go into separate rooms to discuss "arrangements."

Dalton's head was in his hands, listening to the crying of a wife who had just lost her husband. Her sobs as the doctor tried to guide her out of the waiting room made pain radiate through Dalton's chest. He was about to go outside for some fresh air when the automatic doors opened and a familiar face entered the waiting room.

"Keito," Tarrena whispered in relief, standing. The others stood to greet the demon Guardian as he approached them. Dalton could not bring himself to immediately greet his teammate, distracted by the large gash on Keito's forehead and the blood tumbling down the side of his face.

"What happened?" Jikia asked, reaching for the wound. He shook his head, gently pushing her hand away.

"It's nothing. It will heal in a few minutes," Keito said. "Is there any news on Mitoki? What happened?"

"We don't know, yet," Hanyi muttered.

"Was this case related? Was it something else?"

"We don't know," Dalton repeated. "According to the office, his last case was trying to relocate some AWOL demon Guardians that might have been in his realm, but that was over a week ago. He didn't report any injuries on that case."

"Might have been an infection from a smaller injury," Hanyi suggested, just as desperate for an explanation.

"Or maybe he found out something he wasn't supposed to and was attacked," Eclipse grumbled.

Keito's eyes focused on Eclipse.

"What do you mean?"

"Maybe someone didn't want him running his mouth about what he saw when the Kage Lords came to the compound to meet with the Elders. Maybe the same thing will happen to *me*."

The demon remained still and quiet, staring at Eclipse for several long, heavy moments before he spoke.

"The meeting with the Elders was peaceful," he said. "Juki and Rutu did not threaten nor coerce the Elders in any way. I swear on my life."

"Bullshit," Eclipse sneered, standing. "Just being in the same room with them is a form of intimidation."

"Maybe, but it's not the first time the Elders have been in the presence of the Kage Lords. They knew what to expect."

"Then you've done this before?" Eclipse asked, angry. "Called them in when things got a little uncomfortable for demons?"

"I had to get the investigations called off," Keito said. "Turning to them was my last resort. The Elders weren't listening to reason. It would have been disastrous to investigate the demon Guardians."

"Why? Because it would bring to light that you've got ties to some very powerful demons? That you even *lived with* Juki?" Eclipse challenged darkly.

Keito retreated a half-step, his eyes going wide.

"What?"

"Eclipse, you and I should take a walk," Hanyi interjected.

"Shut up," Eclipse snapped, pushing the wolf back as he took a step toward Keito. "Are you going to deny it? Try to tell us that we don't know what we're talking about, *Wandering Child*?"

Keito retreated another step, his head dropping as he stared at the bright hospital tiles under his feet. Dalton was torn, both wanting to stop Eclipse from confronting Keito in such an aggressive manner, and also wanting answers about Keito's friendship with Juki.

"Well, Keito?"

"I…I didn't…"

"You didn't *what*?" Eclipse snapped.

"I didn't have a choice," Keito completed, his voice quiet. He raised his eyes to Eclipse. "No, I won't deny it. I did live in the Kage Palace for many years, but it was not something I wanted. I had nowhere else…"

"Then these investigations would have proven particularly damaging to *you*," Eclipse snarled.

"You don't know anything about it," Keito said sharply.

"Because you won't tell us anything!"

"You don't need to know *everything*!"

"Both of you need to calm down," Hanyi said, pushing them apart and casting a worried eye at those in the waiting room watching the unfolding fight. "This is not the time or place for this."

"Shut up!" Eclipse barked. "Every time we start discussing sensitive things about the past, you get in the way and make up some excuse! You expect me to just let this go?!"

"You will if you know what's good for you," Keito growled.

Eclipse shoved Hanyi away, storming closer to Keito even as the demon retreated. "What the hell does that mean? Is there something else you're hiding? Or," he grabbed the front of Keito's shirt in both hands, stopping his backpedaling, "are you just threatening me?"

"Let me go, Eclipse."

"Or what?" he challenged. "Are you going to go crying to Juki?"

Keito shoved Eclipse backward, but the Antiquan Angel's grip held firm, pulling the demon with him.

"You certainly are getting defensive."

"What do you expect?!" Keito snapped, trying to push Eclipse again. "You're accusing me! I don't have to explain my relationship with Juki to you!"

"Oh, it's a relationship, now?"

"Let me go, Eclipse, or I will force you to do so."

"Seriously, let him go," Hanyi seconded, his hand locking onto Eclipse's shoulder, trying to pull him away from the demon.

"No, I think this is something we need to investigate," Eclipse growled. "You've kept enough secrets. Relationship, is it? What does that mean? You ask him to do things for you and he can call in a debt any time he likes?"

"I will break both of your wrists if you don't let me go…"

"Getting too inquisitive for your liking?" Eclipse asked. "You've been allowed to do whatever you want for a long time, haven't you, Keito DeVero? Everyone has been too afraid to ask you how you have so much influence, haven't they?"

"Dalton, you need to break this apart, *now*," Hanyi said, turning to the leader of the team. Dalton hesitated, trying to sort out his own thoughts. His instincts as a Guardian and the building suspicion in his mind told him to pursue the conversation until they found out why Keito was being so defensive, but he also knew the prying eyes in the room and the worry over Mitoki's well-being was creating even more tension between them.

Eclipse turned over his shoulder to look at Dalton, barking a laugh.

"Looks like the boss also wants to know the truth," Eclipse said, turning his attention back to Keito. He was too enraged to see the way Keito's hands had started shaking on his wrists, or the way the demon's breathing had increased as his eyes looked rapidly around the room. "You saw me and Mitoki standing on those steps and you took off. You didn't want to have to explain yourself to us. You didn't want to explain why the damn *Kage Lords* were meeting with the Elders, or how you even managed to set up that meeting, did you? Makes me wonder if it's a coincidence that Mitoki is now in the hospital with some mysterious injury we know nothing about…"

Keito's eyes widened.

"You…you don't think that *I*…"

"You tell me, Keito," he growled, his hands tightening further. The demon ground his teeth together, pushing Eclipse away harder than before, his nails slicing through Eclipse's sleeves to draw blood as he violently shoved the younger Guardian away. Eclipse started forward again, but Keito shoved him once more, causing him to almost collide with the chairs.

"You think I would be stupid enough to attack Mitoki over something as menial as him seeing Juki and Rutu? Then why didn't I attack you, too?"

"I don't know, Keito, but I'm sure that if Juki asked you to do something, you would," he snarled, holding one hand over the worst of his bleeding. "You believed him when he was trying to drug Dalton last round. You tried to justify that he's not one of our enemies, despite everything that happened with Elder Renard. You even brought him into the damn *compound* to meet with the Elders! I bet you owe him for that one, don't you?"

"I don't need to explain myself to you!"

"The hell you don't!" Eclipse lunged forward, shoving Keito backward until the demon's back hit the wall.

"Eclipse, knock it off!" Hanyi tried to pull the human back from pinning the demon against the wall, but Eclipse shoved his shoulder into Hanyi to keep him away.

"I am so sick of being left in the dark about this shit," Eclipse snarled, his eyes starting to change to dark burgundy as his Antiquan magic caused static to fill the waiting room. "So you're going to *talk*."

"Get the hell off of me!"

"Not until you answer. Did you ask Juki to get the investigations called off for you?"

"Of course I did," Keito snapped.

"And what do you have to do in return?"

Keito's eyes shut tightly. Even around his own confusion and hunger for answers, Dalton noticed the strange way Keito was reacting. Keito had been scanning the room as though expecting someone to leap out and attack him. His breathing was becoming labored, his face paling as his hands quivered.

Keito looked terrified.

His muscles began to tense and he struggled against Eclipse, trying to free himself. "Let me go, Eclipse. I don't want to hurt you."

"Oh, you don't?"

"I do not appreciate you accusing me of some traitorous act!" Keito barked. "I am on your side, damn it! And if you were half the Guardian you should be, you would realize…"

"Realize what?" Eclipse whispered darkly when Keito trailed off. "Now I'm less of a Guardian because I saw another Guardian do something I consider to be dangerous for the Elders? I'm in the wrong for wanting answers? For wanting to know how you're getting *favors* from Juki Kage?"

Keito's head snapped forward, connecting with Eclipse's forehead and causing him to stumble backward.

"Stay the hell away from me," Keito warned, shoving Eclipse a further few steps back before fleeing the waiting room. As the glass doors slid shut, Hanyi went to Eclipse's side.

"Are you okay?" he asked, looking over the slashes on Eclipse's arms. "What the hell was all that, Eclipse? He could have seriously hurt you, you know."

Eclipse yanked his arm away from Hanyi, also leaving, though he turned in the opposite direction of Keito.

The others in the waiting room seemed to relax with both enraged Guardians gone.

Dalton sighed, briefly rubbing both hands over his face as he shook his head.

"What a mess..." he whispered.

"What sparked all that?" Tarrena asked. "Did Keito really bring the Kage Lords to the compound? To meet with the Elders about the demon Guardians being investigated?"

"Yes," Dalton affirmed, closing his eyes and hanging his head. "And I did want to ask him more questions about it, but..." He motioned to the closed waiting room doors. He turned to Hanyi. "Are they going to find one another and kill each other?"

"Keito won't," Hanyi said. "He just needed to get away."

"He looked afraid," Jikia noted quietly, pensive. "Afraid of *Eclipse*."

"Keito doesn't do well when you get in his face like that," Hanyi said. "Eclipse is lucky he didn't get a broken jaw, or at least a broken arm." He turned to Dalton. "I thought I told you not to be worried about Keito's loyalty."

"I'm not...but..."

"But what?"

"You can't fault me for being worried about how easily Keito can call in Juki to help him," Dalton defended.

"You think that was easy for him?" Hanyi asked. "He only goes to the Kages when he has no other choice. And he knows the tension Juki and Rutu create with us. He probably didn't want to tell you because he knew *this* would happen."

Dalton groaned. "I'll go talk to Eclipse," he said. "Even with everything going on, he seems unnaturally agitated. Can you find Keito and talk to him?"

Hanyi nodded, trailing Dalton as they walked out of the waiting room, going their separate ways to find their teammates.

Dalton spotted Eclipse by the vending machines down the hall, sitting on the floor beside them, his head in his hands. Dalton made sure Eclipse heard his footsteps as he approached, stopping in front of the other Guardian and waiting for him to lift his head. Eclipse took a deep breath, discreetly pushing a frustrated tear from his face as he lifted his gaze.

"Do you want to tell me what's really going on?" Dalton asked.

Eclipse turned away from Dalton, taking a few moments before standing.

"It's nothing."

"Bullshit."

"I'm stressed and frustrated," Eclipse said.

"Enough to accuse Keito of treason? To accuse him of *attacking* Mitoki?"

"You know something is going on with him," Eclipse snapped. "Aren't you suspicious?"

"A little, but Keito's right. He doesn't have to tell us *everything* about his past. Not to mention that he's the best Guardian in history and knows more about our mission than anyone else. Pissing him off is not something I particularly want to do."

"He attacked me when I started asking questions." He lifted his arms for evidence.

"You weren't asking questions. You were interrogating him like a criminal," Dalton corrected. "And you scared the shit out of him."

"Like hell I did."

"You *did*." Dalton took a few steps closer, forcing Eclipse to retreat to the wall as Dalton got too close. "So why don't I do this to you and ask what has you worked up enough to lash out at Keito. Do you want to talk to me when I'm in your face like this?"

"Point taken," Eclipse said, firmly pushing Dalton back. "I lost my temper."

"Why?"

"I'm worried about Mitoki, alright? And after everything you said about Keito and what I saw…I just want to know what's going on."

"We're all worried about Mitoki. But that was no reason to attack Keito. He doesn't know what happened, either."

29

Eclipse let out a heavy sigh, turning away from Dalton to lean against the wall, rubbing his face as he tried to hold back angry tears.

"I knew..."

"You knew what?"

"I knew Mitoki wasn't well," Eclipse whispered, his eyes turning to the ground as he shook his head. "I knew he was hurt. I saw that something was wrong."

"When?"

"The same night Juki and Rutu were on the compound," Eclipse said. "He looked pale, paler than usual. And he looked thinner. Weaker. And there were wounds on his wrists..." Eclipse cleared his throat. "I just wonder...if I had pushed him to tell me more that night...if he wouldn't be in the hospital right now."

"...what kind of wounds on his wrists?" Dalton asked carefully.

"I don't know. They were bandaged when I saw them. But he made a point to hide the bandages from me once I asked about them." Eclipse leaned his head against the wall. "Maybe he's suicidal. Maybe it was a mistake on a case. It could be any number of things, but I didn't ask him to tell me more. And I just can't help but feel that Yokouro is behind it somehow. Or Juki and Rutu. It's weird, right? He had to be transferred here because he needed the healers? That's a serious wound."

"I think even if you had asked Mitoki to tell you more, he wouldn't have," Dalton said. "He's pretty secretive. And for all we know, whatever landed him here is completely unrelated to Yokouro."

"You don't really believe that, do you?"

"We don't *know*," Dalton said strongly. "And we can't just make assumptions. I know I'm guilty of that as well, but we need to wait for more information."

"What if he *was* attacked by Yokouro?"

"Then we'll deal with it, but we can't start becoming suspicious of one another, okay? You shouldn't have treated Keito that way."

"He has some kind of relationship with Juki."

"And he admitted that to us. He admitted he lived in Juki's house and that he asked Juki for help with the investigations. He didn't try to hide that," Dalton said. "We have to give him some credit for telling us that much. Attacking him about the information he *is* willing to give is not going to get him to trust us with more."

"We can't rely on the breadcrumbs we're being given," Eclipse groaned. "We need to know, Dalton."

"Then we'll *ask* him about it when tensions aren't so high," Dalton said. "Believe me, I want to know more, too, but we need to find a better time and place. Fair?"

Eclipse bowed his head, grinding his teeth together.

"By the way, I am not helping you apologize to him," Dalton said. "You're doing that on your own."

~/\~

Hanyi was able to follow Keito's scent around the side of the hospital, where he saw the dark-haired demon sitting on a deserted curb, his head low and his eyes distant on the asphalt.

"You caused quite a stir," Hanyi said as he approached the demon. "It's a good thing we're famous Guardians, or security would have kicked us out." He sat next to Keito. "Although, they might have just been too afraid to interfere."

"I was out of line…" Keito whispered.

"He was in your face."

Keito closed his eyes tightly. "Why does this always happen?"

"What?"

"Why is it that Juki and Rutu are always the thing that tips people over the edge? Never mind about Yokouro." Keito angrily pointed at the scabbed-over gash on his head.

"You already know the answer to that, Keito," Hanyi said. "They didn't even know the Kage Lords existed until a few months ago. Seeing you with such favor from Juki is unsettling, even for me. And I know about your friendship." He pursed his lips, hesitating. "Did he ask you to do something for him in return for getting the investigations called off?"

"Nothing out of the ordinary," Keito murmured. "All Demon Realm problems. Nothing I haven't done in the past, nor anything that would concern the others."

"Then you are working for him again."

Keito sighed, lifting his head and leaning back, his eyes turning to the sky.

"*Again* implies that I stopped."

"Probably best you don't tell the boys about that just yet."

"I'd rather not tell them at all," Keito grumbled. "How did they even find out I lived in the Kage Palace?"

"Dalton heard the meaning behind the name Wandering Child."

"How much did he hear?"

"Just the basics," Hanyi said. "Which means they want more answers. Everything they heard was vague. You're going to have to tell them something about Juki. They're not going to let this go."

Keito heaved a deep sigh, rubbing his forehead, wincing when he brushed the scabbed wound. "I'll have to think about what I *can* tell them." Keito hung his head. "Why is this more complicated than before?"

"You say that like it was so easy forty years ago," Hanyi grumbled. "But I think I know what you mean. You trust these humans, don't you?" The wolf smiled, nodding as his eyes became lost in the dark pavement before him. "It's not that the mission is more complicated, just the emotions around it. We both know what it's like when this all goes horribly wrong, and you don't want to go through that again...nor do you want them to feel the same way we do."

"...you know me too well, Hanyi," Keito whispered. "I don't like it."

Hanyi barked a laugh. "Someone has to be your translator."

"I'm worried that I'm going to destroy them," Keito said. "I'm leading them to their doom, and every other demon is just standing on the sidelines waiting to see how long I can keep them safe before they, too, are killed."

"I won't let you do that," Hanyi said. "This has to happen, Keito. But I'm here to help you, to ground you, to make sure that these humans not only survive, but triumph."

"But what if they *don't?*" Keito whispered, his voice so quiet even Hanyi barely heard the question. "What if they do the same thing we did? What if they get to the moment of killing Yokouro, and..."

Hanyi cleared his throat, taking a deep breath as he looked everywhere but at his former teammate.

"It might destroy them, Hanyi."

"It won't."

"How can you be sure?" Keito asked, his voice shaking.

"Because I refuse to let them make the same mistake," Hanyi declared. "We're going to finish this, Keito. I promise."

Chapter Four

After a strained apology where both Keito and Eclipse blamed their agitation on the stress of the situation, another two hours passed before Team Dalton received news of Mitoki's condition.

"Guardian Teban," a doctor called. Everyone waiting for news was on their feet in an instant.

"Is Mitoki okay?" Dalton asked quickly.

"He's doing very well," he said with a comforting smile as he approached. "The healers had to do some extensive work, but he is stable now. He'll be alright."

"What happened?" Jikia asked.

"He had a bad infection. Seems that a small injury on his chest was poorly treated and the infection spread to his lungs."

"What kind of wound?" Dalton asked, his mind flashing to the strange scars he had seen on Mitoki's chest.

"A puncture wound. It's healed now."

"Can we see him?" Tarrena asked.

"Are you immediate family?"

"No, we're the team trainers."

"I'm sorry, but only immediate family and registered Guardians are allowed in outside of visiting hours."

"Can I vouch for them?" Dalton asked.

"I'm sorry, hospital policy."

"It's alright," Jikia said, nodding grimly. "Just go see him. We'll come back during visiting hours tomorrow."

"Let us know how he looks," Tarrena added, visibly upset at having to stay in the waiting room. "We'll wait here."

The paperwork to check in to see Mitoki was familiar to everyone on the team. They filled out the forms mechanically, copying their Guardian ID numbers and picking up their visitor badges before silently following the doctor to Mitoki's room.

The already-pale young Guardian looked nearly as white as the monochromatic walls. The room still sparked with blue healing magic, but even the light energy within the room did not diminish how ill Mitoki appeared. The doctor walked to one side of the bed as the Guardians filed to the other.

"Were there wounds on his arms or hands, doctor?" Dalton asked, trying to make the question sound casual.

"No, none that the healers found. Why? Was he injured on a case?"

"That is something we are trying to determine," Dalton said. "Were there any wounds other than the puncture?"

"No wounds that needed our attention, but we were concerned about the scars on his chest."

"What scars?" Eclipse asked.

"I was actually hoping you would be able to explain them to me," the doctor said, pulling the hospital gown down enough to show several X-shaped scars adorning his torso. The scars were different sizes, some faded from time and others still pink with new skin. Dalton pulled the gown down even further, seeing that the scarring extended beyond Mitoki's ribcage.

"I take it you've seen these before, then?" the doctor said. Dalton quickly looked up, confused by the question, but stopped when he saw the older man was not addressing him. The doctor was looking at Keito, who was staring at the old wounds with fearful understanding in his eyes. He hesitated.

"I...I think so," he mumbled.

"Is this something we need to look further into? The healers could not determine if the wounds were part of a ritual, or were a reason that his infection was so aggressive."

"I'm afraid I don't know much about it, but...it looks like something I've seen before," the demon explained, his eyes scanning the scars.

"What is it?" Hanyi asked.

"A ritual, or at least, I've seen a ritual that left this kind of scarring on people, but..." He shook his head slowly, "this must be something else. If it was the same thing, Mitoki would be long dead."

"Whatever it is, you need to figure out if it's damaging his health," the doctor said. "I've seen enough Guardians and moronic humans tamper with magic too big for them trying to get stronger. If that's what he's doing, he needs to stop now before it does damage we cannot reverse."

"We'll discuss it with him, doctor," Dalton assured. "We'll figure out what caused the scars."

"Good. We're going to keep him overnight for observation, just to be safe. You should be able to pick him up in the early afternoon tomorrow."

"Thank you, doctor."

The older man excused himself from the room. Once the door was closed, Dalton turned his attention to Keito.

"You think this is a different ritual than the one you know?"

"It has to be," Keito said, motioning over Mitoki's chest. "If it was the same ritual, the number of times it's been used on him would have killed him long ago."

"And what is the ritual?" Eclipse demanded.

"It's called *Yua-In Resh*, roughly translated as soul slicing. It's a very damaging means of controlling someone. Not quite as devastating as a draining bewitchment, but more effective in many ways."

"This is something Yokouro could do, then?" Hanyi whispered, voicing the concerns of the other Guardians.

"I'm sure he could, but it's not something I've ever seen him do before," Keito said. "The soul slicing technique gives the caster complete control over the host, body and mind. But it's temporary. It wears off after a few hours. Yokouro would rather use the draining bewitchment because the host never has complete clarity of mind again." Keito furrowed his brow. "This is such an obscure ritual, I don't know who else would know about it."

"If it's so obscure, how do *you* know about it?" Eclipse asked darkly, making no effort to mask his suspicious tone.

Keito opened his mouth, but dropped his eyes to the floor before answering.

"A long time ago, Rutu told me about this ritual."

"*Rutu?*" Eclipse repeated sharply. "So this could be Rutu?"

"If it was, Mitoki would be long dead. Rutu's power would have killed him after the second or third time the ritual happened," Keito said quickly. "We don't even know if this is the same ritual. It's been performed numerous times. It might be some other spell that does make Mitoki stronger, like the doctor said."

"I've heard those spells are very addictive," Hanyi said. "And Mitoki is quite young, and quite physically frail compared to the rest of you."

"That doesn't matter. He's smart and good at thinking on his feet," Eclipse growled. "That's how he became top-ranked. Not because of a spell."

"It's something we should consider, Eclipse," Dalton said as gently as he could.

"He's not some junkie," Eclipse snapped. "We would have noticed by now if he was carving into himself." Eclipse pointed to the marks, shaking his head. "No, this is some other kind of ritual. It has to be."

"Is there any way we can test to be sure it's not a soul slicing ritual?" Dalton asked, turning to Keito, more interested in keeping the obviously-agitated Eclipse calm than immediately finding out the source of the scars.

"The only way I would be able to know for sure is to call Rutu and ask him."

"Like hell!" Eclipse snapped. "You would just *call* and *ask* him? What if it's *him* that's doing this?"

"Then, truthfully, he would have *no* compunction telling me so," Keito said. "But I highly doubt he's the one behind this. And he would be able to tell us if there is any lasting damage or if this is a different ritual altogether."

"We're not calling one of the damn Kage Lords," Eclipse snarled. "Is that your answer to *everything*?"

"Let's not start this again," Hanyi warned.

"I agree," Dalton seconded.

"I was merely saying that the only way we could know for sure if there was severe damage was to ask Rutu, that's all," Keito explained, his voice even. "I did not say that I *was* going to call him."

"Good, keep them out of this," Eclipse said.

"I think we can all agree this is some sort of ritual," Dalton said. "But it's also possible it was from a long time ago. Or at least a few years ago. Some of the scars look relatively new, but it's hard to tell the age of a wound. The first thing we should do is wait for him to wake up and *ask*."

"You really think he'll tell us anything?" Hanyi asked skeptically.

"It's a good first step," Dalton said. "The doctor said the wound was a puncture wound, not an X-shaped cut. There's no reason to suspect that this ritual is still occurring. And we should give him the opportunity to explain himself before we start investigating him like we're suspicious."

The words sat heavily in the room, weighted. Keito lowered his head and Eclipse sighed, busying himself with replacing Mitoki's hospital gown.

"I guess we should have asked the doctor if he'll be fit to compete in the tournament," Eclipse mumbled, finally breaking the tense silence.

"We should also tell Jikia and Tarrena how he's doing," Keito agreed. "I'll go talk to them. I'll keep quiet about the scars. I don't want to worry them more."

"I'll ask the doctor about Mitoki's recovery," Hanyi announced. "I'll see if I can get more answers about the wound and the infection."

"Don't pester him too much," Dalton said. "He's got other patients, I'm sure."

"I never pester," Hanyi said with a broad grin and a mischievous glint in his eyes.

As the two older Guardians left, Eclipse's gaze fell back to the sleeping, pale Mitoki.

"What the hell did you get mixed up in?" he whispered.

"We'll ask him when he wakes," Dalton said. "I'm just going to step out and call my family. They're probably wondering where the hell I am."

Eclipse gave an acknowledging nod, but did not lift his eyes. Dalton only allowed himself to study Eclipse's intense gaze for a few seconds before leaving the room, wondering why the other Guardian looked on the verge of tears.

When he heard his wife's voice over the phone, he could not stop the smile that came to his face.

"Hello?"

"Hey, it's me."

"Hey," Frieda greeted. "We were wondering where you were. I wasn't sure if I should expect you home in time for dinner."

"There was an incident," Dalton said. "Mitoki was transferred to the Guardian hospital and they called me in for paperwork."

"Oh, no, is he alright?"

"He's doing well, now. He's still sedated, but the doctor says he can be discharged tomorrow."

"What happened?"

"A wound became infected. He needed the healers. But he's alright."

"That's such a relief," Frieda said. "Are you going to be coming home tonight? Or are you staying there?"

"I have to be here tomorrow for his discharge, so I thought I would just stay here. I'm sorry, I know I haven't been home much."

"Mitoki needs you, it's alright," she assured with a gentle laugh. "Do you think he'll be up for the trip? Theresa will be so disappointed if even one of your teammates can't join us."

Dalton grinned. "I'm sure he'll be fine. We're waiting to hear from the doctor if he's well enough to compete in the next round, and if he is, he'll be just fine for the trip." He let out a long breath, feeling some of the tension melt from his shoulders. "Did you tell Theresa that if she doesn't keep her room clean and help you around the house, the team isn't coming to the lake?"

"She's been a perfect angel since you said that," Frieda laughed. "I haven't needed to remind her. She's so excited, she can hardly stand it. She's right here. Do you want to say hi?"

"Sure."

"Hello?" Theresa's voice sounded through the phone. "Dad?"

"Hey there," he greeted brightly. "How're you doing, sweetie?"

"Good!"

"Are you behaving and doing everything Mom tells you?"

"Yes," Theresa droned. "I even helped her get the guest rooms ready!"

"Did you? You're awesome. Thank you for helping Mom when I'm not there."

"Are you coming home soon?"

"Soon," he promised. "Mitoki's not feeling well, but as soon as he's feeling better, we'll be there."

"You mean tomorrow?!" Theresa squealed.

"I don't know about tomorrow. It might be the day after tomorrow."

"Aww, but Daaaad…" she whined.

"You wouldn't want Mitoki to travel when he's sick," Dalton said gently. "Then he wouldn't be able to go to the lake with us. I know you've been patient, but it's just another day or two. Okay?"

"Okay…" she grumbled.

"I love you, sweetheart."

"I love you, too."

"Can I talk to Mom again?"

Dalton heard Theresa call for her mother and Dalton's heart warmed at the sound, his eyes closing as he tried to imagine he was back home with his wife and daughter and not under the harsh glare of the hospital's fluorescent lights.

Frieda's bemused laugh came to his ears. "She's so excited," she giggled. "I hope the other Guardians are ready to handle a hyperactive seven-year-old."

"Me, too," Dalton chuckled.

"You sound tired," Frieda said sympathetically. "It must have been a very stressful day."

"It was worse when we didn't know what was wrong. Now that I know he's going to be okay, the exhaustion is hitting me."

"I know you need to stay, but if you came home, you could have a nice home-cooked meal and relax a little."

Dalton smiled, leaning against the wall. "I'm sorry I've been so absent lately. I hope I can spend more time at home after this round of the tournament."

"I hope so, too," Frieda said, her tone gentle. "But the people need you, and I know you'll handle everything just as you always have. You are an amazing man, Dalton Teban."

"You're an amazing woman, Frieda Teban," he whispered. "I love you."

"I love you, too."

"I'll call you later."

"I'll talk to you then."

With hesitant and slow goodbyes, Dalton disconnected the call and closed his eyes, allowing himself to revel in the warmth radiating through his chest before returning to the present moment in the hospital. He wished he could return home, or even that Frieda was there with him as he tried not to let his mind run away with possibilities about Mitoki's wound or the scars on his chest.

When Dalton opened his eyes, a thought struck him.

He went to the nurses' station, smiling kindly to the first nurse that spotted him.

"Can I help you?" she asked.

"Yes, I was wondering if Guardian Ecaep has received any visitors other than us."

She smiled nervously, looking around her to the other nurses, who were occupied with other tasks. "I'm really not supposed to give that kind of information."

"I don't need names, I just want to know if anyone from his family has come to see him. I'm not sure if they've been notified of his hospitalization."

She threw another quick glance behind her before sitting at the computer, her eyes scanning the screen as she typed.

"I don't see any visitors other than you and the others of your team, Guardian Teban."

"Thank you for checking. I'll call his family and make sure they've been notified."

Dalton turned away from the nurses' station and began a slow walk back to Mitoki's room, retrieving his phone from his pocket to make yet another call.

"Dimension Protection Council Guardian Branch. This is Todd," the operator's voice sounded almost immediately after Dalton made the call.

"Hello, Todd, this is Guardian Dalton Teban. Can you transfer me to Operations and Records?"

"Of course, Guardian Teban. One moment please."

The phone rang three times as Dalton slowed his step, being sure no familiar faces were approaching to overhear him.

"Guardian Branch, Operations and Records, this is Cynthia."

"Hello, Cynthia, this is Guardian Dalton Teban. I was wondering if I could get some information from you about a fellow Guardian."

"Which Guardian? Do you have their ID number?"

"I'm afraid I don't, but it's Mitoki Ecaep from the Realm of Light," Dalton said. "He's been admitted to the Jacobsen Guardian Hospital and I just wanted to be sure that his emergency contacts had been notified."

There was a short silence filled only with the clicking of fingers on a keyboard.

"His file shows that both emergency contact numbers were tried earlier today around the same time your office was called. No one answered, but messages were left."

"Are they listed as family contacts?"

"Yes."

"I suppose they haven't received the messages, yet," Dalton mused. "Is his fiancée listed? Could you connect me to her phone?"

"I'll connect you."

The trilling that came through his phone set his teeth on edge. He was not sure why he was so nervous about reaching out to Mitoki's fiancée. In a way, he felt that he was intruding on Mitoki's life, particularly because he did want to ask her about the scars on Mitoki's chest. But another part of him was worried that he would speak to her only to hear that she was not worried about Mitoki and did not want to make the trip to the Middle Dimension to be sure he was alright.

As the phone continued to ring, the more tension took hold of his frame.

An automatic message spoke, asking the caller to leave a message. Dalton was about to introduce himself and ask her to call him back, but as he opened his mouth, he thought better and tried a different approach.

"Hello, this is Jake from the DPC Guardian Branch. I was following up with you to be sure you were aware of Guardian Ecaep's hospital admittance. We have received news that Guardian Ecaep is in stable condition and is expected to be released tomorrow afternoon. If you are unable to be there to sign him out of the hospital, please call the Guardian Branch and inform them so that Guardian Teban can sign the necessary paperwork. If you have any further questions, please contact the Guardian Branch. Thank you."

He hung up the phone, surprisingly unnerved. He did not want Mitoki's fiancée to tell Mitoki that Dalton had called her directly, worried that Mitoki would become more secretive. The fact that she had not arrived at the hospital to check on him made Dalton's suspicions rise. He tapped his phone against his palm, trying not to let his mind run away with possibilities.

When he walked into Mitoki's room again, ready to ask Eclipse if he knew anything about Mitoki's home life considering how much he already knew about Mitoki's past, but when he saw the drawn expression on the other man's face, he refrained.

"How are you holding up, Eclipse?"

Eclipse looked up quickly, startled.

"Fine."

"Still upset? Wanting to throw punches?"

"I'm too tired for that now," Eclipse droned. "It just pisses me off that Keito would say he would just *call* one of the Kage Lords and—"

"He didn't say he was going to call, he just said that was how he would get the information," Dalton interrupted. "And you somehow seem more tense now than you did in the lobby." He watched as Eclipse let out an agitated groan and went to one of the chairs in the corner, sitting heavily. "Is there something else you need to tell me?"

Eclipse's gaze was lost in the boring floor tiles.

"This is Yokouro."

"How do you know?"

"It's complicated. I just know that whatever that ritual is," he pointed at the unconscious Mitoki, "it's linked to Yokouro."

Dalton was silent for two seconds before he walked around Mitoki's bed to the other chair, sitting next to Eclipse.

"You wanna walk me through your reasoning?"

"Not really."

"You have to give me some evidence, Eclipse."

"I just know."

"How?"

"Because...Yokouro already told me."

Dalton's brow crinkled, confused as he looked between Mitoki and Eclipse.

"What does that mean? Did you meet with Yokouro after the last—"

"No," Eclipse snapped. "It...it was in the letter."

It took Dalton's tired and overstimulated brain far too long to remember the letter Yokouro had sent to Eclipse the previous round, announcing his manipulation of Eclipse's path in life. When he did remember the details of the letter, the pieces clicked into place. His jaw dropped and Eclipse's head bowed further.

Dalton leaned back in his chair with a huff.

"Well, that certainly explains a lot," he murmured. "Then, your younger brother didn't die as a baby?"

"For the purposes of keeping him safe, Erik and I agreed that we would say he had died and then cut ties. We figured that keeping distance would be the best option. And I want to keep it that way." He turned his dark eyes to Dalton. "I don't want Mitoki to know."

"But you think Yokouro knows?"

Eclipse sighed, rubbing his face roughly.

"With how much he has been manipulating my life, I'm almost certain he has to know that Mitoki is my younger brother," he said. "Which makes me think that whatever this ritual actually is, and what it does, it has to be linked to Yokouro."

Dalton tried to think of what he could possibly say to Eclipse, but he knew there was nothing he could say to the other man that would be of any comfort. He offered a gentle pat on Eclipse's shoulder.

"Mitoki is going to be fine," he said. "And we'll keep an eye on him and keep him safe."

Eclipse nodded, numb and worried, his mind buzzing with anxiety so intense, he could not think of how to express it.

Chapter Five

The Guardians left the hospital late at night, the long bus ride to Jikia's home feeling even longer in the darkness. Jikia and Tarrena were also silent, more anxious than the others, since they had not been allowed to see Mitoki's condition firsthand.

Dalton did feel better after having something to eat and calling his wife again, and he was even able to sleep decently. He woke with a clearer mind and spent the morning strategizing how to approach Mitoki about the scars on his chest. Even though he knew he had to consider the possibility of Mitoki using destructive magic to make himself stronger, he was more inclined to believe that the odd scarring was the result of an old case Mitoki had taken. He did not want to think that Mitoki was being tortured or controlled by Yokouro, as Eclipse clearly believed.

After a light breakfast, the Guardians were ready to return to the hospital, Jikia and Tarrena also eager to see the youngest Guardian.

But as they were gathering together to leave, there was a knock on Jikia's door.

Tarrena went to answer, returning to the others with a worried look plastered across her features.

"What's wrong?" Eclipse asked. She opened her mouth to speak when a man rounded the corner behind her. The energy that filled the room caused their hair to stand on end and their hearts to race in response to the power the man possessed. The static surrounding them left the lingering taste of copper on his tongue and Dalton felt his head bow instinctively as the unknown dragon entered the room.

"Lord Orkail," Jikia greeted, lowering herself to one knee and bowing deeply, startled by his sudden appearance. Tarrena similarly bowed, leaving the Guardians to wonder if they should do the same. The dragon was clearly of high standing, judging from the intricate robes he wore. His entire being oozed with superiority, his pale blue eyes glancing over the Guardians as though he was inconvenienced being in their presence.

"Rise, my sisters," he ordered, turning to the two female dragons. "You are being summoned for a trial. Lord Kyreane is being tried for conspiracy and high treason. The clan is expected in the Dragon Realm by first light."

"High treason?" Tarrena repeated in disbelief.

"This is not a matter for outsiders," the dragon said, his eyes turning to the Guardians, letting them know without a doubt that they were considered unworthy of hearing more.

"But he was to be the final authority on the Legacy Edict," Jikia said.

"Another will be appointed in his place," Lord Orkail said. "The Legacy Decision has merely been postponed, not forgotten. Now, I am here to escort you to the Dragon Realm."

Jikia opened her mouth, startled. She turned her gaze onto the Guardians, looking between the dragon lord, her daughter, and Team Dalton.

"I apologize," she whispered. "This is something I cannot ignore."

"This sounds important," Dalton agreed. "We'll be alright. They already said they'll likely release Mitoki today. Besides, we're not even competing, yet. You just let us know when you're in the Human Realm when everything is settled."

"I am sorry," she said again.

"There is no need to apologize," Lord Orkail scoffed. "Surely your humans do not need that much supervision. This is far more important than their insignificant troubles."

"Aren't you the sensitive one," Hanyi grumbled.

"We have to prepare the house," Tarrena said. "Talk to the neighbors."

"I have others to collect today. I must insist you come with me now," the dragon said.

"We'll take care of it," Dalton said, trying not to throw an irritated glare at the dragon. "No need to worry. We've got this."

"I could stay," Tarrena offered meekly, dropping her head as Lord Orkail turned to her.

"No," he said. "You are to come with me."

"Thank you, Dalton," Jikia said. "After you, my lord." She bowed her head to the dragon, throwing an apologetic look at the Guardians as she and Tarrena followed him out of the house. They did not move until well after the front door had closed again, waiting for the static to dissipate before turning to one another.

"I've been spending so much time with Jikia and Tarrena that I forget what dragons can be like," Dalton grumbled.

"Not all of them are that stern," Keito said. "But if this is a trial of high treason, that is very serious. And most dragons have a severe superiority complex, so I'm sure he thought we were not worthy to even be in his presence."

"Well, this means we have more things to take care of before heading to the Human Realm," Hanyi declared. "What do we want to do?"

"Even if they release Mitoki today, we'll still have to gather everything we need," Eclipse said. "I'll have to run home and get my bag. I say we go get Mitoki, figure out what the hell that weird scarring is, come back here and prepare the house, and then tomorrow morning we go to the Human Realm after getting our things."

Dalton nodded. "Sounds like a good plan to me. But we can't pester Mitoki about the scars. If he doesn't want to talk about it, we can't push him. Then he'll never talk about it."

"But we have to know," Eclipse insisted.

"And we'll figure it out, but we can't force it."

"Did anyone talk to his family?" Hanyi asked. "I was certain they would show up yesterday."

"I called the branch and his emergency contacts were notified," Dalton answered. "I tried to call his fiancée but she didn't answer."

"Do you think she's okay?" Hanyi asked, looking among the others of the team. "Do you think we need to be worried that they were attacked? Maybe this is more than just Mitoki."

Horrified that the thought had not already occurred to him, Dalton grabbed his phone and made a quick call into the Guardian Branch. After being transferred three times, Dalton finally received the news that Mitoki's fiancée had called the Guardian Branch and asked that Dalton sign Mitoki's hospital paperwork.

"What happened?" Eclipse asked when Dalton thanked the Records secretary and disconnected the call.

"Seems she called and asked that I take care of Mitoki's paperwork," Dalton mused.

"Does that mean she's not coming to see him at all?" Eclipse asked.

"...I think so."

The four men shared glances, equally concerned about the nature of his relationship with his fiancée and the source of the wound that had landed him in the hospital.

There were many instances where Dalton wanted to ask the others what they thought about the situation with Mitoki, but he could not bring himself to start the discussion as they returned to the hospital. The continued silence only served to increase Dalton's anxiety about confronting his youngest teammate.

They signed in with the nurses' station and began the walk to Mitoki's room when Dalton finally spoke up.

"Okay, I know we all want answers and we're a little agitated," Dalton said, trying not to look pointedly at Eclipse as he spoke. "We're not going to ambush Mitoki on this. If he doesn't want to tell us what happened, we're not going to bully him into answering."

"What if he's still in danger?" Eclipse challenged. "What if his family is behind this injury? What if those scars are part of an ongoing ritual?"

"If he's not willing to answer, we'll just be sure to watch his behavior more closely," Dalton said. "He's also probably going to be weak and groggy. We'll just ask him—"

A tremendous commotion further down the hall interrupted Dalton. They turned to see an orderly picking himself from the fallen contents of a rolling tray that had crashed into the wall opposite an open door. Grunts emanated from the open door as another orderly told the person in the room to "calm down." Dalton did not know if he needed to be worried about the fuss happening in Mitoki's hospital room, or if he was pleased that the young Guardian seemed to have retained his strength despite his admittance to the hospital.

"I told you!" Mitoki's voice snapped as the four other Guardians hesitantly approached the room. "I don't need any more pills! I have a birthday party to get to, damn it, so get my damn pants already!"

"I think he's feeling just fine," Hanyi noted, smiling as he strode forward and peered into the open door. "Knock knock!"

"Hanyi," Mitoki greeted, smiling, his eyes moving over the others of the team as the Guardians entered the room. Two orderlies were holding Mitoki's arms, their frustrated expressions flushed with exertion. "Will you please tell these guys I'm fine and get me out of here?"

"Slow down," Dalton said with a laugh, following Hanyi into the room. "What's going on in here?"

The orderlies angrily released Mitoki's arms.

"I swear, you Guardians are worse than those in the violent offenders unit..." one grumbled, leaving the room. The other motioned to Mitoki as he walked closer to Team Dalton.

"He's been trying to take his IV out for the last hour. We were ordered to give him a mild sedative and he lost it."

"I didn't *lose* it," Mitoki defended. "I feel fine and I hate hospitals. I want to get out of here."

"I have to sign for you to leave," Dalton said. He turned to the orderly. "I'm sorry about this. We'll take it from here. Can you call the doctor for us?"

Irritated but eager to leave, the orderly obeyed.

"Quite a fuss, Mitoki," Hanyi noted.

"I *hate* hospitals," he reiterated. "Have you seen my pants?"

"Just wait a few moments," Keito said, gently pushing Mitoki back toward the bed as he nodded to the IV needle still attached to his arm. "They told us yesterday that you can be discharged today, but they still have to follow their normal protocols."

"Also, I don't see your clothes anywhere, so you're going to have to wait," Eclipse added.

"I will walk out of here in the gown if I have to," Mitoki said.

"None of the buses would pick you up like that," Dalton laughed. "Let's just wait for the doctor." He offered a smile as Mitoki huffed, slumping as he sat on the hospital bed. "How are you feeling?"

"I'm feeling fine," he said strongly.

"Do you know why you're in the hospital?" Eclipse asked, trying not to sound too eager to discuss Mitoki's injuries.

"The nurse said something about an infection."

"You had an infected wound," Hanyi confirmed. "But it was a very aggressive infection and they had to transfer you here and call in the healers."

"As your superior, I have to ask if this injury was related to a case," Dalton said tactfully.

"Not exactly," Mitoki said. "I stepped in to help a man being mugged a few days ago and I got stabbed in the process. I guess I just didn't clean the wound as well as I thought."

"Then it has nothing to do with all the other scars on your chest?" Eclipse asked, his eyebrow raised skeptically. Mitoki slumped a little, his eyes turning to his hands. "What are those scars from? The doctor was worried and we didn't know what to tell him," he prompted when Mitoki did not explain.

The youngest remained silent, acutely aware of the eyes on him.

"Mitoki," Dalton said, stepping forward, "I don't want you to feel we're ambushing you, but the scars are troubling. Keito thought it was a mind-control spell of some kind." He took a deep breath. "And I wondered if it was some sort of strengthening spell."

"No," Mitoki said, closing his eyes. "It was a ritual...I was captured and held hostage. I don't know for what reason. I don't even remember most of it. I was delirious by the time I got free."

"I've never read about a case like that in your file," Dalton said. "Those kinds of injuries would be logged with the branch."

"It wasn't a case," Mitoki clarified, his voice quiet, his eyes averted from his teammates. "It was just something that happened to me. I don't even remember getting taken, or the face of the man performing the ritual. I don't even know what the ritual was." He cleared his throat. "When I got free, I just ran. I tried to put it behind me. I..."

The older men in the room were trying not to jump to conclusions based on the limited information, but Dalton was fairly certain that Mitoki was so hesitant to talk about the source of his scars because Mitoki had been attacked, tortured, and then killed the man who tortured him, but did not tell anyone at the Guardian Branch, making it a crime he had covered.

"You don't know anything about why you were attacked? Or what the ritual did?" Keito asked.

Mitoki shook his head. "All I know is that the ritual left me weak. It's why I'm more susceptible to infections and illnesses. I never regained my strength after that."

"And the asshole that did this to you?" Eclipse asked, his voice dark. "Is he dead?"

Mitoki's response was a slow, silent nod.

Dalton let out a long breath.

"Do you think that's why the infection was so difficult to treat from your stab wound?"

"I guess so." Mitoki took a deep breath, finally lifting his eyes to his teammates. "I'm sorry I worried you. Thank you for coming here and checking up with me."

"We couldn't very well just leave you," Dalton said. "The Branch tried to call your fiancée, but I'm not sure if they got a hold of her. I haven't seen her." He tried to make the statement casual, but Mitoki immediately understood the underlying question. He straightened, waving his hand to assure them.

"She won't travel out of the realm," he explained. "Her family was involved in a horrible tram accident between the Realm of Light and the Middle Dimension. She and her father survived, but her mother was killed. She was...actually pulled apart by the energy stream when the tram was damaged. Rebecca watched it happen."

"Holy shit..." Eclipse whispered, horrified at the thought, knowing that an untrained human would be unable to withstand the travel streams between realms if not protected by the specially engineered transportation vehicles meant to bring civilians to and from the realms.

"She's been too afraid to travel out of the Realm of Light since then," Mitoki said. "I'll call her as soon as I get my phone. She's probably frantic."

The doctor entering the room to check Mitoki over for release allowed Dalton a moment to process what he had heard, feeling a little easier knowing the source of Mitoki's scarring and the reason for his fiancée's absence. Still, there was something sitting uneasily with him about Mitoki's explanations.

It was something about the way Mitoki had refused to meet their gaze when he spoke.

Once the doctor had cleared Mitoki for release, his clothes were retrieved and Dalton was pulled away to fill out all the necessary forms. Eager to leave, Mitoki dressed rapidly and then practically ran out of the hospital doors, breathing deeply as though he had not smelled fresh air for months.

"Slow down," Hanyi laughed, jogging to catch up with him on the sidewalk. "You're recently healed from an infection. Take it slow."

"I already feel better," Mitoki said with a smile, turning to his team. "Weren't we supposed to meet up today anyway?"

"I already talked to my family," Dalton said. "I told them that we would be there tomorrow. Jikia and Tarrena were called away to deal with some emergency with the dragons, so—"

"Is everything alright?" Mitoki interrupted, worried.

"One of the higher-up dragons is being tried for high treason," Keito said, waving the question away. "Dragon affairs. Nothing to do with us or Yokouro."

"But that does mean we've been tasked with getting their house in order for their absence," Eclipse said. "We figured we would get our things from home and then go back to Jikia's for the night. Then head to Dalton's tomorrow."

"Oh, okay," Mitoki said with a contemplative nod. "That's good, actually. Then I can check in with Rebecca. Make sure she knows I'm alright."

"You should probably spend a little time with her today," Dalton said. "I'm sure she's worried sick. If you want to meet at my house another day—"

"No, no, it's okay," Mitoki assured. "I'll spend this afternoon with her, but I'll meet you at Jikia's." He grinned at Dalton. "After all, we all promised Theresa we would be there for her birthday party."

"Mitoki—"

"I'm alright," he said quickly. "And Rebecca will be alright, too. I know it. I'll just run home then, get my stuff, and check in with her. I'll see you at Jikia's later tonight."

"…if you're sure," Dalton said slowly.

"I am," Mitoki said. "So, see you tonight?"

"Okay."

Mitoki strode across the parking lot of the Guardian hospital, heading toward the sidewalk while the others remained clustered at the door.

"Is that not sitting right with anyone else?" Dalton asked.

"Me," Eclipse agreed.

"Do you think one of us should go with him?" Hanyi asked.

"I think if we tried, he would become more secretive and sneaky," Keito said, his eyes still following Mitoki through the parking lot. "Best to make him think that we're not suspicious. But we better keep an eye on him. Something isn't right."

Chapter Six

After awkwardly thanking Jikia's neighbors for watching over the animals, the Guardians finally left for the Human Realm the day after Mitoki was released from the hospital. The other Guardians tried not to ask Mitoki more questions about how Rebecca had handled his admission to the Guardian hospital, but they were wracked with suspicions, particularly with how cheerful Mitoki was acting.

As they were on the bus to the portals, Mitoki pat the small duffle bag in his lap.

"Dalton, I didn't know what to bring for the vacation with your family," he said.

"I figured we would end up going shopping before we left," Dalton said. "I don't know if any of you actually own a swimsuit."

"We're going to need swimsuits?" Eclipse gawked.

"I have a lake cabin, of course you're going to need swimsuits," Dalton laughed. "Don't worry, you can pick your own. I'm not asking you to wear one of those revealing ones."

"Why not?!" Hanyi gasped, his eyes brightening.

"Yeah, why not?" Mitoki seconded. "We need commemorative pictures to post during the next Guardian Testing."

Eclipse reached over the back of Mitoki's seat, wrapping his arm around the youngest's neck, holding him in a loose choke-hold.

"You just got out of the hospital, don't make me put you back in there," he warned.

"I have never owned a swimsuit in my life," Hanyi said, rubbing his hands together. "This is exciting!"

"You'll also have to tell us what Theresa wants for her birthday," Keito said. "We can buy something for her when we're out. I didn't know what sort of gift she would like."

"I was going to get her a swing set," Dalton said. "We can make it a joint gift. We'll go shopping tomorrow."

Hanyi seemed to be the only one excited about the promised shopping trip.

They went through the security protocols to enter the Realm of Humans mechanically, knowing exactly what was expected of them as they were funneled toward the busy portals into the city of Kenburough. As Kenburough was one of the largest cities, the portal building was connected to the terminal where civilians could use trams to travel between realms, making the building incredibly crowded with travelers.

Hanyi let out a long breath when they finally left the portal building and stepped into the hot summer sun of the Human Realm.

"There are *way* too many humans…" he groaned. "How can you stand traveling like that all the time, Dalton?"

"I don't even notice it anymore," Dalton said with a shrug, leading the others through the cars parked outside to the long-term parking lot where he had left his car. "I was born and raised in this city. I'm used to the commotion."

There was no relief to the congestion of the city, as once they had piled into Dalton's car and got to the freeway, they hit bumper-to-bumper traffic. Even as the Guardians tried to strike up casual conversation, they could not help but be irritated by the slow moving traffic.

Hanyi leaned forward in his seat.

"Hey, can I have directions to your house?"

"Why?"

"Because I think if I get out and walk, I'll get there faster."

Dalton laughed. "I know, I know, you think humans have a strange way of living."

"More like an *unhealthy* way," Hanyi corrected, bracing himself as Dalton was forced to hit his brakes again in the start-stop traffic jam.

"After the next exit, it should start moving faster," Dalton said easily.

"The fact that you know that means this is something that happens too often," Hanyi groaned, flopping back in his seat. "I don't know how anyone could get used to this."

As Dalton predicted, the traffic eased after another five minutes. It was not long before Dalton turned into an upscale neighborhood on the northern side of the city. Even though there were large houses with sprawling landscapes nearby, Dalton's house was not so lavish. It was a typical two-story house with enough space around it not to be crowded by the larger houses that flanked it.

Dalton pulled his car into the garage and led the Guardians to the door, holding it open as they shuffled inside.

"I hope you don't mind sharing rooms," Dalton said. "We only have two guest rooms and an inflatable bed for the office. One room has two smaller beds and the other one bed. I'll let you decide what you're comfortable with."

"I don't mind sleeping on the floor," Hanyi said. "But I call bunking with Keito!"

"Why?" Eclipse asked, confused by the wolf's enthusiasm.

"Because we've always bunked together," Hanyi said, a confused smile taking over his face. "Why do you ask? Do you want to bunk with him?"

"It's not that. You were just so enthusiastic."

"It did sound like you were disappointed you weren't going to bunk with Keito," Mitoki said with a laugh.

"It's okay if you want to admit it, Eclipse," Hanyi said, squeezing around the younger Guardians as he walked out of the laundry room. "Everyone has a crush on Keito at some point. It was bound to happen."

"Hey!" Keito and Eclipse said simultaneously. Hanyi cackled and darted away before they could throw punches at him. Hanyi leapt through the kitchen, coming to a halt in the living room when he noticed the two people seated on the couch.

"Oh, you must be Hanyi," Frieda greeted.

"Hanyi! You can't just barge into a human's house!" Eclipse barked after him. "Dalton's wife hasn't even met you, yet!"

Eclipse stopped next to Hanyi when he spotted the figures on the couch.

Dalton entered the living room, laughing. "In case you didn't realize it, we're here!" he announced. "Sorry about—oh, Al, I didn't know you were here. I didn't see your car out front."

The man sitting next to Frieda was staring at the Guardians in delight, his hands covering his nose and mouth, causing the multitude of bracelets and rings to glitter as he excitedly tapped his heeled shoes against the floor.

"Mine's at the shop. I'm borrowing my sister's," he said quickly. He lowered his hands, grinning broadly. "Frieda, you didn't tell me the others of Dalton's team were going to be here!"

"I did tell you," Frieda corrected. "That's why I called you over here to pick up the swatches. You're taking over while I have guests."

Dalton leaned down to kiss his wife briefly before turning to the confused and uncomfortable Guardians behind him. "It's alright. Come in, make yourselves comfortable." As the others filed in and took seats around the living room, Dalton briefly introduced Al to his teammates. "Everyone, this is Al, my wife's business partner."

"I'm just so flustered," Al said, fanning his face with his hand. "You all are so much better looking in person. I'm not sure how I'm supposed to handle that."

"Control yourself a little," Frieda laughed, elbowing Al.

"I'll try," Al said, wagging his eyebrows at Frieda before his gaze turned on Dalton. "You look like hell, Dalton."

"Thanks, Al," Dalton laughed.

"I mean, I guess it makes sense with everything going on, but every time I call Frieda, you're off handling some catastrophe. You should leave the demon problems to demons." Al turned quickly to Keito, who had taken the chair closest to where Al sat. "I mean, you're even working with the best demon Guardian in history. You should let him handle the demon problems." Before Dalton could defend that he was just doing his job, Al had leaned over the side of the couch toward Keito. "Now, what's all this about everyone having a crush on you? I mean, I get it, but that must make it difficult to do your job."

"I have no idea what Hanyi was talking about," Keito laughed.

"Like hell you don't," Hanyi scoffed. "I've seen you flirt your way out of *many* situations. And I remember a few times when we needed to get some highly-protected information—"

"Alright, alright," Keito said quickly, interrupting the grinning wolf.

"Nothing wrong with knowing how to use what you've got," Al said. He looked Keito over once more, his grin growing. "I love a handsome Guardian. All that physical activity, those muscles, the little edge of danger…"

"Al, maybe you shouldn't flirt with the best Guardians in the branch," Frieda said with a cocked eyebrow.

"Well, you know what I'm talking about, Frieda," Al said, turning back to her. "I know you have a lot of appreciation for what your man does."

"You're so bad!" Frieda gasped. "You can't say things like that when I have guests."

"Ah, the kiddo's at soccer practice," Al said, waving the statement away. He smiled at Eclipse, who immediately dropped his gaze, clearly the most uncomfortable one in the room. "We're all adults here."

Dalton gave his teammates an apologetic smile, ready to tell them he would show them to the guest rooms, when Al's head whirled to Keito again.

"You know, a girlfriend of mine from college actually married a demon Guardian," he said. "Frieda, do you remember Annette?"

"Vaguely."

"She went to intern at the DPC and met a demon Guardian. They fell madly in love. And she's told me *all sorts* of stories." Al turned to Keito, his grin turning appreciative. "Makes one wonder if all the rumors are true."

"Al, you can't ask that! You just met them," Frieda said, fixing him with a purposeful look. "Keito, I'm sorry."

"It's alright," Keito said. "It's not the first time I've been asked."

"I don't hear about many demon-human couples," Al mused. "Is that uncommon? Is it considered taboo for demons?"

"Most demons do look down on relationships with humans," Keito said. "If a demon were to fall in love with a human, they would have to leave the Demon Realm so as not to incur the scrutiny of other demons. And since demons aren't legally allowed to reside in any realms other than the Demon Realm and the Middle Dimension, it can strain a relationship quite severely and hinder career options for both parties."

"I hope I didn't offend you, or anything, talking about Annette's relationship with a demon."

Keito smiled. "No, not at all. I don't think there is anything wrong with a demon falling in love with a human."

"No?" Al asked, leaning even closer. "You have me intrigued."

"Okay, that's quite enough," Frieda laughed, grabbing Al's hand and pulling him up off the couch.

"I'm behaving!" Al protested, stumbling to his feet.

"No, you're not," Frieda said. "You're hitting on Keito."

"Well, I would hit on the others, but they look afraid of me!"

"As they should be," Frieda jibed, bringing Al to the table next to the front door and picking up a large binder, shoving it into his hands. "You can barely hold a relationship for a month."

"Who said I was looking for a relationship?" Al asked, casting another suggestive glance around the Guardians of Team Dalton.

"Go!" Fried laughed, lightly shoving Al toward the front door. "You're taking over the Matthews' renovation. They still have to approve colors, so don't forget about the meeting with them tomorrow at noon."

"I've got it covered," Al said, hugging Frieda. "Tell the kiddo I said happy birthday. Take care of yourself, Dalton!" he called back as Frieda opened the front door.

"You, too, Al."

"And if any of you want my number, she has it." Al pointed to Frieda, who's eyes went wide as she let out an exasperated laugh and guided him out the door.

"You are impossible," she said. "Go on! I'll let you know when we're back in town."

She called another goodbye as she closed the door, leaning against it and laughing, embarrassed.

"I am so sorry," she groaned, returning to the living room. "What a terrible first impression." She turned her apologetic gaze to Keito. "He's such a flirt. I'm so sorry. I hope he didn't make you uncomfortable."

"Not at all," Keito said.

"I'm so embarrassed," Frieda said, returning to the couch where Dalton placed an arm around her shoulders as she pressed her hands to her cheeks.

"It's alright," he said. "You guys are all okay, right?"

"We're fine," Mitoki said with a laugh. He turned to Eclipse. "Eclipse was the one who ran to the chair furthest away from Al."

"You're not homophobic, are you?" Dalton asked.

"No, I'm just...uncomfortable," Eclipse grumbled, keeping his eyes low.

"That's understandable," Frieda said. "He can be a little overwhelming."

"Keito, you looked like you were flirting *back*," Mitoki noted.

"I did?" Keito asked. He shrugged. "What can I say? I'm a charmer by nature."

"So you *do* know what I'm talking about!" Hanyi said triumphantly.

"You weren't uncomfortable?" Frieda asked.

"No," Keito said again. "Demons are bisexual. It's not a big deal."

The humans in the room straightened, surprised.

"Wait, really?"

"Why is that so surprising?" Keito asked with a smile. "Demon culture is very free when it comes to sexuality. How nervous humans get when discussing sex was one of the most difficult adjustments I had to make as a Guardian."

"So you..." Dalton motioned abstractly in the air, trying to grab the words. "You're..."

Keito laughed. "That's exactly what I'm talking about," he teased. "You can't even say it. I haven't been in a serious relationship with another male before, but I'm not at all uncomfortable with the idea. For demons it's more about connection and trust than gender."

Hanyi could not help but laugh at the startled expressions on the humans' faces.

"Is this some sort of huge revelation?" Keito asked, confused by the silence around the living room.

"No, no," Dalton said, shaking his head. "Sorry."

Keito gave them an incredulous smile. "Seems I keep startling you. You reacted the same way when you heard I had kids."

"You have children?" Frieda asked, smiling. "How many?"

Keito thought for a moment. "Seven."

"*Seven*?" Frieda gasped.

"Why did you have to think about it?" Dalton asked suspiciously.

Keito lowered his gaze, clearing his throat. "It's a little embarrassing to admit that they are not all from the same mother."

"You've been mated *seven* times?" Eclipse gawked. Keito quickly shook his head.

"No, no, that's not what it means to have a mate," he corrected. "You don't need to be official mates to have children. To take a mate is the demon equivalent of getting married, of committing your life to another. I've only done that once."

"Does that mean Yokouro's kids were born without Yokouro being mated? I don't know who would want to marry a lunatic like him," Dalton grumbled.

"Yokouro has kids?!" Mitoki and Eclipse asked simultaneously.

"Yokouro was officially mated for many years," Keito corrected. "Kakuri and Elora are legitimate heirs to the DeVastes Clan."

"Was his mate just as bloodthirsty?"

"Not from what I heard," Keito said. "She died long before I was born, but I heard that she was extremely patient and caring, but certainly not one you wanted to trifle with. I've heard that Kakuri is a lot like his mother, and he is a very patient and understanding demon."

"Opposites attract, I guess?" Hanyi said.

"It's hard to think of Yokouro as a father…" Mitoki mused.

Dalton turned to his wrist watch.

"Theresa should be getting home in about an hour," Dalton said. "Let me show you to the guest rooms."

"I'll make you some lunch," Frieda said, standing with the others and going into the kitchen as Dalton led the other Guardians upstairs.

Once they had set their things in the guest rooms, they gathered in Dalton's dining room for lunch, striking up casual conversation. When Hanyi asked Frieda how she and Dalton had met, they both started laughing. Frieda explained that she had been stressed over a final examination in school and had pulled an all-nighter studying. The morning of the exam, she went to a coffee shop but ended up tripping and spilling her extremely hot coffee all over Dalton—more specifically, all over his lap. After a trip to the hospital and a missed test, the two went to dinner together and had married a year and a half later.

The Guardians tried to help with dishes after lunch until Frieda declared it was too crowded and told everyone to leave, playfully chasing Hanyi out with a dishtowel. She rejoined the Guardians shortly afterward and told them about her interior decorating business, once again apologizing for Al's behavior.

Rapid knocking on the front door made Dalton smile knowingly as Frieda stood to answer.

"I hope you all are ready," he said with a grin.

Frieda opened the door and in burst a young girl, her light brown hair in a ponytail that bounced as she ran toward the Guardians.

"No cleats in the house!" Frieda called after her, laughing as she turned to the woman at the door. "Thank you, Evelynn."

As Frieda thanked the woman for taking over carpooling while Frieda had the Guardians at the house, a young man stepped quietly through the front door, nervously looking over the Guardians in the living room as Theresa bounded into her father's open arms.

Dalton hugged his daughter tightly, though her head was turned over her shoulder to look at the Guardians, grinning broadly and squirming with excitement at meeting them.

"You heard Mom, cleats off," he said, helping her as she clumsily yanked at the laces. "How was practice?"

"Good," she said distractedly, looking among the smiling faces of Team Dalton. "You're all here!"

She stumbled to kick off her second cleat as she ran to the other couch and leapt at Mitoki, hugging him awkwardly as he laughed, surprised.

"Theresa, are you going to introduce yourself?" Dalton prompted.

"I'm Theresa!" she said loudly before hugging Mitoki again.

"It's very nice to meet you," he said, returning the hug. "I'm Mitoki."

"I know!"

"How could you know?" Mitoki asked playfully. "Am I famous?"

"I see you on TV all the time!"

She scrambled away from Mitoki to launch at Eclipse, happily introducing herself as Frieda collected Theresa's cleats, laughing at how affectionately her daughter was greeting the other Guardians.

As she walked toward the front door with the cleats in hand, she smiled encouragingly at the young man lingering on the edge of the living space, wringing his hands nervously together.

"Go introduce yourself," she whispered, lightly patting his shoulder.

Theresa ran to Hanyi next, who hugged her enthusiastically, grinning as she sat back, her eyes dancing with excitement.

"Are you really a wolf?!"

"You wanna see?"

As Hanyi shifted into his wolf form for her to pet and hug, Dalton turned his attention to the young man, motioning him closer.

"Come on," he encouraged. "Everyone, this is my apprentice, Andrew. He'll be joining us at the lake, as well."

"I-It's an honor to meet all of you," Andrew said nervously, stepping forward and offering his hand to Eclipse, who was the closest to him.

"Oh, right, you have an apprentice," Eclipse recalled. "I heard you're taking the oath soon."

"Hopefully," Andrew said quickly. "Master Dalton told me I could be sworn in in a couple months."

"Do you think you're ready?" Eclipse asked with a smile, though there was a very serious tone underlying the question. Andrew gave an enthusiastic nod.

"I've wanted this ever since I was six," he said strongly. "I want to be a Guardian more than anything. I hope to be a Guardian like you guys. I want to make it to top-ranked."

"That just means more stress and more paperwork," Dalton called to his apprentice, chuckling.

Theresa had moved away from Hanyi when her eyes finally rested on Keito. She did not run at the demon as she had the others, slowly approaching as she stared in wonder. Keito waved with a smile, causing her to giggle nervously.

"You're Keito," she whispered.

"Hello, Theresa, it's nice to meet you," Keito said, straightening in his seat and opening his arms to her. She ran to him, throwing her arms around his neck tightly.

"I'm so happy you're here!" she beamed.

Mitoki turned to Andrew with a grin.

"I bet you'd like to talk to him as well," he said.

Andrew nodded quickly, but hesitated in stepping forward to meet the famous demon.

Theresa sat back from the hug, looking over Keito's face.

"Your eyes are so pretty," she said.

"You think so?" Keito asked. "You don't think they're scary?"

She shook her head emphatically. "You're really a demon?"

"I am."

"Then you're really strong!"

"So they say."

"Show me! Show me!"

Keito looked around the living room, trying to figure out how to demonstrate his strength to the young girl.

"Here," he said, standing and setting Theresa on her feet, holding one hand out to her. She put her hand in his. "Both hands. Hold on tight." She clasped her hands over his palm. He lifted her with ease, letting her hang as she wiggled her feet and giggled with delight. Keito lifted her several times with no strain, holding his hand high above his head, stilling when she climbed to his shoulders, laughing and hugging him awkwardly, causing the others in the living room to smile at her enthusiasm.

"Theresa," Frieda said gently, extracting her daughter from Keito's shoulders and bringing her back to her feet. "Come on, let's get that uniform in the wash and let the Guardians get settled."

"But I wanna stay!" Theresa whined.

"The faster you change, the faster you can come back," Frieda said. "I'll race you upstairs."

As Frieda took Theresa from the room, Dalton turned his eyes to Andrew, jerking his head in Keito's direction.

Keito turned to the young Guardian-in-training, smiling.

"It-It's such an honor..." Andrew said, his voice breaking nervously. "I'm Andrew."

"It's very nice to meet you," Keito said.

"Um..." Andrew wiped his hands nervously against his pants. "I'm-I'm sorry, uh, what is the normal way to greet a demon?"

"Normal way?"

"When you greet another demon, what do you do? Do you bow? Do you shake hands?"

"That depends on the demon," Keito answered. "If you were greeting me, because you are younger, you would bow your head. But if you were a lord and had status over me, I would bow or kneel, whichever would ensure that my head was below yours."

"Oh," Andrew said. "So...how should I..."

"There is no need to worry about that," Keito said, extending his hand. "Demons use human customs with humans."

"I've never been this close to a demon before..." the young man whispered.

"That's not necessarily a bad thing," Keito said. "Be careful with demons you don't know. Not all of us are properly socialized."

Andrew let out a breathy laugh. "I have so much I want to ask you," he started. "I want to hear all about the Demon Realm. I want to know everything I can."

"Well, you say that now, but you might regret it."

"No, I think demons and humans can coexist peacefully," Andrew insisted. "I think if we, as humans, made an effort to understand demons and their culture, maybe this thing with Yokouro wouldn't seem so overwhelming. Maybe we can prevent such things in the future. And I think, particularly as Guardians, we have to make an effort to learn about demons and learn how to coexist without fear."

Keito looked at the bright green eyes of the young man before dropping his gaze as he nodded, releasing Andrew's hand.

"We need more Guardians like you, Andrew," he said. "Your generation of Guardians could be the ones to finally bring that sort of peace to the realms."

Chapter Seven

Hanyi had far too much fun the following day shopping with his teammates. When they went shopping for swimsuits, he spent his time snatching things off the rack and asking the humans to try them on, which earned him several punches and Eclipse chasing him around with a hanger twice, threatening to kill him.

Due to the antics, it took them longer to get the shopping done and return to the house. Their final stop had been to buy Theresa a swing set as a birthday present. Since there was no sneaking it past the excited young girl that never wanted to be away from the Guardians, they gave her the present early. What the Guardians had not anticipated, however, was that the young girl would plead that they set it up immediately.

The Guardians spent the better part of the morning fighting about the set-up instructions on the swing set. As they bickered about where certain components were supposed to go, Hanyi did his best to make the assembly even more difficult, hiding screws and handing the wrong tools over when asked. His antics reached a peak when he tried to swing on the incomplete set and caused it to come tumbling down. Once Hanyi was banned from coming anywhere near the swing set, the others managed to get it put together just in time for a quick lunch before they were to load up the car and go to the lake.

As the Guardians were packing Dalton's largest car, the parents of one of Theresa's friends arrived at the Teban house, dropping off Benjamin.

"There are others?" Eclipse asked, turning quickly to Dalton.

Dalton smiled sheepishly.

"Why do you think I wanted you all to join me?" he asked. "Without you, I might lose my mind."

Benjamin was not the only friend Theresa was bringing on the trip to the lake. Emma, another friend from Theresa's school, was dropped off at the Teban house just as Dalton was checking over the house to be sure everything was locked up for their trip. It was another ordeal to get the children to leave the new jungle gym and get into the car for the drive to the lake.

Every seat in Dalton's car was filled. Eclipse and Mitoki shared the first bench with Benjamin between them. Keito and Hanyi sat with Andrew in the middle bench, while Theresa and Emma sat in the far back.

While Eclipse and Mitoki were clearly uncomfortable, unsure how to interact with the children, they did not have to worry during the car ride to the lake—Keito was the center of attention for most of the drive.

"Did you grow up in the Demon Realm?" Emma asked.

"Yes."

"Where?"

"Um...all over the place, I suppose," he said. "No place you would know if I told you. I moved around a lot."

"Were your parents divorced?" Benjamin asked knowingly.

"No, I...I was an orphan," Keito said awkwardly, uncomfortable with the prying questions, but unable to resist the inquisitive glances from the young children. "I just moved around a lot."

"Does the Demon Realm have a king?" Theresa asked.

"No, but...well, I suppose it does. The Demon Realm has three ruling families. I suppose they're a bit like kings of their lands."

"Three kings?"

"Basically," Keito said, figuring he did not need to go into detail about the rulers of the realm.

"Do they ever fight and try to take over?" Benjamin asked excitedly.

"Not often," Keito answered. "It has been many centuries since the last real war between them. But it might happen again soon."

"What do you mean?" Mitoki asked, turning over his shoulder. "Has something happened?"

"There's rumors that Yokouro is preparing his armies for a war with Vestera," Keito clarified. "There's no official declaration, and no confirmation that Yokouro even *will* declare war, but the rumors are circulating, and it is making demons nervous."

"Why didn't you tell us sooner?" Dalton asked from the driver's seat.

"I'm not worried," Keito said with a shrug. "If there is any indication that Yokouro will call Vestera into battle, I'll let you know."

"But what if Yokouro calls in Juki and Rutu to help him fight Vestera?" Eclipse inquired.

"I don't know that they would help Yokouro," Keito said. "Vestera and the Kages haven't seriously tried to kill one another in...well, several millennia, at least."

"Do you have TV in the Demon Realm?" Benjamin burst, catching Keito off-guard with the abrupt subject change.

"Nope, no TV."

"No TV?!" he cried, mortified.

"Nope," Keito repeated. "We have traveling performing troupes. They go around the entire land and perform plays and comedies for entertainment."

Benjamin clearly could not fathom how a band of traveling performers could be the same as watching television.

The first half of the two-hour drive was spent drilling Keito with random and sometimes-confusing questions about the Demon Realm, but when the children ran out of questions, the kids started singing road songs, which had all Guardians, except Hanyi, rolling their eyes and trying not to let the irritating songs grate their nerves. Keito and Andrew made annoyed faces with one another when they made eye contact while Hanyi bounced his head and joined in once he learned the words. Eclipse and Mitoki were looking out separate windows while Benjamin sang loudly between them.

After the road songs came the road games. The Guardians did not participate except for once. As the kids were falling into one another with each turn of the winding mountain road, giggling happily, Benjamin was falling on Eclipse and Mitoki. Keito was begrudgingly playing the game with Hanyi and Andrew, but Mitoki and Eclipse were doing their best to ignore the seven-year-old falling against them at every turn.

After a while, it started grating their nerves.

Eclipse, fed up, pushed into Benjamin on the next turn, who consequently fell heavily against Mitoki. The younger Guardian, caught by surprise while staring dutifully out the window, fell into the door, bumping his head on the glass.

On the next turn, Mitoki retaliated, pushing into Benjamin and pinning the young boy while sandwiching Eclipse against the door panel. The two continued their battle with Benjamin stuck in the middle, unable to do anything but squeak in pain when the turns came. After a few more bends in the road, the Guardians became so agitated they began punching each other over Benjamin while he tried to back as far into the seat as he could.

"Ladies! Break it up!" Keito barked.

"Don't make me come back there!" Dalton scolded.

"He started it!" Mitoki pointed at the other Guardian.

It seemed like far longer than two hours when Dalton pulled into the gated community around the lake and drove to his house. The Guardians eagerly stumbled out of the car when they pulled into the driveway, clustering at the back of the car as the kids excitedly ran to the house, calling for Frieda to unlock the door.

As Dalton opened the back doors of the car, he laughed at the exhausted looks on his teammates' faces

"Five more days!"

"*Five*?!"

The Guardians carried up the bags and groceries, placing them where they were directed around the living room and kitchen as the kids ran about the cabin, Theresa enthusiastically giving her friends a tour.

The main area of the cabin was on the second floor, where a living room and kitchen connected with the deck and hallway leading to two bedrooms with multiple twin beds. In the basement were two more bedrooms and a game room with a few pinball machines and other table games. On the top floor were two more bedrooms, each with one bed.

They were divided into rooms. Benjamin and Andrew immediately called that Hanyi and Keito would share their room with the two bunk beds on the second floor. Theresa and Emma were put in the bedroom across the hall. Dalton and Frieda had their bedroom upstairs and Eclipse and Mitoki divided into the two rooms in the basement.

Everyone got settled as the groceries were put away and dinner was prepared. Those on Team Dalton offered to help, but when Frieda ran out of things for them to help with, Dalton fixed them each a drink and they sat around the table on the deck, enjoying the scent of pine trees and the cooling evening air as the children played downstairs.

"You know what I just realized?" Dalton said, smiling as he watched the colors of the sunset change.

"What?"

"We've never just sat around and enjoyed a drink like this without talking about the case," he said.

"We're workaholics," Mitoki laughed.

"It's nice, though, isn't it?" Hanyi said, smiling as he took a deep breath, filling his lungs with the fresh air. "This is how we become friends, rather than colleagues."

"We are friends," Eclipse groaned, rolling his eyes.

"Really? You consider me a friend?!" Hanyi asked excitedly.

"Don't make me say it again."

Hanyi let out an excited yelp, charging his hands into the air, spilling half of his drink on Keito. "I did it! I'm finally friends with Eclipse!"

The large dinner table was filled with excited chatter as they ate their dinner, the kids talking amongst themselves while the adults and Andrew held their own conversations. Once the plates were cleared, they organized together to play card games, leading to fits of giggles as the adults learned the rules of the games. The kids were loud and enthusiastic, but the Guardians became quite competitive once they learned the rules, and were soon playing the game on their own, snapping playfully at one another whenever they were dealt a bad hand or thought someone had cheated.

As the night progressed and the children began to show obvious signs of fatigue, Dalton sent them to bed, ordering the rest of his team to put the cards away before a brawl broke out. The adults helped Frieda tidy up the kitchen and living room before they decided to go to bed early.

Even though the Guardians were accustomed to waking early, they all commented how rested they felt the next morning. Leaving the kids and Andrew to sleep in, Team Dalton gathered around the table with cups of coffee, enjoying the quiet of the morning and watching as the sky lightened over the mountains, causing the birds to sing among the trees surrounding the cabin.

They were filled with a peace they did not recall ever having before, particularly since taking the case to track down Yokouro.

After finishing his coffee, Dalton stood.

"I think we should go kayaking today," he declared.

"Kayaking?" the others echoed.

"Today is Theresa's birthday, so I think we should go kayaking in the morning and then spend the afternoon here for her party," he said. "Frieda? How does that sound?"

"Sounds good," Frieda said from the kitchen, gathering ingredients to make breakfast. "If you want to get everything ready, breakfast should be ready by the time you're done."

"Do you want help making breakfast?" Eclipse asked.

"No, thank you," Frieda said with a smile. "Dalton will need your help with the kayaks."

The others of Team Dalton needed a lot of instruction to get the trailer hooked up to Dalton's car and load the kayaks that were stored in the detached garage next to the cabin. Most of them were fighting with the straps to secure the kayaks to the trailer, and in the end, Dalton had to go around and check all the straps again, worried that the others had not secured them properly.

As they were gathering paddles and life jackets, Theresa walked outside.

Dalton immediately ran to her, picking her up and spinning her around.

"Isn't today a special day?" he asked her.

"It's my birthday, Dad!" she giggled.

"Are you sure it's today? I thought it was tomorrow!"

"No!" she laughed, hugging Dalton around the neck tightly. "Are we going kayaking?"

"Would you like that, birthday girl?"

"Yes!"

"Are the others up?"

"Yep!"

"Well, then, we better get some breakfast and get to the lake," Dalton declared. "We're just going to gather the paddles and life jackets."

"Can I help?"

Theresa ran to help gather the final things needed for kayaking, but was stopped as each member of Team Dalton scooped her up into a hug and wished her a happy birthday. Dalton could not help but smile at the way his teammates' faces brightened when they spoke to Theresa, noticing that even Eclipse seemed to enjoy hugging his daughter and wishing her a happy birthday. But Dalton did notice that Hanyi was not as lively as usual. While he still picked Theresa up and hugged her, wishing her a happy birthday, he did not spin with her or ask her to race with him to the garage. The wolf seemed a little quieter than usual, but Dalton figured he was just tired from the day before.

Theresa helped the Guardians gather the lifejackets and paddles, placing them in the back of Dalton's car before rushing up to get some breakfast.

Perked up by the delicious food, the kids excitedly changed into their swimsuits and clamored to the car, eager for the adventure of the day. As they drove to a smaller reservoir fifteen minutes from the lake, everyone sang happy birthday to Theresa.

Once again, the Guardians needed instruction about what to do to unload the kayaks and where to place them once they reached the water. The kids entertained themselves by exploring the area under Frieda's careful watch while the adults prepared the boats along the shore. Occasionally, the members of Team Dalton would catch sight of one another and laugh nervously, feeling almost embarrassed doing something so out-of-the-ordinary for them.

Dalton assigned everyone a kayak, putting Theresa and Emma in the double-seated boat while everyone else had their own. Frieda was in the water first, followed shortly by the kids. Dalton then helped Mitoki into his boat and pushed him off the shore, but he pushed too hard and at a bad angle, causing Mitoki to lose his balance and the kayak to capsize.

The Guardians were howling with laughter as Mitoki resurfaced, splashing at his teammates, unable to suppress his own grinning.

"How's the water, Mitoki?" Frieda called.

"Great, actually," he said, watching her paddle toward him. "Wanna join me?" He splashed in her direction as she quickly changed course, laughing.

"No, thanks!"

To make Mitoki feel better, Hanyi—who was going to ride in wolf form on the back of Keito's kayak—allowed the demon to throw him into the water, where he spent time swimming to each boat, visiting everyone until all the kayaks were in the water.

Of course, when Keito pulled him onto his boat, he shook the excess water all over the demon before settling into his position.

The other Guardians had difficulty figuring out how to paddle, despite how much Dalton instructed them. Not only were they trying to figure out how to steer the boats, they were feeling a little ridiculous in their life jackets paddling kayaks through the shallow reservoir. Guardians did not often feel comfortable doing normal recreational activities. Everything they dealt with in their jobs only served to further alienate them from the rest of society, and they felt very out of place.

But as they started to understand how to steer their kayaks and caught sight of eagles among the small islands they rounded, they began to relax and enjoy the morning. The joy of the kids pointing at the wildlife and the beauty of the nature surrounding them soon eased their embarrassment.

Hanyi was continuously shifting on the back of Keito's kayak, trying to put his nose to the water or following the quick movement of a dragonfly fluttering by. He groaned, stumbling as he tried to lower his body to the boat, unable to find enough room to comfortably lie flat.

"Hanyi, quit rocking the boat," Keito said.

"*I'm sorry*," Hanyi told him, though no one else could understand him. "*I'm just trying to lay down.*"

"You're going to nap?" Keito asked incredulously.

"*The sun feels so good*," Hanyi said, lowering his head and closing his eyes. Keito groaned, paddling to catch up with the rest of the group.

"I see Hanyi is pulling his weight," Mitoki teased as Keito came closer.

"He hasn't been feeling well, so I don't blame him, but *really*, Hanyi?" Keito grumbled.

"You could make him paddle the boat back," Andrew suggested with a snicker.

"And what would I do? Swim?" Keito joked. The demon glanced over his shoulder at Hanyi and smirked. Using his paddle, Keito flicked water onto the lounging wolf. Startled, Hanyi leapt up with a high whine, forgetting how narrow the boat was and tumbling into the water with a splash.

Keito smiled innocently as everyone broke into boisterous laughter. Hanyi resurfaced in his human form, his hair a wet curtain in front of his eyes. He turned to Keito slowly, a devilish smirk coming over his face. He launched forward. Keito pushed him away with his paddle and tried to move the boat, but Hanyi grabbed the side of the cockpit and roughly pushed down, capsizing the demon.

"I don't think we've ever had this many swimmers in one trip," Dalton laughed as Frieda turned her camera to the two Guardians in the water.

The demon resurfaced, rubbing the water from his eyes before turning the boat back over and putting the paddle in the cockpit.

"Now, puppy, it's war."

Keito swam after Hanyi, catching him easily and dunking him underwater before swimming backward to escape counter-attack.

"I got twenty bucks on Keito!" Andrew called.

"Go, Hanyi!" the girls laughed, though no one was really taking sides.

"They're acting like children," Eclipse groaned, watching as Keito and Hanyi wrestled and splashed at one another.

Mitoki smiled, deftly paddling his boat to drift closer to Eclipse.

"Is that another eagle over there?" he asked, pointing. Eclipse turned and Mitoki roughly pushed Eclipse over, nearly capsizing himself as Eclipse splashed into the water. Frieda had stopped taking still photos and was now sweeping her camera over the Guardians, capturing video of the wrestling, though her own laughter was causing her hand to shake.

Eclipse rounded angrily on Mitoki.

"What was that for?!"

"Eclipse!" Hanyi called dramatically, swimming toward the other Guardian, one hand outstretched. "You've come for me. I know that Al was smitten with you, but I knew you would choose me in the end!"

"Damn it, wolf! What the hell is your problem?" Eclipse rapidly retreated from the advancing wolf, brandishing his paddle to keep the older Guardian at bay.

"Watch your language around the kids!" Mitoki scolded.

"Hey, are you cheating on me?" Keito growled playfully, leaping on Hanyi and pushing him underwater again.

"You two need help..." Eclipse grumbled, turning back toward his boat. He was greeted with a splash of water in his face.

"You need to lighten up," Mitoki jeered.

"*You*..." Eclipse growled, pointing at the younger Guardian. He waded around his boat, his intent clear. Mitoki tried to paddle away, but Eclipse caught the boat before he could get far. He reached for Mitoki's arm, ready to pull him into the water.

"Wait! Wait!" Mitoki cried. Eclipse paused reflexively and Mitoki tipped sideways, capsizing himself and splashing Eclipse in the process.

"Keito!" Theresa called. He turned as he dunked Hanyi underwater, seeing her reaching her arms out to him. He swam to her boat and gently picked her up, bringing her into the water.

"Be careful, Theresa," Dalton and Frieda said simultaneously.

"Emma, do you want to swim, too?" Keito asked the other girl. She shook her head quickly, giggling. "Are you su—"

Hanyi leapt on Keito's back, yanking him backward and bringing them both underwater with a splash. When they resurfaced again, Hanyi cackled, swimming away as Keito followed. But Andrew paddled his boat in front of Hanyi and then leapt into the water, joining the wrestling.

Dalton watched them with a broad smile, both amused and relieved to see his teammates having such a good time. His realization the previous night of just how little time they had spent together outside of the tournament and the case had stunned him. Seeing how relaxed and happy the others were made him feel like he was spending time with friends, rather than other Guardians, and it allowed him to forget the weight on his shoulders.

"Hold it! Hold it! Hold it!" Eclipse yelled shortly after Keito and Hanyi's wrestling had come to involve him. Everyone stopped, seeing Eclipse pointing at the leader of their team. "Why are you the only one out of the water?"

"I'm not!" Dalton protested weakly. "Frieda, Benjamin, and Emma aren't in the water!"

"The kids have a choice," Mitoki said with a grin, starting toward Dalton's boat. "Frieda is taking pictures. *You*, on the other hand..."

"Don't you dare!" Dalton laughed, rapidly paddling backward.

"Get him!" Andrew called.

The team swarmed Dalton's boat as he tried to ward them off with his paddle, sloshing water at them half-heartedly.

"Just think of it as a team-building exercise!" Hanyi laughed, kicking out of the water and grabbing Dalton's wrist, pulling him in clumsily.

Dalton joined in the wrestling while Frieda continued to film and Mitoki gently splashed Theresa, keeping her away from the roughhousing occurring between the older Guardians.

It took a lot of work to get the Guardians back into the kayaks, but once they were all in their boats again, they paddled to the nearest island, taking time to dry off in the sun and eat a snack after the antics in the water. The kids ran and splashed in the sandy shallows off the island and played games among the trees while the adults lounged and caught their breaths.

"I wish I still had that much energy," Eclipse said, nodding to the children as they chased one another back into the water.

"Don't worry," Frieda said with a grin. "They'll crash as soon as we get back to the house."

Theresa ran to Keito, who was reclined on the ground, letting the sun dry him. She stood over him, holding her hand over his face and letting droplets of water fall onto his cheek. He flinched and opened one eye.

"Be careful," he warned playfully. "I might just throw you back in."

She giggled, but did not move her hand.

"Alright, monkey, you asked for it!"

Keito leapt up and chased her as she tried to flee, laughing in delight. He caught her easily, picking her up and running to the water as Theresa fought playfully. The demon brought her back into the water, swinging her in his arms as he counted down. But he did not throw her. He instead knelt in the water and helped her stand before falling dramatically back, causing her to giggle and leap on him, splashing him.

The wind began to pick up, which prompted Dalton to declare it was time to head back to the cabin. It did not take them long to get back into their boats and paddle the distance back to the car. The Guardians loaded the boats onto the trailer again as the children climbed into the vehicle, their eyelids heavy.

The children were almost completely asleep by the time they returned to the house. The kids went inside to shower, and by the time the Guardians had unloaded everything back into the garage, the three seven-year-olds were fast asleep on the couches in the living room.

The adults sat on the deck, enjoying the mild weather and talking lightly about who had won the water wrestling. As Frieda was sharing the pictures and videos she had taken, Andrew challenged them all to a rematch, saying that he was certain he could take them all on, clearly more comfortable with the older Guardians than he had been upon first meeting them.

The afternoon passed easily, the kids waking to play games downstairs while the adults enjoyed their vacation from their responsibilities.

Frieda eventually started preparing Theresa's birthday dinner of homemade pizza while Dalton called all the Guardians down to the garage. When they met their team leader at the car, Dalton handed Eclipse a card and a pen.

"Here."

"What's this?"

"It's a birthday card for Theresa. I want you to sign it."

"We already got her a gift," Hanyi protested.

"I know, but I can't take all the credit for her other gift," Dalton said. "She'll really love it if you all sign."

As the card was passed around, Hanyi gave Dalton a smirk.

"What did you get her?"

"Something she's been asking for for a long time," Dalton answered. "And we have to go pick it up."

"She really is your princess, isn't she?" Mitoki said.

"As if you could say no to that face," Dalton teased.

Once the card was signed, Dalton led the others down the driveway, telling them that the gift was being held at a friend's house down the street.

"So, did you enjoy kayaking?" he asked.

"I did," Mitoki said. "I don't think I've ever done something like that before."

"Me, neither," Keito said.

"Not going to lie, I felt a bit out of place," Eclipse admitted.

"That's the danger of being a Guardian," Hanyi said. "It's why I always kept my sense of humor. Otherwise, you forget what it's like to have fun!"

"Oh, Eclipse looked like he was having fun," Keito jeered.

"I always found it important to keep doing things as a civilian," Dalton agreed. "Because this job really can drown you."

When Dalton knocked on the door of his friend's house, the amused face of a man greeted them.

"It's not that difficult to wrangle," he teased when he saw all five of them on his porch. Dalton introduced the Guardians to his friend, Jeff, who then invited them in to get Theresa's present. When the other four saw what Dalton had gotten his daughter, they shared knowing looks and smiles.

Putting the gift in the car for the duration of dinner, the Guardians tried to keep the grins off their faces. Everyone ravenously ate the homemade pizzas and eagerly waited for the cake. Once again, they sang happy birthday to Theresa and served the cake as Frieda brought her presents to the table.

Benjamin had gotten Theresa a shirt with a beaded dragon design—something he constantly reminded her *he* had picked out. Emma gave her a friendship necklace that she had the other half to, and Andrew gave her an oversized stuffed bear that she immediately hugged and refused to release. Frieda gave Theresa the usual motherly gifts—socks and underwear—which Theresa refused to show, her face flushing in embarrassment. To make it up, Frieda also gave her a bracelet decorated with horses.

Dalton glanced discreetly at the patio door and then extended a small parcel in front of his daughter with the card the Guardians had signed. He kissed her head.

"Happy birthday, sweetheart."

She opened the card, smiling at the signatures inside.

"Another present from all of you?" she asked excitedly.

"Yes," Dalton answered. Theresa tore through the simple wrapping paper, stopping abruptly when she reached the contents, slowly picking up the collar and leash, her eyes lighting up in excitement.

Frieda's camera was already recording Theresa's reaction.

"Dad?" Theresa turned to him quickly and Dalton motioned for Mitoki to step in from the porch, holding the small dog in his arms. The kids squealed and ran to him as the dog looked over the children, excited but overwhelmed. Mitoki set him on the ground as they knelt to pet him.

Dalton crouched beside his daughter.

"He's about two years old. I found him at a shelter and he asked me to take him home," Dalton told her. She whirled around and threw her arms around her father's neck, spouting ecstatic thank-yous into his shoulder.

"Don't forget to thank everyone else."

She launched to her feet and ran to Eclipse, who was the nearest Guardian, squeezing him in a tight hug and thanking him profusely before moving on to the next member of Team Dalton. Once she had finished her enthusiastic thank-yous, she returned to the dog, who was now excitedly playing with the children.

"That was a very nice gift, Dalton," Keito said with a smile at his team leader's side. "But you do know that you're going to end up taking care of that dog most of the time, right?"

"That's why I got one that was a little older," Dalton said with a chuckle. "I've always wanted a dog, too. He will be my first one. But she's been begging me about getting a dog. Frieda and I decided she was old enough now."

"You're a good father, Dalton," Keito said.

Dalton hesitated, hearing the sad tone in the demon's voice. He cleared his throat, turning to watch his daughter, avoiding eye contact with Keito.

"I know it's none of my business, but I am surprised you don't talk about your kids more," Dalton noted.

"Not all of us are good fathers, Dalton," Keito murmured.

"I'm sure you're a great father, Keito."

The demon snorted. "Most of my children would disagree with you," he said. "Almost all of them were born before my time as a Guardian, and—with the exception of the twins—they all have different mothers. And I was far too young when I had my children. I couldn't take care of them. And believe me, they remember that."

"How young were you?" Dalton asked nervously.

"I was fifteen when my oldest was born," Keito answered, causing Dalton's eyes to shoot wide. "I have never regretted having children, but I do regret that I could not be a proper father to them. I tried, but…" He shook his head, turning back to the human. "Just be what Theresa needs, Dalton. I know that, as a Guardian, you have a lot of responsibility to the realms, but don't miss out on her life. First and foremost, you're her father. Be there. She's the best thing you could ask for. Never forget that."

Chapter Eight

Dalton found himself in a room he recognized, though he could not recall why the lavish gold of the domed room filled with richly dressed people felt commonplace. Despite how familiar the space felt, he was ill at ease, standing in the middle of the grand hall facing several glittering thrones. The middle throne radiated with light and power, the red-robed figure seated there emitting magic so powerful, Dalton had to focus on keeping his feet from leaving the ground from the weightlessness threatening to fly him toward the gold embellishments on the ceiling.

He could not let the magnificent power overwhelm him. He was there to plead his case—an unconscious understanding befalling him that he was there to stand trial.

The gentle weightlessness was soon interrupted by a cold heaviness enveloping him. He turned slowly, sensing he was not alone in front of the occupied thrones. Next to him, Yokouro stood proud, his hands clasped behind his back and his head high, though he was looking at Dalton out of the corner of his eye, smirking triumphantly.

"Honored brothers," one of the other figures in the thrones began, bringing Dalton's attention back to the judges before him. "You have been brought before us on charges of interference with the creatures in dominion over the Realm of Lythehacrentoah, committing acts that threaten the Balance, and treason against our High Lord Vestera. Now that the charges have been stated, you may begin your pleas."

"My honored lords," Yokouro started, stepping forward, "I have no intention of deceiving you by claiming the charges against me are false. However, I will also defend my actions without shame."

"You proudly admit to treason against our leader?" one of the women sneered. "What you have done is reprehensible! You cannot—"

The red-clad dragon in the golden throne raised his hand to silence her. Dalton felt a shiver run through his body, though he was not sure if it was reverence or fear that overtook him.

"You hold a very important position, Yasuain," Vestera said, his voice calm, yet commanding. "You are meant to protect the humans under your care. You are to stand silent watch and be sure that their actions do not threaten the Balance. Yet, you have chosen not only to violate your oath, but to enact your own justice upon the humans. Hundreds of thousands are dead, Yasuain. I cannot overlook such violence against the creatures we are meant to protect."

"My High Lord Vestera," Yokouro said, bowing his head, though Dalton could see that he was reluctant to show submission to the powerful dragon. "I did not create needless violence. I acted within my responsibilities. I saw the humans going astray, and I corrected it."

"That is not your decision to make," another male dragon snapped angrily. "It is the decision of this council whether a human-inhabited world must be curtailed. It is not the judgement of a single dragon."

"I did not trust the council to make the appropriate decision," Yokouro said sharply.

"And that is why you wish to see me removed from power?" Vestera asked.

"You have been ruling for a very long time, my lord," Yokouro continued. "But in all that time, your judgement has been flawed and biased toward helping the scourge that is humanity. When the humans first disrupted the Balance, rather than eliminate them from the universe, you told the clan to watch from a distance, to *guide* them. They are not younglings learning to hunt and fly. They are a disease going unchecked."

"I do not see humanity as a scourge," Vestera said simply. "I am the leader of the clan. I am the heir to the Throne of Chaos. I am very aware of when the Balance is in jeopardy. And killing those humans created a dangerous imbalance. That was *your* doing, not the work of humans."

"These humans were already on the path to destruction!" Yokouro defended. "Just like last time, you refuse to interfere!"

"Unlike last time, we understand precisely the ramifications of humans being left to their own devices. That is why you, as a Watcher, were ordered to guard humanity and report to us when you felt they were getting out of hand. You do not have the authority to pass judgement."

"But you refuse to rain your fire upon the humans," Yokouro insisted. "This moronic plan to drive them to the brink and then connect different human worlds in the *hope* it will stop the impending catastrophe will not work, my lord."

"You can be certain that is not something you will ever know," one of the women snapped. "Yasuain, I see no reason why you should be spared the death penalty. You have broken your oath. You have destroyed the humans in your charge. You have shifted the Balance to the point where Lord Hizoku has needed to interfere to halt an apocalyptic chain of events. I see no reason to show you mercy."

Yokouro turned to Dalton, his eyes hollow and cold, prompting Dalton that it was his time to speak. He felt his mouth open, but no sound came out. There was something in his chest urging him to speak on Yokouro's behalf, though his gut twisted angrily at the thought of the thousands of humans that had died at his hand.

"Does your brother wish to speak on your behalf?" Vestera prompted, turning his ruby eyes onto Dalton.

Dalton carefully stepped forward.

"No, Lord Vestera, not on his behalf," he said carefully. "I do, however, wish to ask that my brother be spared from death. I feel that my brother does not understand why the dragons have been asked to protect humanity, and I wish to help educate him."

"Educate me?" Yokouro growled. "You *child*. Humans think they are the most powerful beings in the universe. They slaughter our kind no matter how we try to guide them. That is why we must take their appearances, and even then, we do not always escape death at their hands. They are vile, destructive creatures. They don't only perform these atrocities on our kind, but even on their own."

"That is why we are supposed to guide them, to help them grow and understand their place in the universe."

"They will never understand!" Yokouro snapped, taking a threatening step toward Dalton. Dalton retreated, turning to face Yokouro fully, ready for a confrontation. "You still wish to protect the plague that is humanity?"

"I see the good in them, Brother," Dalton heard himself saying. "I wish I could make you see it."

"Whatever good is within them does not outweigh the damage they create."

"It will if you give them a chance to show you!"

"Enough," Vestera said at the front of the room, though it took several moments before the angered Yokouro and Dalton could turn away from one another. The old dragon settled back in his throne, letting out a deep sigh. "Yasuain, I understand your fear. Humans, when not properly guided, are extremely destructive, and now that we see the true strength of demons, I understand your fear of the rise of a similar species. But just as the humans kill what they do not understand, you murdered hundreds of thousands to curtail your own fear of their potential."

"I do not *fear* humans," Yokouro scoffed.

"Are you willing to allow them to thrive and flourish? Are you willing to learn the same faith your brother holds in humanity?"

Yokouro turned to Dalton, the hollow, cold look in his eyes turning to rage.

"Until I draw my final breath," Yokouro started, "I will always believe humans are too destructive to be allowed to live. And if Vestera will not act upon his role as the Overseer, and eliminate humanity from the universe, then I will do everything in my power to destroy as many humans as I can."

Dalton raised his chin, turning to Yokouro.

"Then I will do everything in my power to stop you," he said. "Until my last breath, I will protect humans against you."

Yokouro's face broke into a smile, though the look caused a shiver to run down Dalton's spine.

"Are you willing to risk everything, dear brother?"

"Yes."

Dalton could feel the tension in the room rising. The other dragons shivered, turning to one another, reacting to the magic filling the hall. Those seated on thrones at the front of the room straightened. Vestera even opened his mouth to speak but another dragon turned to him.

"This could be a way to keep all the dragons in line," he reminded Vestera.

"Then I ask of you, my brother, will you duel me to the death to protect your humans? Will you allow the good in their hearts to feed your powers to match me in battle, while I am fed by the violence and destruction they wreak?"

"Yes," Dalton said without hesitation. "I accept the conditions, Brother. I will meet you in a duel."

"Lord Hizoku," Yokouro said, turning to Vestera, "do you see our duel? Will you act as our impartial judge and respect the outcome of our battle? Will you bind us together in deep magic and oversee our fight until one soundly defeats the other?"

All eyes turned to Vestera, who remained very still and quiet as the words sat heavily in the air. The dragon to his left leaned over once more.

"My lord, this could put this debate to rest for good," he whispered. "This could unite the clan once again."

Vestera slowly stood, stepping down from the dais to approach Dalton and Yokouro, his eyes scanning each of them in turn.

"Yasuain," he said, turning to Yokouro, "will you allow your powers to be bolstered by the cruelty and violence of the remaining humans under your care?"

"Yes."

"Kuryaoin," Vestera turned to Dalton, "will you allow your magic to be empowered by the goodness and charity of the remaining humans under your care?"

"Yes."

Vestera nodded once, though Dalton could see the conflict on Vestera's face.

"Then I will see and accept your challenge," he said slowly. "You may both choose seconds in your fight, and the battle must be on equal ground. You must allow the humans to replenish and grow until you are both strong enough to face one another. But no judgement will be passed on your humans until, in a mutual battle, one of you is soundly defeated. If you accept these terms, kneel and pledge yourself to the will of your humans."

Yokouro went to one knee in front of Vestera, and Dalton was quick to follow. He bowed his head to the powerful dragon, and when he felt the warmth of Vestera's hand press over his head, he suddenly felt everything around him disappear, leaving him in a black void that had no beginning nor end.

With the dragons and the ornate hall gone, Dalton got to his feet and looked around, waiting, though he did not know for what.

"Seems you're finally ready."

Dalton whirled around, recognizing the voice as the same one that had first come to him in the Beast Realm and visited him again in the Realm of Darkness before the previous round of the tournament.

"Ready for what?" he asked quietly, his voice echoing in the vastness around him.

"To begin your real training," the voice said. Though Dalton could not entirely discern the figure, he could barely detect the dark outline of a man out from the void, slowly making his way toward Dalton. "You cannot continue to ignore this, Dalton."

"Ignore what?"

"Your growing power," the voice said, the figure drawing even closer, though Dalton still could not make out a definitive shape. "That power is the dragon spirit inside of you. But you've kept that power locked away since you were a child. It's now time to awaken it."

"No," Dalton said slowly. "This is just a dream. It's just my brain trying to—"

"It's not a dream, Dalton, it's a memory," the voice corrected. "This is a part of your destiny. And you cannot keep running from it." Something resembling the figure's hand reached out, though the fingers were tipped with long, curled, obsidian claws. Dalton recoiled, but fell heavily, his arms and legs too heavy to lift once he was reclined on the ground. The shape drew closer, the claws reaching for Dalton's face. "Let me in, Dalton."

The clawed digits carefully folded around Dalton's head, covering his eyes, creating pinprick cuts in the skin at his temples.

Fear surged inside Dalton as he felt his powers growing and shifting, swelling to a magnitude he knew he could not control.

"No!"

Dalton bolted upright in bed, disoriented and still half-asleep. The sudden movement startled Frieda out of her slumber. Her tired eyes tried to focus on her husband in the dark as he scrambled out from under the sheets, one hand over his face as he groaned in pain.

"Dalton? Dalton?!"

She rushed to him, but when she put a hand on his shoulder, trying to wake him from whatever nightmare she was sure he was having, searing pain shot through her palm. With a soft cry, she recoiled, holding her burned hand to her chest as she frantically turned on the bedside lamp.

Dalton had collapsed to the ground beside the bed, his labored breathing escaping from clenched teeth. She knelt next to him, hesitant to touch him once more, looking between her shivering husband and the faint burn pattern on her hand in the shape of dragon scales.

~∧~

When Dalton walked to the kitchen, the other Guardians were already awake, sipping coffee at the dining table while Hanyi napped in the spot of sunlight streaming through the deck doors. With a quiet greeting, Dalton went to pour himself his own cup of coffee, hearing one of the other bedroom doors open down the hall. Dalton had barely sat down when Rio ran over to Hanyi, sniffing around the wolf's head as the beast Guardian growled playfully.

Theresa and Emma rounded the corner, both still dressed in their pajamas but not appearing as drowsy as the Guardians

"Good morning," Dalton greeted, forcing a smile to his face as he turned and opened his arms for his daughter to hug him. "Sleep well?"

"Yep," Theresa said brightly. "Dad, can we go on the boat today?"

"Is that what you want to do?" he said. "Well, there are some things we have to do first. Rio has to be taken out, and then we need to wait for Benjamin and Andrew to wake up."

"I can take Rio out!" Theresa declared.

"Go get dressed and I'll go with you."

As Theresa and Emma returned to their room, Dalton laughed and turned back to his team.

"I guess we're taking the boat out today."

"That doesn't mean more paddling, does it?" Mitoki asked.

"Why? Are you sore from yesterday?" Dalton laughed lightly.

"I thought I was in decent shape," Mitoki grumbled. "But I'm still sore."

"To be fair, you all did a lot of wrestling in the water," Dalton teased.

Hearing a noise on the stairs, the Guardians turned to Frieda, greeting her as she went into the kitchen, pouring her own coffee.

"Are the kids still asleep?" she asked over her shoulder. Dalton tried not to show a visible reaction to the edge in her voice, but he was sure that the other Guardians could hear her tone. He turned in his chair to look at her and avoid the concerned looks Eclipse and Mitoki shared. It had not occurred to him until that moment that Hanyi and Keito might have overheard the argument that had transpired earlier that morning.

"Theresa and Emma are awake, but I don't know about the boys," Dalton answered.

"They were still sleeping last I checked," Keito chimed in.

"Theresa wants to take the boat out today," Dalton continued.

Frieda nodded, her eyes averted to her coffee as she turned.

"After breakfast, if you want to prepare the boat, I'll make lunch to take with us," she said, opening the refrigerator and pulling out items for breakfast.

"Is there anything we can help with?" Mitoki asked, his tone light, clearly trying to diffuse the tension between Frieda and Dalton.

"Do you need help with breakfast?" Eclipse offered.

Frieda glanced around the kitchen before putting Eclipse in charge of the bacon and eggs while she prepared the pancakes. Dalton slowly turned away from his wife, letting out a quiet sigh. He was soon distracted by Theresa and Emma returning, dressed and ready to take Rio on a short walk with Dalton.

He left with the girls, though the other Guardians could tell that the smile on his face was forced in order to keep the children from sensing anything wrong. Keito and Mitoki shared a worried glance before Mitoki cleared his throat, turning to the napping Hanyi and trying to lighten the mood of the morning.

"Hanyi, are you going to sleep all day? We're going on a boat. I would think you would be bouncing around the house in anticipation."

Hanyi let out a huff, stretching his paws lazily. Keito cocked a half-smile.

"He's still not feeling very well," he explained.

"Are you alright, Hanyi?" Mitoki asked, peering over the table to get a better look at the sleeping wolf.

"He's fine," Keito said. "He thinks he just caught a little bug. Nothing serious."

With a groan, Hanyi pulled himself upright before standing on two legs as he shifted into his human form.

"It's annoying not being able to talk to you guys as a wolf." He sighed, sitting heavily in the empty chair next to Keito and snatching the coffee mug from the demon's hands.

"Excuse you, that was mine," Keito grumbled.

"Frieda, is there anything else we can help with?" Hanyi asked, raising his voice and ignoring Keito entirely.

Frieda smiled, though it did not bring any light to her eyes.

"After you last tried to help, you are banned from cooking in my kitchen, Hanyi," she teased.

"I thought you were going to teach me how to cook!" Hanyi whined playfully.

"Isn't there a saying about old dogs and new tricks?" she quipped with a wink.

He placed a hand against his chest in mock hurt, but could not stop the smile that came to his face.

Benjamin and Andrew emerged from the bedroom around the same time Theresa, Emma, and Dalton returned. Theresa happily bounded into the kitchen and asked what her mother was making for breakfast before insisting she help make the pancakes. The kitchen quickly became too crowded, and Frieda took over cooking the eggs and bacon from Eclipse, shooing him playfully out of the kitchen as the kids all scrambled to help cook.

Dalton stood to one side of the kitchen, watching the commotion, wondering when he would be able to get a moment with Frieda alone so they could talk about what had happened the previous night. He wanted to ask his teammates to take over making breakfast and watching over the children, but he knew that Frieda was still too shaken to speak with him—she had not once turned to look at him.

"Master Dalton, are you alright?" Andrew asked, seeing the drawn look on his face.

"Yes," he said quickly, shaking himself out of his stupor. "Still waking up a bit. Help Frieda manage them, alright?" he asked, nodding into the kitchen. "I'm going to prepare the boat."

"We'll help," Mitoki offered, standing and throwing an expectant look at the other Guardians. "I feel useless just sitting here."

Dalton led the team to the detached garage, where Dalton opened the large door to reveal an expensive, well-maintained sporting boat.

"Is this what you do with your bonuses?" Eclipse leered.

"Maybe," Dalton played along.

Dalton kicked off his shoes before stepping onto the trailer and climbing into the boat, opening one of the back hatches while the others looked around the lower level of the garage where other equipment was stored, including an enormous triangle-shaped inflatable.

"What is *that*?" Hanyi asked, his eyes dancing with delight.

"That is why we're taking the boat out today," Dalton chuckled, pulling a few lifejackets out of the storage compartment and laying them out in the boat to be sure he had enough of the appropriate sizes. "That is what I will tow behind the boat while you ride."

"The hell I'm riding that," Eclipse snapped.

"Theresa will be so disappointed if you don't ride it," Dalton said with a mock pout. "She'll beg and beg and beg. She wanted so badly for you all to be up here enjoying her birthday celebrations. It will crush her if you don't join in on the fun."

Eclipse let out a heavy sigh, turning away from the inflatable as Dalton asked Mitoki to pass him the cords for the battery charger at the back of the boat.

"Hey, Dalton?" Mitoki started, following the instructions. "I know it's really none of our business, but...Frieda seemed a little upset this morning..."

Dalton sighed heavily, avoiding eye contact as he busied himself charging the battery. "Yeah. She was a bit upset..." he admitted.

"What happened?" Eclipse asked.

"Well, I don't really know," Dalton said, busying himself with another task. "Something weird happened last night."

The four other men turned to one another before slowly turning back to Dalton.

"Oh really?" Hanyi said, unsuccessful at keeping the teasing out of his voice.

Dalton barked a laugh, throwing a playful glare at the wolf.

"I *mean* that I had a very vivid nightmare. And when I woke up…" He hesitated, dropping his gaze to something inside the boat before continuing. "It seems that the magic in my aura was strong enough to burn her hand when she touched me."

"It *burned* her?" Mitoki repeated, mortified.

"Is she alright?" Eclipse asked.

"I healed the burns, but I don't think she's alright," Dalton said. "I haven't really had a chance to tell her about the surge in my powers lately, and when I tried to tell her this morning, she was pretty shaken, and upset I hadn't brought it up sooner."

"Are *you* alright?" Keito asked.

Dalton let out a long sigh, pausing in his busy work.

"To be honest, not really. I know she was shaken, but I'm even more unnerved. I don't understand what's going on with my powers lately. And these damn dreams…" He shook his head, not wanting to go into detail about all the dreams he had been having over the previous month. "I just worry that I'm becoming too dangerous to be around," he finally muttered.

"I mean, as Guardians, we're already pretty dangerous," Mitoki said. "But if you can get a handle on this surge in your powers, I'm sure you'll be fine."

"But how much more powerful am I going to become?" Dalton asked. "Say I take on some training around the tournament, but then in a few months, I get another spike?"

"The only way to know for sure is to train," Eclipse said. "If not for your sake, then your family's."

Dalton paused, his eyes going distant. "I've always been worried I would become one of those Guardians that hurts their family because of night terrors or trauma triggering. But I always thought that would be further in the future, and I would be able to see when I was starting to slip. But now…that reality is a little too close."

"It doesn't sound like the same thing," Keito said. "Your powers are growing, likely in response to the threat Yokouro poses. I think that if you start training and you learn more about your new power, you won't be a danger to your family."

"You think so?" Dalton asked, surprised at the weakness in his tone.

"I do," Keito said with a nod. "I don't think you need to worry, Dalton."

"I could never live with myself if I hurt Frieda or Theresa," he murmured.

"I think that's why a lot of Guardians forgo families," Eclipse mused, leaning against one of the support beams in the garage.

"I think so," Dalton agreed. "But it's been the most important thing in my life," he continued. "Had I not met Frieda when I did, I would not be alive today. I would have put a gun in my mouth long ago. I've never told her, but I was not expecting to last through the month when I met her. When she came into my life, my entire perspective shifted."

"How do you mean?" Eclipse asked.

"You know how it is," Dalton said. "I had put the work blinders on and was taking case after case, but no matter how many people I saved or how many criminals I stopped, it just seemed like there was no good left in the realms. I was angry at the world, and feeling as though I was unable to affect any change. I was wallowing in a very dark place when she came along. My world shifted focus. Suddenly, the good in the realms was everything at home, and my job was to protect that. It grounded me and remotivated me as a Guardian."

"It just seems like such a risk," Eclipse mumbled.

"The risk is worth it," Hanyi said brightly. "I used to feel the same way, Eclipse. In fact, everyone on our previous team made an oath that we would never marry or take a mate because it was too dangerous." Hanyi turned to Keito with a shrug. "Sorry, I broke that oath."

Keito laughed. "I broke it first."

"You'll understand one day, Eclipse," Dalton said, climbing out of the boat and slipping his shoes back on. "When you and Tarrena get married, you'll see what we mean."

"When I what?!" Eclipse snapped. Dalton darted out of the garage with a laugh when Eclipse started toward him, calling over his shoulder that he was going to get the car.

Mitoki sighed, slumping against the side of the boat.

"Maybe Dalton has a reason to be worried by this..." he mused. "His magic became powerful enough to *burn* Frieda."

"If Dalton has not been doing any training over the break, and his powers are growing, the danger is not from the power, but his lack of control," Keito said. "The power spike he had at the tournament last round shows that he has a lot of potential, but if he doesn't do what is necessary to keep it under control, he could be very dangerous to be around."

"Then why did you tell him he wasn't a danger to his family?" Eclipse asked.

"Because at the moment, he's not," Keito said. "And he needed to be reassured. He's terrified, and he has every reason to be, but fear is not going to help him. If he's afraid of his powers, he's going to ignore them, and *that's* dangerous."

"Do you think *we* should talk to Frieda? Explain it to her?"

Eclipse's question was immediately answered by fervent "nos" from all his teammates.

"You do not want to get in the middle of that," Hanyi said quickly. "She has to hear all this from Dalton. We just need to stay out of it and support them as best we can while they figure it out."

It took Dalton a little longer to bring the car to the garage, but when he stepped out of the vehicle, he passed around wrapped breakfast sandwiches that the kids had helped put together for them. They stood around the garage, eating their breakfast and talking lightly about family life and how their jobs affected relationships, trying not to stray into the darker side of the conversation, worried about upsetting Dalton.

Breakfast finished, Dalton instructed Eclipse and Mitoki on how to signal him as he backed the car up to attach the boat. The three humans worked to connect the hitch while Keito and Hanyi watched, laughing at how many times Dalton had to get out of the car to check where he was, unable to make sense of Eclipse's signals.

Finally, after the seventh attempt to attach the boat, Keito walked over, grabbed the tongue of the trailer, and wheeled the boat to the hitch, ending the frustrated bickering.

Chapter Nine

"Are you *certain* you don't need help?"

"For the last time, Acurala, no," Juki laughed, turning to his brother, grinning at the way he was draped over the couch in Juki's office, his head hanging over the side as his foot tapped the nearby bookshelf in boredom. "Don't you have work you can do at the Market?"

"No," Acurala groaned. "The woman you got to replace me is damn efficient at her job. I truly didn't think she would be so good at running the Market. When I first saw her, I thought you hired her because of her enormous tits."

Juki sighed. "I'm glad you think so highly of me."

"Don't tell me you haven't looked at them."

"Of course I've looked," Juki said. "She certainly flaunts them enough."

"How often does she try to seduce you?" Acurala laughed, sitting upright.

"Who says she tries to seduce me?"

"She does," Acurala answered. "She tried to get me into bed a few times. Says that she's determined to have a Kage, and I guess since she couldn't get you, I'm the next best thing."

Juki scoffed. "If you want to take her up on her offer, I have no qualms with that. Just use the appropriate discretion."

Acurala leaned back in his seat, crossing his arms as he smirked.

"You are whipped, *Rau-ka*."

"Damn right I am."

"The thought never crossed your mind to go to bed with her?" Acurala asked skeptically.

Juki shot his brother a glance out of the corner of his eye. "I'm mated, not dead." He leaned back in his desk chair, stretching his arms above his head and rolling his neck, debating if he wanted to bring up what that same woman had told him about Acurala's conduct in the Market. "Are you doing alright, Acurala?"

"I'm fine. Why do you ask?"

"Your temper does seem to be a bit short lately," Juki noted, trying to sound casual. "And Elisa told me about the brawl you had with some lower-level demons in the Market. You're a Kage. You can't pick fights whenever someone looks at you sideways. Our family has a reputation."

"That's the problem," the younger brother grumbled. "I won't have any low-level demon thinking that I'm some pathetic weakling that cannot handle himself. Those morons deserved every broken bone."

"Perhaps it would be best if you were to live here for a while," Juki suggested. "Living at the Market house gives other demons too much access to you."

"I told you, I'm not living here," Acurala snapped.

"I'm just trying to watch out for you."

"I can't stay here, Juki. I hate this place. There's too many memories. I can't stand it."

Juki took a deep breath, nodding knowingly. "Then your recent temper *is* related to Father's resurrection."

"How can you even call him that?" Acurala snarled. "After everything he did to you? To all of us?"

"He's still our father."

Acurala scoffed. "Don't act like you're handling his return so brilliantly. Everyone in the land is waiting for you to falter. Even the low-lives around the Market have heard about your fist fight with Rutu the other day."

"That doesn't surprise me, considering the way the maids gossip," Juki said, turning his attention back to the work on his desk, showing Acurala that he was uncomfortable with the conversation.

"*Rau-ka*, what would be so terrible about letting Rutu kill Kawakara?"

"That is none of your concern."

"It's been centuries since you two have been at each other's throats like this. With the land already in such upheaval, demons are getting nervous, and not in the way Yokouro wants," Acurala explained. "You're a pillar of our culture. If you crumble now—"

"I said this was none of your concern, Acurala," Juki snapped.

"Juki, you're starting to break," the younger brother insisted. "It's one of the busiest times of year for the Trade. Vestera is taking notice of your actions. Yokouro is ordering you to take care of his affairs while he indulges this depressive episode and sleeps the days away. You and Rutu are fighting at every opportunity. And you can't bring yourself to face and kill Kawakara. You can't keep this up for long."

"Are you saying I'm unfit for my position as Old Blood Lord of the Kage Clan?" Juki asked, his tone turning dark, warning Acurala to be careful with his next words.

Acurala stood, walking to Juki's side.

"I'm saying that you don't have to do it all alone. Let me help you. Let Rutu help you. You can't do everything."

"I appreciate the offer, Acurala, but this is something I must do alone."

"*Why*? Give me one good reason why taking on Kawakara alone is something only you can do."

"I don't need to explain myself to you."

"Juki—"

Acurala placed a hand on his older brother's shoulder, but Juki immediately leapt to his feet, grabbing Acurala's wrist, his other hand locking around his neck, turning them both. The younger Kage brother was startled and admittedly terrified at how quickly Juki had moved, but he knew better than to struggle. He stared at Juki, waiting the agonizing two seconds before Juki released him.

He backpedaled, rubbing his neck.

"I'm worried about you, *Rau-ka*," Acurala whispered.

Juki let out a heavy sigh, leaving his office, letting the door strike the wall with a bang. Acurala debated if he wanted to follow his older brother, but eventually decided he needed to keep an eye on Juki.

He caught sight of his brother's robes disappearing around the corner to the main staircase and he immediately rushed forward, nearly colliding with Juki when his older brother stopped at the top of the stairs.

Juki was staring into the foyer, where Rutu stood with two stewards dressed in travel cloaks. Rutu's eyes were turned to Juki, the stare causing everyone around them to shrink away worriedly. Acurala could feel the tension between them, worried he would have to interfere if a fight broke out.

One of the stewards finally gathered enough courage to step forward and bow deeply.

"My Lord Juki," he greeted, forcing Juki to break his eye contact with Rutu.

"What's all this about?" he asked, descending the stairs to join them, Acurala close behind.

"I have brought the caravan from your sister, my lord."

"Caravan?"

"For your Trenrel Banquet."

Juki was taken aback, turning to look at Rutu.

"It's time for that again?" Rutu nodded silently. "I don't suppose I can convince Adriel to forgo the celebrations this year."

Acurala laughed. "You could try. But Adriel will come here herself and smack you for even thinking you would deny her this banquet."

Juki let out a long sigh, nodding once to the steward.

"Very well, you may begin preparations."

"Are you sure?" Rutu asked.

"Do you want to deal with Adriel's wrath?" Juki turned back to the steward. "When can I expect her?"

"Tomorrow, my lord."

"I will be sure we are ready to receive her," Juki said. "Thank you."

The steward, taking his cue, bowed deeply to the three Old Blood Lords before him and left through the front doors of the palace.

"I can't believe it's time for the Trenrel Banquet again," Juki whispered. He motioned a maid to him. "Find Zarina and have her organize preparations for our guests."

"Yes, my lord," she said, rushing to obey the command.

"Just what we need," Acurala groaned. "The entire family in one place getting drunk and bringing up Kawakara every three minutes."

Juki's eyes fell on Rutu once again, though the tension between them had changed, no longer filled with anger, shifting instead to concern.

"It might be best if you weren't at the banquet," Juki said.

"Who would that be best for? Me or you?" Rutu retorted. "What excuse are you going to use when your siblings get drunk enough to accuse me of being a coward for not facing them?"

"You know how they can get, Rutu," Acurala seconded. "With your current stress level, it might be best if you just sit this one out."

"Will you *allow* me to leave?" Rutu sneered, his eyes turning to Juki.

Acurala blinked in surprise at the coldness in his voice, but Juki just closed his eyes.

"Acurala, I need to speak with Rutu in private," he said. "Please go tell my children that I expect them to attend the banquet."

Acurala nodded quietly, his eyes darting worriedly between the two before he turned away and called to another maid to prepare his horse. As he walked away, Juki motioned to the greeting salon off the foyer. Juki and Rutu walked into the salon, Juki closing the doors as Rutu walked to the decanter near the fireplace, pouring the amber liquor into one of the expensive crystal glasses.

"It's a bit early for that," Juki noted. Rutu did not respond, downing the drink as Juki approached him. "We need to call a truce."

"I agree."

"Then why are you still so upset?"

"Because what you're asking of me is unfair," Rutu said.

The older demon sighed heavily, leaning his head back as his eyes looked everywhere but at Rutu.

"I could end him in an instant, Juki," he insisted. "This is not the time to be testing yourself. Let me kill Kawakara and we can get back to managing everything else in our lives. We don't have time for you to take on this crusade of self-destruction."

"It's not worth the risk, Rutu," Juki insisted. "He managed to claw his way to a living plane by latching on to your power. What if that connection to you allows him to push you to the point of losing control?"

"And that is a justified worry, but there is no guarantee that I will keep control of my powers on any day. For all you know, I could wake up tomorrow and decimate everyone in the land. The risks are no different. Let me help you."

"It *is* different," Juki said. "I know what I'm doing. I need you to trust me."

"What happens when Kawakara goes after Kree? Or Shina? Or Kaneuta?" Rutu challenged. "Think of your children, Juki."

"I am."

"By *toying* with Kawakara?" Rutu shook his head slowly. "The longer you drag this out, the more likely he is to find out about them. *That's* not worth the risk."

Two knocks on the salon door interrupted the Kage Lords' conversation.

"Announcing, Lord Dimitre and Lord Van DeVastes," the steward announced through the door, waiting the appropriate three seconds before opening the doors. The two demons who entered the room were dressed in travel clothes, though the simple garments could do nothing to diminish the confidence in their stride or the power of their chilling golden eyes.

"Dimitre, Van," Juki greeted, smiling as they bowed to him. "I was not expecting you."

"Lord Juki, Lord Rutu," Dimitre greeted. "I apologize for arriving unannounced. I am looking for my younger brother. Maids at the palace said he was staying with you."

"He is currently sleeping," Rutu answered. "It would be unwise to wake him. He is not feeling well."

"This is urgent," Van insisted. "I'm afraid I must insist."

"I do not think his irritation will help you with any official matters you want to discuss," Juki warned.

"This is more personal. We must speak with him urgently."

Juki turned to the still-open door of the salon and motioned the steward to him.

"Fetch Lord Yokouro and bring him here," he said. "If he is uncooperative, tell him that I will retrieve him myself if he is not down here in five minutes."

"Yes, my lord."

As the steward hurried away, Juki turned back to the two younger lords, motioning for them to sit on one of the couches, though they refused politely.

"It has been far too long," Juki said. "I hope you are both doing well."

"Thank you, Lord Juki," Dimitre, the oldest, said with another bow of his head. "It has been far too long. I do wish this visit was less formal."

"You know you are always welcome," Juki said courteously.

"I hope all has been well with you, Lord Juki," Van said, trying not to let on that he was well-versed in the gossip rocketing through the Demon Realm about the troubles plaguing the Kage household.

"It has, thank you," Juki said mechanically. "And, of course, congratulations are in order for your newborn son, Van. Did you receive our gift?"

"I did, Lord Juki. Thank you for your generosity."

The four lords fell into a short, uncomfortable silence as the social niceties ran their course. Dimitre cleared his throat.

"I wonder, Lord Juki, if I could trouble you?" he said carefully.

"How may I help?"

"I am concerned about my younger brother's interests outside the Demon Realm," he said. "You know better than most how brazen Yokouro can be when he wants something. I am just trying to understand what it is that he wants."

"I dare say that Yokouro is also trying to decide what he wants," Juki said.

"Surely you know more about his intentions," Van insisted. "He's come crawling back to you like he always does when he's hiding from some sort of consequence. What is it that he thinks he's going to accomplish by causing a fuss in the other realms?"

Juki was silent, knowing that he had no obligation to answer the younger demons, but also knowing that, like their younger brother, Dimitre and Van were quite brazen and could easily step out of line with their questioning.

"Yokouro does not always confide in us," Juki said vaguely.

"I find it difficult to believe that you would allow him to create such tension," Van said coldly. "Perhaps he is taking advantage of your distraction with your father and working behind your back."

Rutu, who had been standing dutifully by the fireplace, straightened and stepped to Juki's side, causing the two younger lords to retreat a step instinctually.

"I would be extremely cautious with your next words, Van," Rutu warned.

"Kawakara is causing chaos through the land," Dimitre said, though his head dipped in a shallow bow as he retreated another step. "It would be very like our brother to take advantage of your distraction in order to further his own goals. You said yourself, you do not know what Yokouro is planning."

"I did not say that," Juki corrected. "But you two are hardly in any position to be demanding information from me."

"He is our younger brother," Van insisted.

"He is also your Old Blood Lord, and therefore, of a higher status. And I hold a higher position, still," Juki reminded the two younger demons. "Now, I understand your concern, considering your brother's previous endeavors, but I am under no obligation to divulge information. And you would both do well to remember your place."

The two demons bowed their heads.

"Forgive us, my lords," Dimitre murmured, hesitant to raise his eyes again.

Several agonizing minutes of silence passed. The two DeVastes demons would occasionally raise their eyes to the Kage Lords, but would immediately lower them again. Through the grueling minutes, the two older demons never moved their eyes from Van or Dimitre, causing the two younger demons to remain as still as possible, worried about angering the powerful Kage Lords.

A guard posted at the door turned and bowed his head.

"Forgive the intrusion, my lords. Lord Yokouro is here."

"Join us, Yokouro," Juki called, his eyes remaining on Van and Dimitre.

Yokouro walked in slowly, rubbing his face.

"What the hell was so urgent?" he asked irritably. When he lowered his hand, he caught sight of his older brothers, their heads still bowed to the Kages, though they had turned their gazes to Yokouro.

Yokouro chuckled darkly.

"Well, well, well, look who's here," he said. "Her highness and her majesty."

"Yokouro…" Van snarled in warning.

"What?" he asked, feigning innocence. "I'm so honored that my two older brothers have traveled across the land to visit me. It's so thoughtful. I know it's not my birthday...nor another family holiday..."

"Enough, Yokouro," Dimitre growled. "You may be our Old Blood Lord, but we are still your elder brothers. You cannot talk down to us."

"Actually, as an Old Blood Lord, I can," Yokouro corrected, stepping to Juki's other side and looking between the four other demons. "Now, I know you're not here just to visit. You only seek me out when you want something. Out with it."

Dimitre slowly raised his head, throwing nervous looks at the Kage Lords.

"Lord Juki, Lord Rutu," he started respectfully, "may I ask that you let us speak with our brother in private? This is a family matter."

Yokouro scoffed. "I should think that they are more my family than you two. Whatever you have to say to me, you can say in front of them."

Dimitre and Van shared a worried look before turning their eyes back to the ground, falling silent.

Juki spoke up when the silence became too heavy.

"It seems they are too intimidated," he noted. "Rutu."

The two Kage Lords left the salon, Dimitre and Van remaining bowed until the guards closed the salon doors, as per Juki's order. The two older DeVastes demon straightened, their shoulders relaxing once Juki and Rutu had left the room.

"How did you manage to piss them off?" Yokouro asked with a laugh, crossing his arms.

"That is not what we're here to discuss," Van snapped. "Has Kokumay come to see you?"

"Why would she come to see me?" Yokouro groaned. "She hates me."

"You *did* leave her to die," Dimitre reminded him coldly. "And if she's not with you, then we have a dire problem."

"And why would our dear baby sister be a problem?" Yokouro asked, leaning against the fireplace, bored.

"We told you that your return to power would create problems with her," Van warned.

"Well, if she wants revenge, she knows where to find me. If you two can track me down so easily, so can she," Yokouro said, shaking his head, disinterested in the conversation. "Like I told you before, I'm not afraid of Kokumay."

"She actually could kill you, you know," Van reminded him.

"Dimitre, Van," Yokouro said, his tone becoming condescending, as though he were teaching them a subject they were struggling to understand, "Kokumay is the weakest in the entire family. With her little dagger or not, I can overpower her easily. And if she does come after me with that little trinket, then I'll possess it once she shows her face and I end her. Again, I'm not concerned with whatever trivial plan she's cooking up against me."

"Perhaps you should be," Dimitre said. "Because if she hasn't already come after you, and if you haven't already killed her, then that means she's left the Demon Realm."

"What are you talking about?"

"She's gone missing. We went to see her and she was gone. When we tried to track her down, she was nowhere to be found."

"I'm sure you realize that that means she likely left the realm," Van said, smiling when he saw the way Yokouro's expression became stony, clearly understanding that their younger sister actually *could* become a problem for him. "Tell me, do you know where your new human toys are? Do you think Keito is with them?"

"We all know that Kokumay is quite weak, particularly after you left her to die all those years ago," Dimitre continued. "I wonder if she would go directly after those humans rather than waste her time with you. Could you imagine if she brought that dagger with her? Keito could probably overpower her with the right motivation, don't you think?"

"Do you want that in his hands?" Van concluded.

Yokouro took a deep breath, finally turning his eyes to the ceiling in irritation.

"Fine," he snarled. "I'll find her."

"Keep us informed, baby brother," Dimitre said with a cold smile. "We'll show ourselves out."

Chapter Ten

It was slightly chaotic to get the excited children, the dog, and the Guardians onto the boat and away from the dock with the large inflatable attached, but they managed to get to the lake before the hottest part of the day. The Guardians sat near the back of the boat with Andrew and Frieda while the children and the dog sat in the bow, enjoying the rushing wind and the bouncing of the boat as Dalton drove onto the expansive lake.

Once again, the other Guardians felt both out-of-place and oddly-at-ease being on the boat under the sun, enjoying a day without worrying about their jobs or Yokouro. Occasionally, each of them would think about how they should be working, but the stunning day and the joyous giggling of the children would bring them back to the moment and they would push the dark thoughts away, enjoying their break from their lives as Guardians.

Dalton slowed the boat in a near-deserted part of the lake, asking his daughter if she was ready to ride the inflatable.

She quickly agreed, leaping toward the back of the boat with Benjamin and Emma. Frieda double-checked their lifejackets as Dalton prepared the inflatable. The Guardians were a bit over-protective of the children as they clambered onto the large, triangular tube and slowly drifted behind the boat, the rope uncoiling as Dalton waited to start the boat again.

Dalton started slowly, watching Theresa for the hand signals he had taught her that would indicate when she was ready for them to go faster. Even over the growing sound of the boat's engine, the laughter and exhilarated screams brought grins to the Guardians' faces as they watched the inflatable trail in and out of the boat's wake.

After a few turns and one particularly hard bump, Emma tumbled off the inflatable, Theresa barely managing to hold on while Benjamin clenched the handles so tightly his knuckles were turning white. Emma pulled herself back onto the platform and the children, once again, squealed in delight as Dalton pulled the inflatable over the gentle waves on the lake's surface.

Emma and Benjamin both fell off on the next big bump and then asked if they could get back on the boat for a bit. The Guardians helped pull the children onto the boat while Theresa proclaimed that she wanted to remain. Dalton pulled the large tube to the back of the boat while Theresa pouted that she needed two more people on the inflatable to keep it balanced.

"Then pick who you want to join you," Dalton said, turning to the rest of his team with a broad smile. Theresa's eyes immediately locked onto one Guardian.

"Uncle Keito?" she asked.

Keito straightened, not expecting the affectionate name.

"Me?"

"You and Hanyi should ride!" she exclaimed.

Keito turned his eyes down to the sleeping wolf next to him.

"I think we're still waking up a bit, Theresa," Keito said.

"That's why you should ride!" she said. "When you fall in the water, it'll wake you up!"

"Oh really?" Keito teased, standing. She nodded enthusiastically. "Well, then." Keito peeled off his shirt and darted to the back of the boat, diving into the water as the others laughed in surprise. Keito disappeared under the water, swimming toward the back of the inflatable before resurfacing. Theresa was giggling happily as Keito climbed onto the tube and playfully grabbed her ankles to pull her into the water.

"Your turn!" he laughed.

As she squirmed away from the demon, Dalton turned to Hanyi, though the wolf was still lounging on his side on the floor of the boat.

"Looks like Hanyi's not ready yet," he said. "Eclipse? Mitoki?" he turned to the two younger men, raising an expectant eyebrow.

"Why don't you go?" Eclipse said.

"Someone has to drive the boat."

"Which one of you is joining us?" Keito called.

Eventually, Eclipse was persuaded to climb onto the tube to join Keito and Theresa.

As the tube drifted out and Dalton resumed his seat at the wheel, he turned his attention to Hanyi.

"Hanyi? Are you sure you're alright? I thought you were excited about tubing."

Hanyi groaned, sitting upright before shifting into his human form and nodding, stretching his arms above his head.

"I'm fine," he assured. "It's nothing serious. Just feeling a bit off. And it takes a lot of energy to be in a human form all the time, so I'm saving my energy as much as possible."

"Oh no," Dalton chuckled worriedly. "Keito was sick last round. Don't you dare get sick."

"I'm sure I'll be fine," Hanyi said with a smile, but Dalton could tell that the expression was forced. "I'm just enjoying the relaxing time out here. It's helping a lot, actually. But if you're worried, you can always check my nose and see if it's cold."

Dalton laughed at the devious look on Hanyi's face. "Check your own nose," he said.

Dalton drove the boat slowly to allow Keito and Eclipse to get used to tubing. When he got the signal from Theresa, he picked up speed, going as fast as he knew his daughter could handle. Secretly, he had made it his goal to get one of the Guardians in the water.

He continued to turn the boat, creating larger waves, hearing Theresa's excited screams and yelps as they went over the bumps in the water. Even though Eclipse had been hesitant about tubing, everyone could see the broad smile on his face as the tube bounced and Theresa giggled loudly in delight.

Dalton eventually turned the boat in three circles, creating large enough waves to launch the tube into the air, bouncing again when it hit the water. Eclipse tumbled off the inflatable with Theresa. Dalton cut power to the boat and watched the waves settle. Eclipse resurfaced and swam toward Theresa, who was coughing, but smiling broadly. Eclipse and Keito helped Theresa back onto the inflatable before Eclipse fixed Dalton with a glare, settling back onto the inflatable's platform.

"You did that on purpose!" he called.

"You have no proof!" Dalton defended with a broad grin.

Eclipse lasted another turn on the inflatable, but when he decided he was done, Hanyi joined Theresa and Keito. Dalton managed to get Hanyi into the water quite easily, but the wolf climbed right back on and ordered Dalton keep going, because he was determined to conquer it. When he found himself in the water again, he leapt back onto the tube and demanded another try.

The day continued in that fashion. Everyone other than Dalton and Frieda took turns on the inflatable, and the day flew by with broad smiles and loud laughs.

Andrew, Eclipse, and Keito were the last ones on the inflatable. Dalton was driving the boat a little slower than before, aware that everyone was tired. Hanyi leaned over to Dalton, smiling devilishly.

"Flip them."

"Eclipse will hold me down while Keito kills me," Dalton objected with a broken chuckle.

"I'll take the blame," Hanyi said. "I promise. And then you can laugh at me while they kill me."

"They'll blame me because I'm the one driving," Dalton said. "And I really like my head where it is. It fits nicely on my shoulders."

"Please?" Hanyi whimpered.

Dalton stared at him for a moment before his own mischievous side began to take interest.

"You're nothing but trouble."

Dalton picked a good spot on the water and made two loops before turning the boat sharply in the opposite direction. When the rope snapped tight, the inflatable hit the rolling hills of water at just the right angle. With Andrew on the front of the triangular platform and the two heavier Guardians on the back, the front popped upright, sitting perpendicular in the water and launching everyone aboard backward.

The younger kids began laughing hysterically. Frieda and Dalton were pursing their lips against their own boisterous laughter while Hanyi chuckled deviously.

Dalton turned the boat around and turned off the engine when Eclipse began swimming toward the fantail, Andrew close behind. They both climbed onto the back of the boat, proclaiming they were too tired for another run. As Frieda handed them towels, Keito swam to the side of the boat, where Hanyi was leaning over with a grin.

"Hanyi," Keito said suspiciously, "why do I get the feeling that *you* told him to do that?"

"Oh, the ideas that come out of your head."

Keito launched out of the water and grabbed the front of Hanyi's shirt, yanking him over the side of the boat. Eclipse laughed triumphantly as a new round of giggling overtook the others at Hanyi's punishment. Hanyi resurfaced in wolf form, paddling to the fantail, Keito following. The demon helped the wolf back onto the boat where he shook dry, the water droplets soaking Keito. Hanyi shifted back into his human form, giving the demon a triumphant nod.

"Serves you right."

Eclipse darted to the fantail, pushing Hanyi back into the water.

The wolf was greeted with even more laughter when he resurfaced, once again in his wolf form. He had Keito pull him back onto the boat before he leapt toward the seats, laying on Eclipse's shirt as the Antiquan Angel yelled at him.

Hanyi changed back into his human form once more.

"I'm going to get you for that," Eclipse warned.

"Come on!" Hanyi whined. "I've been thrown in the water twice already! No more revenge!"

The inflatable was secured to the back of the boat and everyone found a spot to sit, drying in the sun and eating the sandwiches Frieda had prepared, chatting lightly and enjoying the warm weather.

After lunch, Dalton took them to a dock on the opposite side of the lake, where the kids ran into the fueling station to get ice cream. Rio loved running around to the other families on the dock and greeting them with a wagging tail. But once Rio had gotten the attention of the others around the dock, Team Dalton was spotted and nearly swarmed. Many recognized the Guardians from the coverage of the Guardian Tournament. Pictures were taken and autographs were given, but the Guardians were quick to find any opening they could to return to the boat and get away from the crowd. The kids became bored waiting for the Guardians so they returned to the boat before them, waiting with the laughing Frieda, who refused to save her husband from some of the women openly flirting with him.

Once they were able to escape the dock, Dalton drove the boat to a cove where a river fed into the lake, anchoring the boat and allowing the kids to swim in the shallow water while the adults relaxed. Rio, Hanyi, and Frieda sat in the shade of the boat's roof while the others sat in the sun's rays, enjoying both the peace of the lake as well as the excited laughing of the playing kids.

"Dalton," Mitoki said, causing his team leader to turn, "I don't know if I've thanked you for bringing us out here. It's really nice to have a break from everything."

"That's why I have this place," Dalton said. "Sometimes, we just have to get away from it all."

"You have found a very good balance," Keito agreed.

"I feel like I should be concerned with how out of place I feel out here," Eclipse murmured, his eyes distant on the water. "I don't think I've taken a vacation since I joined the Guardians. Apart from medical leave to heal."

"I understand the feeling," Dalton said. "So when all this business with Yokouro and the tournament is over, I expect you all to join me up here a few times a year."

Mitoki laughed, nodding. "Sounds like a plan to me."

Frieda, sitting in the driver's seat of the boat, looked among the four Guardians sitting in the sun, feeling her heart fall. One of the most difficult things in her relationship with Dalton was his job as a Guardian. She had managed to live with the fear that he might not return home any time he left for work, but she had been unable to ignore the toll his work brought upon him. She had seen the way the mission with the tournament and Yokouro was wearing him down, and hearing the others of his team, she knew that the other Guardians understood, better than she ever could, how Dalton was feeling. She was certain that he had already discussed his power increase with his teammates, while she had been left in the dark until the previous night.

For the first time since they got married, she felt as though Dalton was too far away for her to reach.

When she dropped her head and turned to her water bottle, she saw Hanyi looking at her, giving her a questioning glance. She forced a smile and then turned away, hoping he had not seen her inner turmoil on her face.

"Keito!" Emma called, waving to him from the shallow water. "Come swim with us!"

"Why do they only pick on me?" Keito groaned half-jokingly. "They think I'm so full of energy…"

He dove into the water and swam toward the children, grabbing Andrew and wrestling with him as the others joined in on the fun. The human Guardians laughed.

"He's complaining, but clearly he's enjoying himself," Dalton said. "I don't know that I've ever seen Keito have this much fun."

"I didn't know he *knew* how to have fun," Eclipse seconded. "He's like a different person."

"That's because he's happy," Hanyi chimed in from his seat in the boat, causing them to turn around. "Happiness is a luxury Keito doesn't often have. He's been fighting for survival since he was an infant and he never really had time to be a kid. He actually told me once that he was afraid to be happy because he never felt he deserved it, and whenever he allowed himself to be happy, that was when horrible things would happen to those he loved."

"Wait, he *told* you that?" Eclipse asked skeptically. "He *communicated* with you about how he was feeling?"

Hanyi barked a laugh. "Well, to be fair, he was drunk off his ass at the time and fighting with himself about whether or not to tell Sadee he was in love with her."

The humans straightened quickly.

"Wait, with *Sadee*? Your teammate?"

"Yep. One and the same," Hanyi said. "He spent so much time overthinking it and fighting with himself about whether or not to let himself be happy and admit his feelings to her. I made sure to take the opportunity when he was smashed to get him to open up a bit."

"Did he tell her?"

"I should hope so. She was his mate," Hanyi laughed.

"I didn't know *Sadee* was his mate," Dalton said quietly. "And to lose her the way he did…"

Hanyi sighed heavily. "It basically broke him," he admitted. "But, after he had grieved for her and we started talking again, he told me that he had made the right choice. That no matter the risk, no matter the pain, the happiness he had found with her was worth it, because she was worth everything to him."

The water wrestling did not last much longer, as the children were also feeling the exhaustion settling in from the full day on the lake. When they returned to the house, the Guardians helped Dalton put the boat away while Frieda and the children went inside, preparing for an early dinner.

Once everyone's bellies were full, the sleepiness began to take hold. The children wanted to stay awake and watch a movie, but when Frieda saw they were falling asleep during the first twenty minutes, she turned off the movie and told the younger kids to get some sleep.

While the Guardians were doing the dishes and helping Frieda clean up the kitchen after dinner, Andrew asked Keito stories about his old missions, begging him to recount every detail while Dalton, Mitoki, and Eclipse tried to pretend they were not as interested in the demon's stories.

Frieda excused herself to the balcony, leaning on the railing and looking up at the stars, trying to ignore the heaviness in her chest.

"Do you mind if I join you?" a voice asked. She turned quickly, startled, smiling as Hanyi closed the door to the balcony and approached her.

"Oh, Hanyi, no, not at all," she said.

He stepped next to her, taking a deep breath as he, also, leaned on the railing.

"Thank you so much for dinner. It was incredible," Hanyi complimented. "Sorry I'm such an idiot in the kitchen, or I would help more."

"It's my pleasure, Hanyi," Frieda said. "I'm just happy that you're all having so much fun up here."

"I can't tell you how nice it's been to get away from work," Hanyi agreed.

"…I can imagine," Frieda murmured, unsuccessful at keeping the sadness out of her voice. Hanyi looked her over as she turned her gaze to the railing under her hands.

"You've been quiet all day. Are you alright?"

"Yes, I'm fine," she said. "I'm sorry. Just a little tired today, I guess."

"Okay." He fell silent, looking into the dark trees around the house, feeling the tension in Frieda's being. She hesitated, taking a deep breath, too nervous to lift her head as she spoke.

"Hanyi, can I ask you something?"

"Of course."

"Why did you choose this job?" she asked. "Why did any of you choose this? It's a horrific way to live and it brings so many Guardians so much pain. Why not just get out?"

Hanyi thought for a moment, a sad smile tugging at the corners of his mouth. "It's not that simple..." he started. "Once you're a Guardian, there's no way to go back. Sure, you can quit, but that doesn't change how you look at the realms. Nothing looks the same after being a Guardian."

"But you still choose it?"

"For some, being a Guardian is the best thing they can do. It gives us a purpose, makes us feel we can accomplish something, that we can help people."

Frieda placed her elbows on the railing, rubbing her face roughly.

"I would never presume to ask Dalton to quit his job. I know how important it is to him," she said, her voice strained. "But sometimes...I feel like he's purposely trying to bring evil toward him. If he wasn't a Guardian, then Yokouro wouldn't be so interested in going after him, and he wouldn't be struggling to find a way to kill this demon. Dalton's putting himself through all this pain, and I don't know how to help him."

Hanyi was silent for a few moments, thinking about how to respond.

"Dalton is one of the most incredible people I have ever met," he said. "Despite his job and the pain it brings, he hasn't lost sight of who he is and what he wants to achieve with his life. He wants to protect people. To make them happy. If he can see people living a peaceful life, smiling, having families, that's all he needs." His eyes turned to Frieda, his smile growing. "He's amazingly strong. Yes, Yokouro is catching us off guard, but through all of that, Dalton has managed to keep a level head and hold this team together. Even Keito couldn't manage that when we started going after Yokouro. He has strength even he doesn't know, and after coming up here, I can see where he gets it. He's so resilient because of you and Theresa. Because of how much you support him. Not many spouses are as supportive as you've been."

"Sometimes I wish I wasn't," Frieda chuckled, shaking her head. "Not that I don't want to support him in whatever he does, I just wish I could tell him that I don't want him to be a Guardian. But if he wasn't a Guardian, he wouldn't be Dalton."

"You're an amazing woman, Frieda," Hanyi said. "I hope you know that. The fact that you understand that about Dalton makes you truly remarkable."

Frieda pursed her lips, lowering her head, her voice becoming choked.

"Then why am I so afraid?" she whispered. "Why am I so afraid that he's becoming someone I don't know? That I'm losing him?" She pressed her hands over her face. "He's pushing me away. He doesn't talk to me about these things anymore. He didn't tell me that his powers were growing, or that there's some connection between him and Yokouro. All I see is him in pain and his magic becoming so strong…" she trailed off. "I just don't know what to do."

Frieda's body trembled as she tried to contain her sobs. Hanyi put a hand on her shoulder, squeezing gently.

"Are you afraid that he's going to hurt you or Theresa?"

"No, no, he would never do that," she said quickly, pushing her tears away with the heels of her hands.

"Then he's not becoming someone you don't know," Hanyi said. "Believe me, he's terrified about what's going on with his powers, but he's trying to figure it out. He probably didn't tell you much because he doesn't know much himself. But you can trust him. You can trust that that worry about his magic is going to be the thing that helps him master it."

"But how do I not be afraid of that?" Frieda demanded.

"It's okay to be afraid," Hanyi assured. "It's better to be honest about being afraid than pretending you're not."

"But if I let him know how scared I am, he won't talk to me. He gets more support from you and the other Guardians," she said. "You understand this mission and what it's doing to him."

"All the more reason to talk with him and tell him about your fears," Hanyi said strongly. "We're Guardians, Frieda. It's different with us. Dalton is the top-ranked Guardian in the branch, and he's our superior. He feels like has no room to be vulnerable with us. But if you let him know that, despite the fear, you're there to support him, he'll let you see how he's truly feeling. He won't let us see it."

Frieda sniffed, trying to push her tears away, though they stubbornly continued to trickle down her cheeks. Hanyi looked around quickly.

"Sorry, I don't have any tissues," he said. "You can use my sleeve, if you want." He turned his shoulder to her, causing her to let out a bark of laughter and shake her head. She swallowed hard, sniffling once more.

"You're pretty amazing, too, Hanyi," she whispered. "You knew exactly what I needed to hear."

"Wolf intuition," he said, beaming. "But now you need to talk with Dalton. I don't like seeing the tension between you. I want you both to be having as much fun out here as we are."

"I'll talk with him," Frieda assured. "Thank you for looking out for Dalton…and for me."

Hanyi grinned. "Hey, I have a title to live up to."

"Title?"

"Man's best friend."

Chapter Eleven

Hanyi clearly was feeling unwell the following morning. When everyone heard that he was sick in bed, they crowded around the lower bunk bed where Hanyi was reclined in a human form.

"Are you gonna be okay?" Theresa asked worriedly. "You didn't want breakfast."

"I-I don't know..." the wolf said dramatically. "It's hard, but...I will try to pull through." The Guardians looked to one another, rolling their eyes. "If...if I don't make it...please, tell my family I loved them..."

"Knock it off," Eclipse groaned. "Keito said you have a fever. You're not suffering some ancient tragedy."

Hanyi laughed. "Yeah, I know. No one cares that much."

"If I didn't care, I would have kicked you out of the room for tossing and turning so much last night," Keito said, returning to the room with a damp towel and placing it around Hanyi's neck. "What is with this fever?" he grumbled. "It should have broken by now."

"Is there anything I can get you, Hanyi?" Frieda asked. "We have a pretty big first aid kit here."

"There's no need to worry," Hanyi said with a smile, ignoring the way Keito's fingers prodded into his neck. "It's just a fever. It will break."

"And what's that going to take?" Keito asked, taking Hanyi's chin. "Open your mouth."

Hanyi complied, but Dalton raised an eyebrow.

"Keito, what are you doing?"

"Checking him for normal ailments," Keito explained, peering into Hanyi's mouth.

"You're not a doctor."

"No, but I have quite a bit of medical training," Keito explained, trapping Hanyi's wrist in his fingers while pressing his other hand to the center of Hanyi's chest. "Deep breath."

"How do you have medical training?" Eclipse asked skeptically.

"My mother taught me quite a bit when I was young. And then Juki taught me the rest," Keito said mechanically. He cringed as soon as the words left his mouth. "Sorry...I forgot that that was a sore subject."

"Why am I even surprised?" Eclipse mumbled.

Keito's hand against Hanyi's chest began to glow with a faint blue light that was common with healing energy, but the light only lasted one moment before Keito lifted his hand and narrowed his eyes. He opened his mouth, but hesitated.

"Everything okay?" Mitoki asked.

"Could you give me a moment?" he asked, nodding to the door.

Even though Dalton wanted to ask what Keito was worried about, he turned his eyes to the young children in the room and nodded, helping to usher them out before closing the door and leaving Keito alone with Hanyi.

"What do you think that was all about?" Eclipse asked.

"Is Hanyi going to be alright?" Benjamin asked.

"He'll be fine," Dalton said with a comforting smile. "You wanted to go into town today, right?" Theresa and her friends nodded enthusiastically. "Well, since Hanyi isn't feeling well, I think we're going to stay here and look after him, okay?"

Frieda let out a disbelieving laugh, staring at Dalton as he smiled sheepishly.

"Is that okay?" Dalton asked Theresa.

"Uh-huh," she agreed. Dalton turned to Andrew.

"Go with them? Help Frieda out?"

Andrew sighed heavily before begrudgingly agreeing.

"Can we take Rio, Mom?" Theresa begged.

"No, we're going to leave him here with Dad," Frieda said. "It's too hot for him to stay in the car. And he can keep Hanyi company until he feels better." Frieda bent down and kissed the top of her daughter's head. "Go get your shoes on."

As the kids scrambled away, Keito opened the door and joined them in the living room just as Benjamin and Andrew went to retrieve their shoes.

"Is Hanyi alright?" Mitoki asked.

Keito nodded hesitantly. "Yeah, he's okay. It's nothing physical, exactly."

"It's mental?" Dalton asked, confused.

"No, it's…" Keito took a deep breath. "It's Xana. Apparently, she's pretty sick. She was sick before Hanyi left and her illness is putting a strain on their mate bond."

"Xana?" Dalton repeated. "Then he should go back and take care of her."

Keito pursed his lips, his eyes remaining downcast.

"I don't think that will help," he said quietly.

The words were thick as they hung in the air. Dalton was about to ask Keito how serious Xana's illness was when the children returned to the living room, excited about going into town and seeing the candy factory Theresa had told her friends about.

"Frieda, if you're going into town, can I trouble you for a few things?" Keito asked. "There are a few herbs that I can give to Hanyi to ease the worst of the discomfort and break his fever."

"Of course," she said. Keito disappeared into the kitchen to write down the things he needed as Frieda told the children to get in the car, causing a flurry of activity as they rushed to the driveway. Dalton extracted his wallet and passed her a few large bills of money, kissing her on the cheek.

"Have fun."

Keito returned with the folded piece of paper, handing it to Frieda. When she opened it, she saw several more large bills inside.

"Oh, no, Keito, it's alright. I've got it," she said, trying to hand the money back. Keito retreated several steps.

"I won't take it back," he laughed.

She sighed, grinning. "Thank you." She turned to Dalton and kissed him. "We'll be back later. Call me if you think of anything else we need."

She also left the living room as Mitoki smiled at Dalton.

"I'm glad to see you and your wife made up," he said.

"Indeed," Keito said with a laugh.

Dalton turned to the demon.

"What is that supposed to mean?"

Keito raised his eyebrows. "Do I *really* have to say?" Eclipse and Mitoki started chuckling at the embarrassment that overtook Dalton's face.

"Wait, how did you…" He shot the demon a suspicious look.

"Never question how I know something," he said. "There is a very *healthy* spark in your aura that is unmistakable."

Dalton opened and closed his mouth a few times before shaking his head and changing the subject as quickly as he could.

"Enough about…that. Is Hanyi going to be okay? Is Xana going to be okay?"

Keito's face fell.

"I don't know about Xana," he said truthfully. "Hanyi is physically fine. But from what he told me…it doesn't sound like Xana is doing well. She wasn't doing well when he left. Both he and Xana are quite old, even by Treneke wolf standards."

"He should be at home with her," Mitoki insisted.

"He'll know when things are getting dire," Keito said. "But with Yokouro and the tournament, it's going to be hard to convince him to go home. That's why he didn't say anything before. Just don't let him know that you know what's going on. It will be better for him. He'll tell us if he needs to go home."

Yokouro bowed his head even further against the howling wind slicing into his face. He had finally caught sight of his destination ahead, but his horse was even more eager to seek shelter in the large cave opening. His horse's hooves slid over the loose rocks on the mountain path as he rushed forward, finally stepping into the maw of carved stone. The horse dropped his head and snorted, stubbornly refusing to move until the elements improved.

Yokouro dismounted, unwinding the fabric from his face and brushing the remaining snowflakes from his hair and shoulders as the other three horses stepped into the opening, just as eager as their own riders to get out of the blizzard.

The horses were tied to a wooden post stationed outside the large door sitting against the carved rock face.

"Did she carve this out herself?" Acurala asked, shaking his head to loosen the snow clinging to his hair.

"I doubt it," Yokouro sneered, taking hold of the heavy handle and pulling the door open to lead them into the cave home. "Kokumay was always notoriously lazy. She probably paid or seduced others into doing this for her."

The four demon lords stepped into the cave home, Yokouro motioning his hand over the room to ignite the candles scattered throughout, illuminating the rough walls covered with simple tapestries.

"Hard to believe a lady of the DeVastes Clan would live in a place like this," Acurala noted, walking among the primitive furniture scattered in the spacious cave. "How long has she been living here?"

"Only a few centuries, I think," Yokouro answered.

"Looks like she cleared out in a hurry," Juki said, kicking the ashes in the fire pit near the door. "And recently. She hasn't been gone more than a week, I'd say."

"We already know she left the realm. Why did we come here?" Acurala asked.

"We're here in the off-chance that she left her dagger here." Yokouro turned to Rutu, his anger causing his nostrils to flare and his eyes to shimmer. "Rutu, can you sense it?"

"It's not here, Yokouro," Rutu said, standing by the door.

"Do you want to actually *look around* before you answer?" Yokouro snarled.

"Do you really think I need to look around?" Rutu challenged. "That dagger contains very potent magic. I would be able to sense it from outside. But it's not here."

"She could have warded it to keep it hidden from me," Yokouro snapped. "Now, help me look for it."

Rutu groaned, stepping over to the mattress piled high with blankets behind a thick, tapestry screen. Crouching, he pushed the blankets aside before shoving his hand into the large tear he somehow knew would be there. He pulled out a narrow, black box, carved with intricate symbols that had been inlaid with gold. Rutu set the box on the ground, flicked the latch, and opened it to reveal the contents had been removed, leaving only an empty dagger cradle.

"Anything else you need me to do for you?" Rutu growled.

Yokouro's foot kicked the box to the side as he loomed over the crouching Rutu.

"If you're so powerful, why don't you just track my sister? Tell me where she went and what she did with the dagger?" he snarled.

Rutu stood slowly, the air around him becoming dangerous as his own temper rose to match Yokouro's.

"I've tried to tell you where she is, but you don't want to hear it," he growled. "Ignoring the truth doesn't change it, you insolent brat."

"Rutu," Juki said with a warning tone.

"I'm not ignoring the truth," Yokouro defended, leaning forward to challenge Rutu. "I am trying to find my sister and keep her from meddling."

"And how do you plan to do that?" Rutu asked coldly. "Are you going to kill her? Are you going to risk a mark on your neck that will put you down for months?"

"Well, I didn't think I could ask *you* to do it," Yokouro snapped. "You won't even kill Kawakara."

Juki was about to speak when Rutu grabbed Yokouro's neck and shoved him against the nearest wall, knocking over a small table and causing the books atop it to tumble to the floor.

"You have caught me in a very unforgiving mood, Yokouro," Rutu growled. "I have warned you time and time again not to get sloppy when it comes to the Guardians, but you have refused to listen to me. Now, you drag us all the way into the mountains when I have *told* you that your sister is likely already tracking Team Dalton. So do not waste any more of my time by asking me questions you don't want to hear the answers to."

Yokouro stared at the angry Rutu, but rather than back down as he knew he should, he snorted, shaking his head.

"Then why don't you go crawl back to your palace, Rutu?" he sneered. "I'll deal with Kokumay myself. You should go back to sulking and hiding from Kawakara, even though it was *your* power that brought him back to begin with."

Juki flinched away from the words.

"Yokouro is going to get himself killed..." he whispered.

Yokouro knew that Rutu often left a confrontation when he became too angry, since he could not let his emotions get the better of him at his power level. But when Rutu's face softened into a cold smirk, Yokouro knew he had stepped too far over the line.

"Fine," Rutu said gently. "You kill Kokumay and get your dagger back. But let me remind you of what will happen when you do so."

An agony that had Yokouro's knees buckling radiated through his body from Rutu's hand around his neck. He reached up to claw at Rutu's hand, but the older demon released him. Yokouro fell heavily to the floor, his nails scraping along his neck and face as the dark, cursed markings all over his body began to shine with a bright orange light, pulsing in time with his quickening heartbeat.

"Do you remember that pain, Yokouro?" Rutu hissed, leaning over the groaning demon on the ground. "How it was a hundred times worse than any of your other marks?"

Yokouro's teeth were grinding so hard together Juki and Acurala could hear it from across the cave. Acurala looked between Rutu and his brother, wondering if Juki was going to step in—though he was not sure it was safe to even approach Rutu when he was so enraged.

"That's because your clan loved sneaking into family members' rooms at night and slaughtering them in their sleep just for an easier shot at the throne," Rutu growled, crouching next to Yokouro. "So if you think you can bear up to this pain while I sulk at home, then don't let me stand in your way."

Yokouro let out a shout of pain, his claws leaving deep gashes in his neck as he scraped at the agony burning his neck and chest.

The sound prompted Juki to step to Rutu's side.

"Alright, that's enough," he said. "You've proven your point."

"I'm disciplining an unruly pup," Rutu corrected, his eyes never leaving Yokouro's agonized expression.

"There's a difference between discipline and torture," Juki whispered. Rutu slowly turned his gaze to Juki. "You've proven your point."

Rutu was still for a very long moment before he stood, turning away from Yokouro. Yokouro let out a long breath and his body slumped, his breathing labored as he tried to collect his bearings from the searing agony that had suddenly vanished. Rutu walked to the door, slamming it shut behind him when he stepped outside.

"Rutu?" Acurala started toward the door when his brother's voice stopped him.

"Acurala. I wouldn't."

The younger Kage was clearly torn, unsure if he should stay with Juki and Yokouro or be sure that Rutu had not left the mountain entirely in his anger.

Juki helped Yokouro to his feet, watching as the youngest Old Blood Lord healed the wounds on his face and neck.

"Does Rutu know what Kokumay intends to do?" he asked, trying not to sound breathless.

"No," Juki said.

"What do *you* think she'll do?" Yokouro asked.

"I have no doubt that she's trailing Team Dalton, and she clearly took the dagger with her. But I doubt she'll just hand it over to them."

"Does Keito know she has it?"

"I don't know," Juki admitted. "But if he spots it, you can be sure he'll take any opportunity he can find to take it from her. You know her strength better than I. Do you think Keito can overpower her?"

Yokouro turned to look at the empty box that had fallen near the middle of the cave.

"Get Rutu under control," Yokouro ordered, turning back to Juki. "I want his eyes on her at all times. If she makes a move against Dalton, I'll interfere. We can't let Keito get his hands on that dagger."

~∧~

Later in the day, after Frieda and the kids returned, everyone agreed to head back into the nearby town to the movie theater. The rest through the day had done wonders for Hanyi, but Dalton wanted to keep the day low-key, so even though the kids wanted to go bowling, he promised they would do so the following day, desperate to keep Hanyi quiet while trying not to show his worry.

The children opted to see the latest action film that had been released two weeks previous to rave reviews. Dalton got the children snacks and drinks and then helped Frieda wrangle them into the theater, where they picked their seats and waited for the movie to start.

It was impossible for Team Dalton to keep a straight face through the movie.

The story was about a demon Guardian named Kido LaPyro—a loose cannon who had no respect for authority—who had to thwart a plot to open holes in the dimensions and let loose demons on the human race.

As soon as the character was introduced on screen, Keito groaned and hid his face in his hands, curling into his seat as the others desperately tried to stifle their laughter in their hands. Others in the theater were shushing them, but it was extremely difficult for any of the Guardians to hide their amusement, particularly when the character did anything Keito-like.

The story was very simple. Kido was a demon Guardian with a dark past where his parents were brutally murdered by other demons when he was young, so he became a Guardian to find the killer and bring them to justice. Kido was secretive about his life, but when asked, he was also willing to explain his trauma with a quiet, brooding expression on his face that had the Guardians nearly rolling on the floor. He teamed up with a beautiful half-demon Guardian named Hannah, though he was cold to her and often put her down, even when she had good ideas about how to handle the case.

In the climax of the movie, there was a breach in the realms that linked the Demon Realm to the Human Realm, and the demon responsible for the plot was the same demon that had killed both Kido's parents and Hannah's family. They beat the comically-inept villain and the two Guardians ended up together in the end.

Part of the fun of watching the film was trying not to laugh at it. They were repeatedly shushed and shot dirty looks, but there were moments where the Guardians could not help themselves, even going so far as to bite their hands to keep from bursting out with laughter.

When they left the theater, they were practically in tears as the humans continued to tease and reenact certain lines in front of the extremely embarrassed Keito. By the time they reached the car, the children had realized that the story was based around Keito and began asking him about the case the movie had shown.

"I suppose it could have been a real case," Keito finally admitted. "A hole opening up between the Human Realm and the Realm of Demons is something I dealt with constantly. But if that was based on a real case, it was nowhere *near* what happened."

"Who was Hannah?" Theresa asked.

"I have no idea," Keito groaned.

"Oh, please!" Hanyi barked. "Great sense of humor? Gorgeous? Put up with your crap when she should have walked away long ago?" He pointed at himself. "*Clearly*, it was me!"

The laughter started anew as Keito shuddered.

"They made us into a couple," he pointed out.

"Come on, that was a rumor for decades," Hanyi said.

"It was not!"

"Yes, it was!" Hanyi defended. "Do you know how many people asked me how we managed to stay professional on cases when we were sleeping together?"

Keito choked. "No, they didn't!"

"Keito," Hanyi said with a disbelieving laugh, "I was *kidnapped* because Arena Buchant thought that it would be a way to get to *you*. Remember?"

Keito's eyes began rapidly flicking back and forth on the floor of the car as he thought. The kids were howling with laughter while Mitoki was holding his stomach and wiping tears from his face as his giggling refused to subside. Eclipse was trying very hard not to join in the laughing, his face turning red as he pursed his lips so hard they nearly disappeared.

"I know she used you as *bait*," Keito said slowly.

"She kidnapped me and told me that she was waiting for my lover to come and rescue me," Hanyi said with a grin. "I spent the entire four hours until you showed up explaining to her that we were not a couple. She *refused* to believe me."

"Why didn't you tell me about this before?" Keito gasped.

"I assumed you knew," Hanyi said. "And, there were many times where I pretended it was true so people would give me access to Archives. I figured there was no point in trying to correct it after a certain point."

When they reached the house, Dalton had the younger kids take Rio out for a walk before bed, asking Eclipse and Mitoki to keep an eye on them. Rio sniffed around the trees, looking for a particular place while the kids laughed and talked about the movie. Eclipse and Mitoki, both exhausted from laughing so hard at the film, tried not to let their giggling get a hold of them again, hanging back and watching the kids from a distance.

"Did you see the tail tonight?" Mitoki finally whispered.

"Yeah, right about the time we entered the gates they took the turn off toward the lake," Eclipse said, recalling that, once they had been able to stop laughing about the movie, he had spotted a car following them to the gated community where Dalton had his house before pulling off the side of the road. "Dalton saw it, too. He was changing pace to see if they were following or not."

"What do you think?" Mitoki asked.

"Well, with our jobs, it could have been anyone," Eclipse said, stopping when the kids halted to allow the dog to sniff around some bushes on the side of the road. "It has been a little quiet for all of us being together. I've been wondering if one of our *friends* would make an appearance."

"That's what worries me," Mitoki agreed. "We're sitting ducks out here, more or less. And we have a bunch of little kids. We're really not in a good position if someone decided to attack."

Rio lifted his head suddenly, his ears pointed into the dark shadows within the trees. His hackles raised, his teeth showing as he began growling. He barked angrily, leaping backward from the side of the road as Theresa tried to soothe him.

"Theresa? What's wrong?" Mitoki asked, rushing to the kids.

"I don't know," Theresa admitted, struggling with the leash. "He just started freaking out."

Eclipse turned to the bushes that had startled the dog, reaching out with his magic to sense if there were any people or demons nearby. He could not ignore the nervous knot in his stomach, particularly after his conversation with Mitoki not a half-minute previous. There was nothing immediately threatening that he could sense, but there was a strange odor he could not entirely place.

Mitoki told the kids to stay where they were as he stepped to Eclipse's side.

"Can you sense anything?"

"No," Eclipse whispered. "Can you?"

"No," Mitoki said. "But I am noticing the smell...and the crickets."

"Crickets? What crickets—oh..." Eclipse stopped, realizing that the area around them was eerily silent. Moving as slowly as he could in hopes of not making noise, Eclipse stepped into the shadows of the trees, Mitoki close behind, listening carefully, breathing deep as he tried to place the stale, sweet smell.

The moment they left the road, they could feel their skin prickling at the energy surrounding the area. Eclipse turned to Mitoki, communicating silently as he motioned to the children. Neither of them had their gun with them, but there was magic trailing from their fingers, ready to defend if they were suddenly attacked. They could feel the energy around them, heavily sitting in their lungs and causing the shadows to shroud their eyes, making it even harder to see.

As Mitoki turned to follow Eclipse's motion to get the kids to the house, a snap in the tree above them caused them both to look up. A shower of pine needles fell near Mitoki, but the younger Guardian rolled out of the way as a man descended from the branches, landing in the spot where Mitoki had once been standing. Mitoki got to his feet only to have Eclipse push him roughly out of the way when another dark figure fell from above, landing on Eclipse, pinning him to the ground and brandishing a knife.

"Mitoki! The kids!"

The younger man turned just in time to see a third attacker leaping over the bushes toward the seven-year-olds. The children began screaming and running as the dog growled angrily, barking at the figure. Mitoki leapt over the bushes and grabbed the back of the man's shirt, pulling him sharply backward and pinning him to the pavement, trying to avoid the daggers in the attacker's hands.

He managed to knock one of the blades aside, but was distracted by Eclipse's pained cry in the tree line. Exploiting his distraction, the man flipped them both, pinning Mitoki and raising his remaining dagger. The children screamed loudly at the sight.

Mitoki grabbed his wrist, twisting his hand and forcing the dagger into the attacker's diaphragm, making one sharp slice sideways and pushing the man away, holding the dagger so he would have a weapon if he was attacked again.

Satisfied that his attacker was dead, Mitoki turned to look at the children.

"Are you okay?" he asked quickly.

Theresa and Emma were crying, holding onto each other and to Rio. Benjamin's eyes were locked on the dagger in Mitoki's hand. The Guardian walked closer, worried, and ready to rush the kids back to the house. Benjamin backed away from him, his eyes still locked on the blade.

Mitoki crouched next to the kids, placing a hand on Theresa's shoulder, not sure how to stop her shivering or crying. When he turned to Benjamin and saw the pale look of terror on the child's face, his heart sank.

"Benjamin?"

"You...you killed him..."

Eclipse had been trying to keep his ground fighting the other two attackers. They were fast, and both still held two daggers. It was very clear with their speed and strength that they were not human, but they were not lethal enough to be demons. Eclipse was already considering removing his power limiters and using his Antiquan magic to defeat them.

Taking a chance, Eclipse launched at one of the attackers, redirecting the blade to take it as his own, but the other was immediately at his side. He barely had time to move, the dagger he had tried to take burying itself into his thigh. He let out a shout of pain before shouldering the attacker, shoving him to the ground. Before he could make a decisive move to kill the one he pinned to the ground, the other was at his back.

A heavy weight crashed into him and sent Eclipse flying to the side as Mitoki rolled away with the second attacker. Eclipse forced himself to his feet and leapt at the man trying to get off the ground. He got behind the man, wrapping his arms around his neck and sharply tugging, breaking the man's neck and letting him drop to the ground as Mitoki struggled with the final attacker.

It was a team effort for Mitoki to pin the final man down and Eclipse to stab him in the chest. As the last attacker slumped to the ground, Mitoki turned to Eclipse, propping him up as his attention was brought to the bleeding wound in his leg.

"He got you?" Mitoki asked.

"Just my leg," Eclipse said with a tight nod. "The artery is safe." He took a few deep breaths to steady himself. "Well, Mitoki, this should teach you a very valuable lesson."

"What the hell are you talking about?"

"The appropriate phrase is speak of the devil and he shall appear," Eclipse sneered. "You said we were vulnerable to attack, and what happens? We get attacked not twenty seconds later!"

"Oh, right, of course I knew that these guys were in the trees waiting to attack," Mitoki groaned, helping Eclipse to his feet. "We have to go check on the kids."

Mitoki quickly returned to the street, rushing to the children, who had not moved from their spot on the road. Theresa and Emma had calmed slightly, though their breaths were still shuddering out of them. Benjamin could not tear his eyes away from the dead man on the pavement. Eclipse looked between Benjamin and the third attacker.

"I'll move him. See if you can calm them down and get them back to the house," Eclipse said, grabbing the wrists of the dead man and pulling him off the road.

"Is everyone alright?" Mitoki asked, approaching them. "Are you hurt?"

Trembling like a leaf, Theresa shook her head. She shakily walked toward Mitoki, hugging close to him as the adrenaline wore off. Emma went to Mitoki's other side, hiding her face in his shirt to keep herself from looking at Eclipse dragging the body away.

Benjamin, however, began backpedaling.

"Benjamin?" Mitoki asked. "What is it?"

The young boy turned and began running down the street as fast as his wobbling legs could carry him.

"Benjamin! Stay here!" Mitoki called, running down the street after him and grabbing his wrist. "It's not safe!" The boy screamed, his legs giving out from under him.

"Please don't hurt me!" Benjamin screamed. Mitoki immediately released him and retreated a step.

"Benjamin, I'm not—"

"You killed that guy! You just killed him!" Benjamin cried.

"Benjamin..." Mitoki started, trying to reach out again. The boy flinched away, tears flowing down his face. Mitoki was frozen to the spot, his brain going blank, unable to decide how best to calm the young boy. Slowly, trying not to feel his heart sink at the way Benjamin flinched, Mitoki crouched to him.

"I'm sorry I scared you. I was just trying to protect you. I won't hurt you."

He did not respond, crying and trembling on the pavement.

"We're going to go back to the house. Come on," Mitoki said, gently wrapping his hand around the seven-year-old's arm and pulling him to his feet, though Benjamin's entire body was tense with fear and he walked as far away from Mitoki as he could as the Guardians made their way back to the house.

Chapter Twelve

"They attacked you out of nowhere?" Dalton asked.

"I didn't even sense anything until I was off the road," Mitoki said with a heavy sigh. "The magic was intense, but it wasn't like anything I'd ever felt before. It felt almost...muted, somehow? It's difficult to explain. They weren't strong enough to be demons, but they were damn close."

Frieda stepped out of the girls' room and sat next to Dalton on the couch.

"They finally fell asleep," she said. "I gave Benjamin something to calm him down, so he should sleep through the night. He'll feel better in the morning."

"Master Dalton," Andrew started, "is there anything besides demon, beast, human, and dragon magic?"

"Not that I know of, but I'm sure there is," Dalton said.

Keito walked down the stairs and everyone turned to him for news on Eclipse, who the demon had been treating in the room upstairs.

"He's alright," Keito assured. "The wound was deep, but missed both the artery and the bone. His Antiquan Angel magic already healed most of it. He's just resting for a moment." The demon sighed as he sat on one of the couches. "How are the kids holding up?"

"Honestly, not too great," Hanyi said. "Benjamin was a mess. The girls were a little calmer, but they're all very frightened."

Mitoki dropped his head. "It's my fault. I should have pulled him back into the trees and killed him there. I didn't mean for them to see that."

"Mitoki, you were attacked. It wasn't something you could control," Frieda said gently.

"You were protecting them," Dalton added. "They don't understand entirely, but you saved their lives. They just need time to process."

"They're going to be scarred for life."

"You can't blame yourself, Mitoki," Hanyi said. "They're young, and the young are surprisingly resilient. As they get older, they'll realize that you saved their lives."

"These people didn't give any indication of what they were after?" Keito asked, diverting Mitoki's attention, seeing the defeated look on the young Guardian's face. Mitoki shook his head.

Once Eclipse felt well enough to stand and walk around, the Guardians and Andrew returned down the street to the brightly-illuminated magic barrier Mitoki had put up to keep everyone away from the bodies, marking a Guardian crime scene. However, even with the bright barrier, there was no one on the streets of the quiet, spacious community to question what the Guardians were doing.

As soon as they stepped through the barrier, the Guardians could feel the bizarre energy that Mitoki had described.

"I'm…not sure what that is," Dalton murmured.

"It's not just one type of energy," Keito noted, looking around the trees before glancing down at the three bodies. "I sense some underlying demon energy, but not from them. I almost wonder if these three were tracking a demon when you stumbled across them."

Andrew also walked closer to the men, crouching down to look over the three that had attacked Eclipse and Mitoki. His face pinched in confusion, his eyes darting to the three faces before he turned to Dalton.

"Master Dalton, these men all look exactly the same."

Team Dalton gathered around the men, using their magic to light the bodies and get a better look. As Dalton studied their faces, he could see that the men did not merely look similar—they were identical.

"That's not normal," Mitoki muttered.

"Triplet assassins?" Hanyi suggested. Everyone turned to him with a skeptical eyebrow. "What? It could happen."

"They also don't look…real?" Eclipse said, turning back to the men. "Does that make sense? They almost look *too* much like a human."

"I see what you mean," Dalton agreed, noting that the hair seemed to have fallen in exactly the same fashion despite the different positions they had died in, and their skin had no texture.

Keito turned one of the men's faces, looking over the oddly-too-exact features.

"I think I know what these are," he mused, wrapping his hand around the man's neck and squeezing. A strange crunching sound came to their ears, though it was not the sound of breaking bones, but of cracking cement. When the demon loosened his grip, his skin was covered with a fine, red dust and thick crumbles of clay. Keito yanked down the man's collar, exposing a dark, circular mark against the pale, too-smooth skin.

"What is that mark?" Andrew asked.

"It's the mark of the person puppeting them," Keito said. He looked over his shoulder at the other two fallen figures. "These are *ubetin*, or Scouters."

"This is a spell, then?" Eclipse deduced.

"The *ubetin* are creatures created from clay and decayed flesh that can act independent of the one who raised them, but they have no soul or free will. They're meant to perform simple jobs and tasks, and the one who created them can see through their eyes at any time."

"Hence the name Scouters," Andrew murmured with a nod. "But if they were just tracking us, why did they attack?"

"We don't know that they were tracking us," Eclipse said. "And something like animating clay and dead things sounds like the powers of a Soul Summoner, but as far as I know, they've all been wiped out of existence."

"All but one," Keito agreed.

"Please don't tell me that Yokouro is a Soul Summoner..."

"He's not," the demon said. "But Rutu is, and this," he pressed his finger into the dark, circular mark on the *ubetin*'s neck, "is Rutu's mark."

"Then Rutu is actually the one who attacked us," Eclipse said.

"I highly doubt Yokouro would order him to attack you at all," Keito said. "It doesn't make sense. Yokouro wants you alive." He stood and shrugged, wiping the dust from his palm. "You must have startled them."

"Yeah, *we* startled *them*..." Mitoki groaned.

"What direction did they come from?" Andrew asked.

"Up," Eclipse said, pointing into the dark tree boughs.

"Do you remember which tree?"

"No."

Keito jumped to the lowest branch near him and easily climbed. The others watched, though they quickly lost sight of him in the dark shadows, tracking his ascent by the soft cracking of smaller twigs as he moved. When he went silent, Mitoki turned his eyes back to the fallen *ubetin*.

"If this is Rutu's doing, then for sure they were tracking us," he said.

"But Keito's right," Dalton said, slowly shaking his head as he thought. "Yokouro said that he wanted to train us, and keep us alive. Why would three of Rutu's men suddenly attack? And if they can't do anything without their master's say, Rutu ordered them to attack."

"It doesn't sound like Rutu," Hanyi said. "Believe me, if Rutu wanted us dead, he would not give us an opportunity to fight back.

He'd end us in an instant. These three didn't say anything to you? They didn't seem like they wanted to pass a message along?"

"No," Mitoki said strongly. "They were very clearly attacking us and the children."

A loud snap above them startled them. The rustling of Keito's descent from the tree was far louder than his ascent, and when the branches began to part, the Guardians backed away from the tree, startled when the demon landed on the ground with a branch in his hand.

"What did the tree do to you?" Hanyi asked, looking between the branch and the demon.

"Rutu wasn't following us," Keito said. "He's tracking someone else who's following us. That's why there's a demon energy here as well as the *ubetin*'s magic."

"Wait, the demon energy isn't Rutu's?" Dalton asked.

"No, no, it's not powerful enough," Keito said, crouching by the fallen branch. "Look at this."

He lifted the splintered base of the branch and used his magic to light the area so they could all see the X shape carved into the base. Keito turned his gaze to Dalton. "From where this branch was, I could see right into the living room and kitchen of the house."

Dalton's stomach dropped.

"Another demon, not Yokouro, is stalking us up here?"

"Keito, this mark smells burned," Hanyi said, leaning close and taking a deep breath. "This looks like a knife cut, but it smells like it was branded into the bark."

"Like a curse-infused blade?" Andrew asked.

Keito's eyes went wide.

"Dalton, do you have a piece of paper?"

Dalton tapped his pockets, extracting the receipt for the movie. Keito smoothed the paper out on his leg before holding the back of the receipt close to the small X carving. Steam began to rise from the underside of the paper as dark char slowly burned onto the receipt. Keito pulled the receipt away before it caught fire and turned it over.

"I didn't know you could do that with hexed weapons," Eclipse whispered, leaning over Keito's shoulder. The receipt now had a dark X shape burned into its surface, but around the X, in intricate, tiny patterns, were symbols encircling each point of the shape. "I don't recognize those symbols," Eclipse said.

"I do," Keito whispered. "This is a demon weapon." Keito turned to Hanyi. "This is the Sien-Raa dagger."

"Are you sure?" Hanyi gasped.

"It has to be."

"What's that dagger?" Dalton asked.

"I've been searching for it for centuries," Keito explained. "It's a hexed blade that can kill Yokouro. For good."

"Can't we kill him with any knife?" Eclipse asked skeptically.

"Yes, if you did enough damage, or managed to take his head off," Keito agreed. "But the problem with these incredibly powerful Old Blood Lords is that, unless you make the killing shot immediately, they can heal. We could stab Yokouro thousands of times, but unless we instantly end him, he can heal the damage."

"That would have been good to know when we started this mission," Dalton groaned.

"The spell on the Sien-Raa is believed to be powerful enough to stop Yokouro from healing the wounds it inflicts," Keito continued. "If you stab him in the heart with this, it should kill him, unlike a regular blade would."

"But why would it be *here*?" Mitoki asked. "I guess I can understand why Rutu's men would be tracking whoever has that dagger, if that's what made this mark, but why would the demon who has a dagger that powerful be after *us*? Why not go after Yokouro directly?"

"Maybe they're waiting for Yokouro to attack us so they can have a shot at him," Eclipse guessed. "Draw him out into the open."

"I think that if Yokouro knew where the dagger was, and he sent Rutu to retrieve it, Rutu wouldn't waste time tracking the demon, he would kill him and take it," Hanyi said. "And Rutu would be able to do all this without attacking *us*."

Keito looked between the *ubetin* and the branch, finally glancing once more at the receipt in his hand. He stood, walking to the fallen men and glancing over their wounds, which were devoid of blood.

"But Rutu must be trying to keep us away from the dagger," Mitoki said. "Which is why they attacked us."

"But you didn't know they were here," Keito said. "Even if you had walked over here, they had no reason to attack you and give away their presence." He turned to the rest of his team. "And not that I doubt your abilities, but you shouldn't have been able to kill them so easily."

"What do you mean by that?" Eclipse asked.

"Rutu ordered them to attack, but he wanted you to kill them," Keito said. "He must have wanted us to know that this demon was tracking us."

"But why?" Hanyi said.

"Maybe he wants us to go after this demon and get the Sien-Raa," he guessed.

"He *wants* us to have a dagger that could kill Yokouro?" Mitoki asked. "I thought he was working *for* Yokouro. And I know, I know, he has his own agenda, but to blatantly sabotage Yokouro? Seems a little too good to be true."

"Keito, do you know who would have the dagger?" Hanyi asked. "Is it something we could take from them? Bribe them for?"

"I don't know," Keito admitted. "Yokouro has so many enemies, I really have no idea who it could be. And I didn't recognize the demon power in the tree. It wasn't potent enough to be recognizable."

"Then that's a good thing," Hanyi said with a strong nod. "Maybe they're not that powerful."

"But if they only attack Yokouro when Yokouro shows up to attack us, we have no chance of getting that dagger," Eclipse said. "Yokouro will kill them easily, and then he'll have the dagger and then we'll be fighting Yokouro. We'd have to track down this demon and take the dagger from them before Yokouro decides to come after us again."

"Do you know how we could track this demon?" Mitoki asked.

"Everyone, stop," Dalton said strongly, holding his hands up to stop their planning. "We're making a lot of conjectures about what Yokouro's intentions are, what this demon with the dagger wants, and why Rutu wanted to *warn* us about the demon tracking us. But regardless of *any* of that, this all puts everyone with us in incredible danger."

The Guardians remained silent, a little embarrassed that they had forgotten the civilians with them at the lake cabin.

"We're not going to take the chance of poking at these demons while we have the kids here," Dalton declared.

"We might not get another opportunity," Keito murmured.

"The way I see it, if this demon wants to fight Yokouro, or attack us, or whatever their plan is, they'll follow us back to the city," Dalton said. "I refuse to put my wife and those children in any more danger."

"We don't know that they will follow us," Keito said.

"It is possible that they are actually trying to attack *us*, not Yokouro," Eclipse agreed. "Maybe they'll kill others in this community to draw you back here."

"If that happens, we'll come back and deal with it," Dalton said. "But right now, I have to think about the children. I can't put them at risk, no matter how important that dagger is to us. Rutu's men attacked you while the children were with you. Clearly, the safety of the children is not important to Rutu, either. We're not going to risk their lives for a small advantage over Yokouro."

Keito stared at Dalton's determined expression, clearly not wanting to let the opportunity slip. He eventually dropped his head and nodded.

"I understand."

"We're going to go back to the house and call Guardian Forensics to dispose of these *ubetin*," Dalton said. "And then we're packing up and heading back to the city."

Chapter Thirteen

Even though Dalton tried to tell the children as lightly as possible that they were returning to the city, it both eased their minds and worried them more—they knew that the Guardians would not leave the area unless there was a real threat. But Emma and Benjamin were visibly relieved to be returning home.

There was a lot to do before leaving, as the cabin would be left uninhabited for quite some time, which meant it was not just a matter of packing up clothes and getting into the car. Dalton and the Guardians handled properly storing the boats, kayaks, and trailers while Frieda helped the children pack and then clean up the cabin and pack out the food they had brought with them.

Team Dalton and Andrew met with Guardian Forensics down the street when the young children were occupied with packing. They met with the small team and their van next to the area where they had been attacked, briefly explaining to the team what had happened while leaving out the details of the demon lords they believed to be linked to the attack. Then they left the forensics team to collect the bodies of the *ubetin* and file their reports.

The Guardians were quick to pack their own things, accustomed to quickly moving from place to place on cases. They then stationed themselves near the car, keeping an eye on the surrounding trees and distant cabins in case they were attacked again. Andrew stood watch from the house, standing on the deck to scan the area.

"What is taking them so long?" Dalton groaned, trying to tell himself that his growing sense of unease was nothing more than unchecked paranoia.

"I don't know," Eclipse said. "But I'm about ready to get my gun from my bag. I think our window for leaving is closing fast."

"You feel that, too?" Mitoki muttered.

"Keito?" Dalton asked, all three humans turning to the demon. "You feel that, right?"

"I do," he said. "I think the demon tracking us sees us leaving. I think they're going to try and stop us."

"What should we do?" Hanyi asked.

Keito hesitated, looking between the house, the car, and the surrounding woods. "Dalton, if this demon attacks while we're driving, there's the added danger of a severe car crash."

Dalton took a moment to contemplate his options, looking among the faces of his team before turning to Andrew.

"Keep them inside for the next fifteen minutes," he said. "Maybe get them all into one room while we see if we can lure this demon out and deal with them."

Andrew nodded obediently, ducking back into the house as Dalton took a deep breath and stepped away from the car, raising his voice.

"Well?" he called loudly. "You want us to stay? Why don't you come out and tell us what the hell you want?"

Their ears were carefully listening for any response, but Keito and Hanyi were the first to notice the sound of footsteps amid the fallen pine needles behind the house. They turned quickly, bringing the attention of the human Guardians to the same spot.

Casually, hands at her sides, a female demon stepped out from behind the house. She walked confidently, a smirk teasing at the corners of her mouth as she approached. Dalton had to do a double take when he noticed the bright silver hair, chilling golden eyes, and the dark line under her eyes and over the bridge of her nose. She was dressed in tight, black clothing, her arms and midriff bare to show off the few dark markings she sported across her skin.

"Kokumay?" Keito breathed, confused.

"Mutt," she growled, stopping a few paces from the Guardians.

"I thought you were dead," Keito said.

"Try as they might, it's hard to kill a DeVastes these days," she said. Her cold gaze latched onto each of the Guardians, unimpressed with what she saw. "What pathetic weaklings…"

"You're a DeVastes?" Mitoki asked.

"Kokumay DeVastes, disgraced lady of the DeVastes Clan, thanks to my moronic brother." She crossed her arms. "I'm sure you know *him*."

"You're Yokouro's *sister*?" Eclipse asked.

She scoffed, rolling her eyes. "What brilliant deductive reasoning."

"What are you doing here?" Keito asked. Once Dalton realized he was looking at one of Yokouro's siblings, his mind ran rampant with possibilities about her strength. But seeing Keito relatively unconcerned with her appearance eased his nerves—though only slightly.

"Seeing what has my brother so fascinated," she said, scrutinizing the Guardians once again. "He must be truly bored."

"What do you want with us?" Eclipse demanded. "Why have you been following us?"

"I was just observing," she said. "I'm wondering how you knew I was following you, though. Seems I did something to spook you, since you're all scurrying like terrified rats."

"It was only a matter of time before you attacked us," Dalton said.

Kokumay looked as though she was pondering something before she nodded reluctantly.

"I suppose you're right," she said. "But I was going to wait until Yokouro crawled out of whatever hole he's been hiding in lately. Then I was going to gut his new toys in front of him."

"He would kill you if you tried," Keito said. "You're not strong enough to challenge him."

"I know," she said, shrugging one shoulder. "But I do take some pleasure in knowing that when he does kill me, I'll cause him an incredible amount of pain."

"I take it you're not fond of him," Eclipse noted.

"Well, I used to be just as strong as that lowlife," she said. "And thanks to him, I'm now irreparably damaged. For fourteen years, my powers were slowly carved away from me and now I live with not only my family curse," she prodded one of the dark markings on her belly, "but another parasitic curse that is eating me from the inside. So even if I just disrupt whatever plan he has with you, I'll consider it a victory. As long as I can cause him as much pain as possible before I die."

"Kokumay," Keito said, raising both hands, "we could help one another. You want him to pay for what he did? We're trying to kill him."

She barked a laugh, raising an eyebrow at Keito.

"Are you? And do you think *you* can achieve such a feat, you pathetic mutt?"

"Perhaps with your help," Keito said. "You have the Sien-Raa dagger. We can kill him with that."

Her eyes narrowed.

"Who says I have it?"

"You used it to mark the tree you were using to spy on us," he said. "If you give it to us, we can kill him for you."

"Why would I want *you* to take that honor from me?" she sneered. "Haven't you already taken enough from the DeVastes family, Keito? You would also want to take Yokouro's death for yourself?" She smirked. "No, I would much rather take your lives and watch him wait another however many decades until yet another human takes his fancy. Such a stupid game he enjoys."

128

Dalton regretted not grabbing his own gun from his bag, but he had been worried about upsetting the children with the sight of the firearm. Realizing that Kokumay was so weak, he wondered if a few bullets would slow her down enough to either capture her...or maybe even kill her. He did not know, were they to fight her there, if they were going to try and capture her or if they were trying to end her life.

But before he could even glance at his teammates, Keito lunged forward. She dodged, but Keito anticipated it, grabbing her wrist and twisting it behind her back. His sudden movement caused the others to leap forward as well, figuring they would just react to Keito's actions, despite wishing they could discuss whether it was worth it to keep Kokumay alive.

Keito pulled her around as Eclipse and Dalton rushed forward. Dalton tried to restrain her other hand, but she pulled a simple dagger from the sheath strapped to her thigh, swiping at him. He retreated clumsily, forcing Mitoki back as well as they were both fended away by the dagger.

Kokumay jerked her head backward, connecting with Keito's jaw. Startled, he released her, retreating a safe distance to regain his bearings. As she turned toward him, Hanyi launched at Kokumay, his teeth closing around her upper arm as the force of his attack knocked them both to the ground. Eclipse wasted no time pinning Kokumay's other arm as Hanyi's teeth sunk deeper into her flesh.

Dalton took the opportunity to pin Kokumay's flailing legs, but once he had one pinned to the ground, her other foot connected with the side of Dalton's head, sending him crashing into Hanyi. As the two fell to the gravel on the side of the driveway, Kokumay lifted her free hand and punched Eclipse hard enough to nearly break his jaw.

She turned onto her hands and knees to get up, but Mitoki leapt on her back, wrapping an arm around her neck and putting her into a chokehold, pulling her backward until she was on top of him on the pavement.

As he struggled to keep her on the ground, the other Guardians rushed to help. Keito hesitated a moment as the others tried to pull her hands away from Mitoki's arm. He glanced Kokumay over before grabbing her left ankle, pinning it to the pavement and running a hand up her calf. The older demon stilled instantly, understanding what Keito was doing. Ignoring the other Guardians, she lifted her right leg and put all her strength into kicking Keito. Keito turned just in time to wrap his arm around her leg, though he still fell heavily to the ground, Kokumay's body twisting to press her knee into Keito's throat.

Holding her ankle, his other hand ran up and down her calf, clawing at the object he felt strapped under her clothing.

Dalton and the others had no idea what had happened, but Keito's pained shout was followed by a disorienting rush of air as the others were flung in various directions. Eclipse collided with the car while Mitoki and Hanyi were forced into the nearby tree line, barely missing the trunks as they fell heavily to the pine needles. Dalton tumbled backward on the pavement, sliding to a stop as he tried to orient himself.

Keito was holding his hand tight to his chest, blood pouring through his fingers as he growled through his teeth. Kokumay had leapt to her feet, snatching up her fallen dagger and kneeling over Keito, one knee pressed into his chest as she leaned over him, the blade biting into his neck.

"Did you really think I was that stupid?" she said with a dark smile. "The dagger is warded, mutt. Your filthy hands should never touch such a powerful weapon."

Keeping her knee on his chest, she whirled around and raised a hand to the Guardians coming to Keito's aid. Her magic rushed forward, filling the air with near-suffocating heat as the spell coiled around their chests and forced them to their knees.

"I'll get to you," she said. Her dark smile turned back to Keito as she grabbed his bleeding hand sharply, pulling it away from his chest to look over the dozens of small gashes in his flesh. "I guess it's too bad you didn't touch it directly. I was hoping to do more damage." She pinned his hand to the ground as she returned her dagger to his throat. "I guess I'll just have to carve you apart myself."

Dalton continued to struggle against the magical binds around his torso, realizing that the strength of the spell was quickly diminishing. He knew he should have put some thought into why Kokumay was so much weaker than her brother, but he could only focus on getting free. Using his own magic, he strained, feeling the fibers of the spell splitting.

Before Kokumay could drag her dagger further down Keito's arm, Dalton barreled into her, knocking them both to the ground in an ungraceful heap. Adrenaline rushing through his veins, he ignored the scrapes and cuts he received, his magic sparking around his hand as he punched her in the abdomen. She curled around his fist, grabbing his forearm and pulling him even closer as her head collided with his.

As Dalton reeled backward, his head spiraling with pain, Hanyi's teeth clamped around Kokumay's arm, pulling her away from the human as she tried to fight off the wolf. Mitoki went to Dalton's side to help him up as Keito also got to his feet, holding the large gash on his arm and watching as Eclipse and Hanyi wrestled with Kokumay, waiting for an opening.

Eclipse managed to pry her dagger away from her fingers, though their position against the pavement made it impossible for him to make a decisive hit with the weapon. He swung angrily at the demon, feeling the blade sink into flesh and hearing Kokumay's enraged shout of pain in his ears.

He backed away, being sure to keep hold of the dagger, trying to see where he had stabbed Kokumay, but she grabbed his ankle, pulling him back to the ground and causing the others of Team Dalton to rush to his aid.

The fight became disorienting. Magic was sparking in the air around them, causing crackling electricity to snap at their skin and leave them wondering if they had been injured. Each Guardian was trying to pin one of Kokumay's limbs to the ground, but despite how much weaker she was than Yokouro, her demon strength still gave her the advantage. When Keito tried to kick her leg, hoping to dislodge the hidden dagger, the warding on the weapon sent them flying once again.

But that time, Kokumay did not give them time to regain their bearings.

She turned onto her hands and knees, snatching the dagger from Eclipse and leaping at Dalton, pinning him on his back as she raised the dagger to stab him in the chest. He barely managed to catch her wrist, his magic helping to keep the dagger from plunging into his heart.

A dark blur barreled into both of them. Dalton rolled onto his stomach, his muscles slowly relaxing from the grip he had held on Kokumay's arm. Certain that Keito had attacked Kokumay once again, he took a few moments to catch his breath before turning back to the fight.

But Keito was not the one struggling with the thrashing and growling Kokumay.

Five strangers had interfered with the fight, each dressed in the same black clothing, their hair sitting too still on their heads and their skin too smooth to look natural. The stunned members of Team Dalton stared in silence as the five identical men hauled Kokumay upright as she screeched and struggled.

One man wrapped a piece of cloth around her mouth, forcing it between her teeth and yanking her head backward. Another man raised an uncorked vial to her face, shoving it under her nose. Within moments, Kokumay's eyes rolled back and her body went limp, despite how she tried to fight the sedation.

The silence that fell over the area was deafening.

Keito helped Dalton to his feet, though both of them were watching the *ubetin*, worried they were now going to fight the five strange men. The Guardians gathered together quietly, on-edge, ready for another confrontation.

Two *ubetin* kept Kokumay upright as the one in front of her corked the vial and placed it in his pocket. He then held his hand out, palm facing the unconscious demon, and began a sweeping motion over her. It was when he fell to a crouch and his hand hovered around Kokumay's right calf that the Guardians realized the *ubetin* were looking for the Sien-Raa dagger.

Dalton's mind raced. If Keito had been correct about what the dagger could do, they could not let Rutu's *ubetin* take the weapon back to Yokouro. But Dalton was also certain trying to interfere with Rutu was a death sentence. He turned to Keito, silently questioning if they should step forward and try to take the dagger. Keito was clearly struggling with the same dilemma. The warding around the dagger made Keito hesitant to try for the weapon again.

The *ubetin* yanked up Kokumay's pant leg to reveal the intricate black sheath strapped to her calf. But when his fingers made contact with the straps, the same powerful shockwave radiated outward, pelting the Guardians with fine gravel as they tried to remain standing. The *ubetin's* fingers cracked and disintegrated into clumps of red clay, falling to the ground as his arm, up to his elbow crumbled.

But the magical creature was not deterred, not even showing pain at the injury the warding had caused. He, instead, hooked the fabric of Kokumay's clothing over the top of the dagger and used his only hand to make a fist, holding it as close to the dagger as possible.

The air became heavy. The Guardians felt as though they were breathing in water as the magic swelled around them. Despite the lack of clouds in the sky, the light dimmed, and a soft rumble sounded under their feet. The dagger began to bounce and shudder against Kokumay's leg, jittering in the sheath until the dagger threatened to dislodge itself entirely.

The *ubetin* opened his fist and the straps around Kokumay's leg snapped, the dagger violently launching away from the demon to clatter to the gravel a few feet away.

Eclipse almost took the opportunity to sprint forward and take the dagger, but the *ubetin* was faster, snatching the weapon off the ground with his only hand before turning to face the Guardians.

The black eyes of the *ubetin* made the dissipating magic in the air feel like ice and Dalton shivered instinctively. Then the strange man's eyes blinked, and the black color had been replaced with a powerful hazel that Dalton knew immediately belonged to Rutu.

Everyone was deathly still for two agonizing seconds.

The possessed *ubetin* took a measured step forward, slow, trying not to startle the Guardians. Keito growled, lowering his head as he prepared to fight. But Rutu's step was unthreatening as he closed the space between them, stopping two paces away. The *ubetin* spun the dagger carefully in his hand so the hilt was in his palm, the rest of the sheathed blade resting against his forearm.

Then, he extended his arm to Dalton.

Dalton was too stunned to move at first, staring at the black sheath with the intricate gold designs and the golden hilt inlaid with precious stones. His gaze slowly raised to meet the hazel eyes of the demon lord possessing the *ubetin*, silently questioning Rutu.

The *ubetin's* hand remained steady.

His hand shaking, Dalton wrapped his fingers around the cold sheath and lifted it from the *ubetin's* grasp.

The man's hand dropped to his side and his eyes blinked back to the chilling, empty black. He turned and nodded to the other four, who had gathered Kokumay on one *ubetin's* back. The five men ran into the tree line, moving faster than any human but not quite at the speed of a demon. They disappeared from sight within moments.

Dalton's eyes fell to the dagger in his hand. The weapon was heavy and cold, despite how close it had been to Kokumay's skin. The delicate gold patterns were so precise they did not befit the severity of the weapon within. The golden hilt was partially wrapped in pristine black leather, allowing the gems to glitter in the sunlight through the few braided openings. As though hypnotized, Dalton slowly removed the blade from the sheath, amazed at the smooth finish, and the soft pulsing he could feel from the spell within.

When he slid the dagger back into place, it broke the other Guardians out of their own stupefied scrutiny. Dalton let out a shuddered breath, turning to Keito.

"Why did he just hand this over?"

Keito shrugged one shoulder, shaking his head. "It's Rutu. Who knows?"

Dalton turned back to the dagger, a profound sense of destiny falling heavy on his shoulders as he looked at it, as though he could already see the moment when he would plunge the blade into Yokouro's chest.

"Master Dalton?"

He jumped, turning quickly to see Andrew peering cautiously over the deck railing.

"Is…is everything alright? What happened?"

"Uh…" Dalton said, trying to pull some of his scattered thoughts together to form an explanation. "It's…difficult to explain," he finally said. "But we're safe now. Let's get the kids into the car and head back."

Andrew nodded, turning back into the house to gather the others as Dalton's fingers tightened around the dagger.

"Let's get out of here before Rutu has a chance to change his mind," he added under his breath.

Chapter Fourteen

Kokumay woke up cold and confused. A quick glance around her confirmed that she was in chains in a dark, dungeon-like room, but it took two long hours for the fog in her mind to dissipate enough for her to recognize the symbol carved into the rock above the cell door—the DeVastes family seal.

The realization that she was back in the Demon Realm and imprisoned in the palace of her birth had her heart racing and her brain scrambling to put together a plan of escape. She yanked and pulled on the chains, even using what little magic she could collect around her exhaustion to try and break the bindings. But the spell in the iron swelled, siphoning her magic away the more she struggled, leaving her drained.

She did not know how long she had been there. She could hardly remember the fight with the Guardians. She did not know how she had fallen unconscious, or if she had even seen her brother come to capture her.

Her stomach was growling angrily—evidence of the hours passed—when the cell door finally opened. The screech of the hinges set her teeth on edge and she flinched away.

"Finally awake, I see," Yokouro noted, stepping into the cell.

Upon hearing his voice, she lunged forward, gnashing her teeth together as she yanked her restraints, nearly dislocating her shoulders when they stopped her advance. Yokouro stood confidently just out of reach, smiling darkly at his younger sister as Rutu also entered the cell, not bothering to close the heavy door behind him.

Yokouro watched as Kokumay thrashed and fought to attack him, though she did not have the strength to do so for long. She eventually retreated, breathing hard, though her eyes were still full of fire as she glared at her older brother.

"It has been a very long time, dear little sister."

"You are not my brother," she snarled. "You ceased being my family when you left me to die."

Yokouro groaned, rolling his eyes. "Are we still gnawing at that bone, Kokumay?"

"I vowed to kill you, Yokouro."

Yokouro cast a smug look around the cell, a smirk quirking at the side of his mouth.

"Then how did you end up my prisoner?" he asked.

She growled again, trying to push forward once more, but the jolt to her wrists and neck stopped her and she stumbled backward again.

"Kokumay," Yokouro said, irritated, "I don't want to waste my time trying to rebuild our relationship. Frankly, I don't give a damn about what happens to you after I leave this cell. But while you are in this cell, you are my prisoner, and I promise that whatever fate you have once I leave will be infinitely less painful if you just answer my questions."

She scoffed. "What could you possibly need to ask me that you don't already know?" she sneered. "You have the omniscient Rutu Kaneaka right behind you."

"I'm flattered you think I'm all-knowing, but you are incorrect," Rutu said with a soft laugh.

"Where is the Sien-Raa?" Yokouro asked.

"What's that?" Kokumay asked mockingly.

Yokouro nodded, licking his lips briefly.

"I see." He took a step forward, allowing his magic to fill the cell, causing Kokumay to choke as she retreated by instinct. "You know, you used to be one tough bitch," he said. "So sad how the mighty have fallen."

Kokumay pressed her back to the cell wall.

"At least *I* managed to survive when they tried to tear me apart."

"Do you really think it's in your best interest to taunt me?" Yokouro asked coldly.

"What are you going to do? *Kill* me?" Kokumay laughed. "That's rich. You wouldn't risk the mark. Are you going to torture me? You think you can throw anything at me I haven't already survived?"

Yokouro's smile widened as he stepped to the side and motioned to Rutu.

"Why do you think Rutu's here?"

A look of genuine terror crossed her face as her eyes turned to Rutu. Yokouro reached forward, taking his younger sister's chin and focusing her attention back on him.

"You can't play this game with me, Kokumay. I'm the one who taught it to you," he said. "But I'm on a schedule, so you can cooperate with me, or I will ask Rutu to rip the answers out of you as slow as he possibly can."

"You coward," she snarled. "If you're going to torture or kill me, do it yourself."

"I'm giving you a chance, dear sister," Yokouro said. "Tell me where the dagger is."

Kokumay stared at her brother's cold expression, her breathing becoming heavy as her anger swelled. She wanted to oppose him, to spit at him and drag on the interrogation because she knew that he would not risk the pain that came with killing her. But she was also acutely aware of the notorious Rutu Kaneaka-Kage standing by the open door of the cell—a well-known master of torture. She glanced at him briefly before lowering her gaze to her feet.

"I'm waiting," Yokouro prompted.

"I don't know where it is," she growled. "I was fighting your human toys when your henchman interfered." She nodded dismissively to Rutu. "If you didn't find it when you searched me, then the Guardians must have it."

Yokouro turned, looking at the older demon expectantly. Rutu blinked in surprise.

"I didn't sense it there. I followed Kokumay's energy, not the dagger's magic."

Yokouro rounded on Kokumay again, wrapping a hand around her neck and squeezing tightly.

"For your sake, you better be lying," he snapped.

She shook her head as much as she could in his vice grip.

"I...had it...strapped to my...leg..." she choked.

Yokouro released her neck, but she had no time to collect her bearings before he turned her to face the wall, hooking an arm around her elbow and pulling her restraints taught, straining the bones in her forearm.

"Try again," he growled.

"I swear!" she burst. "That disgusting mutt was trying to take it from me! He probably has it now!"

"How did he know you had it, Kokumay?!"

"I don't know!" she cried, shaking as she tried to adjust her body to ease the strain on her bones.

"I thought *you* wanted to kill me," he said. "But you want the mutt to do it for you, don't you? You've sunk low."

"I was trying to get them out of the way!" she screeched.

"Stop lying to me!"

"I'm not!"

Yokouro's arm jolted and Kokumay's right forearm snapped in a clean break. She screamed loudly, the sound reverberating off the cold stone walls as Yokouro released her. She fell heavily to the ground, shivering and crying in pain. Yokouro looked her over, trying to determine if she was lying, while Rutu watched emotionlessly from the door.

Yokouro walked to Rutu.

"Do you think she's telling the truth?" he whispered.

"I did not sense the dagger when the *ubetin* took her," Rutu said. "It's possible that Keito got it from her in the fight and warded it."

"But how did he know she had it?" Yokouro asked. "Unless she was trying to use the dagger on *him*."

Rutu's eyebrows rose as he thought over the possibility.

"I suppose it's possible," he said. "But Keito and Kokumay are about the same strength. He could have taken it from her and tried to use it on her, instead."

"She didn't have any unhealing wounds…" Yokouro noted, turning back to his sister, who was slowly calming as her body acclimated to the pain of her broken bone. "You don't think she *gave* it to him, do you?"

"Kokumay hates Keito almost as much as you do," Rutu said. "I doubt she would assist him."

"Do you think Team Dalton has it?"

Rutu took a deep breath. "If she's telling the truth," he started carefully, "and she had it before I interfered in her fight with Team Dalton…then very likely, yes."

"Damn it," Yokouro grumbled.

He turned to face Kokumay again, trying not to smile at the way she shied away from him as he approached.

"Do you swear, on your family name, that you had the dagger during your fight with the Guardians?"

She swallowed hard. "Yes."

"You swear that you did not hide it from all of us?"

"I swear," she whispered.

"Then I see no reason to keep you alive," Yokouro said. He stepped back. "Rutu."

Kokumay pressed herself as close to the back wall of the cell as she could, her chains rattling, hissing through clenched teeth as her movement jarred her broken arm. Rutu stepped forward, but stopped when he was next to Yokouro, as if hesitating.

"What is it?" Yokouro asked.

"Yokouro," he said quietly, dropping his head and turning to the younger demon, "I don't think you should order me to kill her."

"You were the one who reminded me of why I can't be the one to kill her," Yokouro snarled. "So you will obey my order and end her life. We have a schedule. I don't have time to waste on moral conflicts."

"It's not about who ends her life, it's about where," Rutu whispered.

"What the hell are you—" Yokouro stopped when he saw that the older demon was not looking at him. His eyes were turned to the open cell door, where three DeVastes Clan soldiers were lurking, peering in curiously to see what the fate of Yokouro's younger sister would be. Yokouro hesitated as well, suddenly realizing that the gossip of Kokumay's death by Rutu's hand would rocket through the entire land in mere seconds.

Yokouro curled his lip at the soldiers.

"See something interesting?" he snapped.

The soldiers ducked away from the door, though Yokouro did not hear footsteps retreating, telling him they were still lingering nearby, eavesdropping.

"You need to be very cautious," Rutu whispered. "She is still considered a member of the royal family to many in the clan. If you order me to kill her, within the DeVastes Palace, you may turn many in your court against you. I don't know that you can afford that right now."

"What do you suggest I do?" Yokouro asked. "I can't just let her go. Her actions are considered treason. And she can't stand trial because she denounced the clan. The Justices would just send her into exile again, and we're back to square one."

"I know you can't kill her yourself, and ordering her death by your guard would also divide the clan. And you can't ask me to do it without making everyone in the clan think that the Kage Clan is secretly running the DeVastes land. I suggest you make an example of her."

"An example?"

"Show your court that there are things worse than death," Rutu said. "Particularly if they try to work against you."

Yokouro shifted his eyes to his sister, who was looking between the two older demons rapidly, unable to conceal her horror at their conversation.

"Rutu," Yokouro said, raising his voice to a normal level again, "I recall you saying that this was one of the busiest times of the year in the Trade. Perhaps you could use another laborer."

Kokumay's face paled several shades as her eyes went wide.

"No," she whispered. "You cannot ask me to—"

"You've never had to work a day in your life, dear sister," Yokouro said with a broad, cold smile. "Imagine how accomplished you will feel when you're able to get your hands dirty sewing fields and laying bricks. The harvest is coming up soon. There's plenty to do."

"You better just kill me, Yokouro," Kokumay snarled. "A lady of the DeVastes Clan? Property of the Trade? That will sully our family name!"

"Will it?" Yokouro asked. "Or, will it send the message to everyone in the clan that their status does not immediately offer them protection?" His smile grew. "Rutu, I give her to you."

Rutu stepped forward again. Kokumay began kicking her legs at him angrily.

"Stay away from me, you evil monster!" she screeched.

"Why should I?" Rutu asked with a laugh, crouching and grabbing one of her ankles when she tried to kick his head. "I have to get you to the Trade as soon as possible. I have a lot of customers that would love to have a lady of the DeVastes Clan working their fields."

"I won't obey you," she snapped. "I'll fight you until you kill me."

"Then you'll be fighting a very long time," Rutu said. "Because I'm not going to kill you, Kokumay."

She scoffed. "Softened up in your old age?" she jeered. "So much for the legends of Rutu Kaneaka. I guess it was all myth."

Rutu reached for the larger rings on the wall that secured Kokumay in the cell. She lunged toward his hand, her teeth bared, ignoring the way her broken bone made pain ricochet through her body when she moved. She tried to bite his arm, but his other hand grabbed her hair, twisting her to the ground, pinning her face down on the cold cement.

She laughed, turning her eyes as far as she could to look at him, struggling against his strength.

"This will go much easier for you if you cooperate," Rutu said.

"Why should I be afraid of you?" she cackled. "You're clearly very well trained. Once the prince of the greatest demon clan in history, and now the tamed attack dog of Juki Kage." She twisted her head up, grinning coldly at him. "Are you anything more than that, Rutu Kaneaka?"

"As of today, I am your master," he said. "And you would do well to remember that."

"You'll never be my master, you demented freak!"

"No?" he challenged.

He pushed her head to the floor, yanking the back of her shirt collar until it ripped, exposing her back to him. Rutu pressed his hand against her right shoulder blade, but before Kokumay could struggle, burning pain shot through her. It was a pain similar to the searing agony of her curse marks, but it was more acute, and it left the smell of burning skin in the air.

She stilled in terror, realizing that Rutu was branding her.

Yokouro laughed in the doorway, shaking his head. "You should have just listened to him," he said. "But I'm sure he'll train you to keep your mouth shut and follow orders. It was always something you struggled with."

When Rutu pulled his hand away, Kokumay was too shocked at what had happened to fight him as he unchained her from the wall and stood, gathering the chains in his hands.

"Get up," Rutu ordered.

"How long will it take for you to take her to the Trade?" Yokouro asked. "I need you in the Human Realm in two hours."

Rutu sighed, glancing down at the shivering Kokumay, who was struggling to get to her feet. Her ripped shirt was falling off her shoulders and her head was bent in shame, her frame trembling from the pain of the brand on her shoulder and her broken arm.

"I'll contact Dynam at the Trade and ask him to meet me. He can take her the rest of the way and get her processed."

"She's tricky, Rutu," Yokouro warned. "I'd give Dynam some *ubetin* to help him contain her."

"I'll take them along, then."

Kokumay did not want to follow Rutu's guide out of the dungeons. She did not want to be subjected to the staring and pointing and whispering as she was paraded, almost half-naked, through the palace hallways to the front of the estate, where a valet held Rutu's horse, surrounded by six eerie *ubetin*. But she needed time to think, so she followed him quietly, her head down, trying to concoct a plan around the pain in her body and the shame threatening to cripple her.

Even when Rutu mounted his horse and she was forced to walk beside the animal, she did not raise her head. The brand on her shoulder was akin to a death sentence for her. The Trade rarely branded their workers—those who were branded were those who were to be property of the Trade until their dying breath. She could not stand the thought of being laughed at, degraded as she toiled away in the fields, or on the buildings of lesser lords in the Demon Realm. Her stomach was twisting angrily and her heart was beating so fast, her body was practically vibrating.

But she walked obediently beside Rutu's horse, because she knew, of all the demons in the realm, Rutu Kaneaka-Kage was the last demon to fight against.

But as an hour of walking passed and her acute fear changed to fiery rage, she decided it was better to be killed by Rutu than subjected to the Trade.

Treading slowly along a quiet, forest path, she lifted her head.

"I bet you're really proud of yourself, aren't you, Rutu Kaneaka?" she hissed. "You really screwed my brother up. You raised him to be just as disturbed as you."

Rutu scoffed. "Believe me, he's nowhere near my level of disturbed."

"Oh, so you still have more to teach him?" she laughed hollowly. "It's a wonder your children are as sane as they are. Of course, your youngest is a little shit, isn't he? Wonder where he got that…"

"That is absolutely none of your concern."

"What? Does it hurt to hear that?" she challenged. "When it's a poor orphan boy beaten and then exiled by his family, it's fine to raise him to be a murderer. But when it's your own flesh and blood, you can't bear to think that you were a horrific parent?" She laughed, shaking her head. "Although, why would I try to reason with a Kaneaka?"

"I am no longer a Kaneaka," Rutu said. "I haven't been for a very long time."

"Then why do you keep the name?" she said shortly. "Can't let go of the glory days of savagery and butchering any demon that stood in your way?"

Rutu sighed heavily, stopping his horse.

Even though Kokumay shivered, knowing she had finally struck a nerve, she was thrilled that he was angry enough to kill her rather than take her to the Trade.

He unwound her chains from his saddle and dismounted, yanking her toward him. She stumbled, practically falling into his chest from the force of the tug. She looked up at him quickly, unable to suppress the instinctive shiver that radiated through her at the power of his stare.

"Oh," she said shakily, forcing a smile. "I see. Are you going to teach me a *lesson*?"

Rutu was still for two agonizingly long seconds before he turned her around, grabbing her long braid and winding it around his fist. She trembled, terrified, though she tried to hide it. She forced a laugh instead.

"Fine," she said, though the contempt in her voice was weak from fear. "Show me how you're superior because you're a man."

"You are definitely a DeVastes," he whispered, reaching for his dagger as he pulled her head back so she would look at him. "That shitty attitude and loud mouth runs in your bloodline."

"I knew you wouldn't be able to keep up that unfazed façade," she said. "At least I didn't have to bring up the new drama with Kawakara to get you to show me who you really are, you Kaneakan monster."

Rutu pressed his dagger to her jugular. Her body tensed.

"You talk too much."

He moved quickly. She expected to feel the bite of his dagger, to feel warm blood trickling down her chest. Instead, there was the brief smell of burning hair before the pressure on the back of her head released and she stumbled forward, confused.

She whirled around, her chains jingling as her eyes turned onto Rutu.

In his hand was her long, silver braid.

Before she could grasp the magnitude of what he had done, she jumped in surprise at seeing one of the *ubetin* collapse to the ground with a gash across his throat. One-by-one, the *ubetin* fell, various wounds manifesting over their bodies, Rutu's twitching fingers casting spells to kill them in ways that looked like an attack.

When the last man fell, Rutu sheathed his dagger again and went to the nearest *ubetin*, yanking the shirt off his body before turning to Kokumay.

"I...I don't understand..." she whispered. She nodded to the long braid he clutched in his other hand. To cut the hair of an Old Blood demon was blasphemous, as it was a symbol of their high social status. "You...you cut my hair..."

"I freed you," he corrected. "Hide your family mark. Take a new identity. Renounce your Old Blood status and live the rest of your life in peace. But you must stop pursuing your brother. You will not seek to reclaim the Sien-Raa. You will take this moment," he showed her the braid, "to begin again. Don't be a DeVastes anymore. Believe me, you will be happier."

As he extended his other hand, passing her the shirt, the cuffs around her wrists, ankles, and neck popped open and fell to the ground with a clatter.

But Kokumay could not move. She stared at Rutu, dumbfounded, unable to even take the shirt he was offering her so she could cover herself. When he stepped forward and offered her the shirt once more, she retreated.

"It doesn't matter if you release me," she whispered. "You *branded* me."

143

"No, I didn't."

She quickly reached for her shoulder, running the pads of her fingers over the area she was certain he had branded. Her skin was smooth.

"I had to make it believable for your brother," Rutu explained, extending the shirt once again. She was hesitant, but her fingers slowly closed around the fabric and she pressed it to her chest, her broken arm hanging loosely at her side. Rutu took another step forward, gingerly raising her arm and placing his hands around the break. She flinched as his magic easily healed the broken bone, creating only a brief stab of pain before the throbbing ache eased.

"I don't understand…" she repeated.

"I don't expect you to," he said.

She blinked in realization. "You gave them the dagger," she whispered. "You want them to win."

He did not speak, watching as she pulled the shirt over her head, tossing her torn clothing to the ground with a soft laugh.

"I guess you're not as well trained as I thought," she said. "Finally tired of being on Yokouro's leash?"

"I'm just trying to be useful," he murmured.

"Useful?" she repeated, confused.

"Never mind," he said, waving the statement away. "You better leave quickly. Dynam will be here soon."

"You actually called someone from the Trade?"

"I have to make it look as though you overpowered him and escaped," he said, raising her severed braid and using his magic to burn it in his palm. "I'll have to rough him up a bit to cover my ass."

"You're going to beat him up without explanation?" she asked.

"He doesn't need one," Rutu said. "It's not the first time I've done this. He knows that the less he knows, the safer he is."

Kokumay straightened, opening her mouth to say something, though it took her mind several moments to find the words.

"I've misjudged you," she whispered.

"Many do." He let the final tendrils of hair fall to the ground, leaving a smoldering pile of ash on the side of the forest road. "Go, Kokumay. Find a happier life than the one you've known."

She remained still as her brain tried to wrap around what Rutu was doing for her. She let out a disbelieving chuckle, dropping to one knee and bowing her head to him before running into the trees.

Chapter Fifteen

The car ride back to the city was not as lively as the car ride to the lake. The Guardians were tired, trying to ignore their wounds from the fight with Kokumay and hiding the dagger as quickly and effectively as they could. They had rapidly donned layers of clothing to hide the bloodied spots from the distressed Benjamin and Emma. Benjamin refused to sit anywhere near the Guardians, making seating difficult as the young boy would start crying in fear whenever he looked at them. The only time he relaxed a little bit was when Rio climbed onto the seat next to him. He hugged the dog tightly, just as Emma and Theresa were doing to Hanyi, who was seated between them in his wolf form.

Because of his high state of distress, Dalton took Benjamin home first.

He called Benjamin's mother to let her know they were returning early, and even though she asked about the strain in Dalton's voice, he did not tell her the specifics. When they pulled into the driveway of Benjamin's house, the young boy ran to the front door, knocking hurriedly. The Guardians were slower to get out of the car, Dalton taking Benjamin's bag from the back with a heavy sigh.

"I better go talk to her," Dalton said.

"I'll come with you," Frieda offered with a reassuring smile.

"We'll come, too," Eclipse said. "We'll explain what happened."

"I should stay behind," Keito murmured. "If she takes this badly, she's going to immediately blame you for having a demon anywhere near her son."

Dalton wanted to say that Keito did not need to stay behind, but he knew the demon was right. He threw a quick glance at the front door when he heard Benjamin's mother open it and hug her trembling son tightly.

"Sorry, Keito."

"It's alright," he said. "I understand."

"Andrew," Dalton called into the car. His apprentice stepped out slowly. "You better join us, as well. This is something you will have to do at some point as a Guardian."

Keito quietly got back into the car, trying not to disturb the sleeping Emma and Theresa, while the others approached the front door. When Benjamin's mother saw them approaching, she ushered her son inside before standing straight to greet Dalton with a tight nod.

"Guardian Teban," she said curtly.

"Irene," Dalton greeted. "May we please come in? There are a few things we need to discuss."

She hesitantly stepped aside, motioning them into the living room, though no one sat down. Dalton placed Benjamin's bag by the side of the couch, casting a worried glance around the rest of his teammates before turning back to Irene. He slowly and carefully explained the incident at the lake, being sure to be as truthful as possible without terrifying her or giving her any particularly brutal details.

By the time he had finished speaking, her jaw was clenched tightly and her nails were digging into her crossed arms.

"You're telling me that my son saw one of you *kill* a man?" she growled.

"I am so sorry, Irene," Dalton said. "We were just trying to protect him. We didn't mean for him to see something so horrific."

"Why would you take him with you if there was a threat that you would be attacked?" she snapped. "You would endanger, not only your own daughter, but my son and Emma as well?"

"Irene," Frieda started gently, "there was no way we could have known that would happen. And I don't appreciate your accusations against us as parents. We should be thankful that they were there to protect the children."

"But who protects the children *from* the Guardians?" she snarled. "You? Your husband and his colleagues *brought* the trouble with them to begin with."

"Ma'am," Mitoki said, clearing his throat and stepping forward nervously. "I am sorry. This was entirely my fault. I was the one Benjamin saw."

"*You?*" Irene hissed. "You're just a child yourself."

"Mitoki," Dalton said, raising his hand to stop the youngest Guardian from trying to explain further. "I am his superior, and I am the one who asked him to walk with the kids that night. The blame rests with me, not him."

"As far as I'm concerned, it rests with all of you," Irene snapped. "Even you, Frieda. How could you subject children to such a horrible spectacle?"

"If I may," Hanyi started. "We did not *subject* them to anything. We had no way to reasonably believe that we were in danger. There had been no previous threat, and we were confident that we would be able to discern when a threat was credible."

"Do you have children? Would you want them to see something like that when they are only *seven* years old? The world is already falling apart, and he's already terrified by everything he hears from the news. And now, you Guardians make it even worse. You killed a man in front of my son. What do you think that does to a child? You Guardians should be out doing your jobs to make these realms safe for children again, not scarring them for life."

"Enough," Eclipse growled, stepping in front of Mitoki as she pointed, hurling her accusation directly at him. "What happened was unfortunate, but we got him back home safe and unharmed. Mitoki risked his life getting between that attacker and the kids, and you, instead, tell him he did something *wrong*? Would you have preferred he missed the opportunity and endanger your son further?"

"How dare you speak to me that way?" Irene gasped.

"Eclipse, maybe you and Mitoki should wait outside," Dalton suggested gently.

"Yes. Get out of my house. You are not welcome," Irene said, pointing to the door.

Frieda stepped forward to get Irene's attention as Eclipse led Mitoki out, glaring at the woman as they left.

"Irene, please, try to understand," Frieda started cautiously.

"Understand what?" she snapped. "Am I the only one who sees what happened as problematic? My son is just a boy! He shouldn't have seen that. Do you know what happens to kids who are exposed to that kind of violence? They become like *him*." She pointed at Andrew, who blinked and retreated a step, startled. "They decide to train to become murderers themselves."

"How can you say that?" Andrew whispered. "How can you call Mitoki a murderer when he saved your son's life? I have never looked at Master Dalton as a murderer, even though I saw him kill when I was six years old."

"And look at where you are now," Irene sneered. "Do you think your mother would be happy to see you training to become a Guardian?"

"My mother was just happy to see me alive," Andrew said. "Even as she was dying, she was thanking Master Dalton over and over again for saving my life. She didn't think about the kind of memories I would have, she was just happy I was still alive. Can't you just be thankful for that? Your son is alive. He's with you now. Could you imagine if he had been with people who weren't trained to protect him?"

"Andrew," Dalton said in gentle warning. Irene was silent, staring at Andrew, her eyes brimming with tears.

"I want all of you out," she whispered.

"Alright, but before I go." Dalton reached into his pocket and pulled out a card. "Here is my card. My ID number is listed there, as well as the number for the Conduct Board of the Guardian Branch. I take full responsibility for what happened. If you think I did not act accordingly, you may submit a complaint."

Irene snatched the card out of his hand, glaring.

"Again, I am very sorry, Irene."

"I won't have him anywhere near you or your daughter," Irene said. "Guardians shouldn't be around children. And they sure as hell shouldn't raise them if this is what happens."

She ushered them out of the house, closing the door sharply behind them. Dalton sighed heavily as he put an arm around Andrew's shoulders, pulling him into a hug.

"Thank you for what you said in there," he said.

"How could she...*why* would she say something like that?" Andrew asked in disbelief.

"You mustn't be too hard on her," Frieda said. "She's terrified. Her child was in danger and she wasn't there to protect him. She feels helpless, and angry, and Benjamin is very upset, which makes her feel even worse. They both need time to process. I'm sure they'll be alright, in time."

"But she had no right to call you murderers."

"Technically, Andrew, it's true," Hanyi said. "Mitoki didn't arrest that man, he killed him. Well, I guess it wasn't really a man, it was reanimated clay and dead stuff in the form of a magical spy..." Hanyi gave a strong nod. "I think it's a good thing we didn't mention that."

Mitoki and Eclipse turned to the others as they approached the car.

"I'm sorry," Mitoki said. "If she files a complaint, I'll be sure to take the blame."

"It's alright, Mitoki," Dalton said. "And there is no blame in this situation. You saved Benjamin's life. His mother is just upset."

"But you shouldn't have to take the heat," Mitoki insisted.

Dalton shrugged one shoulder. "It's no trouble," he said, walking around the front of the car to climb into the driver's seat. "I only have one other cite against me right now. I'm alright taking another in this situation."

"Only one?" Eclipse teased, climbing back into the car with the other Guardians. "Aren't you a goodie-two-shoes."

"Why? How many do you have?" Keito chuckled behind him.

"Four."

"Be careful," Mitoki warned with a grin. "Two more and you'll get a suspension."

"Humans are lucky," Keito groaned. "You get six cites before a suspension. Demons get three and they stay on our record for seven years instead of five."

Andrew turned to Keito as Dalton backed out of the driveway.

"Isn't that unfair to the demon Guardians? I thought there was supposed to be equal treatment."

"There's supposed to be," Keito agreed. "But the public is not as accepting of demon mistakes as human mistakes. When I first became a Guardian, cites for demons lasted ten years, and it only took two before that demon Guardian was suspended. It took a lot of arguing, but I managed to get it to three cites for seven years."

"Were you ever suspended?"

"Sixty-eight times," Keito declared without hesitation. Andrew barked a disbelieving laugh as the other Guardians in the car whirled around.

"Sixty-eight?!" Mitoki and Eclipse asked in unison.

"And how many of those cites were just because of your cold, unfeeling demeanor?" Hanyi jibed, laughing when Keito punched him lightly in the arm.

"How did they not fire you?" Dalton asked.

"Oh, they threatened plenty of times," Keito said. "But I was top-ranked and I was more efficient than any other demon Guardian at the time. They almost always shortened my suspension time to two months. They couldn't afford to have me out of the field for long."

"You must have been damn good at your job if they didn't fire you after all that," Mitoki said with a laugh.

"What would you have done if they had fired you?" Eclipse inquired.

"Probably gone back to Benny's gang," Keito said with a devilish grin. "Or started my own bandit clan and raised a bit of hell in the Demon Realm."

"Gang? Were you a criminal before you were a Guardian?" Andrew asked.

"I was," Keito said. "I actually built a pretty notorious reputation."

"Did the DPC know that when they allowed you to take the oath?" Dalton asked, raising a questioning eyebrow.

"Oh, they knew," Keito said. "It caused a lot of controversy."

"Then you had a record with the DPC?" Andrew asked.

"My record outside the Demon Realm was pretty small," Keito admitted. "But they heard my reputation and it stopped them from accepting me for three years. I kept applying, but they kept refusing, saying I was too dangerous and could not be trusted because of my history."

"What finally changed their minds?" Andrew asked excitedly.

"I broke one of their biggest cases," he said proudly. "There was a demon in the Realm of Light that was causing all kinds of trouble, but she had been impossible to bring into custody. She had killed four demon Guardians, and most of the other demon Guardians were refusing to take the case. I struck a deal that if I could bring the demon into custody or kill her, they would allow me to finally take the oath and be a Guardian. They took the deal immediately because they were certain I was going to be killed."

"Did you kill the other demon or bring her into custody?"

"I killed her," Keito said. "And it was not easy. She was a Trade Mercenary."

"One of Juki and Rutu's disciples?" Eclipse asked. "Like the one we faced?"

Keito nodded. "This Trade Mercenary had been hired by another demon to go after a handful of humans he believed had wronged him. And she was damn good at her job. I chased her for months around the Realm of Light, but I knew how the Trade Mercenaries were trained, so I was able to better track her movements and defend myself against her. Eventually, she decided she was going to send a message to the DPC and she attacked the compound. I was able to finally bring her down there." He laughed. "Needless to say, I impressed a lot of people and was able to take the oath."

"You managed to kill a Trade Mercenary?" Mitoki asked in disbelief.

"I was a lot younger then," Keito said playfully. "But it was only because I understood her training and how she was likely to plan her attack. That was when the DPC realized that my criminal past and my…connections, were actually an asset."

"Juki must have been pissed you killed one of his mercenaries," Dalton noted.

"He was not pleased," Keito agreed, though he was smiling. "But I don't often get to screw over Juki, so it was a victory for me, regardless."

Eclipse turned almost completely around in his seat to look at Keito.

"Do you like Juki? Or hate him?"

Keito's face turned pensive momentarily.

"It depends on the day," he said vaguely. Eclipse rolled his eyes. "Care to elaborate?"

"I *respect* him," Keito said. "I respect him immensely. We certainly have had a very strained history together, but he has taught me a lot, and he has been willing to help me when I need it. But I know better than to push my luck with him. I would rather maintain a relationship with him that is more to my benefit than my detriment. Believe me, you do not want Juki as an enemy."

"He *is* our enemy," Eclipse pointed out.

"No, it's not that simple," Keito insisted. "I actually think that, right now, Juki and Rutu are on our side. We should enjoy that while it lasts."

"They did help us survive Yokouro's test last round," Mitoki pointed out. "And Rutu just handed that dagger to us a few hours ago. I think it's safe to say that they are on our side right now."

"I just don't understand how you can trust them so easily," Eclipse said to Keito. "I thought you were afraid of them."

"I'm terrified of them," Keito said with a bark of laughter. "But I respect them, and there is a certain level of trust that comes with that."

When they pulled up to Emma's house, they gently woke her and brought her to the door, where her parents greeted her, worried, but thanking the Guardians profusely for saving their daughter and bringing her home. After what happened with Irene, it eased the Guardians to have Emma's parents so grateful despite their concerns about the long-term effects of Emma's trauma.

Dalton dropped Andrew off at Master Bowen's Guardian Training Center—the same facility where he had completed his own training. Andrew was reluctant to leave the older Guardians, wanting to pose a million more questions, but Team Dalton agreed to all train with him one day, which caused him to walk into the large, domed training center with a broad, excited smile plastered across his face.

The Guardians finally made it back to Dalton's house. Frieda immediately brought Theresa into the kitchen to make her a quick lunch to keep her from becoming too irritable, leaving the Guardians to unload the car. It took another hour for the Guardians to distribute the bags into the rooms, start laundry, and eat lunch, finally taking some time to tend to their more serious wounds.

In the early afternoon, the Guardians sat around the living room, enjoying a light drink and taking a moment to relax from the stressful fight earlier that day.

"Dalton," Hanyi said, catching Dalton's attention. "Thank you for taking us up to the lake. I know things got a little...well, I had fun anyway. So, thank you."

"Thank you for indulging me and Theresa," he said with a laugh.

"It was an experience I was not expecting," Mitoki added. "I don't think I ever would have gotten into a kayak or gone tubing in my life if you hadn't brought us up there."

"Can you imagine if we told the other Guardians in the branch that we went tubing during the break between tournament rounds?" Hanyi laughed.

"I need to start exercising immediately for the tournament," Keito groaned, rubbing his hands over his abdomen. "Your wife is an incredible cook," he told Dalton. "I ate way too much. I'm going to lose my killer abs."

"You do not have killer abs," Eclipse scoffed, rolling his eyes.

"Well, they may not be my *best* feature," Keito agreed. "Most have said that my ass was my best feature."

"You're proud of that, aren't you?" Mitoki teased.

"I've never not been proud of my assets," Keito played along. "All that criminal activity kept me in pretty amazing shape and gave me that rugged look that I've always been able to attract people with."

"Show them your scars and tell them all the eccentric stories?" Dalton leered.

"Actually, demon bodies don't scar," Keito pointed out. "Not unless a lot of damage was dealt with spells or magic. But if I did have scars, I would absolutely tell all my wild stories to anyone who wanted to see them."

"You really do know how to use your assets to your advantage, don't you?" Hanyi said with a chuckle.

"I better use it while I got it," Keito laughed.

A knock on the door surprised them, but no one was particularly worried. Dalton stood to answer, laughing at Hanyi's comment about Keito's baby-smooth skin as he reached for the door knob. He opened the door to see a woman standing on the front porch, her back to him as her hands fiddled with the zipper on her purse nervously.

"Can I help you?" Dalton asked.

The anxious woman spun around, her wide blue eyes meeting his.

Dalton's heart fell into his stomach and his blood ran cold.

"Dalton?" she whispered. "Dalton, is that really you?" She pressed a hand to her lips, tears welling in her eyes. "Oh, you've grown up so much."

Dalton's voice was weak and choked when he spoke.

"...M-Mom?"

Chapter Sixteen

The air in the living room was heavy and uncomfortable. The Guardians sat stiffly, keeping a closer eye on Dalton than on the woman who had turned up on his doorstep. When Frieda had come to see who was at the door, she had taken charge of the situation, putting Theresa down for a nap before putting herself between Dalton's mother and her husband. Even as they sat on the couches around the living room, she was sitting closer to the older woman than Dalton, holding Dalton's hand protectively.

Dalton's mother was extremely uncomfortable under the scrutiny of everyone in the house. She twirled her fiery red curls and kept her chilling blue eyes averted to the ground whenever she caught the gazes of the other Guardians.

"I'm sorry to show up so suddenly, and unannounced," she murmured. "I wasn't sure if you would even see me."

"May I ask…" Keito started, looking at her expectantly.

"Shannon."

"Shannon," he continued, "what prompted you to suddenly show up on Dalton's doorstep?"

"I've been fighting with myself about the decision for months," she said with a nervous laugh, more afraid to meet eyes with the demon than any of the others in the room. "I've been watching you compete in the tournament."

The Guardians, all trained in reading body language, saw Dalton tense at the words, turning his head away from his mother, trying to pass the action off with a casual sigh.

"I just couldn't believe how handsomely you've grown up, and how strong you are…like your father was."

The others of Team Dalton did not know much about the abuse Dalton had suffered at Shannon's hand as a child, but they knew that a lot of her anger and abusive behaviors had been related to Dalton's father's death and the fact that he had been a Guardian, and seeing Dalton's anxious reaction to the words confirmed the severity of the abuse.

Dalton's fingers tightened around Frieda's hand.

"Dalton, please, look at me."

He obeyed, but it was difficult for him to raise his eyes to hers.

"I need to tell you that I'm sorry," she said, her voice choking up. "I hope you realize…that I had to leave…I had to leave for you. To keep you safe."

"You left in the middle of the night," Dalton whispered. "You didn't tell anyone else you were leaving, either."

"I know...I-I did call your grandfather, though, when I could. I knew he would take care of you."

Dalton scoffed, though his voice was shaking.

"A week later?" he hissed.

"I was drunk, Dalton. I'm clean now. Seven years sober." A wobbly smile took over her face. "I needed to get help, Dalton. And I fell off the wagon several times, but I think I'm finally in a place where I can see you again. Where I can tell you that all the things I said to you...all the things I did..." She trailed off, letting out a shaking breath. "I loved your father so much...and that attack was so violent and traumatic...I took out my pain on you. And I'm sorry."

Dalton let out a long breath, but did not speak.

"I'm not asking for you to immediately forgive me, but...I really hope you'll give me a chance to show you how much I've changed. I really want to get to know you, Dalton."

"Why?" he asked. "I'm a Guardian. You hate Guardians."

"I don't hate Guardians," she said. "I hate the job that can so easily take away those you love."

"It didn't take Dalton away from you," Keito noted coldly. "You left him. Are you saying that you didn't love him enough to stay? William is a part of him."

Shannon turned to Keito.

"You knew William?"

"Not well," Keito said, which caused Dalton and the others to straighten, surprised he had not mentioned it before. "I only met him twice before he was killed."

Shannon's face brightened and she nodded, motioning to Dalton.

"Then you see how much Dalton looks like him."

The anger that had been building in Dalton's frame changed to fear again, causing him to shrink away on the couch.

"And you're just as strong as your father. Probably even stronger," she continued, smiling at Dalton despite the way he refused to meet her gaze again. "Watching you in the tournament was quite thrilling. It was almost like seeing him again."

"Please, don't," Dalton whispered.

"Shannon, I don't mean to sound suspicious," Hanyi said, trying to keep his tone light. "But how did you know where Dalton lived?"

"Oh…" She suddenly became nervous again, dropping her gaze. "I went to the Guardian Branch at the compound and asked to see you, actually. But they said that you were away on a vacation, but they gave me your home phone number. From there, I was able to figure out the neighborhood based on the area code…then I did a little digging and asked around. Eventually, I called your grandfather and he told me." She raised her hand to Dalton, apparently oblivious to how the motion made him flinch. "I know, that sounds horrible, but I just had to see you again, while I had the courage."

Frieda squeezed Dalton's hand, but she did not take her eyes off the older woman, her back straight to show Shannon that she was not afraid of her.

"I was so happy to hear that you had a family. Beautiful house, beautiful wife, even a daughter," Shannon pressed her hand to her chest, shaking her head with a smile. "I would love to meet my granddaughter."

"She's taking a nap," Frieda said. "It's been a very big day. She's quite tired."

"How did you know all that about Dalton?" Mitoki asked. "Just how much did you ask about him before you came here?"

"I haven't seen him in two decades," Shannon said. "I wanted to know how my son was doing."

"Wouldn't it have been better to just call *him*?" Hanyi asked pointedly.

Shannon dropped her gaze again. "I figured he would hang up on me if I tried to call." She turned back to Dalton, taking a chance and standing, walking around the coffee table to sit on Dalton's other side, surprising all the Guardians at how bold she was being. She sat next to him and took his other hand. He tried to back away from her, but he could not bring himself to take his hand away.

"I know that my coming here is a shock." She patted the back of his shaking hand. "But I want to get to know you, Dalton. I know I can't make up for the time we've lost, but I hope you'll give me a chance to be a part of your life now. Losing your father was the hardest thing I ever had to handle. But I could not bear it if I lost you, too."

Dalton pulled his hand back, clearing his throat nervously.

"I-I'll have to think about it."

"Please, give me another chance," she said, leaning closer. "I have changed. I really have. I've even bought tickets to see you in the next round of the tournament. I'll finally be the mother I should have been, cheering on my son and supporting him."

"You don't have to do all that," he said, clearly becoming more flustered and uncomfortable, unable to look into her eyes as she stared at him expectantly.

"Oh, but I want to," she insisted. "I want to be there for you, Dalton. Please, just let me—"

A chiming in Dalton's pocket cut her off, but it took Dalton's clumsy fingers a few seconds to pull out his phone and see who was calling him. He was confused when he saw Hanyi's work phone number on the screen. He looked at Hanyi quickly, who minutely jerked his head to tell Dalton to leave the room and collect himself.

"I'm sorry, I have to take this," he murmured, getting to his feet and answering the fake call, pretending to talk to someone as he stepped down the hallway and into his office, shutting the door.

Shannon looked in the direction he had gone before turning back to the other faces in the living room, who were staring at her like angry lions. She slumped back a little, wringing her hands together nervously as she looked at her lap.

"I suppose...he's told you stories..." she whispered.

"He didn't need to," Keito said.

Shannon turned to Frieda, but of all the angry eyes in the room, Frieda's were the darkest.

"...thank you for taking care of my son, and being a better mother to his child than I was to him," she said. "I hope that I can show you that I'm a different person, and that I can be another support to Dalton."

"You'll have to forgive my skepticism," Frieda said coldly. "He may have not told *them* what you did to him, but he has told me. And I would *never* be able to leave my child, alone and terrified, for five minutes, let alone for a *week* before I called for help." She scoffed. "And who do you call? Jonathan, a man so wrapped up in his own career, he barely remembered he had a *son*, let alone a grandson."

"I wasn't right after William was killed," Shannon insisted, though she did not drop her head as she had with every other accusatory remark. "I knew I was hurting him. I left him to protect him."

"So he could wonder for *years* what he did wrong?" Frieda snapped. "What he did that was so terrible you would leave him? And then he was dropped off at a Guardian training center. Master Bowen raised him, not you, not Jonathan. And then he became the thing you never wanted him to become—a *Guardian*. You're the one who made him believe he had to prove that he was worthy to be alive. I don't know how you plan to undo that damage. The scars

157

you left on him are nothing compared to the insecurity you planted in him."

"Could you imagine if you lost him?" Shannon whispered. "Could you handle it?"

"No," Frieda said honestly. "But I would *never* take it out on my child. And I would never make her think that she was the *reason* her father was gone."

"I know I can't take any of that back," Shannon said. "But I want to try and build some sort of relationship with my son. Maybe I can't undo the hurt, but I don't want to live the rest of my life wishing I could have at least told him how sorry I was for what I did to him."

"I think it's time we call bullshit," Keito said darkly. "Why are you really here?"

Shannon turned to him, startled.

"What do you mean?" she asked. "I just said, I'm here—"

"No, no," Keito said quickly. "I don't buy it. I don't think you've changed at all."

"You're hardly in a position to be making that judgement," Shannon said, not dropping her gaze from the demon for the first time since she arrived. "You don't know me."

"No, but I don't need to," he said. "I know your type."

"*Type?*" she said indignantly.

Keito did not respond, his eyes locked with hers. She scoffed lightly, causing the other Guardians turn to one another in surprise at her attitude.

"Do you think you might be projecting your own issues a bit, Keito?"

"And what issues do you think I'm projecting?" he challenged.

"Your own childhood, perhaps?" she asked. "Perhaps wanting apologies from your own parents?"

"I never wanted an apology from my father," Keito said with a smirk. "But I find it interesting that you're so confident I was abused as a child as well. Any chance you've been talking to some demons? Do you know more than you should?"

Shannon's momentary hesitation was not lost on anyone.

"You're the one who said you knew my so-called type," she defended. "Is it really so hard to believe that I merely want to have some sort of relationship with my son now that I've straightened myself up a bit?"

"I find the timing to be a bit too perfect," Keito said. "And I don't buy anything you're saying."

She shook her head. "How am I supposed to respond to that?" she asked quietly. "And I'm not looking for *your* forgiveness. I'm here for my son."

"Shannon," Frieda said, cutting Keito off, "I think what Keito means is that, right now, with the tournament and the current state of affairs with this demon causing chaos in the realms, your arrival might be a little much for Dalton to handle. Perhaps, it would be better if you were to leave your contact information with us and he can call you when he's ready."

Shannon faltered, noticeably caught off-guard by the proposition. She slowly dropped her head, tears gathering in the corners of her eyes.

"Yes...I suppose..." Her voice became choked. "It was too much to assume he would let me into his life. I just...I really wanted to show him how sorry I am." She let out a long breath. "Do you know of anyone who would want a ticket to the tournament?"

"You can still go to the tournament," Mitoki said. "It's fine to support him, just let him gather his bearings and deal with all we're working on with the Guardian Branch."

Shannon's demeanor changed again to meek and nervous, her eyes on the floor as she shook her head.

"I would love to be there for Dalton, but...I came here so suddenly, I don't have any place to stay. I'll need the money from the ticket to return home."

"You came here without making arrangements at a hotel?" Hanyi asked, startled. "Even around tournament time?"

Shannon laughed nervously, shrugging. "I didn't think this through, I guess. I suppose there aren't going to be any rooms left in the city."

"This is a full house, currently," Keito said, unable to hide the ice in his voice. "With all of us staying here."

"I'll call the Regency Hotel," Dalton said, leaning against the opening of the hallway, having been quietly listening. Everyone jumped, turning to him, having been too wrapped up with watching Shannon to notice his return.

He walked slowly into the living room, but he did not resume his seat, standing next to the couch as he spoke.

"Mother," he said, "I know it must have taken you a lot of courage to come and find me. I have always wondered how you were doing, and you look like you've been doing well. And if you want to come to the tournament, you should. You already bought the ticket. I'll call the general manager at the Regency Hotel. He owes me a favor. I'm sure he can set you up with a room."

"Really?" Shannon asked, standing slowly, her eyes filled again with tears. "You...you're giving me a second chance?"

"No," he said. "I'm...deciding to get to know you. We'll just have to start there."

"That's perfectly fine with me," Shannon said, stepping forward to hug Dalton, though he retreated, raising a hand to keep her at a distance. She paused, stunned, and then dropped her head. "Thank you, Dalton. You don't know what this means to me."

"I'll call you a cab to take you to the Regency," he said. "And I'll call the hotel and have them set you up with a room. But it has been a very long day, so perhaps we could meet up another day?"

"Of course, of course," she said, still beaming from the kindness Dalton was showing her. "If it's alright with you, I just need to use your restroom."

He nodded, stepping aside and telling her where the guest bathroom was located. As she left the room, Dalton called for a cab to come to the house, trying to ignore the way his team watched her with dark, suspicious glares.

As soon as the call was complete, his team stood to gather around him.

"Dalton, I don't like this," Keito said.

"And I do?" he asked.

"We do have a lot to worry about as it is," Eclipse agreed. "And...there's something off about her."

"There always has been," Dalton agreed.

"Dalton," Frieda said, taking his hand gently. "You have no obligation to set her up with a hotel room, or endure her trying to intrude on your life. You can send her home. It's okay."

"You want me to just throw her out?"

"I would," Eclipse said.

"That's like what she did to me," he said quietly. "If I turn her away, and she really wants to make amends, then it makes me no different from her."

"That's not true, Dalton," Keito protested. "She showed you who she was when you were a kid. You don't owe her anything, not even the benefit of doubt."

"I would just..." Dalton closed his eyes, taking a deep breath to steady himself, "I would rather have her somewhere where I can keep an eye on her. And she can't just turn up again and surprise me."

Even though they all heard the bathroom door open down the hall, no one moved away from Dalton, making a show to Shannon that they were discussing what to do about her sudden visit. But she seemed unfazed when she returned to the living room.

"Thank you again, Dalton," she said, readjusting her purse on her shoulder and smiling gently at him. "I can't tell you what this means to me."

He merely nodded before motioning to the front door.

"I'll wait with you for your cab."

With a bright smile, Shannon walked toward the front door, opening it and stepping outside, Dalton trailing behind her.

"Keito," Hanyi said quietly when the front door was closed, "you don't think Yokouro had anything to do with bringing Shannon here, do you?"

"Really?" Eclipse gawked. "Not everything has to be related to Yokouro."

"No, but I'm pretty sure this is," Keito said.

"You might be overreacting," Mitoki added.

"Yokouro was the one who killed Dalton's father," Keito reminded them. "He's also the one who's been manipulating Eclipse's life since childhood." He shook his head slowly. "I would be more surprised if Yokouro *wasn't* somehow involved in this reunion."

Dalton walked his mother off the porch, standing with her on the curb, his hands shoved deep into his pockets.

"I'm sorry I didn't call before showing up," Shannon said. "I just felt that, if I was going to make an effort to reconnect, I better show you how committed I was."

Dalton forced a smile, but could not bring himself to respond.

"I, uh," she opened her purse, pulling out a small, black pouch and extending it to him, "I wanted to give this to you."

He was certain she saw the way his fingers trembled as he took the pouch. He opened it and pulled out a simple watch, the leather band soft and well-worn, and even though the watch face was scuffed and scratched, it had clearly been recently cleaned.

"It was your father's," she said tenderly. "They gave it to me before he was cremated. I've held onto it all these years. The only real memento I have of him. But I think you should have it."

Holding the watch was oddly surreal. Dalton had heard many stories about his father as a Guardian, and when he was younger, he always imagined what he and his father would have done together. But as he had matured, he had lost touch with the childish imaginings of his father. Holding the watch, a small glimmer of those memories resurfaced.

"Thank you..." he whispered.

The taxi pulled up to the curb, breaking his attention from the watch.

"When you get to the hotel just ask for Jason Getty, the general manager. I'll set everything up with him."

She beamed at him. "You're such a good man, Dalton." She stepped forward, opening her arms and hugging him, as though forgetting how quickly he had retreated before. He stood stiffly in the hug, trying to slow the fear that rocketed through his body, telling him to get away from her.

Shannon held the hug much longer than Dalton anticipated, increasing his anxiety and causing him to flinch when she pulled away and placed her hand gently against the side of his face.

"I'll call you," she said, turning and climbing into the cab. Dalton watched her get into the car and watched the vehicle drive away. He let out a long sigh, his body going slack as he spared one more glance at the watch before pocketing it and returning to the house, trying to ignore the sick feelings churning in his stomach.

Chapter Seventeen

Even though they saw the toll it was taking on Dalton, the team discussed the timing of Shannon's arrival. Keito insisted that Yokouro had to be involved somehow, and while all of them were suspicious of that fact, they also were desperate for Yokouro to *not* be involved in something. Dalton hardly participated in the conversation, still in shock from seeing his mother after two decades.

The following day, Dalton was acting more like himself, though he was clearly tired, so the Guardians avoided the subject, opting instead to spend the day relaxing around the house and spending time with the energetic Theresa, who seemed to have overcome her fear quite quickly and spent a lot of time in the backyard on her new swing set and running around with Rio.

The day after, the Guardians went to the training center where Dalton had completed his training, meeting with Andrew to train with him as promised. The famous Guardians were quickly ushered into a private training room to keep the entire center from descending upon them. Andrew was eager to prove his strength to the Guardians, even though he still had much to learn. Team Dalton left the training center—through the back of the facility to avoid a scene—impressed with Andrew's potential and his determination to be one of the best Guardians in history.

Just before dinner, Jikia and Tarrena called Dalton, telling him they would be in the Human Realm the following morning. Dalton gave them directions, but had to arrange a room for them at one of the smaller, nearby hotels due to the limited space in his house.

The two dragons arrived at the house after settling at the hotel and immediately asked how the visit to the lake had gone. They filled them in on all the antics of kayaking and boating, but agreed to tell them more about why they had left the lake early once Theresa went to bed to avoid upsetting her.

"What was going on with the dragons?" Mitoki asked.

"Oh," Jikia said with a sigh and a roll of her eyes, "Lord Kyreane, who was a dragon of very high standing, was put on trial for plotting the murder of Vestera Hizoku."

While the humans were mortified at the thought, Keito let out a soft laugh.

"What a moron," he said. "Vestera's basically indestructible."

"Why would he want to kill Vestera?" Dalton asked.

"There's been some trouble in the dragon clan lately," Jikia explained. "But what it boils down to is that Vestera has no young. He is the only direct descendant to the four original dragons left, so the clan is pushing for him to have young, but he refuses to take a mate. This has made many dragons nervous about what will happen when Vestera is no longer around. Dragons are jockeying for positions of power in preparation and Lord Kyreane thought it would be easier to just removed Vestera and start a new dragon order."

"Can Vestera even be killed?" Mitoki asked. "And wouldn't killing him upset...*everything*?"

"Killing Vestera would send everything into chaos," Tarrena said with a strong nod.

"And, in theory, Vestera *can* be killed," Jikia said hesitantly. "He is considered the first *mortal* dragon, but his power is so great, he's practically immortal. But the clan is very traditional, and rather than start a new regime, they want Vestera to continue his bloodline. So with this newest attempted treason, there is a decision in the works to make Vestera have young, so things should calm down now."

"Force him to have a kid?" Eclipse asked. "Is that even possible? I thought he was your ruler. He could just say no, right?"

"He has been saying no for a very long time, but I'm sure he'll notice the tension in the clan and finally agree to produce an heir. But it is difficult because of his power level and his age. It is almost impossible to find a female that is able to bear his young, so he cannot put it off much longer. That's why Lord Kyreane thought it was the perfect time to plot against Vestera."

"Was he imprisoned?" Mitoki asked.

"Killed," Tarrena corrected. "The clan decided that if he wanted to kill Vestera, he should challenge him in a duel. Unsurprisingly, Vestera won."

Theresa was fascinated with the dragons in the same way she had been fascinated with Keito. But when the adults started watching the news, she quickly got bored and went to help her mother and Tarrena in the kitchen preparing dinner.

The news stories were covering riots breaking out in the Darkness Realm due to a recent demon scare, but the local Guardians and law enforcement were doing a good job keeping the situation from getting too out of hand, so the Guardians were only half-listening. When Keito's phone rang, everyone turned toward the noise, seeing the confused expression that came across Keito's face when he saw the number on the screen.

"Hello?" he answered hesitantly. Dalton muted the television and Keito's eyes widened. "Oh…" The demon began speaking in another language, standing and excusing himself while his teammates watched him, not bothering to turn the sound on the television again.

They did not speak until he returned a few minutes later, looking torn.

"Everything okay?" Mitoki asked as the demon resumed his seat.

"Yes, everything's fine," he said, his eyes distant. "I just…I forgot about something back home. I might have to disappear for a few hours and go back to the Demon Realm in a few days."

"Is it serious?"

Keito hesitated, glancing worriedly at Eclipse before he answered. "There's a banquet at the Kage Palace. It's a traditional event that the Kage family hosts every century to celebrate Juki's reign. It's a big deal on the Kage Territory."

"How big of a deal?" Mitoki asked.

"Any event that gets all Juki's younger siblings in the same room is a big event," Keito said with a hollow laugh. "It used to be a way for the clan to celebrate having Juki as their Old Blood Lord rather than his father, but now it's become an established Kage banquet that I think they hold just for the sake of tradition."

"How long has Juki been in power?"

Keito had to think for a moment before he spoke. "I think his most recent reign is about seventy millennia?"

"Seventy millennia? Juki is *seventy-thousand* years old?" Mitoki gawked.

Keito let out a laugh. "I guess I forgot to tell you how old Juki is. No, he's *much* older than that. He's the oldest living demon in the realm, and is actually millions of years old. I think about sixty-three million."

The shock that gripped the living room had everyone speechless.

"*Million?*" Eclipse choked.

"Juki and his living younger siblings are survivors from the Demon Realm's feudal period. That's why this is such an important, traditional event for the Kages. Juki is something of a pillar in demon culture."

"Wait, if he's that old," Mitoki started, "why did you say his most *recent* reign has been only seventy thousand years?"

Keito sighed heavily.

"Because Kage politics are a *mess*," he said with a groan. "I told you about the Old Blood Lords and how the DeVastes Clan has the leaders that make the most noise, but they don't hold a candle to previous Kage leaders. And Juki's father, Kawakara Kage, is the most notorious and most hated demon in the history of our land."

"Worse than Yokouro?"

"Easily a thousand times worse," Keito said. "It was said that he used to make the entire Kage household, even his own children and mates, kneel and face the walls when he passed them. He was known to walk through the villages of the realm and single out entire families to kill for no reason. And he played mind games with *everyone*. Even millions of years later, demons are afraid of the name Kawakara Kage. Even Yokouro would know better than to mess with Juki's father."

"How long was he in power?"

"A few thousand years," Keito said. "But the transition to Juki's reign was not easy, and even today, the things Kawakara did affect the Kage Clan."

"How so?"

Keito hesitated, glancing toward the kitchen to be sure that Theresa was occupied with other things so she would not walk in and hear anything he was about to say.

"Kawakara was a tyrant, and he was involved in a very dirty war with the Kaneaka Clan through most of his reign. And that war between the Kages and the Kaneakas tore apart the entire land because they were the two most powerful families at the time. He committed horrible war crimes and he really should have been executed a thousand times over, but everyone was too afraid of him. And he was incredibly powerful, so not many could stand up to him. So the clan let him get away with his crimes, mostly by trying to cover them up or denying they even happened."

"I'm going to assume he eventually stood trial and was executed," Mitoki said.

"No. Never," Keito corrected. "And the reason the clan was so quick to cover all of Kawakara's crimes was because they became accomplices." Keito threw another quick glance at the kitchen and lowered his voice slightly. "Because Juki ended up making a deal with his father that benefited everyone in the palace."

"What kind of deal?" Dalton asked nervously, wondering why Keito was being sure to keep his voice so low.

"Juki made a blood oath with his father to basically become the scapegoat for the entire house," Keito explained. "Kawakara used to kill members of his own house on a whim. He would abuse and torment anyone who managed to catch his eye. So, to protect his younger siblings, Juki made an agreement with his father.

Kawakara imprisoned Juki in one room of the palace, and every day, for over twenty years, he would torture Juki, but he was not allowed to lay a hand on anyone else in the house. So, from the time Juki was ten, until he was over thirty, he was kept in that room and brutally tortured until he eventually snapped and killed Kawakara."

Dalton knew his jaw was wide open, but he could not hide his mortification.

"And no one thought to *help him*?" he snapped. "Not even Juki's *mother*?"

"Unfortunately," Keito said, "everyone was willing to let Juki be the palace scapegoat because it kept them safe. Kawakara honored the deal. He almost killed Juki in the process, but he didn't harm anyone else in the house because of the oath, so everyone turned the other way." Keito let out a long sigh. "Of course, that does mean that the entire clan was in hot water when Kawakara was finally killed. They tried to sweep the entire thing under the rug by exiling Juki from the clan and pretending it never happened."

"After all that, they exiled him?" Eclipse asked, disgusted.

"Like I said, the Kage politics are a mess," Keito said with a broken chuckle. "But Kawakara didn't name any of his other children as successors to the clan—only Juki. So the clan was without a leader. Half the clan wanted to bring Juki back, half wanted Acurala to take the throne, but Acurala didn't want it, and on and on the problems went. The Kage Clan almost collapsed. Juki eventually came back and took control. But there are still those in the clan that think Juki is not fit to rule. He's been stripped of his title and reinstated many times due to one reason or another. This banquet will be a milestone of consecutive years to have him seated in power."

"That sounds like a lot of drama," Dalton groaned.

"Believe me, that's only a fraction of it," Keito said. "But this celebration is a very big deal for the Kage Clan."

"Then why do you have to be there?" Eclipse asked. "Is Juki your Old Blood Lord?"

"No, Vestera is," Keito answered. "But…as you know, I did live in Juki's house. And it would be considered very rude of me not to go."

"I don't like it," Eclipse said. "Juki is our enemy, and you want to go to a banquet in his honor?"

"I don't see him as the enemy," Keito said.

"And that's part of the problem!"

"Eclipse," Mitoki started slowly, "it might be more dangerous for Keito *not* to go if he's being asked to attend. Juki is a very powerful demon, and if Keito doesn't show the proper respect for him, it could be dangerous for all of us."

"How big is the banquet?" Dalton asked. "Is everyone across the Demon Realm invited?"

"No," Keito said. "This is a very Kage-focused event. Juki will be there, his kids, his siblings, Rutu, some of the lower lords of the Kage Territory, but if you're worried about Yokouro showing up, I'm almost certain he won't. I wouldn't even think of going if there was a chance of him making an appearance."

"But if there's only people from the Kage Territory going, you don't need to go," Eclipse said shortly.

Keito hesitated. "It's not that simple. Yes, technically, I pledge to Vestera, but everyone in the Demon Realm knows that I'm…"

"That you're what?" Eclipse pressed.

"That I've had past relations with the Kage Clan," Keito completed carefully.

"Relations that you won't share," Eclipse pointed out sharply.

"You did say you would explain more eventually," Dalton said. "How long did you live with Juki?"

Keito was very hesitant to respond. He cast his gaze around the expectant faces before his eyes went to the floor.

"Many years," he admitted. "I was first brought to Juki's palace shortly after I left Benny's gang. I think I finally left the palace when I was in my early twenties, so I was there for at least ten years."

"Ten years?!" Eclipse gawked. "It took you ten years to run away?"

"I was safe at Juki's," Keito murmured, refusing to lift his gaze. "I've made a lot of enemies, but no one would dare come after me if I was with Juki."

"But why would Juki want to protect you?" Mitoki asked.

Keito was becoming more uncomfortable by the minute, his eyes flicking around the room as he rubbed his hands together nervously.

"I first met Juki when I was about four years old, and as I was being passed around the different territories, being hunted by the purists on the DeVastes land and then seeking refuge with Vestera, the Wandering Child title made him interested in why Vestera and the DeVastes Clan were so invested in me. So, Juki and Rutu ended up keeping an eye on me as well. That's why I was able to stay there."

"Just…live with Juki?" Eclipse said. "He just let you stay there?"

"…no," Keito finally said. "Juki did have me working for him. I started out as a servant, cleaning the palace, but when I had gained more of his trust, Juki sent me on some other jobs…jobs that my days as a thief made me qualified to do."

"You worked for him," Eclipse said shortly. "You actually *worked* for Juki?"

"What was I supposed to do? I was just a kid and he's one of the most powerful demons in existence. Was I supposed to tell him no?" Keito challenged. "Do you know what happens to people who tell Juki no?"

"But you *did* leave," Dalton prompted.

"There were a lot of factors to me leaving," Keito said. "I told you that I had my children very young. It was during my time in Juki's palace, but I was under Juki's thumb, and I was more or less stuck there. When Vestera heard about my children and the work Juki was ordering me to do, he interfered and I was taken out of the Kage Palace."

"You travel in some very elite circles," Jikia noted warily.

"But I'm not part of the nobility, which is why it's so important that I keep my relations with Juki and Rutu civil and respectful. I don't have the protection of a title."

"But that means you have to go to a party with Juki and his family? Rutu will be there, too, along with a bunch of demons who support them…" Eclipse let out a long sigh. "I still don't see why they expect you to be there."

"How many children does Juki have?" Jikia asked curiously.

"Three."

"Does Rutu have children?" she asked.

Keito blinked, confused, and then pursed his lips and rubbed his face.

"Oh no, I forgot to tell you…"

"Tell us what?" Dalton asked.

"Juki and Rutu have three children *together*. They're mates."

Another stunned silence fell over the room, leaving only the distant sounds of Frieda, Tarrena, and Theresa in the kitchen.

"You just *forgot* to mention that fact?" Mitoki hissed, his eyes wide.

"They've been together for an eternity. I truly forgot that not everyone knows," Keito defended. "I mean, didn't you think it was strange that they were always together?"

"No!" Eclipse said.

"They didn't really act like a couple," Dalton noted, trying to think through his limited interactions with the Kage Lords.

"I guess they're not as openly affectionate as human couples," Keito agreed. "But they're closer than any couple I've ever known."

"Wait, they have children?" Jikia asked. "Which one is the biological father?"

"They both are," Keito said, trying to keep a smile from pulling at his lips, knowing he was about to shock the other Guardians even more.

"How is that possible?" Dalton asked slowly. "They're both male, right?"

"Keito, you've seen them naked, haven't you?" Hanyi said, turning to the demon. Keito glared playfully.

"It wasn't that kind of job, Hanyi," he said. "But, yes. They're both male. Their children were created through deep magic, but they've always been very secretive about how they managed to perform the spell. They don't want that magic getting into the wrong hands."

"And that's…that's acceptable in the Demon Realm?" Eclipse asked. "For someone as powerful as Juki to have a male mate?"

"Lords and ladies take same-sex mates all the time. It's not a problem until the question of a blood heir comes up," Keito explained. "Juki and Rutu found a way around that. Vestera knows how they managed to have children and he has permitted their children to be named as the heirs of the Kage Clan."

"But, considering Juki's age, Rutu must be much younger than him," Jikia noted.

"No, I think there's only about twenty years between them."

"That *is* a big age difference," Mitoki noted.

"Not when they're both in their millions," Keito said with a laugh.

"But wait…" Dalton said, raising his hand to get Keito's attention as his brain tried to take in all the new information. "You've always called it *Juki's* palace, not Juki and Rutu's palace."

"That's a formality thing," Keito said. "*Technically*, Rutu is not a Kage Lord, even though he has the name."

"Because he mated into the family?"

"Yes, and because the Kage Clan has taken every opportunity they can to completely screw him over," Keito groaned, rolling his eyes. "Everyone knows that Rutu is the most powerful demon in the history of our species. And before he mated Juki, he was the most powerful politically, as well."

"Why did his status drop?" Jikia asked.

"He's as purebred as demons come," Keito said. "Rutu's family, the Kaneaka Clan, was the first demon family and the first Old Blood Clan. When Juki and Rutu were children, Rutu's family was the most powerful clan in the realm."

"Wait, you said Kawakara committed war crimes against the Kaneaka Clan," Dalton recalled.

The demon nodded. "The Kaneakas and the Kages were bitter enemies. The Kaneakas had the most land, the most money, the largest population, and Rutu's father was an incredibly powerful Old Blood Lord. But the Kaneaka Clan collapsed."

"Because of Kawakara?" Mitoki guessed.

"Actually, no one knows why," Keito said. "The disappearance of the Kaneaka Clan is the largest mystery in the Demon Realm. Everyone assumed that the Kaneakas had been wiped out of existence, but then Rutu turned up. As he was the prince of the Kaneaka Clan before the collapse, he immediately became the Old Blood Lord of the Kaneaka Territory, so he had the right to reclaim the territory and rule as his father had. But he refused."

"The entire clan just disappeared?"

"Legend goes it was almost overnight," Keito said. "There are thousands of theories about what happened, but no one knows for sure. The Kaneaka Palace is long abandoned and said to be so cursed that, if you even look upon the walls, you will die an agonizing death, so no one investigates it. Demons are quite superstitious."

"Do you think Kawakara was responsible?"

"I've always thought he had a part in it," Keito said with a nod. "But Rutu won't talk about what happened. All he's ever said is that his family's curse caught up with them. They were all killed and he ran. He was eventually discovered as a kitchen servant in the Kage Palace, which was how he met Juki and how they became friends and, eventually, mates."

"Did he give all his royal titles to Juki, then? Is that why his status dropped when he mated into the Kage Clan?" Jikia deduced. Keito nodded.

"And because the Kaneaka Clan was a long-time foe of the Kages, Juki's siblings do everything they can to make Rutu's life hell. They also blame him for the death of their youngest sibling, so there is a lot of hatred."

"Why would they blame him for the death of the youngest sibling?" Dalton asked, unable to rein in his curiosity.

"The deal Juki had with Kawakara was that he was never allowed to leave the room where he was imprisoned, but Rutu began sneaking him out whenever Kawakara was away," Keito explained. "I don't know the details, but basically, Kawakara found out and he attacked the entire household to punish Juki, and that included killing the youngest of his children. It's said that that was what made

Juki snap and finally kill Kawakara, but the surviving siblings blame Rutu for even taking Juki out of that room. They've even gone so far as to beat him down and humiliate him in revenge, bringing up her death at every opportunity."

"And Rutu lets them get away with that?" Eclipse asked with raised eyebrows. "Even though he's such a powerful demon?"

"He's loyal to Juki," Keito said with a shrug. "He's more concerned with Juki's status as an Old Blood Lord than his own reputation. Demons make up all sorts of crazy rumors about Rutu as it is. He's used to it. It's how demons handle the fear they feel at just how powerful Rutu is."

"If he had the power to create life *three times*..." Jikia shook her head in disbelief. "That sort of magic is beyond anything I've ever seen. I don't know if *Vestera* would even try magic that volatile."

"No one knows the full scope of Rutu's power, but every demon knows that Rutu could kill them in an instant if he wanted to," Keito said. "He's seen more as the enforcer of the Kage Clan. Because of his reputation, his family's reputation, and his incredible power, he's always been seen as Juki's attack dog, because if you don't listen to what Juki orders you to do, Rutu comes in to enforce Juki's word." He laughed quietly. "And apparently, that's the way it's always been with them, even before they were mates. When Juki was exiled, Rutu was right there by his side. They went rogue together, which means they gave up their titles and went to the lowest rung of the social ladder. From there, they took over the Market—which is a central marketplace in the Demon Realm. They built up a notorious reputation as the Market Kings, and they ran the Market with an iron fist. Then they went on to create the Trade. And once the Trade was well-established, Juki returned to take control of the Kage Clan again."

"They must be the wealthiest demons in the realm, then," Dalton concluded.

"Yes," Keito affirmed. "Vestera, obviously, comes from very old money, but Juki and Rutu built their own empire from the Market and then from the Trade. They also had their family money once they reclaimed the title of Old Blood Lord." Keito smiled, lowering his gaze. "Honestly, that's one of the reasons I respect them so much. Juki and Rutu literally clawed their way to their positions. They've been in poverty with other demons. They've had to struggle to survive. They cleaned up the Demon Realm like you would never believe. They centralized everyone and solidified the social ladder. Their work in the Market and the Trade created a single currency for the Demon Realm and made the land a cohesive culture. They built the modern day Demon Realm, and made the land safer than ever before—with Vestera's help, of course. But even then, Vestera is a dragon. He doesn't understand demon culture like Juki and Rutu."

"And it's because of this culture that you have to go to this banquet?" Eclipse asked.

"Yes, and I would like to show my respect to Juki. He may not be my Old Blood Lord, but he has done a lot for me—for *us*."

Dalton sighed, nodding slowly. "Okay," he said. "But I'm putting a curfew on you."

"Fair enough," Keito chuckled.

Chapter Eighteen

"I would really rather you didn't do this…" Rutu murmured, shaking his head disapprovingly.

"Yes, you've been saying that all morning," Yokouro groaned. "But if I do this, it will make things far simpler, which means I can focus better."

"But does it have to be *today*?" Rutu asked, following Yokouro as the younger demon walked to the back corner of the DeVastes Palace gardens. He was making his way toward the large meditation labyrinth, which Rutu was eyeing nervously.

"No time like the present."

"Yokouro, do you not *feel* the tension in the air today?"

Yokouro's step halted and he closed his eyes, trying to sense the same thing that had Rutu so on-edge.

"What tension?"

"There is strain on the dimensional fabric today. Can you not feel it?"

"I don't feel any tension," Yokouro said, exasperated.

"With Vestera's seal broken, the realms are going to shift against one another when tension builds high enough," Rutu explained. "Just like an earthquake. But that is when holes rip in the dimensional fabric. And today, there is a lot of strain. If you go through with this, you could trigger a shift."

Yokouro smiled, resuming his determined pace.

"Even better."

Rutu fought against the irritated growl threatening to bubble out of him, turning to follow Yokouro.

"Yokouro, please, I will only ask you one more time."

"Good, because I'll only hear it one more time before I try to do this without you," Yokouro said, smiling over his shoulder at Rutu. "Would you rather I try this alone? I could cause even more damage."

Rutu let out a defeated sigh, coming to a stop next to Yokouro at the entrance of the meditation labyrinth.

"Then you'll help me?" Yokouro asked.

"Yes, I'll help you," Rutu groaned, aggravated.

"You don't have to be so enthusiastic…"

"Just start the damn labyrinth. I'll wait for your call," Rutu said, his tone clipped. Yokouro decided not to respond, convinced that Rutu was unreasonably paranoid. He turned his attention to his feet, taking three deep breaths before stepping onto the large, flat stone at the beginning of the labyrinth. His eyes remained cast to his feet as he took rhythmic steps along the twisting and winding paths of white stone. He listened to the breeze passing through the nearby trees, took in the fragrances of the colorful flowers in the garden, and felt the molecules of air passing over his skin and rustling his hair as he walked.

After years of practice, he was quite adept at clearing his mind and slowly transitioning to the Antiqua-Kel subrealm. Being the successor to Antiquan the Third, his magic was already closely tied with the plane, meaning he could traverse there whenever he pleased. But that day, he knew he needed his mind and magic as quiet and collected as possible so as not to raise suspicions. So he stepped over the stones and followed the turns and bends in the path until he felt his aura reach a consistent, quiet level. Only then did he allow his mind to wander to the Antiqua-Kel plane, and he soon found himself stepping off the white stones of the meditation labyrinth and onto the harsh, red rocks of the Antiqua-Kel plane.

Yokouro had no fondness for Antiqua-Kel. Despite being chosen as Antiquan the Fourth, and completing his duties associated with the position, he tried to avoid traveling to the stale, dark plane. The mountains were too jagged, the air too sharp, and the sky too dark for him to feel comfortable. It was one of the reasons he had always been hesitant to show an interest in Antiquan's position—he did not want to live there. He preferred the majestic beauty of the Demon Realm to the barren land of the subrealm.

He stepped to the edge of a steep, dark canyon slicing into the red rocks, easily finding one of the many spiraling paths that led into the canyon. The further he descended, the wider the paths became, passing in front of doors crammed into crudely cut holes in the canyon wall, where the lowest class of the Antiqua-Kel plane resided. He could feel their nervous energy as they watched him pass, some slamming their doors shut loudly the moment they spotted the silver-haired demon standing in sharp contrast to the darkness of the canyon.

Yokouro had already learned to ignore the terrified glances and hurried retreats—many demons reacted the same way. He kept his mind calm and unbothered as he walked down the well-worn path, descending deeper into the canyon.

The air was thicker in the canyon, becoming nearly suffocating as Yokouro left one of the branches and entered the main gorge that extended for thousands of miles across the crust of Antiqua-Kel. The river below was a surging, heaving mass of nearly-black water, its roar echoing off the sheer walls of rock and covering the bustling of those who lived in the subrealm. Life could only sustain itself in the canyons of Antiqua-Kel, so the canyon was alive with movement.

Yokouro's training as an Old Blood Lord had taught him to never lower his head, but he did so as he continued his descent. He could not allow himself to be distracted by all those bustling around the canyon.

He finally found himself at the lowest level, about a hundred feet above the raging waters of the river. He crossed one of the bridges and came upon the ornate gate blocking others from getting close to the residence of Antiquan the Third—the ruler of that realm.

But Yokouro merely had to place his hand upon the lock and it swung aside for him. It was only when the gate was closed again that Yokouro lifted his head, walking confidently along the front of the ornately carved home embedded into the canyon wall. Statues of past Antiquan Angels stood in silent watch over the home, their carved eyes cast to Yokouro as he approached the enormous, thick drapes that acted as a door to Antiquan's home.

There were three layers of curtains before Yokouro found himself in the foyer, acting as sound buffers for the raging river outside. It was quieter and much cooler in the ornate residence, allowing Yokouro to breathe a little easier as two young servants rushed forward and bowed in greeting.

Yokouro followed the servants deeper into the home, breathing evenly with the number of steps he was taking to keep his mind calm. He forced Rutu's warnings to the back of his mind, knowing he was too close now to allow doubt to stop him. Even though Rutu had immense power, and had never been wrong about a premonition or bad feeling, Yokouro knew he had to do this.

He could not afford to stall any longer.

The servants parted in front of another set of thick curtains, turning and bowing to Yokouro as he stepped through them into Antiquan's audience chambers. He heard their bare feet striking the smooth, mosaic floor as they scurried away, leaving Yokouro and Antiquan the Third in privacy.

Yokouro smiled gently and bowed his head to the figure sitting in the carved, stone throne. The audience chambers were much smaller than any of those at demon palaces, which had always given Yokouro a claustrophobic feeling. But that day, the room seemed even smaller than usual.

"Master," he greeted.

"Yokouro," Antiquan greeted, motioning him to the stool that had been placed before the throne. Yokouro moved slowly, studying the slumped posture of the ruler of Antiqua-Kel. He was wearing a loose-fitting robe, as opposed to the ornate, layered vestments Yokouro was used to seeing. He was also cradling his head tiredly in one hand, looking more unkempt than the demon had ever seen before. His red eyes were watching Yokouro move, but they showed his exhaustion.

"I heard you were ill..." Yokouro said, sitting on the stool. "But I did not want to believe it."

The older man smiled tiredly.

"It will be difficult for you to understand until you sit in this throne, Yokouro, but my ailments are not physical." He groaned as he lifted his head. "There is great tension in the universe right now. Lord Vestera's seal may have greatly disrupted our way of life, but once it was in place, it kept everything quite stable. Now that it has fractured, there is a gaping wound in the universe, and my powers are directly affected."

"Rutu mentioned something about a building tension..." Yokouro murmured.

"That demon really is something else," he chuckled weakly. "I have always been curious just how far his awareness stretches." He shifted in his chair, letting out a long sigh. "When you are tapped into the celestial magic, you will understand how unstable everything can become. The Balance has tipped, but in a most unusual way. Souls with certain destinies must often follow a set path to keep the Balance aligned, and right now...it appears that is not happening."

"I know this lesson, Master."

"You know it, but you have never felt it," Antiquan said. "Not the way I do. I know you have conflicting destinies, which means you are stuck in your own limbo, never sure which path to follow at which time." Antiquan motioned Yokouro closer to him. The demon stood and walked to the front corner of the throne, kneeling by Antiquan the Third's feet, as was custom. "I do apologize," Antiquan murmured. "Had I known your soul had another destiny aligned, I would not have chosen you as my successor. I imagine it has been hell."

"I do not regret that you chose me, Master," Yokouro said quietly.

"Nor do I regret choosing you," Antiquan said with a smile. "You are powerful, cunning, and you have been a brilliant student. You were the right choice for my successor."

Yokouro smiled.

"You have been a remarkable teacher, Master," Yokouro complimented. "Is there anything I can do to aid you in healing?"

"No, this is something that not even the dragons could ease. They're likely feeling it, as well." Antiquan closed his eyes, rubbing them tiredly. "Do you remember when the realms were connected four thousand years ago?"

"Yes."

"Do you remember how powerful I became at that time?"

"Yes."

"That was because my power is directly linked to the Balance. When the energies of the larger realms became entwined and the realms connected together, power spiked for anyone connected to the Balance, such as Vestera. That is why Vestera was able to so easily put the seal on the realms, and it is also why he cannot fix the seal now. The Balance is in a downturn. And it feels as though the souls in the Balance have been interrupted on their paths. Something has taken place out of turn, and the entire universe is suffering for it."

"Something out of turn?" Yokouro asked. "Such as?"

"I do not know," Antiquan the Third said with a soft smile. "My power may be great, but I cannot see into the future. You will have to ask your own oracle."

"He hasn't told me anything, yet," Yokouro grumbled.

"I believe that the universe is heading toward an apocalypse," Antiquan said. "A total reset of the Balance. It was supposed to happen four thousand years ago, but something stopped it."

"I thought the realms connecting *was* the apocalypse," Yokouro murmured.

Antiquan's smile grew, the secrecy in the grin causing Yokouro's hair to stand on end.

"You do not understand what an apocalypse is. It's not fire raining down on the land, or horrific natural disasters sweeping over the lands. It's far more efficient and devastating. And what happened when these realms connected was too methodical and careful to be apocalyptic." Antiquan reached forward, placing one sharp nail under Yokouro's jaw and lifting his head to look at him. "Tell me, my apprentice, did *you* break Vestera's seal three hundred years ago?"

Yokouro remained silent for several long moments.

"Not directly," he answered.

"Did you order Rutu to do it for you?"

"No," Yokouro said with a sigh. "I asked, but he outright refused, no matter how I tried to convince him."

"Then you used your vessel as a conduit of some kind to cause just enough strain in the seal."

"My vessel had just met Vestera, and still had traces of dragon magic within him," Yokouro said with a nod. "It was the best option at the time."

"Quite cunning of you."

"Master, about this power shift," Yokouro started. "If my destiny with the dragons plays out in my favor, that means the shift in the Balance would be dramatic enough to be a true apocalypse, correct?"

"It is possible, but nothing is set in stone."

"What if it *doesn't* play out in my favor?"

Antiquan sighed heavily.

"I would ask your own oracle, but mine tells me that it will merely be a delay in the reset of the Balance. Eventually, nothing will stop the universe from collapsing in on itself and starting again, but for the time being, there are powerful entities holding everything in place, trying to keep the universe in this state. If your foe triumphs over you, then those entities will remain in power, and they will continue to hold the Balance in this position until the time comes to release control and let everything fall apart."

"Powerful entities? You mean Vestera?" Yokouro mused. "Then, if I win, Vestera will be removed from power. And with no young to succeed him, the dragon regime will crumble."

"Not necessarily." Antiquan shook his head. "Yes, removing Vestera from power would severely weaken the dragon clan, but it will unlikely crumble. If Vestera were to have young, then it would decrease the chance that your victory would cause an apocalypse."

"How so?"

"Vestera is the Overseer. He keeps control over everything in the universe and tweaks and pushes things in certain directions when needed to maintain the Balance. If he has young, then there will be another Overseer, and even if you wanted a dramatic power shift, Vestera's descendant would have the power to stop you."

"Then I need to take Vestera out before he finds someone to bear his young."

Antiquan chuckled, a quiet cough following the sound.

"You are filled with ambition, Yokouro. It's very admirable. But you will need a lot more power before you can even think about going against the dragon clan."

"I know. I would need celestial magic," Yokouro agreed.

He sat back on his heels with a sigh and a smile, reaching into his robe pocket and extracting a pouch, offering it to Antiquan. "I apologize for being so inquisitive when you are ill. This is some Tak-Nei root, to restore some of your strength."

"You are good to me, Yokouro."

He took the pouch, opening it and pinching the hair-thin root strands, extracting them from the bag. He hesitated as he looked them over, casting a quick glance to Yokouro's face. He then offered the root to Yokouro.

"You first."

The demon lord grinned.

"You are a wise man, Master."

He opened his mouth, allowing Antiquan the Third to place the bitter root onto his tongue. He chewed and swallowed, the corners of his lips still curved in a smile.

"I have been alive for ten thousand years," Antiquan said, pinching another bit of the root and withdrawing it from the bag. "I have known a few poisonings."

"Poison is so petty, though," Yokouro said with a sigh. Antiquan placed the root on his tongue, some falling onto his robe. Yokouro immediately rose to his knees again, wiping the fallen root away. "There are better ways to kill someone."

"Very true," Antiquan agreed.

Yokouro took the pouch with one hand as he leaned closer, his other hand stealing inside his robes to draw the dagger he had concealed there. In a quick motion, he pushed the dagger deep into his master's diaphragm, looking into the surprised red eyes as Antiquan's hands tangled in the robes on Yokouro's shoulders, trying to push him back.

"Shh, shh," Yokouro cooed. "I want you to die on your throne."

"You think…this will…" Antiquan's voice became choked and his expression became confused. He could feel his magic trying to circle around the blade, ready to heal him, but his powers were also being diverted, the root Yokouro had given him upsetting the flow of his magic. He felt a deep fire radiating through his abdomen, realizing that his magic was not working fast enough to counteract the poison Yokouro had coated on his dagger.

"Poison…is…too petty…is it?" Antiquan choked.

"I never said I wasn't petty enough to use it," Yokouro said, leaning closer as Antiquan's struggles waned. He felt the twitching of the older man's muscles, saw the way his chest heaved as he tried to take in air, and smiled wider when blood began to seep from the corner of his mouth, black and viscous, dribbling down the front of his robes.

"You...still won't...have enough power..." Antiquan gasped.

"No," Yokouro admitted. "But this is a start. And once I am Antiquan the Fourth, I can focus all my attention on Dalton. No more conflicting destinies. No more limbo. Once I take care of you, I will only have one path."

To Yokouro's surprise, Antiquan smiled.

"I guess he was right all along..."

"Who?" Yokouro asked.

Antiquan's eyes went glassy, his body slumping further as his final breath left his body. Yokouro stared at the dead man for two long seconds before he began to feel the fire building in his veins.

"R-Rutu..." he called, backing away from Antiquan, his entire body beginning to shake.

In an instant, Rutu was in the room with him, grabbing his wrists as his trembling became almost violent.

"This is going to be painful, Yokouro," Rutu warned.

"I know."

Yokouro grit his teeth, his legs giving way under him. He fell to his knees, Rutu holding his wrists tightly as the fire grew to encompass him entirely. Yokouro had thought that the pain of assimilating the powers of the Antiqua-Kel plane would be similar to the pain of his cursed markings, but it was a very different sort of agony that bounced along his nerves. It was not unbearable. His body was accustomed to pain.

But his mind was bending and stretching in ways he had never known before. His eyes were closed but he could see more than he had ever seen before. His vision was wider, more encompassing, searching outside the residence, outside the canyon, through the vast lands of the Antiqua-Kel plane to the bright bands of magic that kept it mostly sealed from the Darkness Realm. He could see the bright energy radiating from the large Realm of Darkness beyond, holding gentle ties to the subrealm that were just enough to anchor it in place. His thoughts stretched in thirteen different directions at the barrier to the Darkness Realm, reaching out to his Antiquan Angels, connecting with them in a sharp focus that made Yokouro's head nearly split open. His magic was morphing and spreading, pulsing out of him to cover the land and claim it as his own.

While Yokouro was groaning and cursing on the ground, trying to understand the new powers and incorporate them, Rutu was holding him steady, keeping him from hurting himself. He was also blanketing Yokouro's new powers with his own magic, softening the shockwaves radiating from the younger demon, being sure that the sudden change in power did not annihilate everyone in the canyon.

The position of Antiquan had never passed to a successor following a sudden death before. When the prior ruler had grown tired and weak, he would perform months of rituals to slowly pass the celestial magic onto his successor. Celestial magic was potent and dangerous, and to suddenly take on the amount Antiquan possessed would normally overwhelm and kill a successor.

But Yokouro was a powerful demon, and Rutu's immense power made sure the magic did not rip him apart.

Rutu tempered the celestial magic flowing into Yokouro and radiating out into the land, regulating it while Yokouro came to terms with his new powers and his new awareness. To Yokouro, the process lasted for days, but it was only three minutes later that Rutu felt the magic settling, and crouched in front of Yokouro, releasing his wrists but keeping his arms extended to catch the younger demon from falling if needed.

"Can you open your eyes, yet?" Rutu asked gently.

"They are open."

Rutu smiled, reaching forward and placing his fingers over Yokouro's closed eyelids.

"Come back to the physical, Yokouro."

Yokouro's eyes flashed open, briefly shining a bright ruby color before fading back to the chilling gold. He stared at Rutu for a few moments before laughing in disbelief.

"What…was that?"

"You have a lot to learn about these kinds of powers," Rutu said. "The first should probably be how to tell your physical awareness from your celestial awareness."

The curtain behind them flung open as a group of servants rushed to the audience chamber. They looked hurriedly between Yokouro and Antiquan's body.

Then, the yelling began.

The younger servants screamed in horror, while older ones began yelling about the murder, rushing out of the room to alert the rest of the land the reason for the shockwaves of magic.

"But I'll teach you that back home," Rutu said quickly, yanking Yokouro to his feet. "Let's go before we have an angry mob."

Yokouro merely nodded, his head still spinning. The quick dimension hop to the Demon Realm did nothing to orient him, and he fell heavily to his side on the smooth stones of the meditation labyrinth, greedily gulping down the comforting, fresh air.

"Yokouro? Look at me," Rutu said, crouching over him again.

Still dizzy, Yokouro slowly propped himself up. He looked around, startled to see the energy radiating from every living thing around him. The flowers were more vibrant, the towering trees exuding a golden aura that he had never seen before, and the cool, steady vibrations of the earth below him, humming in tune with his racing blood.

"How do you feel?" Rutu asked.

"Incredible…" Yokouro whispered. "Everything is so…"

There were no words he could find to describe what he was feeling or seeing.

He reveled in the beauty around him, feeling connected to everything, causing his nerves to sing in harmony. But it did not take long for him to become accustomed to the feeling, and realize there was looming heaviness encompassing all the majesty around him.

"What is that?" he whispered. "The heaviness? Is it a storm?"

"That's the tension I was talking about," Rutu said. "Do you sense it now?"

"It's…weighing down on me."

"I told you it was bad today," Rutu said.

"But…the realms didn't shift."

"It's a ripple effect. It might take a few minutes before things shift. Until we're certain that—"

Rutu stopped abruptly, his gaze going distant. Yokouro did not need to ask what was wrong. He felt it as well. He could almost see himself soaring over the Demon Realm, scanning the land, drawn to a very specific spot where everything was straining to remain in place. At the center of that weakened point, there was a darkness that was so acute and strong that it was painful to look at. His mind could not handle the shape or the scope of it.

He was brought back to his body when the land rumbled, shaking the trees and flower beds, some of the older tree trunks groaning. A sudden gust of wind tore through the gardens, forcing both Old Blood Lords to shield their eyes from the grains of sand pelting their faces. The air became electric, sparks dancing over their skin.

Yokouro raised a finger to Rutu.

"Don't you dare say I told you so," he growled.

Rutu was not about to gloat. He had turned in the direction of the wind, his face creased with concern.

"How bad was that shift?" Yokouro asked.

"A hole opened up to the Human Realm," Rutu whispered, his eyes seeing something Yokouro could not. "But it was not a natural tear. It was forced." Rutu cursed colorfully, scrambling to his feet. "That was Kawakara. He's going to attack the Human Realm."

Chapter Nineteen

The morning had been relatively uneventful.

Theresa had soccer practice, so the house was quiet and the adults were enjoying the peace, trying to gather the motivation to go to the training center and prepare for the tournament.

But as they were planning a time to leave the house and train, Eclipse began getting anxious.

"What's wrong?" Hanyi asked when he saw Eclipse stand and let out a nervous breath.

"Nothing," he said too quickly, shaking his head. "Something...just doesn't feel right, that's all."

"What do you mean?" Keito asked.

"I don't know," he said. He placed his hands on his head and let out another long breath, beginning to pace behind the couch. "I just feel uneasy." He shook his head quickly. "Maybe it's just something with the Antiquan Angels. I should call One, see if he feels the same."

Dalton was about to speak when his breath left him as though he had been kicked in the stomach. He clutched the front of his shirt, doubling over in his chair and spilling the half-full mug of coffee he held.

"Dalton?!" Frieda gasped.

Before the team could focus their worries on Dalton, Eclipse also fell to a crouch, his hands clasping his head and his teeth set against an agonized scream.

"What the hell is going on?!" Mitoki snapped, turning to Eclipse. "Talk to us. What's wrong?"

Dalton groaned, breathing heavily through grit teeth, his eyes tightly shut.

"I have no idea," Keito said, looking between the two pained Guardians. "I don't feel anything."

"Neither do I," Tarrena and Jikia seconded.

"Just Eclipse and Dalton," Hanyi noted. "This has to be Yokouro."

"What is he doing to them?" Frieda asked, petrified.

"He took the throne..." Eclipse growled, his hands slowly coming away from his head. He turned his wide eyes to the rest of his team, his face pale and his breathing shallow. "Yokouro killed Antiquan the Third."

"What does that mean?" Frieda asked before anyone else could.

"I...I don't know what it means for Dalton, but it does mean that Yokouro just became a lot more powerful," Eclipse said. "*Celestial* magic powerful."

"The destiny he shares with Dalton," Hanyi murmured half to himself. "If Yokouro had two destinies, and he's completed one of them..."

"...then his entire focus is going to shift to Dalton," Keito completed, nodding to the now-calming leader of the team. "Dalton, what did you just feel?"

"I-I don't know," he said weakly. "Heaviness? Power? It was...indescribable."

"Are you alright?" Frieda asked, rubbing his back.

"I think so..." he said, slowly straightening, rubbing his chest as he shook his head. "That was...like a kick to the chest but...I think it's done."

Eclipse leaned on the back of the couch, slowly shaking his head.

"This is...not good."

"How much damage did Yokouro do taking the throne of Antiquan?" Keito asked.

"It's an entire sub-celestial shift in power," Eclipse said.

"Wait, doesn't that mean that the realms—"

A sharp crack inside the house interrupted Mitoki before the house groaned and shook on its foundation. Everyone crouched, feeling the magic change dramatically around them as a gust of wind tore past the house, rattling the windows and causing the lights to flicker before they went out.

"—are going to shift?" Mitoki finished his sentence slowly.

"That wasn't just a shift," Hanyi said, standing as the house began to settle once more. "That was a tear in the fabric." He looked to the other Guardians. "And it has to be pretty close."

"We should go see if we can help," Dalton said, standing, quietly assuring Frieda that he was alright as she supported him upright. "Frieda, get to the basement and stay down there. Lock the door. We'll get you when we know it's safe."

"What about Theresa?" she gasped.

"I'll go and get her right now," he said. "Just get to the basement and lock the door."

"I'll stay with her," Tarrena offered. She took Frieda's hand, but Dalton's wife lunged forward and hugged Dalton before she could be led away.

"Please, be careful."

Dalton kissed her forehead.

186

"I will."

Tarrena guided Frieda away as the Guardians rushed to the front door, worried what they would be confronted with outside. Jikia trailed behind them as they stepped onto the front porch.

"That's demon energy..." she noted.

"It's a hole to the Demon Realm," Keito agreed. "That makes this even more dangerous."

As Dalton and the others went to the sidewalk, trying to sense in which direction the tear was, Dalton's neighbors began stepping out of their houses, wondering what had happened. A few called to Dalton, asking him what was going on. When he saw more of his neighbors starting to walk to him, he raised his hands and his voice.

"Everyone!" he called. "It's best to get inside and stay there. If you have a basement or a storm cellar, that is the safest place to wait until you hear the announcement that everything is alright. This is a tear in the dimensional fabric. Please return to your homes and find a safe place to wait until the hole is repaired."

Even though they were horrified at the prospect of another hole ripping in the dimensional fabric, they were quick to obey the order, ushering their families out of the street and rushing to their homes.

"The DPC already knows, right?" Jikia asked worriedly.

"A disturbance that large would trigger the warning system," Keito answered with a nod. "As soon as they've pinpointed the tear, they'll scramble everyone they can. They'll likely also send Demon Control Units once they realize it's a demon problem."

"It seems very quiet, though," Hanyi noted. "Maybe the hole opened up in an uninhabited part of the realm and no demons were pulled in."

"Let's hope," Keito whispered. "There is a lot of energy coming into this realm, though. It feels like Kage energy."

"Does that mean Juki or Rutu—"

"No," Keito interrupted Eclipse quickly. "It just means that the tear happened somewhere on their territory. Hopefully closer to the north where there aren't as many demon settlements."

"How far away is Theresa?" Mitoki asked Dalton.

"She'd be at the public park. It's about seven miles that way," he pointed up the street.

"We better take your car, then."

"Dalton, I can fly ahead and see what's going on where she is," Jikia offered.

"You might get shot down," Mitoki warned. "A dragon flying around during a demon scare might cause chaos and you might get hurt."

"I'll be fine," Jikia said. "I can get to Theresa and keep her safe until you arrive."

"Please do," Dalton said quickly. "But be careful. Try and get all the kids someplace safe, if they aren't already."

As Dalton ran back into the house to retrieve his car keys, Jikia darted to the middle of the street and shifted into her dragon form, taking to the skies with a powerful stroke of her wings, her sleek, black scales shimmering in the sunlight as she flew.

Taking Dalton's car, the Guardians were looking out each window to see if they could spot the tear, though nothing appeared out of the ordinary, other than the sparking magic filling the air.

"Dalton, I'm sure she's alright," Hanyi said, noticing how tightly Dalton was gripping the steering wheel.

"All the same, we better get there soon." He ducked his head to look up at the sky. "I don't see the break anywhere. There's no visible energy streams in the sky."

"It must be behind us," Eclipse said. "Maybe—"

"Dalton!" Hanyi cried.

Dalton turned back to the middle of the road and slammed on the brakes, trying to avoid the demon standing in the middle of the road, stopping traffic in both directions. Dalton's car skidded, but before it could strike the simply-dressed demon, his hand fell upon the hood, bringing it to an abrupt halt and crushing the front end, bending the vehicle upward. The rear wheels fell back to the pavement, jarring the Guardians further.

Dalton tried to collect himself, studying the unfamiliar, dark-haired demon in front of his car. Drivers in the opposing lane scrambled out of their vehicles, trying not to scream as they fled from the demon.

The demon smiled darkly, raising his hand and crooking a finger to the Guardians.

Keito cursed colorfully under his breath.

"You know him?" Eclipse whispered.

"Just move very slowly and don't attack him," Keito replied, carefully extracting himself from his seatbelt, his eyes never leaving the demon. "This is an extremely dangerous demon and he can very easily kill us."

Before they could inquire more, Keito shoved open the buckled passenger door and stepped slowly onto the pavement. The others followed, surprised by how acutely they could feel the painful static in the air surrounding the demon.

"Introduce yourselves," the demon ordered.

"We're Guardians of the DPC," Dalton said, closing the car door.

"Guardians?" the demon scoffed. "Three pathetic humans, a wolf, and a filthy demon mutt," he noted, his eyes scanning over the five men before him. With a smirk, he lifted his foot, pressing it against the dented bumper of the car and kicking it back. It skidded along the pavement, colliding with another stopped and abandoned car behind it with a deafening crunch. Team Dalton retreated a few steps, casting a quick glance at their surroundings to be certain bystanders were at a safe distance.

"Demons are not allowed in the human realms," Dalton told him. "We'll escort you back to the Demon Realm. It is in your best interest to cooperate."

The demon leaned his head back with a boisterous bark of laughter.

"You little vermin," he said. "You think *you* are in any position to be commanding me? I am Lord Kawakara Kage of the Kage Clan. You should be groveling on your knees, not giving orders." One side of his mouth quirked upward in a smirk. "But it does seem that you five will do quite nicely."

The Guardians looked at one another, hoping that Keito would understand what the demon lord meant, but Keito appeared just as confused.

"Do nicely for what?" Mitoki asked, too worried about the dangerous magic emanating from the demon to wonder why Kawakara—who they knew to be dead—was standing in front of them.

"My son appears to have taken an interest in you," Kawakara said. Dalton could feel the magic in the air around Kawakara swelling, bombarding his exposed skin like thousands of icy needles. He barely managed to suppress his wince of pain.

"Your son? Juki?" Dalton asked.

Kawakara's eyebrows rose. "You address my son, the Old Blood Lord of the Kage Clan, so informally?"

"I could have sworn I heard you were supposed to be dead," Hanyi chimed in. Keito instinctively raised an arm in front of Hanyi, worried that the unpredictable Kawakara would leap forward and attack at the slightest provocation.

"Yes. I was," Kawakara said with a laugh. "It has been very disorienting, returning mega-anna after being brutally murdered to find that my son has not only survived this long, but he has made friends with *humans*." The contempt dripped from his tone, though Dalton could not tell if it was disgust with the humans or with Juki.

"What makes you think that we mean anything to Juki?" Eclipse challenged, knowing they were merely trying to buy time for civilians to flee the area while they came up with a plan for containing the extremely volatile demon.

"I can feel his magic all around you," Kawakara said, as though the answer was obvious. "He feels some sort of obligation to protect you, it would seem. So you will do well enough."

"Well enough for what?" Keito asked.

Kawakara outstretched a hand to them, then angrily clenched his fist in the air.

Dalton felt as though bony, sharp fingers had grabbed his ribcage, crushing his ribs and sternum together in a vice grip. He gasped, crumbling to his knees as his lungs were constricted and his bones threatened to break. The agony was so acute that he could not even turn his head to see that the rest of his teammates had also collapsed in similar pained positions, struggling to breathe.

"Juki has become very devious as he's aged," Kawakara said, taking a slow step forward, grinning broadly as he watched the Guardians writhe on the pavement. "And he's not as willing to give his old man the time of day anymore. Tormenting and killing you should be just the right motivation for Juki to get his pathetic ass out of hiding so we can have a chat."

Dalton's fingernails scraped along the asphalt, trying to anchor him as the pain in his chest radiated through his body. His head was going light, his veins bulging as his heart struggled against the growing pain. He could feel the air around him becoming even sharper, stinging his throat with every choked inhale.

Something deep within him strained against the attack, but Dalton quickly pushed the instinct away, knowing he did not have enough control over his growing powers to safely use them in the presence of other humans.

"What's this?" Kawakara asked, the grin evident in his voice. "What is that sparking in your aura, human?" The demon lowered his fist, crouching in front of Dalton, reaching a clawed finger out to press into the bottom of Dalton's chin, lifting his reddening face. "How fascinating…" he murmured. "Is that the reason Juki's so interested in you? Do you have some potential you have yet to discover?"

Dalton could hardly hear the words, his vision tunneling as the pain became so overwhelming he could hardly feel his body anymore—his entire being had become an embodiment of agony.

"Why don't we crack that potential wide open?" Kawakara whispered, gently running his nail along Dalton's jaw as his sickening smile dropped the temperature of the entire neighborhood several degrees. "Don't resist. I specialize in breaking individuals to the core."

Dalton could feel the demon's magic prodding deeper, slicing away at his very soul.

In an instant, Kawakara was sent flying backward, letting out a startled shout as he fell heavily against the hood of one of the abandoned cars, leaving a sizable dent.

The acuteness of the pain eased immediately, and the Guardians became able to breathe, gasping as they watched a familiar figure walk slowly in front of them, focused on Kawakara. Juki's hand reached back to the Guardians, dark streams of magic escaping the Guardians' chests as Juki removed the suffocating spell. The magic collected in Juki's palm, though he did not turn to see if the Guardians were alright, even as the last of the spell created a sparking, black orb in his hand.

"There he is," Kawakara said darkly, straightening from the car. "You've been avoiding me, Juki. I had to get your attention somehow."

Juki remained very still, but when Kawakara took one step toward him, the older Kage demon collapsed with a wail of pain. Once he was on his knees, the shadow he cast upon the pavement reached up with distorted fingers, yanking his arms down and holding him in place. Juki moved the orb of dark magic in front of him, encasing it in both hands gently.

"What are you doing, Juki?" Kawakara asked with a condescending laugh, struggling half-heartedly against the shadow restraints. "Trying to show off for your humans?"

Juki crushed the black orb in his palms, the spell shattering like a splintered gem.

Kawakara's body went rigid, another yell of pain escaping his lips as his head was forced back and the heavy, sharp magic that had engulfed the area surged toward Kawakara. Thousands of needle-sized blood droplets collected over the demon's skin as the magic hit him, combining to form narrow rivulets of red down his face and hands.

Dalton had been unable to stand, watching in confusion and fascination as Juki commanded the magic with ease, surprising even Kawakara. Keito appeared at Dalton's side, helping him to his feet, though everyone was transfixed by the confrontation.

Kawakara's pained groans and grunts turned into breathless laughter.

"Really? Is that the best you—"

From the resurrected demon's chest, sharp spikes of black magic protruded violently, contorting Kawakara's body as his eyes went wide and his jaw dropped in shock and pain.

Everyone watching had gone deathly still, staring at Kawakara, the spears of black magic resembling swords protruding from his body. And while the Guardians were certain that the dangerous demon had been killed from the internal attack, they noticed there was a lack of blood. Even the blood that had collected on his skin from the previous magic had already run dry, turning to a dull rust color.

Kawakara's head slowly moved, a smile overtaking his lips once more as the spikes retreated into his body, the squelching of his flesh causing Dalton's skin to crawl.

"Still don't want to land that killing blow?" Kawakara jeered. "What's the matter? You did just fine last time."

Juki remained eerily silent, watching as Kawakara slowly stumbled to his feet, laughing breathlessly.

"You and I are very much alike," he noted. "You're dragging this little quarrel out for a very long time, Juki. You want to make me suffer? Do you want revenge, my son?" He tilted his head, waiting for Juki to speak, but still, the younger Kage demon remained silent. "Or are you just stalling?"

The anticipation hanging in the air was suffocating the Guardians.

"You know I'm not a patient man, Juki," Kawakara warned. "I had to drag you all the way to this pathetic realm because I was getting bored. And I don't like being bored." His dark smile sent a shiver down everyone's spines—even Juki's back stiffened at the look. "Remember how much fun we used to have together? You were always my greatest source of entertainment. Watching you try so hard to fight against me when you knew you stood no chance." Kawakara lifted a hand, his smile becoming unnervingly wide when he saw the way Juki flinched. "So entertain me, Juki."

Kawakara snapped his fingers and a shockwave of energy radiated from him. Not only could Dalton and the others feel the power, black jagged fingers of magic rocketed along the ground in all directions, spearing through the ankles and calves of everyone it touched, moving as fast as lightning.

Dalton fell to the ground once more, but the magic was now able to spear through his torso.

Dalton was about to use his own magic to put up what small barrier he could when the light above him seemed to dim. He turned his head, watching as the black lightning bolts of magic arched over his head before descending like a flurry of arrows onto Juki. From the pain in their own legs, they expected Juki to be riddled with bloodied gashes and deep wounds from the attack, but even as each tendril embedded itself into his body, he did not flinch, nor make a sound.

That was when the Guardians realized that Kawakara was not commanding the magic to hit Juki, but Juki had redirected it and was absorbing the magic—all without saying a word or moving.

Kawakara lowered his hand when the magic had fully absorbed into Juki's body.

"How did you manage that?" he asked, sounding somewhere between impressed and concerned.

Finally, Juki spoke, though it was merely a muttered spell that no one could decipher.

A dark shadow slid across the pavement too fast for Kawakara to react. His body gave a jolt, horrible cracking and crunching sounds setting Dalton's teeth on edge as the resurrected demon collapsed to the ground, writhing and wailing, blood pouring from his nose, the corners of his mouth, his ears, and running down his cheeks like tears from his eyes.

The longer Kawakara writhed, the closer curious bystanders came, some fishing for their phones only to find that the magic emanating from Juki had shut their devices off, making it impossible for him to be caught on camera.

The resurrected demon began laughing again, even as he writhed and twitched on the ground.

"That's it, Juki!" he bellowed with a sadistic laugh. "This is all I ever wanted from you!"

With a heavy sigh, Juki snapped his fingers and the spell lost its power, dissipating into the air around Kawakara as the older demon groaned.

"Just when it was starting to get interesting," he grumbled. He slowly turned over, getting to his feet, his smile still unnervingly dark. "But I will say, Juki, this is *nothing* like what you've been showing me over the last few months. You've been holding back on me this whole time, haven't you?" He laughed. "You've been using me to *train*." He clicked his tongue against the roof of his mouth. "That's very deceitful, my son. Looks like I've taught you well."

"You have two choices, *danra*," Juki said.

"Oh, he speaks," Kawakara gasped, his tone dripping with mock surprise.

"You can follow me, *quietly*, back to the Demon Realm. Or you can wait for Vestera to come and collect you."

Kawakara scoffed. "Are you commanding me?"

Juki had fallen silent again. The Guardians could not see the expression on Juki's face, but something Kawakara saw made his smile grow.

"I've always been amazed by you, Juki. That's why I always showed you so much attention. I knew that you would become great." He shrugged one shoulder. "But I guess I knew that, without me there to keep you in line, you would become too full of yourself."

"Make your decision," Juki said. "I won't fight you here and endanger thousands of humans. Follow me, or wait for Vestera."

"You're really not as impressive as you think, Juki," Kawakara continued, ignoring Juki's command and taking another step forward. "You certainly look the part. I bet everyone cowers when they see you." He took another step. "Empowering, isn't it?" He took yet another step. "Do they avert their eyes? Do they turn the other way? Do they fall to their knees?"

When he took one more step, Juki retreated, his head dropping as he turned his eyes away from his father.

"Ah, there it is," Kawakara said triumphantly. "All that power, but you still know your place. I trained you perfectly, didn't I?"

Keito growled before he could help himself, attracting Kawakara's attention immediately. Dalton and the other humans could not even register that the older demon had moved before Juki's arm wrapped around Kawakara's torso and flipped him to the ground, stopping him from attacking the Guardians. But Kawakara was just as quick, yanking Juki down with him and flipping them both, pinning Juki face-down on the pavement. Kawakara wasted no time grabbing Juki's arm, hooking it at the elbow and violently breaking the bone.

Even though Juki flinched, he grit his teeth against making a sound.

"Good boy," Kawakara complimented with an impressed laugh. He leaned forward, his dark smile causing everyone who could see it to shiver. "I made you, Juki. And now, I'm going to break you."

Kawakara's hand wrapped around Juki's neck, yanking his head back as he raised his other hand, but before he could strike Juki once more, a warmth spread through the area and two arms locked around Kawakara's chest, hauling him off of Juki.

"How about you and I talk first?" the man who had interfered said.

Dalton's body both relaxed with relief and tensed with amazement when he caught sight of the man he instinctively knew to be Vestera Hizoku. His bright ruby eyes were filled with the dragon's immense power, but his robes and the braided, unnaturally red hair made him look more like the other demon lords than a dragon.

Kawakara looked over his shoulder and laughed hollowly.

"Nice to see you look exactly the same, you dragon bastard."

"And it is the same displeasure to see you again, Kawakara," Vestera growled. "Juki?"

"Just get him out of here, please," Juki groaned, turning onto his side, carefully cradling his broken right arm, wincing in pain.

Vestera spared a glance at the Guardians, his eyes finally resting on Dalton. The human stared at him, his eyes wide. He could feel his magic shifting in response to the dragon's proximity, trying desperately to surge forward. But before Dalton began to worry about his control over his new powers, Vestera nodded once to him and, with a pop of displaced air, he vanished, Kawakara with him.

It took the Guardians a few moments to let out relieved sighs, as they could not completely relax until all traces of Kawakara's oppressive presence had dissipated into the air. Juki remained on the asphalt, cringing as he turned onto his back, his eyes tightly shut.

Dalton did not know if he should move to Juki and help him up or not. He was still frozen to the spot from the surge of power he felt at seeing Vestera Hizoku. But as his feet began to shift forward, a figure darted to Juki's side, falling to her knees next to him.

"Papa? Are you alright?" she gasped, helping him sit up as he stared at her with wide eyes.

"What are you doing here?" he gasped, wrapping his unbroken arm around her when she hugged him tightly. "I told you to stay away from Kawakara."

Dalton turned to ask Keito if the woman was Juki's daughter when another figure walking toward Juki caught him by surprise.

Rutu approached the two, silently watching as Kree broke the hug and looked over her father.

"I couldn't just sit back and do nothing," she said. "I was keeping shields around the humans, but I was ready to step in and tear that bastard to shreds."

"Listen to me, Kree," Juki said, placing his hand on her shoulder, "I really appreciate your help, but I cannot fight if I'm worried about your safety. That's why I need you to stay away from him." He turned his gaze to Rutu. "You should have told her to stay home."

Rutu scoffed, helping Kree to her feet before taking Juki's arm and pulling him up.

"She's an adult. She's allowed to make her own decisions," he said. "Shina and Kaneuta have the breach well contained. She wanted to help."

"I stayed back," Kree reminded him. "But like hell I was going to just sit by uselessly." She hugged him again. Juki cringed in pain as his arm was jarred, which prompted Rutu to step forward and take his broken arm between his hands to heal him.

Dalton jumped slightly when Kree turned to look at them. He had been studying her already, startled to see that her dark hair and facial features strongly resembled Juki, but her eye color and shape was identical to Rutu's. There was no doubt in his mind that she was their daughter. But she was dressed simply, not donning the same regal robes as her parents, and her long hair was not intricately braided, framing her face in gentle waves.

"Papa?" she asked, turning over her shoulder. "Are these the Guardians?"

He nodded.

"It's so good to finally meet you," she said with a bright smile, stepping up to them and extending her hand to Dalton. "I'm Kreeanya Kage, eldest child of Lord Juki Kage and heir to the Kage Clan."

"Uh, I-I'm Dalton Teban," he said, taking her hand while also bowing to her awkwardly. "This is Eclipse Retani, and Mitoki Ecaep," he introduced the others. "I assume you know Keito. And maybe Hanyi?"

"Yes, I know them," she said with a smile. "Keito. And Hanyi, very nice to see you again."

"I'm surprised you remember me," Hanyi laughed, bowing his head. "We only met once."

"Of course I remember you," she said. "You're the one with the great sense of humor."

"I knew I liked you," Hanyi said.

"Oh, I'm just so happy I finally get to meet you. My sister and I have been dying to see you in person," Kree said, turning her attention back to the humans as Juki and Rutu slowly approached them. "She's going to be so disappointed she wasn't here."

"She'll get a chance, I'm sure," Juki said with a smile, placing his arm around her shoulders and turning his eyes onto the Guardians. "Thank you, Guardians, for stalling. I tried to get here as quickly as I could."

"It...wasn't really planned," Dalton said nervously, glancing around the sidewalks as he saw the growing crowd of curious humans accumulating on the sides of the road.

"Regardless," Juki said, extracting a large stack of folded bills from his inner robe pocket, offering it to Dalton, "I apologize for the damage to your car and the injuries he caused."

Dalton stared at the money for a long moment before hesitantly taking it.

"Thank you," he said slowly. "But I thought your father was supposed to be dead…"

"He was dead," Juki agreed. "But he was accidentally resurrected a few months ago. I've been…trying to deal with him."

"Why not just kill him?" Eclipse asked. "I saw what you did just a few minutes ago. You could end him easily."

"Not necessarily," Juki said vaguely. "I'm just sorry he came after you. Are you badly injured? We can heal you."

"No, we're fine," Mitoki said. "But he did say that he found us because your magic was around us. That you're…protecting us?"

"Maybe a little," Juki said. "Mostly, I'm just keeping track of you."

"Oh, great…" Eclipse groaned.

Dalton could not stop studying Kree, and she finally laughed nervously when she caught his scrutiny.

"Why are you staring at me?" she asked. "I have a to-be mate."

"No, no," Dalton said, shaking his head quickly. "I'm sorry. It's just…you really look just like both of them," he said, looking between Juki and Rutu.

"Well, they *are* my parents," she laughed.

"Yeah, we didn't know about that until yesterday," Mitoki said, throwing a sideways glance at Keito. "We didn't even know that you two were mates, let alone that you had somehow had children."

"Really? You didn't know that?" Rutu asked.

"I assumed that was common knowledge by now," Juki added.

"We certainly didn't know," Eclipse said. "Came as a bit of a shock."

"Why?" Rutu laughed. "I didn't realize humans were still so uptight."

"They are," Keito said strongly.

"I think the bigger shock is that you two had children," Hanyi said with a laugh. "Hence the staring."

Juki nodded, tightening his arm around the grinning Kree.

"I suppose that makes sense," he said. "Even demons struggle to wrap their heads around how the two of us managed to have three amazing children."

Kree giggled, resting her head against her father's shoulder.

"Because it's never been done before," Eclipse said strongly.

"We did have to bend some laws of nature for them," Rutu admitted.

"We should move this conversation elsewhere," Keito said, noting the growing number of gawkers on the sidewalks. "Demon Containment should also be here soon."

"We should actually head back to the Demon Realm," Juki said. "Help Shina and Kaneuta close the breach."

"Are you certain you don't have injuries that need to be healed?" Rutu asked, looking among the Guardians.

"Just some small cuts, I think," Dalton said, looking among his teammates for confirmation. "What about other demons that got into the Human Realm?"

"The tear was in the middle of the plains," Rutu said. "Uninhabited. And our children are keeping any curious demons from getting too close. Kawakara was the only one who came to this realm."

"Are you going to seal the breach? Or do we need to call in the DPC to do it?" Keito asked.

"Now that Kawakara is contained in the Demon Realm again, I'll seal it back up," Rutu answered.

"He shouldn't cause you any further problems," Juki said. "But I'll still be keeping an eye on you, just to be sure."

Dalton did not know if he should thank Juki or not, thankful that Juki had interfered earlier, but worried about how much Juki was going to be keeping track of them.

"Could I ask a favor of you, Dalton?" Juki said.

"Sure?"

"If there are any pictures or video of me or my father, could you see to it that they are deleted?" Juki asked. "I'm sure you understand that it's in the best interest of all the realms if my identity remains secret."

"Uh, sure, I can do that. Once the emergency crews arrive to contain everything, I'll make sure they check everyone's phones."

"I appreciate it," Juki said.

"Is that your car, Dalton?" Rutu asked, pointing to the crushed and mangled car collided with another two abandoned cars on the road. Dalton turned, cringing when he saw the damage.

"It used to be," he grumbled.

"Do you live far?" Kree asked.

"No, not far," Dalton said.

"I don't think there's any saving it," Rutu said, looking over the vehicle. He turned to Juki. "Did you give him enough for a new car?"

When Juki nodded, Rutu turned to Dalton. "Do you need a car in the meantime? We have several if you want to borrow one of ours."

"Thank you, but I have another car," Dalton said quickly.

The wailing of the emergency crews could be heard rapidly approaching. Dalton's phone also began ringing, but when he extracted his phone to see his grandfather's personal number, he heard a pop and looked up to see Juki, Rutu, and their daughter had vanished before the emergency crews spotted them.

Chapter Twenty

Dalton was eager to finish processing the scene with the emergency crews that had responded to the tear in the dimensional fabric, but there were numerous statements he had to give about why they did not need to find someone to repair the damage. He did everything he could not to drop Juki's name, and had difficulty talking around the problem without explaining his own mission with Yokouro. Unfortunately, all the others of Team Dalton were struggling with the same problem, meaning that questions were asked over and over again, leading them to talk in circles.

They did not realize how long they had been at the scene where they had faced Kawakara until Dalton spotted Jikia walking along the sidewalk with Theresa's hand in hers. Theresa ran to her father, confused, but also unconcerned with any possible danger. He picked her up and held her as he tried to finish another conversation with his grandfather, who was also trying to understand what the DPC needed to do in response to the shift in the realms.

When he was finally able to go to the sidewalk, Jikia nodded to the various damaged and abandoned cars on the road that were being slowly cleared away.

"What happened?" she asked.

"Uh…" Dalton turned to his car before shrugging one shoulder, "you know, normal Wednesday." He squeezed Theresa's hand. "Are you okay, sweetheart?"

"I'm fine," she said. "'What happened?'"

"There was a little emergency, but everything's alright now," he said. He glanced around his teammates. "Do we need to stick around here?"

"They said we could go," Hanyi said. He looked at Theresa. "You okay to walk the rest of the way home?"

By the time they reached Dalton's house, Theresa was on Eclipse's back, complaining about her tired feet but eagerly rushing into the house to see her mother. Tarrena and Frieda were waiting in the living room, having received a short call from Dalton that everything was alright before he had been pulled away to answer more questions.

The Guardians did not say much about their encounter with Kawakara Kage, mostly because they were not entirely sure what to make of it. It was several hours before anyone could talk about it.

"So…" Mitoki finally said, "what the hell was all that about?"

"I have no idea," Eclipse groaned. "I don't know what to be more worried about. Yokouro taking over as Antiquan, the fact that Juki's insane father was resurrected, or that Juki has his magic surrounding us all the time to keep tabs on where we are."

"Did you know Kawakara was alive?" Dalton asked, turning to Keito. The demon dropped his eyes, a guilty expression settling over his face.

"Yes, but I really didn't see any point in telling you," he said. "Even if I had told you about his resurrection, you wouldn't have known who he was. And I never thought he would *ever* go after you." He turned his gaze to Dalton. "And now I'm wondering what it is he saw in you."

"Yeah, he did mention you had some untapped potential," Hanyi agreed. "He must have sensed your growing magic."

"As concerning as that is, we should probably figure out how to keep Juki from tracking us," Dalton said, eager to switch the subject. "And we should put some thought to what's going to happen to us now that Yokouro's the new Antiquan."

"How much more powerful did he become?" Mitoki asked, turning to Eclipse.

"He's now in control of an entire subplane," Eclipse said. "And he can now access celestial magic. But, hopefully, because he didn't go through the proper rituals to gain his power, it will take him some time to be able to properly command his celestial magic. That should give me time to talk to the other Antiquan Angels and see what they know."

"Dalton," Jikia said, leaning forward in her seat to fix him with a steady glare, "you need to begin training and growing your new magic."

"I will, I will," he said quickly, waving the statement away.

"When?" she demanded. "They're not going to go away, Dalton."

"I'll...figure it out," he said. "Right now, we need to prepare for the tournament. It's the day after tomorrow. We should go back to the training center and spar a bit."

"Dalton, sparring is not the same as training," Jikia said. "And you can't put it off forever. And I can't help you if you're not willing to show me these new powers."

"I haven't been doing anything with them," Dalton said. "I know they're there. I know I need to train. But I can do that after this round of the tournament. One thing at a time, as much as possible."

"This case is going to take up all your free time," Jikia insisted. "First it's this first round of the tournament, then it's going after Yokouro, then it will be another crisis. You need to get yourself right, first."

"I'm fine," he said strongly.

"For *now*," she agreed. "How long do you think your luck will last?"

"Dalton," Keito started, "Yokouro isn't going to wait for you to be ready."

"I can't just disappear for a few months to train. Not now," he said. "I know I need to. And I told you, I'll figure it out. I just—"

The doorbell rang, startling everyone. Frieda poked her head out from the office and slowly walked into the living room as Dalton opened the front door.

There was a man in a crisp black suit on his doorstep, holding his phone in one hand and a set of car keys in another.

"Dalton Teban?" he asked, glancing at his phone and then up at Dalton's face.

"Yes?"

The man extended the car keys to him. "Courtesy of my masters," he said.

Dalton stared at the keys, perplexed.

"What?"

"They asked me to bring a temporary vehicle for you," the man said, motioning to the driveway. Dalton peered around the man to see a car—very similar to his destroyed car, though newer and more expensive—sitting in front of his house.

"I...don't understand," he said slowly. "I told them I didn't need a car."

"Clearly they felt differently," the man said, extending the keys one more time. Dalton slowly took them, casting a confused glance back at the others in his house. "Here is my card," the man said, producing a business card from his pocket. "Once you have your new car, just call me to pick this one up."

"I...I mean..."

"Enjoy the rest of your day."

The man turned and easily walked off the front porch, approaching a sleek car idling on the curb, getting in and driving off as Dalton stood, dumbfounded, in the doorway.

"Dalton?" Frieda asked.

He finally closed the door, lifting the keys.

"What the hell?" he asked.

Keito chuckled. "I think this is Juki and Rutu trying to apologize for Kawakara destroying your car."

"You should put some serious thought to what kind of car you're going to buy," Hanyi said excitedly. "I mean, if Juki's paying for it, there's no reason not to get an awesome one."

The excitement and stress of the day caused the Guardians to turn in early that night, which allowed them to get an earlier start on training the next morning, securing a private training room at Master Bowen's center to spar and get their heads back in the tournament. Andrew also joined them, mostly watching from the sidelines and learning as much as he could from afar.

Team Dalton spent most of the day at the training center, returning home in the late afternoon to rest. But it was not going to be an early night for the Guardians.

"What time is my curfew?" Keito asked as they were clearing the plates from dinner.

"Is that tonight?" Dalton asked. "The tournament is tomorrow."

"I know, but I'll be fine," Keito assured. "I just need to run home and change into some more formal clothes. I also thought I would take the Sien-Raa dagger to Vestera so he could keep it safe for us for the time being."

"What time do you think the banquet will be over?" Hanyi asked.

Keito glanced at the clock on the wall, doing some quick calculations in his head.

"I really just need to show my face for a little bit. I don't have to stay for the entire celebration," he mused. "I could be back here by three in the morning."

"Can you make it two?" Dalton asked. "I really don't want you tired for the tournament."

Keito thought for a moment before nodding.

"I'll make it work," Keito said.

Keito left shortly after helping clear up after dinner. The others occupied themselves by watching the pre-tournament news coverage. Jikia and Tarrena left for their hotel late that night, agreeing to meet the Guardians at the stadium the following morning. Frieda went to bed shortly after they left, leaving Team Dalton to watch the late-night news. When the coverage ended, the Guardians began watching infomercials, laughing at the absurdities of the products, trying to keep themselves entertained until Keito returned.

Mitoki and Hanyi had drifted off by the time the front door opened. Dalton, who was bordering on unconsciousness, straightened, startled. The others also woke quickly as Keito walked into the house.

"Sorry," he said with an apologetic smile. "I didn't think you would wait up for me."

Dalton stretched, blinking his heavy eyelids several times before glancing at the clock to see it was four minutes past two in the morning.

"You're late," he said.

Keito also glanced at the clock.

"By four minutes, Mom. Sorry," he teased. "You could have gone to bed."

"We wanted to see how your date went," Hanyi said with a sleepy grin.

Keito groaned, flopping into one of the seats with a heavy sigh.

"It was an evening filled with typical Kage family drama," he said. "When all the Kage siblings get together, and the alcohol starts flowing, everyone starts getting stupid."

"How many siblings does Juki have?" Eclipse asked.

"Full or half?"

"Both?"

"Five full siblings. And seventeen surviving half-siblings."

Dalton's jaw dropped at the number, mirroring the other expressions around the room.

"Kawakara had that many kids?!" Dalton gawked.

"Well he had nine different mates," Keito said. "And several of his children have died. I think he had about thirty children all together."

"*Thirty?*" Eclipse gasped. "That's insane."

"That's Kawakara," Keito agreed. "And he was, of course, a hot topic tonight. All of Juki's younger siblings started screaming at him to just kill Kawakara. He said it wasn't that simple. Then they started throwing glasses and bottles at one another. It was a mess."

"Damn," Hanyi said. "Anyone get hurt?"

"Not severely," Keito said. "One of the sisters had a violent breakdown. Two of Juki's brothers began threatening to contest Juki's reign. Another sister was taken away with a mild concussion from taking a wine bottle to the head. I left shortly after Rutu had to excuse himself. I figured it was best to duck out before I got roped into any of the confrontations."

"That's something I've been wondering," Mitoki said. "If Juki is saying it's too complicated for him to kill his father, why doesn't Rutu do it for him?"

Keito laughed hollowly, shaking his head.

"That's the question that's been on everyone's minds since Kawakara was resurrected," he said. "I don't know. Juki and Rutu have been fighting about that for months. One of the worst fights they've been in in centuries. Believe me, that gossip rockets around the Demon Realm at the speed of light."

"It's important gossip to know if Juki and Rutu are in a fight?" Dalton asked.

"It's a favorite topic for demons," Keito said. "Their disputes are actually quite famous. They do not fight like a normal couple. They were both raised in a very brutal time in the Demon Realm, and they had warrior fathers who basically taught them to never back down or show weakness. So, they start throwing fists. And they're not afraid to hurt one another."

"What a healthy relationship..." Hanyi groaned.

"Based on what I saw tonight, I don't think they're that angry with one another anymore, but there is still some tension," Keito said. "But hell, I'm okay with that. If they're worried about their own drama, they'll leave us alone to deal with the tournament."

"You really think they'll leave us alone?" Eclipse asked skeptically.

"For now, I think so," Keito said. "They have enough to deal with as it is." He drummed his fingers along the arms of the chair. "We should get some sleep. Third round of the tournament is in a few hours. We need to be as rested as possible. Who knows what's waiting for us in the ring..."

Chapter Twenty-One

Dalton was surprised to find himself feeling rested the following morning as they drove to the larger of the two stadiums in Kenburough. Despite having so little sleep, he felt ready to handle the tournament—which was a little alarming. He felt like kicking himself for not being more anxious.

It was more start-stop traffic to get to the stadium, particularly because the stadium had sold out for the third round of the Guardian Tournament and the audience was eager to file to their seats. Young men and women dressed in reflective vests were guiding cars into different sections of the parking lot to keep the crowds as manageable as possible, but it did lead to some confusion about where the participants were to park to avoid being mobbed by excited audience members.

When Dalton parked the lavish car Juki and Rutu had loaned him, Hanyi stumbled out of the backseat, moaning dramatically.

"I hate cars…"

"Be dramatic inside," Keito said, looking around the parking lot nervously. "We need to get inside the stadium before we're spotted."

The five Guardians hustled to get out of the car and rush to the participant entrance. But Dalton could see long before they reached the door that the press had crowded the area, barely held at bay by over a dozen burly security guards.

"Team Dalton has arrived at the stadium!" one of the excited reporters called, pushing his cameraman closer to focus on the Guardians. "Guardian Teban! How does it feel to be the favored team for the new Guardian Tournament?!"

Keito managed to put himself as close to Dalton's back as possible without bumping into him, quickly guiding him toward the door as Dalton lowered his head against the barrage of press questions.

"What do you think was the cause of the tear in the dimensions the other day?"

"Do you think the tear should have postponed the tournament?"

"There are rumors of foul play outside the tournament. Have you experienced any of that?"

Dalton barely heard their questions as they overlapped one another, creating a cacophony of words that were too loud and disorienting to discern. When he managed to open the door to the stadium, he let out a long breath, shaking his head of the buzzing in his ears as he turned to his flustered teammates.

"Are we going to have to deal with that from now on?" Mitoki groaned, jerking his thumb over his shoulder toward the door.

"I hope not," Dalton sighed.

"If you had shown up earlier, you wouldn't have had to deal with that," a voice teased down the hall. Jikia laughed as she walked toward them. "Did you get caught in traffic?"

"It's a zoo out there," Dalton grumbled.

"Seems the traffic is causing a lot of problems. There's been a delay in getting the fights started," Tarrena noted. "Our team room is in the Corner again." She jerked her head for them to follow her.

"They haven't called the demons for examination, yet?" Keito asked, turning over his shoulder to the small clock above the door. Tarrena shook her head with a shrug.

"Not yet. I think they're waiting for other teams to arrive."

Because of the large crowds entering the stadium, Team Dalton had to navigate the narrow, dark hallways under the stands to Hall D and their team room. Even though the room was relatively silent, they could still hear the dull rumbling of the audience rushing to their seats, eager for the start of the fights. It became white noise as the five Guardians meditated to focus their magic and prepare for whatever they might face in the tournament, trying not to wonder how many teams in the arena might be working for Yokouro.

When ten more minutes had passed with no announcement as to the start of the fights, Dalton's anxiety began to creep further up his chest.

"Is it normal to delay the tournament like this?" he asked.

"It does happen on occasion," Jikia said. "Although, normally they make an announcement."

"They probably don't want to give a reason for the delay," Keito said. "It could be something as simple as the Tournament Board being stuck in traffic."

That eased Dalton's mind a little.

It was only a few minutes later that there was an announcement apologizing for the delay and calling for the demon Guardians to be examined.

"I'll see if I can figure out the reason for the delay," he said as he left the room.

Only two minutes after Keito left the team room, there was a knock at their door.

Confused about who would be visiting them, Mitoki opened the door hesitantly, freezing when he saw the familiar fiery red curls of the woman standing outside.

"Oh, good morning," Shannon said with a bright smile. "Mitoki, right?"

When Hanyi and Eclipse recognized the voice, they turned to Dalton with stunned and worried expressions, though Dalton did not notice. He was staring at Mitoki's back, frozen, wondering why his mother was outside the door.

"Shannon? What are you doing here?" Mitoki asked, being sure to place himself in the opening of the door to keep her from seeing in. However, she took a step forward, getting so close to Mitoki that he instinctively retreated a step, giving her just enough of an opening to push her way into the room.

"The energy is really electric in the stadium. It's so exciting," she said with a giddy grin as she entered the team room. Eclipse and Hanyi scrambled to their feet, trying to make the way they flanked Dalton appear casual, though they were carefully watching both their team leader and his mother. The two dragons did not know who Shannon was, but they responded to the immediate tension in the Guardians, also approaching cautiously.

"Excuse me. Who are you?" Jikia asked.

"I'm Shannon Marrone. I'm Dalton's mother."

Everyone could see the way the pieces fell together for the dragons as they straightened, adopting a more defensive stance as they took another step closer to Dalton.

"I'm surprised security let you through," Tarrena noted. "Only participants and trainers are allowed in the team rooms."

"I told them I was family and the guard let me through," Shannon said easily.

"That's generally not allowed," Jikia said, her tone cold and guarded.

"Oh…" Shannon pursed her lips. "I hope that guard doesn't get into trouble. He must not have known." She waved the statement aside. "Sorry, I know you're probably getting mentally prepared for the tournament, but I wanted to come down here and wish you luck," she said to Dalton, reaching forward in an attempt to place a hand on his shoulder, though he retreated, startling everyone. Shannon's hand hovered in the air before she let out a dejected sigh, tears gathering in the corners of her eyes.

"You know…I've been thinking a lot about what everyone said at your house the other day," she said slowly. "And…I'm sorry that you feel that you have to prove that your life is meaningful because of things I said to you when you were a kid."

"This really isn't the time for this," Hanyi interrupted. "Dalton said he would contact you when he was ready to talk to you."

"I know, I know, I'm sorry. I'm being pushy again." Shannon reached forward once more, placing her hand on Dalton's arm despite the way he flinched. "I just can't imagine how lonely you felt at that Guardian Training Center…wondering where the hell I'd run off to. Were they at least kind to you there?"

Something about the way she asked the question made everyone uneasy, particularly when they noticed Dalton's paling face as he stared into her eyes.

"Master Bowen took very good care of me," he whispered. "But…that's something we can talk about at a different time. We need to prepare for the fights."

"Right, of course." She squeezed Dalton's arm and nodded. "Good luck. I'll be in the stands cheering you on. I can't wait to see how strong you've become."

She turned and left the team room without a second glance, not even acknowledging the others on the team.

"She sorta leaves a heaviness in the air, doesn't she?" Hanyi noted.

Dalton let out a long breath, rubbing his face with a groan.

"You okay?" Eclipse asked.

"I think so," he said. "But she has a way of catching me off guard. It's so weird to see her after so many years."

"You didn't mention you had seen your mother again," Jikia noted. "When did she show up?"

"Just before you came to the realm," Dalton explained. "It's fine. I'm alright. Just…I think I'm going to need a little more meditation before I go into the ring."

Shannon walked down the dimly-lit hallway toward the door that would lead her to the audience stands, but as she reached for the doorknob, the door opened and she nearly collided with Keito's chest. Her eyes turned up to his, expecting him to step aside and let her pass, but instead he straightened his shoulders, stepping forward so she had no choice but to retreat as he closed the door behind him, blocking her exit.

"I was wondering where you were," she said. "You weren't in the team room."

"Convenient timing for you," Keito said. "Care to explain why you're down here, Shannon?"

"Not that it's any concern of yours, but I came to wish my son luck," she said coldly. "I would wish you luck, but I'm sure the famous Keito DeVero doesn't need it. So, if you'll excuse me…"

She started toward him, ready to push him out of the way when he grabbed her arm and forced her to turn to him.

"Listen to me very carefully," he growled.

"You're hurting me. Let me go."

"Stay away from Dalton. Do you understand?"

She scoffed. "I'm his *mother*. Who are you to tell me to stay away from my son?"

"You may have given birth to him, but that does not make you his mother," Keito said sharply. "You think I don't see what you're doing?"

"Still so suspicious," she sneered. "You need to get some therapy for your issues, Keito. You're projecting them."

Keito yanked her close again when she tried to break free from his grip.

"There's no need to pretend. Not with me," he snarled. "I know you're purposefully distracting Dalton. What perfect timing for you to find your way to the team room just before the match so you could distract Dalton and bring up all sorts of painful memories for him. And I'm not there to interfere and keep you from even coming into the room. You've been well trained, it seems."

"Let me go, you son of a bitch," she snapped. "How dare you accuse me? How can I make amends with Dalton when you're filling his head with doubts about me?"

"You did that all on your own," Keito said.

"But you're convinced I'm trying to *sabotage* him somehow?"

"Do you realize just how much perfume you wear?" he asked coldly. "And that the scent is from a Demon Realm flower?"

"What the hell are you talking about?"

"Are you trying to cover his scent on you?" Keito asked. "I know how he plays, Shannon."

"Who the hell are you even talking about?! Let me *go*!"

She yanked her arm away from his grip, though his claws sliced into her skin as she freed herself. She let out a yelp of pain, pressing her hand to the wounds as she glared at Keito. The demon stared calmly back.

"I wonder what would happen to Team Dalton if I showed this to the Tournament Board and said that Keito DeVero cornered me and attacked me."

Keito leaned in, his eyes boring into hers.

"Go ahead."

Keito could see the anger building in Shannon, but they both knew that she stood no chance at intimidating or harming Keito. She glared at him for three long seconds before turning on her heel and leaving the hallway, slamming the door behind her.

Keito stepped into the team room, seeing the tension around the room and noting the dark look in Dalton's eyes.

"Why did Shannon come here?" he asked.

"She said she came to wish Dalton luck," Hanyi said. "But it was...not a pleasant conversation."

"What did she say to you, Dalton?" Keito asked.

Dalton shook his head. "Nothing. It's not a big deal. Like I said, I'm just not used to seeing her after so long. She caught me by surprise."

"Are you certain?" Jikia pressed. "You need to keep your mind focused on the tournament."

"I'll be alright," he said again.

Keito nodded knowingly.

"I know that phrase," he said. "I won't press you about it, Dalton, but if you need to take time during the tournament to collect yourself, for whatever reason, just let me know. We've all got your back."

"Thank you..." Dalton murmured.

"On a different note," Keito started, "I know why the tournament was delayed."

"Traffic?" Hanyi guessed.

"That's what they thought," the demon said. "But it turns out there were some different problems with the other teams."

"What kind of—"

"May I have your attention, please?" a female voice called over the speakers, interrupting Mitoki's question. "We apologize for the delay and now ask that the Guardian teams come to the ring to begin the third round of the Guardian Tournament."

The exhilarated cheering rumbled through the stadium as Team Dalton waited for Keito to explain.

"Come on," he said, turning to the door. "You'll see what I mean."

While the stadium was a little smaller than the one they had competed in for the second round in the Darkness Realm, the ring felt enormous surrounded by thousands of excited spectators. Dalton led his team toward the center of the ring as Jikia and Tarrena went to their assigned team box, looking over the other teams filing to the center of the ring.

Dalton took immediate notice of the five other teams around him. As he scanned the stadium, noting there were no straggling Guardians rushing to the center of the ring, he realized that there were five Guardian teams absent.

"Looks like we're missing some people…" Hanyi noted sarcastically.

"The delay was because the Tournament Board had to get in contact with the Guardian teams to make sure that the missing teams were still alive," Keito explained. "Seems that all the missing teams have at least one member that was hospitalized."

"Why?" Dalton asked, mortified.

"I don't know. They wouldn't give me any details," Keito said. He drew in a deep breath. "But that's not the only problem."

"Of course it's not," Hanyi groaned.

"I don't see anyone from Yokouro's ranks here to challenge us," the demon elaborated. "But every team here has at least one demon. And that team," he motioned across from them, "is all demon Guardians."

The reality of the number of demons in the ring did not hit Dalton at first. He was startled to see faces he recognized, even among the all-demon team. But he was just thrilled that the demons competing were actually Guardians, rather than demons working for Yokouro with fake papers to compete in the tournament.

"Welcome, everyone, to Stadium H-2 in the beautiful city of Kenburough. How's everyone feeling today?" the announcer called, greeted by a round of excited cheers. "My name is Sammy and I will be your announcer today. We apologize for the delay. Several teams have been disqualified for being unable to show up for the tournament. Even though there aren't as many teams as usual, this promises to be an incredible round of the Guardian Tournament! Give it up for our six competing teams!"

Dalton had to make a conscious effort not to search for his mother amid the cheering audience.

"The first match will be Team Mariko versus Team Darin. All other teams, please exit the ring."

Team Dalton joined Jikia and Tarrena in their team box, feeling relatively relaxed about what promised to be a short day in the stadium. But Keito was not at all relaxed. He was glancing around the stadium, sharing silent conversations with the other demon Guardians. Even as the others of Team Dalton sat on the bench and waited for the first match to start, Keito remained standing in the far corner, scanning the demons.

"Keito," Dalton said, noticing the tension in his teammate's shoulders, "with the way things have been with the demon Guardians, is it going to be a problem having so many demons competing today?"

Keito did not respond.

"What's going on?" Eclipse asked, worried that Keito was noticing something they could not sense.

"I'm worried things will get political," Keito whispered. "There are members from each territory here." He turned over his shoulder to look at Dalton. "I'm concerned."

Magic began to fill the stadium as Sammy asked the two teams in the ring for match conditions. The static curled around everyone in the stadium, permeating through the barrier around the ring to engulf the audience in excited energy. The Guardians noticed it first, becoming uneasy at the growing tension while the audience leaned forward in their seats, apprehension gripping them for a reason they did not understand. Dalton's hair stood on end as a shiver passed through his body.

Keito's magic also radiated outward, matching the energy of every demon in the ring, pushing against the others as the demons tested one another, scoping out the competition.

"I can already tell things are going to get ugly..." Hanyi murmured, watching Keito.

The tensions rose even higher when it was decided that the teams in the ring would have an exclusive fight between the two demons of their teams before the humans finished the match. As the two demons were left in the center amid the thrumming of the excited crowd, the spectating demons were scrutinizing the combatants closely.

Dalton could also sense that things were about to get very ugly.

He could only watch Keito nervously while hoping the barrier around the ring would protect the audience from the demons battling. He was not sure the combined magic of the human Guardians would be enough to interfere if the demon Guardians got out of hand.

As the two demons were asked about conditions for their exclusive fight, Keito went to the back door of the team box.

"I'll be back," he muttered rapidly, exiting the team box and hurriedly striding toward another team box, where another demon stood to greet him, both demons ignoring the front row of spectators reaching out to try and touch Keito, though the security guards kept them from getting too close.

Dalton was more concerned with Keito's behavior than the way the two demons in the ring were glaring at one another.

"I would like to think that we can trust these demons to fight fairly," Dalton said slowly. "They are Guardians, after all."

"I hope so, but we should prepare for the worst," Jikia said. "Having a lot of demons competing like this at once is dangerous.

And in previous tournaments when there were a lot of demons in the stadium at the same time, this kind of tension would reach a fever pitch and that was when the most accidents would occur." The older dragon sighed. "Demon culture is very complex, and I think that plays into the tension more than we will ever understand. We're actually quite lucky that Keito knows so much. I would venture to say he understands the culture better than most *demons*. He should know when things are getting too dangerous."

Dalton turned his attention back to Keito, who was speaking with the demon that had stood to greet him. He recognized one of the human members of the team as Lukas, a Guardian he had worked with a few years previous. Lukas gave him a thin, nervous smile and shrugged, casting an eye at the two demons. Dalton smiled and nodded in understanding, relieved that he was not the only one nervous about the mounting tension.

"Jikia?" Hanyi asked. "Do we have any cards against us, yet?"

"Two," she answered.

"Cards?" Dalton asked.

"Just warning cards. We're not being penalized," Jikia said. "We got two cards against us in the last round."

"Why? Aren't they supposed to tell us about stuff like that?" Eclipse asked.

"Not necessarily," she said. "They weren't cards they wanted to give in view of the audience. They were warnings during the two fights with Yokouro's teams. But there is no reason to be concerned. We're allowed ten warning cards through the season before we get any restrictions." She turned back to Hanyi, suspicious. "Why do you ask?"

The wolf sighed heavily. "Because I know Keito…"

"Please remember that animal forms have not been approved for this fight," Sammy reminded the demons in the ring. "You may begin!"

The two demons leapt at one another, appearing as two blurs around the ring as Dalton tried to keep up with their movements. The cameras were panning all around, trying to capture as much as they could of the fast-moving battle. The audience was on their feet, screaming themselves hoarse as they cried out encouragement to the two demons. Occasionally, the Guardians would pin one another to the floor or the wall, allowing everyone to catch brief glimpses of the fight before the demons took off at their normal, explosive speed once again.

While Dalton could not see the brutality of the fight, he noted the amount of blood soaking into the dirt.

He turned to Keito. The demon's eyes were glued to the fight, his frame stiff as his eyes flicked around the ring to follow the battle. Another demon had joined at Keito's side, watching the fight with the same anxious expression.

"They are brutalizing each other..." Tarrena whispered. "They're going to kill each other at this rate."

Jikia looked torn.

"I can't call a foul," she said. "Neither of them are on our team."

"There's a lot of blood on the ground," Mitoki noted. "Someone should stop them."

Dalton turned in time to see Keito rush to the announcer's side, leaning over to whisper something in her ear as he motioned over the ring. Covering her microphone, Sammy spoke to Keito, who was becoming increasingly agitated. She shook her head, her eyes wide, and Keito straightened, glancing among all the other demons in the stadium, as though debating if he should be the one to interfere.

Sammy watched Keito before turning back to the ring. She uncovered her microphone.

"Both Guardians have been ordered to stop the fight for an investigation," she announced as boldly as she could manage around her own nerves. The audience turned to her with angry boos and shouts, infuriated that she would dare stop such an exhilarating fight. But their disapproval waned quickly when they realized the two demons had not obeyed the order. Their magic was beginning to strain the barrier around the ring, and when one demon was violently flung into the warding, the audience screamed at the crackling of lightning that radiated from the impact.

Keito watched the two collide in the center of the ring again, scraping and biting, their magic flaring high on instinct and making the pressure almost unbearable. He shifted his weight back and forth, breathing hard, fighting with himself as Sammy tried to call the fight to a halt a second time.

Still, the two demons did not obey.

Keito leapt over Sammy's desk, slamming his hand on the wall surrounding the ring to break the barrier with a counter seal as he leapt into the arena. The magic that had been contained spiraled outward, knocking the breaths out of the humans as the enthusiastic cheering changed to terrified and confused screams.

Three other demon Guardians leapt into the ring after Keito, creating more chaos among their human and beast teammates who did not know if they should also interfere. A few demons sat in their team boxes with a smug look of triumph painted on their expressions while a few demon Guardians watched on in concern.

"Wait! You can't interfere!" Sammy yelled after the demons.

Guards of the stadium swarmed toward the arena, barking orders. Keito ignored their commands to stop and barreled into the fight, knocking both demons to the ground and finally stopping their continuous movements. The demons following Keito pulled the two demons apart, struggling to keep them separated.

Dalton was horrified at the state of the two demon Guardians.

One was struggling to stay standing as he was pulled away. His face had four large scratches down the left side, the blood running down his chest to join the blood pouring from the gaping wounds across his torso. The other demon was also substantially injured, but he was fighting against the two demon Guardians holding him back, hungry to continue the battle.

"Enough!" Keito snapped, standing between them. "You were ordered to stop."

"Stay out of this, mutt!"

"Have you forgotten where you are?" Keito growled at the struggling demon. "You were about to *kill* one another."

"*And?*" he spat. "I wouldn't expect you to understand what it means to defend your lord, Wandering Child. You'll support whoever is most convenient for you at the time, right? Whose side are you on at the moment?"

Keito's lip curled in a warning snarl as he loomed over the younger demon, growling deep in his chest.

"How dare you speak to me that way?"

"As if you have any status over me," the other demon snapped.

"I am a member of Demon Council," Keito reminded him. "I hold rank over you. And I am ordering you to leave Demon Realm politics out of the tournament. Do I make myself clear?"

"Back off!" the demon barked. "I don't have to listen to a damn word you say. You're nothing without the Old Bloods standing behind you. You don't scare me."

"Keito!" another demon called as the second Guardian in the match collapsed limply in their arms. As he was lowered to the dirt, Keito knelt next to him, shaking him lightly.

"We need a medic!" Keito called to the announcer.

The audience was on their feet again, though their cheering had disappeared, replaced with worried muttering as they tried to see what was happening in the ring. The cameras focused on Keito and the fallen demon, displaying the horrific injuries for the entire stadium to behold. The guards tried to push the other demons crowding around Keito back as they approached.

One fell to his knee next to Keito. "We'll take it from here," he said, his hand going to Keito's shoulder. The demon growled and shook off the hand.

"Get the medic out here. We can't move him," he ordered.

"We can't treat him in the middle of the ring. There are cameras broadcasting this to millions of homes," the guard retorted.

"Just let him die," the Guardians who had been fighting snorted. "He would be doing Vestera a service. Vestera wouldn't want such a weakling as a supporter. He's a disgrace to his Old Blood."

"Will you shut up?" one of the other demon Guardians snapped. "You know nothing about honoring your Old Blood. What sort of display was this?!"

"Can we ignore the politics right now and save his life?" the demon helping Keito groaned, exasperated.

"Roll him on his side," Keito said, helping to turn the shaking demon as he began to convulse, choking and spluttering, blood gushing from around his clenched teeth.

"You are all ordered to leave the ring," one of the guards barked, turning to the demons that had interfered in the fight. "Your teams will receive yellow cards for your interference. If you do not obey this command, I will be forced to give you another one."

"Three," Hanyi murmured.

"You're all pathetic!" a demon who had not entered the ring yelled from his team box. "You're making spectacles of yourselves!"

"Stay out of this, you Kage-boot-licker!" another demon bellowed.

"You want to get in the ring, you damn DeVastes?!"

"Let's go!"

"Stop!" another guard bellowed, holding his hands up to the arguing demons. "That's another yellow card. One more slip up, and—"

"Shut up, human! This doesn't concern you!"

"Four..." Hanyi said with a heavy sigh.

"Are you keeping track of the cards?" Mitoki asked. The wolf nodded solemnly.

"I just hope Keito doesn't do anything to give us another..."

Keito and the other demon looking over the convulsing Guardian on the ground seemed unconcerned with the angry bellowing occurring around them. They whispered to one another as they both tried to heal the demon's gaping wounds, but there was something about the desperation of their actions that had Dalton's stomach twisting itself into knots.

The audience was getting more and more nervous as the angry demons defied the orders of the guards, barking at one another about the others' loyalties. The human Guardians could feel the nervous energy rolling through the stadium, creating an unbearable atmosphere of anxiety that weighed heavily in the air.

"They need to get this contained…" Jikia said, casting a worried eye at the apprehensive audience members.

"Is there anything we can do?" Eclipse asked, trying not to let the anxious energy seep into his bones.

"No, just stay out of it," Jikia said strongly. "The last thing we need is for human Guardians to try and interfere with demon politics."

The medic team finally ran into the ring, bringing a stretcher and a few medical care boxes to the fallen Guardian. They went to a crouch next to the demon, looking him over to assess the damage.

Keito put his hand on one of the medic's arms and shook his head slowly.

Dalton's heart plummeted.

The other demons were too wrapped up in screaming at one another and challenging the authority of the guards to see how things had turned for the worst for the demon convulsing on the ground. The guards were trying to get the demons under control, but their own fear made them yell louder, increasing the chaos and undermining any chance they might have had at containing the demons.

Keito jumped to his feet and turned.

"Shut up!" he bellowed, his magic amplifying his voice to echo around the entire stadium, leaving a short, whining feedback from the speakers as the demons fell silent in surprise. "Enough bickering like spoiled children! Your petty arguments aren't going to heal his wounds, and they sure as hell aren't going to help your Old Blood Lords. So shut the hell up and get back to your team boxes, *now*! That is an order."

Silence gripped the area as the demons stared at Keito, finally hearing the strained, choking sounds of the demon on the ground. The three demons who had jumped into the ring after Keito slinked away, throwing worried looks at one another as they left. Those who had been shouting from their team boxes sat once again, avoiding eye contact with the other demons and their confused teammates.

As the demon from Team Darin began to turn away, Keito grabbed his arm.

"Not you." he snarled. "Come here."

Keito yanked the younger demon closer and pushed him violently to his knees, placing a hand on the top of his head and turning him to face the demon on the ground.

"I want you to watch him," Keito growled. "You killed him. You should at least pay him the courtesy of seeing him to the end."

It was mere seconds later that the demon stopped choking and went still, his eyes remaining wide as he stared into nothing.

The audience was in shock. The other Guardians were just as stunned. There was always the possibility of a mistake leading to a death in the ring, but it was very different to see the reality. Dalton's mind was spinning with thoughts—the cameras were still focused on the dead demon, displaying the cold reality of death, not only to the audience in the stadium, but to anyone watching the live coverage from home. Things with demons were already strained, and Dalton knew that seeing such a brutal fight and a disregard for the rules and authority figures of the tournament would only help to build a case against demons. It also told Dalton that the tension between the demon Guardians was much higher than he believed.

The medical team covered the dead demon, breaking the trance of the audience. Many let out stunned breaths, unsure how to respond to the barbaric death. Keito released the demon's head and backed away, but the demon did not move, staring at the sheet-covered face, his shoulders slumped as he, too, understood the bigger implications of his actions.

It was not until the medical team had turned the demon's body to load him onto the gurney that he was able to move. He stood, keeping his head bent in shame as he slowly moved out of the ring.

"Due to the death of Guardian Paxal from Team Mariko, this match has been ruled as a double-loss. Both teams have been disqualified," Sammy said, her voice quiet, just as jarred by the death as the audience members. "Let us share a moment of silent for Guardian Paxal."

The stadium fell silent, watching the body be wheeled out of the ring, away from the blood-soaked dirt.

Chapter Twenty-Two

Everyone was more subdued by the time Keito trudged back to the team box and the dead Guardian had been removed from the ring. The demon slowly ascended the steps and opened the door of the team box, his eyes low.

"Sorry you had to see that," he whispered.

"Are you alright?" Jikia asked

"I'm fine."

"Did you say you were a member of Demon Council?" Eclipse asked as Keito grabbed one of the bottles of water under the bench.

"I'm just an honorary member. It's not much of a title, but sometimes it gives my word a little more weight," he answered.

"What was all that?" Mitoki asked, motioning to the clean-up that was happening in the ring. "Was that all because of the Old Blood Lords?"

"Yes," Keito said. "Paxal was pledged to Vestera, and Kier is part of the DeVastes territory. With the tensions between Vestera and Yokouro right now, a lot of demons are taking it upon themselves to squabble in the name of their Old Blood."

"Is that going to be a running theme today?" Dalton asked warily, looking among the demons around the ring, his eyes finally settling on the all-demon team two team boxes away.

"I hope not," Keito said, also scanning the demons. "There is only one other Vestera supporter left besides myself. And with Kier gone, there is only one DeVastes supporter left."

"The rest are under Juki and Rutu?" Mitoki deduced.

Keito nodded. "Two of them were born in the Middle Dimension, but their families are Kage-based," the demon explained. "A few of the other Guardians have worked with them before and said they have no investment in the Old Blood quarrels. Which was proven when they did not interfere in that fight."

"Then you're certain Juki and Rutu didn't smuggle anyone into the tournament to challenge us?" Eclipse asked.

"I'm certain," Keito said. "If Juki and Rutu were at all involved with the tournament today, that fight would have never gotten that out of hand." Keito sat on the bench with a heavy sigh. "I think Paxal's very public death probably knocked most of the demons back to their senses. I don't think we have to worry about something like that happening again."

Dalton hoped Keito was right.

Though there were still some pools of blood remaining in the dirt, the cleaning crews rushed out of the ring as Sammy spoke into her microphone.

"Alright, everyone. We're ready to get moving again. The next match will be Team Riley versus Team Dalton. Will those two teams please step into the ring?"

As Dalton led his team out of the team box, he began to feel extremely uneasy. He had felt alright when he first arrived at the stadium, and even with his mother dropping by the team room unannounced, he had felt confident that he would be able to handle that round of the tournament.

But sometime from the beginning of the first fight to that moment, he began to feel heavy, as though he was dragging an enormous weight as he walked. There was a burning sensation in his chest that he could not name, nor could he dispel the worry around the feeling. He attributed the anxiety wracking his bones to the magnitude of demon magic that had filled the stadium during the previous match, but even as everyone calmed into the subdued silence following Paxal's death, the swell of worry in his chest only grew.

Something inside him was telling him that he was in danger.

The sparking magic deep within him was struggling to come forward, desperate to protect him from the unseen danger.

But Dalton knew he could not risk tapping too deep into his magic for the match. Following the death of one Guardian, Dalton was sure that any brutality resulting from his new magic could lead to horrific repercussions.

Team Riley was led by a demon Guardian who immediately squared off to Keito. Dalton tried to get Riley's attention away from Keito, but even when Sammy asked if the two teams had any conditions, Riley's eyes never moved from Keito.

"Do you have any conditions, Dalton?" Riley said. Dalton turned to Keito, who was also staring at the opposing demon, though he appeared calm and unbothered by the fire in Riley's glare.

"I can't think of any conditions," Dalton said, still trying to get Riley's attention. "And you?"

"I don't want to limit the supposed-best team in the tournament," Riley said darkly. "I want you to be at your best when we beat you."

"What makes you think you can beat us?" Eclipse scoffed.

"Unlike most Guardians, I'm not intimidated by your position as top-ranked. Everyone else has been so worried about defeating you because you are their bosses. Not me. I'm not going to let you depend on your status for this fight."

"In my experience, this kind of posturing leads to more crushing defeats," Keito said.

"Says the demon who will bow to anyone with the title of Old Blood Lord," Riley sneered. "Council should have left you in retirement, Keito. Sanyai is more of a Guardian than you'll ever be."

"I couldn't agree more," Keito said. "And yet, they wanted me."

"Because of your connections, no doubt."

Keito barked a laugh. "It must hurt you to know that your lords actually took the time to train me."

"I can only imagine what you had to do to gain such strong favor with them," Riley growled. "Dalton," he finally turned his eyes to the human Guardian, "do you have any conditions or not?"

"Can I request that you keep your mouth shut for the rest of the match?"

Riley smirked. "If you really want to, go ahead."

Dalton turned to Sammy and shook his head. When Riley stated he had no further conditions, Sammy spoke again.

"Demons, you are not allowed into your animal forms for this match. As there are no conditions for the fight, you may begin!"

Dalton was startled when Riley lunged at him, but Keito intercepted the other demon, bringing them both to the ground. The distraction Riley had caused made it easier for the tiger Guardian on Team Riley to pounce on Dalton, her claws digging into the human's flesh as they fell heavily to the dirt. Eclipse and Mitoki locked eyes with the two humans of Team Riley as the eagle Guardian swiftly took to the air, circling above the fight as the cheering crowd rattled the stadium.

Hanyi worked with Dalton to fight the tiger, but the eagle continued to dive into the wolf, his claws clenching around his fur and leaving large gashes as he pushed him away from the tiger. Hanyi tried to lock his teeth around one of the eagle's wings, but a magically-amplified screech directed at Hanyi brought the wolf to the ground with a whimper, while everyone in the stadium covered their ears from the piercing cry.

Not only was the eagle providing distraction, but Riley continued to bring his fight with Keito as close to the humans as he could, startling the humans when the two demons would sprint between them at the pace of a blur.

The audience was still cringing whenever the deafening screech of the eagle sounded, but they continued to cheer whenever they could, excited to see Team Riley doing so well fighting Team Dalton.

Even Keito was surprised by how fast Riley moved. He tried to keep his fight with the other demon away from his teammates, but before he could register how close they had moved, Riley was weaving around the other Guardians, taunting Keito. Even when Keito had caught up to the demon, he found it almost impossible to land a serious attack without possibly colliding with his teammates.

Both Eclipse and Mitoki were doing well in their fights, though they were distracted with Hanyi and Dalton trying to fight the tiger while also fending off the eagle. Mitoki managed to knock his opponent out with a magical binding attack, but that was when the youngest of Team Dalton realized he was still not fully recovered from his stay at the hospital. Physically, he was feeling just fine, but his magic had yet to properly replenish, and the attack left him feeling dizzy and momentarily confused.

That was when the eagle turned his attention onto the youngest Guardian. With a powerful stroke of his wings, he dove toward the ring, his claws extending to latch onto the back of Mitoki's neck and his right shoulder. The force of the collision brought him to the ground, but before Mitoki could understand what had happened, the eagle let out another bone-rattling screech. Mitoki could feel the magic hitting him in shockwaves from the sound, and his own weakened magic was struggling to bear up to the force of the attack.

But Eclipse managed to grab the back of the eagle's neck and force him to the ground. Desperate to get out from the larger Guardian, he shifted back into his human form, but Eclipse still had superior strength, and began punching the eagle Guardian repeatedly until he worriedly called his surrender, his hands covering his broken nose and split lip.

Dalton and Hanyi were trying to get the tiger to surrender, but she was much stronger and faster than either of them. Dalton spent more time avoiding the swipes of her claws than attacking, and Hanyi was circling with his head low and hackles raised, looking for an opening. The wolf darted forward, managing to get his teeth around the underside of the tiger's neck, but rather than thrash and pull away, she fell forward, nearly crushing Hanyi under her weight.

Hanyi's high whine forced Dalton into action. He ran forward, lowering his shoulder and nearly falling on top of the tiger as he pushed into her side, in turn releasing Hanyi. As the tiger turned her head, her jaw found Dalton's arm and her teeth began to sink into his flesh.

But Dalton only felt the smallest pressure from her sharp teeth before he heard an unsettling crunch and a howl of pain. The tiger released her hold from Dalton's arm, parts of her teeth falling to the ring as she retreated. Dalton quickly looked between his barely-bleeding arm and the fallen teeth, fear surging through him as he wondered when he had willed his magic to form such a strong barrier around him.

The tiger, now enraged, charged him again, swiping at him with her claws and bringing him to the ground. But when he pushed his hand into her side to try and keep her weight off his chest, he felt her bones give way, and with another pained sound, she fell to her side, growling on every exhale, slowly shifting back into her human form.

Hanyi leapt toward her, snarling, his head low, but she lifted her hand, wrapping her other arm around her chest as she felt along her three broken ribs.

"I surrender…" she whispered.

Dalton could only stare at her, feeling the heat surrounding his hands from the magic he had never called upon.

Keito and Riley, now having the entire ring, finished their fight quickly. No longer worried about running into members of his team, Keito put his all into winning the fight, finally knocking Riley out by using their combined speed to run the younger demon head-first into the wall surrounding the arena.

Even as the audience cheered themselves hoarse from the thrilling fight and Sammy called the victory to Team Dalton, the five Guardians did not look pleased with their win. The deep gashes were treated and stitched shut, some of the more serious wounds healed with the dragons' healing magic. But the Guardians remained silent, feeling something unsettling in the air. It was not the same feeling they had when Yokouro was nearby, but it was equally concerning—particularly since the feeling was emanating from Dalton.

The fifteen-minute break passed too quickly, and Dalton was just rolling his sleeve back down from his now-bandaged arm as Sammy spoke into her microphone again.

"Ladies and gentlemen, thank you for your patience," she said with a broad grin. "We're now ready to start the semi-finals of the first set of matches in the third round of the Guardian Tournament!"

The audience let out excited cries, eager to continue the thrilling fights.

"The semi-finals will see Team Matthew fighting Team Dalton! Will those two teams please step into the ring?"

"Again?" Hanyi groaned.

Dalton was trying to hide his shaking as he approached the other Guardians. He continued to replay the way he shattered the tiger's teeth and broke her ribs without commanding his magic, and it made him worry that his powers were already out of his control and were now a danger, not just to his opponents, but to everyone in the stadium.

His worries only grew when Team Matthew's condition was that no weapons of any kind could be used and they wanted all physical attacks to be coupled with magic. Dalton wanted to find a way to contest the condition, but he could feel the worried eyes of his teammates boring into his back, so he accepted the condition quietly.

Dalton had been in the tournament long enough to expect the demon of Team Matthew to lunge at Keito while the others divided up among the rest of Team Dalton, but when Sammy called the match to start, Team Matthew did not move at all.

Not accustomed to attacking first, all members of Team Dalton hesitated, and in the hesitation, crushing weight fell over all of them.

The magic that descended over the five Guardians of Team Dalton was certainly human in nature, but it was powerful and stifling. They fell to their knees, feeling as though the weight of the magic had draped over their shoulders and encased their arms in concrete. Dalton tried not to panic, tried not to let his own magic react to the attack, but the others on Team Dalton were struggling against the binding.

But their magic only seemed to strengthen their confinement.

"Struggle all you want," Matthew laughed, raising his hands to them. "The more you struggle, the more magic I'll drain away from you and the closer to the ground you'll become."

"Focus on Keito," the woman behind Matthew whispered to the other woman next to her. The demon of the team stood casually to the side, waiting to step in as needed.

Mitoki barely had any magic to put into the bindings, and it was not long before he could feel his energy seeping out of his bones, dragging him closer and closer to the ground. Hanyi turned when he saw Mitoki lean forward with a groan.

"Mitoki! Stop! You'll pass out!" he snapped.

Keito was straining more than any of the others, thrashing as much as the magic would allow, but while Matthew was focused on the four weaker members of Team Dalton, the three other humans were concentrating entirely on keeping the demon contained in the powerful spell, knowing he had enough magic to overwhelm the binding enchantment.

"Now, this is how this is going to work," Matthew said simply. "One at a time, I'll release you and you and I fight. And I'll keep going until I have defeated your team."

"Presumptuous of you," Eclipse growled, his eyes beginning to shift into the deep burgundy of his Antiquan Angel magic.

"You'll get your turn, Eclipse," Matthew said, his eyes falling on Dalton. "I want to take out the team leader first."

The pressure around Dalton's chest and arms released so fast that he barely caught himself on his elbows before hitting the dirt. He stopped, unsure if he should meet Matthew's challenge or call his own surrender to keep him from seriously harming the older Guardian.

"Come on, Dalton," Matthew said, stepping forward and tapping his side with his foot. "Get up and face me. Who knows? You might beat me and then your teammates will be free to fight the rest of my team."

Dalton was still slow getting to his feet, his heart racing, fear filling every muscle in his body.

"Is this how you've handled all your other matches?" Dalton asked.

"Just the powerful teams," Matthew said. "I make sure to check the lineup at every stadium and then research at the branch to see how powerful my possible opponents will be." He smirked. "I bet you don't take this competition that seriously, huh? You're Dalton Teban, after all. Who could beat the best Guardian in the branch?"

Dalton spared a glance at the three humans behind Matthew, seeing them straining to restrain Keito, and the demon watching very carefully, ready to leap at Keito when he broke free.

"So, Dalton, think you can beat me? You look almost afraid to face me," Matthew laughed.

"I'm not."

"Good." With a rapid step forward, Matthew threw a punch at Dalton's face. Dalton barely leaned far enough back to avoid the hit, but the sparking energy radiating from the fist left small slices on his chin and neck. He stumbled, trying to regain his balance as Matthew followed him, throwing punches, trying to get Dalton to retaliate.

The four other members of Team Matthew remained in their spots. The humans had taken over the binding spell while their team leader fought, but they were struggling to keep the others of Team Dalton contained—most noticeably, Keito and Eclipse. Hanyi and

Mitoki had ceased their own struggles, though they found it difficult to raise their heads against the oppressive weight of the spell, their own magic already weakened from previous fights. Conversely, Eclipse was fighting so strongly that his fingers had already started to lengthen and his horns began to protrude from his hair, laying close to his skull behind his ears.

His Antiquan magic was putting an enormous strain on the entrapment spell.

"Focus on Keito..." the man growled through his teeth. "We can't let him interfere..."

"Screw Keito," one of the women snapped, flinching. "Eclipse is going to overwhelm the spell and rip through it. Focus more magic on him."

"I can handle the Antiquan Angel," their demon teammate said coolly, stepping forward and shaking out his hands in preparation for the fight. "If he can rip through that spell, then he should be most entertaining to fight."

Dalton was dodging and avoiding attacks from Matthew, terrified of breaking bones if he tried to retaliate. He could hear the impatient audience becoming bored with the fight, screaming at Dalton to do *some*thing. But all he could think about was how his mother was seated somewhere in the audience, likely waiting for him to slip up and use too much magic on another human, proving the danger he posed.

Reflex eventually led to him catching one of Matthew's punches and redirecting it to shove his shoulder into the other man's chest, pushing him away. But when he tried to release Matthew's fist, another hand latched on his wrist, pulling him close.

"I feel your magic, Dalton," Matthew whispered with a grin. "Do you want to feel what it's like to be on the other side of it?"

His freed hand pressed into Dalton's chest, and Dalton could feel a rush of magic moving out of his arm, through Matthew's body and back into his chest with the speed of a bullet. He was violently launched backward, pain spiraling like fire through his chest and neck as the magic ran along his nerve endings, creating painful sparks under his skin.

"Come now, Dalton," Matthew tutted. "You can use more magic than that. Don't you think it's important to understand how your opponents feel?"

Before Dalton got to his feet, Eclipse let out a loud screech, his wings ripping from his back and propelling him forward as he tore through the entrapment spell and moved to attack the humans confining his teammates. The demon of Team Matthew intercepted him, laughing as he brought Eclipse to the ground and began wrestling with the Antiquan Angel.

"Well, seems I should have freed Eclipse first," Matthew said, throwing a cursory glance at the other fight, "since he does seem to be the strongest human on your team."

"Then why don't you focus on him?" Dalton suggested. "Let my team fight your team in a normal five-on-five."

"Oh no, I'm far more interested in why you're so afraid to fight me, Dalton," Matthew said. "Could it be that you're worried people will finally see you're not as strong as you claim to be?"

Deciding to pretend he was interested in the fight, Dalton stepped forward with an open palm filled with sparking magic, hoping to tire Matthew and the rest of his team to the point that his own teammates would break free of their bindings.

"That's a little better," Matthew said condescendingly. "But I know you can do more, Dalton. Come on, you know magic, *use it.*"

With Hanyi and Mitoki no longer struggling, the other humans on Team Matthew were able to focus their attention on Keito. They could feel that Mitoki and Hanyi were nearly drained of energy, but Keito's magic was far more than they anticipated, and even though his magic was strengthening the binding spell, there was a saturation point when he would begin to overwhelm it—and that moment was rapidly approaching.

Eclipse and the demon were scraping at one another, growling and baring their teeth in a vicious battle that had captivated the audience's attention. The simple attacks and slow movements of Dalton and Matthew were nothing like the spectacle of Eclipse fighting a demon Guardian.

The excitement of the crowd was building, and the enthusiasm permeated into the ring, causing Dalton to take the fight a little more seriously, seeing that Matthew was not concerned with the growing intensity of Dalton's attacks.

On one more occasion, Matthew redirected Dalton's magic back to him, and while it was painful, Dalton also felt it feeding back into his magic, fanning the flames that were rushing through his veins as he stood back up and went to face Matthew again, putting more force into his punches and kicks.

Eclipse looked as though he was dominating the fight with the demon until the demon's head connected with Eclipse's and stunned him just long enough for the demon to flip them over, grab one of Eclipse's wings, and snap it in his hands.

Eclipse's screech of pain was ear-piercing, and the audience gasped and cringed at the sight of the protruding bone projected on the monitors around the ring. Dalton and Matthew turned quickly, startled, seeing Eclipse flailing against the demon, trying to strategize around the pain.

Matthew chuckled, turning back to Dalton with a smirk.

"And that takes care of..."

The words died on his tongue. Dalton's eyes had gone dark.

Dalton remembered the screech of pain when Eclipse had been blinded the previous round. He recalled the broken wing and the savagery of the Trade Mercenary that Yokouro had ordered after them. He recalled the way Yokouro had toyed with them the previous round, never giving them a moment's rest, only to toy with them further by watching them squirm from afar as they wondered why he was not more involved in the third round of the tournament.

His anger swelled.

Faster than Matthew believed a human could move, Dalton stepped forward and landed a brutal punch to his jaw, but before he could fall to the ground, Dalton's fingers grabbed the front of his shirt and hauled him back to his feet, punching him once more, his magic slicing open Matthew's skin as the spells radiated down his neck and chest.

"You know, that's an interesting trick you've learned," Dalton said, holding Matthew's throbbing jaw in one hand to force the older Guardian to look at him. "Redirecting my magic back to me. I wonder if I can do that to you."

Dropping Matthew to his knees, Dalton retreated two steps before falling into a crouch and placing his hand against the dirt. He could feel the pulsing magic across the ground, reaching from the members of Team Matthew to the confined Guardians of Team Dalton, holding them in a vice grip, feeding off their magic. He locked onto the rhythm of the pulsing, and then sent it in the opposite direction.

As though he could see the energy streams of the spell, Dalton felt the tendrils of magic retract like snakes, turning around to coil around Team Matthew with such terrifying speed, they did not realize they had lost control of the spell until it was too late.

The crushing weight descended on them. They let out choked cries, falling to their knees. Matthew's back went rigid as he screamed, the magic coiling around his arms with such ferocity that his forearms both snapped under the pressure, bringing his wrists to the ground limply. The demon was pulled to the ground face first, held against the dirt as he struggled to breathe, his own magic strengthening the spell.

Eclipse dragged himself along the floor away from the writhing members of Team Matthew, both impressed and horrified at what Dalton had managed. Now freed, Hanyi was helping Mitoki to his feet, though they were both shuddering, watching Dalton with a mixture of concern and awe.

"How much magic do you have to feed this spell?" Dalton asked, his fingers flexing over the dirt, tightening the binding around the other Guardians. A new round of screams made the audience's excited cheering turn to concerned murmuring. "Shall we see just how much of your own magic you can stand?"

"I surrender! I surrender!" Matthew bellowed, his eyes closed tight in agony.

The others also sounded their defeat, panicking as they felt the magic straining their ribs, threatening to snap more bones.

Dalton's hand left the ground and the spell vanished in an instant.

"And with that incredible turnaround, Team Dalton wins the match!"

Reverberating cheers shook the stands, but Dalton could hardly hear them over the ringing in his ears. His vision had tunneled, his blood racing through his veins as he stared at his hands. The rage inside him was still licking at the walls of his stomach, and he could see the sparking black magic dancing over his fingertips.

"Dalton!"

Finally hearing Hanyi, Dalton straightened and turned, seeing that Hanyi was still supporting the pale Mitoki as Keito guided Eclipse to his feet, though the broken wing of the Antiquan Angel was dragging limply on the ground. He watched numbly as Jikia and Tarrena rushed into the ring to look over Eclipse, asking if he was still conscious and aware of his surroundings.

Though Eclipse said he was still fully in control of himself, Dalton knew he could not say the same.

~∧~

Team Dalton opted to go to the team room after the fight with Team Matthew. The medical team followed them there, worried about the severity of the wounds the Guardians had received.

Hanyi sat in one of the chairs in the corner, exhausted and holding his head as his dizziness became overwhelming. Eclipse was being fussed over the most, his broken wing hanging loosely while Tarrena tried to stabilize it and the medical team tried to decide whether to surgically remove the broken wing or not. Mitoki was struggling to catch his breath still, his body shaking and sweat beading over his brow.

Keito and Dalton stood to the back of the team room, trying to stay out of the way, watching the medical team check over the other three members of Team Dalton.

"Ladies and gentlemen," Sammy's voice sounded over the speakers, "due to the fact that Team Dalton will be fighting three matches in a row, the Tournament Board has requested that all members submit to a medical examination to determine if they are fit to continue. Also, a twenty-minute rest period will be granted. At this time, we would like to remind you that the concession stands and drink bars are located in the second floor hallways for your convenience."

Dalton closed his eyes, leaning his head back on the wall with a heavy sigh.

"What would happen if we were disqualified from the tournament?" he asked.

"I do not know," Keito muttered.

"Do you think Yokouro's controlling the Tournament Board?"

"Actually, no," Keito answered. "I think Yokouro has tweaked a few things for this round, such as making sure there were so many demons in the stadium, but he's been surprisingly absent. I don't see a lot of his influence."

"…why does that worry me even more?" Dalton whispered, hanging his head.

"It worries me, too."

The medical team finally concluded that Eclipse needed to be taken to the medical room to have his wing removed surgically, as he was struggling around the pain to successfully lower his magic levels.

"Does that mean he's ineligible for the finals?" Jikia asked worriedly.

"Unfortunately," the medical advisor said. "We'll have to use light sedation and we cannot allow a Guardian to fight after that. The rest of the team can fight, but for the rest of this round, he'll have to sit out."

Dalton let out a worried sigh, his head still bowed.

"We might have a bigger problem," one of the medical staff said, turning to the team leader. "Mitoki Ecaep's energy reading is too low for competition."

"As is Hanyi Treneke's," one woman added, lifting the aura reading device to show the frighteningly low numbers on the screen.

"Three of my Guardians will be ineligible to fight in the finals?" Jikia asked, her eyes wide in horror.

"We're facing disqualification," Dalton muttered, his stomach churning angrily as he tried to think what Yokouro's next move would be if they were no longer in the Guardian Tournament.

"That is up to you and your team," the medical team leader said. "We'll take Eclipse for now, and you discuss what you want to do, but I must disqualify Eclipse, Mitoki, and Hanyi from the finals. If they fight, they're likely to be killed or suffer permanent injury."

The medical team left with Eclipse, Tarrena trailing behind. Jikia turned to Dalton as the door closed, a heaviness falling over the team room.

"Dalton?" she asked.

"I don't know what options I have," Dalton said. "Being disqualified from the tournament would free up our time to go after Yokouro, but what if Yokouro decides to attack a stadium because we're no longer in the tournament?" He looked between Keito and Hanyi. "What do you think Yokouro will do?"

"It's impossible to say," Keito said. "If I thought he was behind the Tournament Board, I wouldn't even worry, because he would never let us be disqualified. But…"

"It doesn't seem like he's involved today," Hanyi agreed with a short nod. "Being deemed unfit to fight after a match does not immediately mean disqualification. Because we all showed up and we all fought, even if a member is too severely injured to continue, the rest of the team is allowed to keep fighting that round if they so choose."

"But that means it's just me and Keito against a team of *five* demons," Dalton said with high eyebrows. "Keito, do you think there is any hope for the two of us to win a match like that?"

"Two of us against five demons? It would be a very difficult match," Keito admitted. "The five of them can easily overwhelm us if they all attack at once." The demon looked to Jikia. "What do you think?"

"Both being disqualified and trying to fight two-on-five is a very risky gamble."

"What about that thing you did with Team Matthew?" Mitoki asked, motioning to Dalton. "If you managed to do that again, you could keep them from attacking you all at once, and you can take them out one at a time."

"I don't know how I managed to do that," Dalton said quickly. "And even if I could do it again, I don't know that I could control it to the point where I could keep them still while we turned it into a one-on-one match."

Hanyi's face lit up. "Wait," he interjected. "You can ask for one-on-one fights because a majority of the team has been ruled unfit to continue. Rule 49-6, subsection F."

Dalton had forgotten that his wolf teammate was basically a walking rulebook for the Guardian Tournament.

"That could work," Keito said, nodding. "If we use that rule, I can fight the demons one-on-one."

"Do you have that kind of stamina?" Jikia asked, raising a quizzical eyebrow. "Five demons, one-on-one, after the fights you've already been in? You could become severely injured, as well."

"I can at least take as many as possible and Dalton can take over if needed," Keito said.

"Dalton fighting demons one-on-one?"

"If he taps into that power, he probably would do just fine. He was able to overpower the *jjanye* demon last round," Hanyi reminded them.

"No, no," Dalton protested. "I didn't do that. You told me that was Vestera's interference."

"You have been tapping into that power little by little," Keito said.

"That doesn't mean I can control it!" Dalton burst. "What if I kill someone?"

"That's a hazard in the tournament, of course, but if you're defending yourself—"

"No, I won't do that," Dalton snapped, cutting Jikia off. "I won't."

Keito crossed his arms, narrowing his eyes at Dalton.

"What do you suggest we do, then?" he said, unable to keep the bite out of his voice. "You have been off all day. What is wrong with you?"

"Really?" Dalton gawked. "We're facing a demon team two against five, and you're talking about taking as many on as you can until, what? You get too injured to continue? Or they kill *you*? I'm rightfully concerned."

"No, that's not what I mean," Keito said. "You're irrational today. You have no sense of the situation. You're frantic in the ring. Something is going on, Dalton."

"Nothing is going on, I just don't want you taking such a big risk."

"Then you want to quit?" Keito asked shortly. "You want to bow out of the tournament and go after Yokouro, hoping he doesn't decide to set fire to another stadium?"

"What other choices are there?" Dalton demanded.

"The one we were just discussing!" Keito said, exasperated. "Look, I told you this morning that if you were feeling uneasy or off-balance because of everything else going on, I would cover for you. You don't want to use your powers. We're going up against an all-demon team. I'm not seeing an alternative if we want to stay in the tournament."

Dalton opened his mouth, ready to protest, but he could form no argument. There was something stirring in his chest, but he could not tell if it was a bad feeling about how the finals were going to progress, or if his new magic was responding to his stress and trying to surge forward to fight whatever threat Dalton was facing. He could feel his heart racing, his blood beginning to turn to fire. The room felt as though it was getting smaller, and before he could help it, he saw his mother's face in his mind, saying: *I knew you were too dangerous. Your powers are the reason that demon came after us. You're the reason your father is dead.*

"Dalton, you need to make a decision," Jikia said. "We're running out of time."

Dalton's breathing became labored and he shook his head.

"I need some air."

"No." Keito grabbed his arm before he could get too far away. "Whatever this is, Dalton. You need to deal with it."

"I just need some air," Dalton growled, trying to yank his arm away from Keito. "This is not something I can decide so easily."

"What else is there to think over?" Keito asked.

"I just need a moment to think!" Dalton barked, freeing himself from Keito's grip. "Back off, Keito. You're not the team leader. This isn't your choice to make."

"Maybe not, but I am the one putting my ass on the line taking on this team one-on-one," Keito said. "And I'm willing to take that gamble. I don't know whatever the hell is wrong with you today, but this conflict you've got isn't about the tournament. And it isn't about Yokouro."

"Screw you, Keito. I just don't want you risking your life." Dalton turned away, but Keito grabbed his arm again. He whirled around, his eyes growing dark as he balled his fists and shook free of the demon's grasp once more. "Touch me again, and I swear…"

"What?" Keito challenged. "You'll punch me? Go ahead," he spread his arms, "take a swing if that's what you need to do. But you need to be *here*, Dalton."

"That's the problem!" Dalton barked. "I am here, and I'm too dangerous to be here! You saw the faces of Team Matthew. I don't even know how I *did* that! I can't control it. And if I get into that ring again, I'm terrified that the next tournament catastrophe is going to be because of *me*!"

"That's why I'm going to fight as many as I can—"

"That's not the point!" Dalton snapped. "The point is that I have these powers, and I can't control them. And that is putting you in danger, and if I have to fight, it's putting the rest of the stadium in danger." He let out a broken laugh. "And hell if I know how much worse it's going to get. Soon, my family will be in danger, too, probably."

"You can worry about that later," Keito said. "And if you end up fighting a demon, I'm sure some of that magic will come second nature in order to keep you alive and help you win."

"I don't want it to become second nature," Dalton growled. "I can't lose myself to this magic. I don't know how to control it, and I don't want to use it."

"Well, too damn bad, because you're going to have to learn some time. That magic is not going away," Keito said. "But right now, the decision you have to make is very simple. Do you want to stay in the tournament, or not?"

Dalton wished he saw the decision as that simple. But there was so much tangled up around the tournament that he could not think straight—as Keito had said. He was too worried about his growing powers, the strange tidal wave he could feel building in his chest, how Yokouro would react if they backed out of the tournament, and how difficult it would be to keep his powers in check if he did find himself in the ring again.

He could almost feel Yokouro watching him, smirking as he grappled with his decision, waiting for him to make the wrong one.

"...I think...we need to stay in the tournament."

Keito relaxed slightly, and even though the others in the team room were also concerned with the two-against-five finals, they were relieved that Dalton had made the decision they all knew had to be the correct one.

"Then I'll take on as many demons as I can. And if needed, you can take over after me," Keito said. "I told you I would cover for you, Dalton. I'll do my best to keep you out of the ring if you're that worried, but this is a gamble, and if you want to stay in the tournament, you have to be willing to take the risk."

Dalton could not respond. He did not nod in acknowledgement, nor did he shake his head to say that he was not willing to continue with the risky plan.

"Then we better tell the Tournament Board our decision," Jikia said quietly, glancing over Dalton for a brief moment to see if he would change his mind, but when he remained staring distantly at the ground, she left the room to tell the Tournament Board that Team Dalton was going to compete in the finals with only two of their members.

Chapter Twenty-Three

"May I have your attention, please?" Sammy started, though her voice was barely heard over the excited muttering of the audience as everyone watched Team Dalton return to their team box—though Eclipse was nowhere to be seen. The crowd whispered theories to their friends and family about what was going to happen to Team Dalton, a few even standing to try and get a better look at the Guardians, despite the angry hisses of those seated behind them.

"Eclipse Retani, Mitoki Ecaep, and Hanyi Treneke have been deemed unfit to fight in the final match by ruling of the tournament medical team," Sammy said, having to wait until the angry shouts quieted to continue her announcement. "However, using rule 49-6 subsection F, Dalton Teban and Keito DeVero can still compete, but the match with Team Keelan will proceed in a series of one-on-one fights."

Their disappointment forgotten, the spectators cheered, knowing that one-on-one matches would be easier to follow and more exciting to watch with so many demons in the ring.

"Each team will send out one member to fight. With each subsequent victory, the teams will have five minutes to pick their next fighter, and the fights will continue until a team has secured at least four wins," Sammy explained. "So, to start the finals, will Team Dalton and Team Keelan please send out their first fighters?"

As Keito walked toward the team box door, Jikia grabbed his arm.

"Fight intelligently," she warned. "Save your strength. You can't push yourself or act recklessly."

"I'll be careful," Keito promised, looking back at Dalton with a nod before stepping into the ring amid the excited bellowing of the crowd.

"The first fight will be Kamio of Team Keelan versus Keito of Team Dalton," Sammy announced. "Are there any conditions for this fight? If you wish to fight in your animal forms, you will need approval from the Tournament Board."

Kamio quirked a smile, rolling his eyes. "Think they'll ever learn how painful it is for us to fight in our animal forms?"

"Not likely," Keito said with a broken laugh. He looked at Sammy and shook his head.

"I have no conditions," Kamio called back to the announcer.

"Then you both must remain in your human forms," Sammy said. "If there are no other conditions, you may begin!"

Kamio lunged at Keito and the cheering audience got to their feet, flicking their eyes between the screens and the blurs darting around the ring as the two demons began the fight.

Keito spent much of the fight defensively evading Kamio's attacks. When he found an opening, he would try a counter attack, but Kamio was sure to never stop moving, forcing Keito to remain defensive for extended periods of time, hoping he could wear down the older demon and cause him to make a mistake.

But Keito was reading the younger demon's style and recognized his pattern quickly. When Kamio started to change directions, trying to force Keito to retreat further into the ring, Keito dug his foot into the dirt and met the younger demon full-force. His opponent scrambled to turn, not expecting the sudden change. Keito's fingers coiled around his wrist, yanking him closer as they both spun, falling to the ground, Keito trying to pin Kamio.

But he missed the other demon's hand, giving Kamio an opportunity to punch Keito in the side, rolling them both. Before Keito could defend, the other demon's magic created a sharp, sparking point, which Kamio stabbed into Keito's left side.

With the two demons in one place, the cameras were able to broadcast the attack, and it immediately caused an uproar in the stadium. Audience members leapt to their feet, screaming encouragements to both demons in a muddle of sounds, while Dalton flinched away, seeing the blood that was slowly leaking to the ground from Keito's wound.

But the demon of Team Dalton did not seem worried about the wound. He sat upright, his head striking Kamio's and stunning the younger demon enough for Keito to scramble away. He did not even flinch at the pain in his side, keeping his attention on Kamio as the other demon rubbed his head, standing.

"It would be something else to fight you in the field, Keito," Kamio said slowly. "It'd be amazing to see what you were truly capable of, considering your reputation."

"It wouldn't be much of a fight," Keito said simply.

"I suppose that confidence is well-founded," Kamio agreed. "Considering the bodies strewn behind you."

"Are you waiting to see if I become weak from blood loss? Why are you talking so much?" Keito chuckled darkly.

"I'm waiting to see how long until you make the first move."

Taking the invitation, Keito surged forward, but when Kamio went to block his obvious attack, Keito ducked under his arm, circling behind the other demon. His magic swirled from his hands, creating a tight braid of dark purple energy that he pulled tight against Kamio's throat.

"I don't have any interest in drawing this out," Keito whispered into his ear, straining as Kamio kicked and thrashed against the pressure on his throat. Keito pulled tighter, but could not hold the younger demon long. Kamio's magic coiled around Keito's arms, pulling taught just as Kamio's face began to turn red from his restricted breathing. Keito's arms were forced straight, releasing the pressure on Kamio's neck. Kamio spun, kicking Keito's legs out from under him.

"You want to end this quickly?" Kamio laughed, stepping on Keito's chest when he tried to get up. "Then you better show me more than this."

Keito grabbed his ankle, pulling the other demon down and starting another chase that was too fast for the humans and the cameras to follow, though that did not curb the enthusiasm in the audience.

Dalton had to turn away, guilt sitting like a stone in his gut. He did not know if he should focus on Keito's match or on focusing his mind so that he could fight if needed. Seeing the speed and power in the fight, he did not know how he could fight a demon Guardian without the use of his magic—and the thought of using his powers petrified him.

His eyes caught sight of a red-headed woman seated near the front of a nearby section in the stands. She was not watching the two demons in the ring. She was not on her feet like those around her, cheering on the Guardians. She was watching Dalton, sitting calmly as though the enthusiasm of the crowd or the danger displayed in the ring had no effect on her. She just smiled softly at Dalton.

The expression was anything but soothing. Dalton's mind was filled with the times his mother would smile at him, often when she was drunk, and pull him into a hug, petting his hair and telling him that if he ever became a Guardian, or tried to use magic like his father had, she would break however many bones necessary to make him too weak to be a Guardian.

His body started to shake, reminded of how terrified he had been as a kid when he started training as a Guardian. He had feared for years that his mother would return, find him at Master Bowen's, and keep her promise.

Dalton's staring was interrupted when Hanyi walked to his other side, planting himself on the bench in Dalton's eye line. He smiled broadly.

"Don't look over there," he said. "Watch the fight. And every time you feel like looking over here, you're going to see this handsome face." He flashed another grin, which brought a breathy chuckle out of Dalton. He nodded silently, turning his attention back to the ring.

The fight between the two demons had slowed, but that was because Keito had trapped Kamio's ankles in a binding spell, bringing the younger demon flat to the ground, though Keito still had to avoid the claws swiping at his face. Kamio's hand made contact, leaving four long slashes down the side of Keito's head, but he shook off the pain, finally grabbing Kamio's wrist and pinning it to the dirt at his side, turning his opponent in an awkward position.

"Surrender, or I break your arm," Keito warned.

"You don't have the balls!" Kamio spat.

Keito proved him wrong. Pushing hard on Kamio's elbow, Keito yanked his wrist backward, the snapping of bones masked by Kamio's pained roar.

"First time with a broken bone?" Keito noted, seeing the way the demon shuddered once he stopped screaming. "Not to worry. We heal quickly." He pressed his hand into Kamio's elbow again, jarring the broken bones as he wrapped his hand around the young demon's bicep, the sparking magic from his fingers burning Kamio's skin. "Surrender, or I break another bone."

Kamio tried to mutter the counter spell for the binding magic, but Keito released his elbow and wrapped a hand around his mouth.

"I can knock you out, if you want," he said, his magic pooling around his hand in a dark cloud of blue and purple. "Your choice."

Kamio shook his head. When Keito removed his hand from Kamio's face, the younger demon yelled his surrender.

Ignoring the cheering of the audience, Keito released the younger demon and then helped him to his feet. He tried to take Kamio's broken arm to look over the damage, but Kamio retreated from him, leaving the ring with a dark glare over his shoulder, making his way for the medical room so that the bone could be reset before his accelerated healing healed it incorrectly.

Sammy announced that there would be a very short break before the next Guardians would fight, but the others in the team box were worried it would not be enough time to see to Keito's wounds.

The demon stepped slowly into the team box, trying to wipe the sweat from his brow though he flinched when he grazed the scrapes along his face.

"Tarrena, treat those cuts," Jikia ordered, guiding Keito insistently to the bench as she yanked her supplies box closer. "Let me see the stab wound."

Keito lifted his shirt, giving everyone a clear view of the circular wound that was only lightly bleeding.

"Have you already healed this?" she asked, tenderly pressing her fingers to the edge of the wound.

"Just the damage to my kidney," Keito said. "I'm trying to preserve my energy as much as possible."

"I'll clean and bind this wound, but you might make it worse in the next fight," she mused, grabbing the cleaning solution from her supplies. "Do you want me to heal it?"

"You might want to preserve your healing magic," Keito said. "This is going to be a long fight."

Dalton knew he should say something to Keito. He met eyes with the demon, but no words would form. His more logical brain said that he could take the next demon and let Keito rest and heal so they could alternate fights, but the thought stayed stubbornly stuck in his throat, his fear of his growing magic seizing his tongue. Keito just gave Dalton a short nod and closed his eyes, allowing Tarrena to dab at the slashes on his face.

A soft commotion behind them brought their attention to Eclipse, who was being led to the team box by four burly security guards keeping the excited audience away from the injured Guardian. Eclipse stepped unsteadily into the team box, Mitoki immediately guiding him to sit on the bench.

"Are you alright? I thought they would put you out to remove your wings," Hanyi asked.

"Funny thing, they didn't have anything strong enough," Eclipse said. "They spent ten minutes going over every form of sedation they had on the phone with Dr. Grant. So they numbed me as much as they could and I just had to bear the rest of it." He forced a smile when he saw the horrified look on Tarrena's face. "I'm alright. The wings are gone, I'm stitched up, and I'm on as many painkillers as they can legally give me."

"Just sit here and try to drink this," Mitoki advised, putting a bottle of water in his hands.

"How are we still competing?" Eclipse asked, looking among his teammates for an explanation of how they were going to fight the final team. Keito remained quiet and still as he was treated, preserving his strength as Hanyi explained the specifics.

Dalton could not bring himself to speak at all.

241

The short break was over in a flash, and the next fighters were called into the ring. Keito left the team box without saying a word, walking out to meet the next demon from Team Keelan in the center of the ring.

The second fight was faster than the first, but it was brutal.

Jikia was half-way out of the team box when Keito approached, helping him up the steps and to the bench as he held the stab wound from the first match, wincing at the new injuries he had to his back and left arm. He kept his eyes closed, breathing hard as Jikia yanked up his shirt to see the gauze she had taped to his side already saturated with blood.

"You've torn this further open," she said, removing the gauze as carefully as she could. Catching sight of the new gashes and deep bruising on his chest, she helped him remove his shirt so she could see the extent of his injuries. "You need to heal some of these, Keito."

"I'm alright…" he whispered, his eyes still closed, his breathing coming in labored pants.

"You sure as hell don't look alright," Eclipse noted.

"Keito, you're shaking," Tarrena said, grabbing a cold compress and holding it to his bruising shoulder. He shook his head with a short growl, pushing her hand away. "Keito?" she murmured, surprised by the growl.

"Just…give me a few seconds…"

"What's going on?" Mitoki asked.

"That fight just…" Keito took a deep breath, growling quietly as he exhaled. He still had not opened his eyes. "My adrenaline is a little high, that's all."

"What does that mean?" Eclipse asked worriedly.

"Keito…" Hanyi started, "should we be worried about you becoming too dangerous to your opponents?"

"I'll be fine once I calm down," Keito said slowly. "He just really had me running ragged. I started to feel a little desperate to end the match."

"Are you going to fly into a blind rage?" Eclipse asked, trying to make the serious question sound like a joke.

"Hopefully not," the demon said.

"I don't think it's a good idea for you to fight again so soon," Jikia said, looking him over. "You're quite wounded, Keito."

"It looks worse than it is," he assured. "I'm more worried about losing control of myself."

"We're all worried about that," Hanyi agreed quickly. He looked at Dalton, who shied away from the look as though Hanyi had raised a hand to strike him. "Dalton?"

He could not lift his head.

"It's fine, Hanyi," Keito said. "I just need a few minutes to be quiet." He opened his eyes briefly to nod to Tarrena. "Sorry."

She replaced the cold compress to his shoulder as Jikia reluctantly went to cleaning the new wounds on the demon Guardian. She did use a bit of her healing energy to close the worst of the stab wound, but she still placed gauze over what was left, worried he would rip it open again in the next fight. She tried not to look over at Dalton, but everyone could feel her frustration.

Dalton felt it acutely. He could feel waves of anger radiating from her, causing his own stress to rise and the guilt to sit heavier inside his body.

He was feeling his own adrenaline coursing through him, making him feel jittery and panicked, and no matter how he tried to slow his breathing or focus on something other than the feelings in his chest, his new magic was rising closer to the surface, instinctively trying to protect him despite how he fought.

"Keito," Eclipse started with a worried shake of his head, "I don't think you should go out and fight again. There has to be another way to do this."

"I'm fine," Keito said again.

"I'm struggling to believe you," Eclipse retorted. "This tournament is not worth killing yourself over. We've got bigger problems to worry about."

"I've made up my mind, Eclipse," Keito said. "And if you think you're stubborn, I assure you, my stubbornness far surpasses yours."

"May I have your attention please?" Sammy said into the microphone, bringing a round of excited cheers from the audience, drowning out the rest of her announcement. "We are ready to continue. Would the next two Guardians please enter the ring?"

Keito stood, pulling his shirt back on as he left the team box, ignoring the surprised whispers of everyone wondering why Keito was fighting yet again.

As he met the female demon in the ring, Jikia stepped in front of Dalton, crossing her arms with a huff.

"...I'm sorry, Jikia," Dalton whispered.

"I'm not the one you have to apologize to," she said. "Keito is killing himself out there."

"If I fight, I might kill someone," Dalton hissed.

She leaned toward him, looking far larger than her short, stocky frame as Dalton shied away from her.

"And if you *don't* fight, you might kill Keito," she snapped. "You are the leader of this team, Dalton. You're acting like a child hiding from a monster in the closet. Whatever fear you have of these powers, you need to let it go. Because Keito's right. They're not going away. They're there for you to use to protect those you care about. And Keito needs your help."

"You don't understand—"

"No, I don't!" she snapped. "This is Team *Dalton*. Take control, and help drag your team through this. Keito is not going to be able to take all five of these demons on at this pace. You're going to have to step up."

"Mother," Tarrena said quietly, trying to pull the other dragon away from Dalton.

The words struck him deep. He wanted to fight. He wanted to give Keito a reprieve. He wanted to help. But he knew from experience that using his powers could be lethal if he lost control of them—with his magic growing by the day, he was certain that risk had become far greater.

Keito was fighting his own battle for control of his power. He knew he was not in danger of death from any of his opponents. He still had a power limiter keeping most of his powers on reserve, which could allow him to heal if a serious wound was inflicted. But his blood was racing, his nostrils flared, taking in all the scents around him. His fight or flight instinct had kicked in, reacting to the pain in his body and the threat of having to fight yet again. Like a wounded fox backed into a corner, he felt himself growling as he faced the female demon.

"Getting tired, Keito?" she asked. "You're looking a little desperate. It might have been better for you to sit this one out."

"I'm fine," Keito repeated yet again.

"Are there any conditions for the fight?" Sammy asked. Both demons shook their heads and she called the match to commence.

As usual, Keito waited for his opponent to make the first move.

"It's fascinating watching you fight, Keito," she said with a smile, grabbing two small daggers from her hips, twirling them with a flourish before gripping the hilts. "I wondered how the Wandering Child would fight. I thought you would show more of the western Demon Realm fighting style, but when you go on the offensive, I can see the eastern style in your moves."

"I just react to my opponents," Keito said. "I've picked up techniques everywhere. I don't have a particular style."

"You do," she said, brandishing one dagger in front of her as she bent her knees in preparation for attack. "And I know what to watch for."

She sprinted forward, beginning the match. Keito stood his ground, watching her form as she moved to swipe at him. He ducked her hand, turning to grab her other wrist and push it away, bringing his elbow across her face. She dropped from the impact, but when Keito moved to pin her to the ground, she planted her foot into his abdomen, kicking him over her head so that he was the one on the ground. She leapt on him, raising one of her daggers.

Keito deflected it, the weapon flying to the dirt as she tried to stab his side with her other weapon. When he grabbed her hand and tried to pry the dagger from her fingers, she punched him with her other hand and leapt away, retreating as he followed with a loud growl that his teammates could hear from the team box.

As the fight continued, Keito pushed his body even harder, feeling his natural defenses kick in. Adrenaline filled his veins. His focus narrowed only on his opponent, blocking out the audience, the stadium lights, and the worried expressions on his teammates' faces. Part of him knew that he was pushing too hard, but his rational thoughts were being pushed aside in favor of ending the fight quickly, no matter how brutal his attacks became.

The female demon took a sharp turn, watching as Keito followed her like a starving predator. She saw the desperation in his eyes, realizing he was more interested in ending the fight than forming a strategy for defeating her. She used his intense focus to lead him around the ring in different patterns, trying to tire him or get him to make a simple mistake.

Placing her remaining dagger between her teeth, she stopped running, turning to face Keito. As she expected, he did not slow, intent on tackling her to the ground. She lowered her stance, watching him mirror the position, but she leaned into the attack, her feet sliding backward as she reached as far down as she could with her right hand, her claws digging into Keito's back before she scraped her claws upward, forcing him to circle away when the deep gashes reached his neck.

Keito rolled on the ground, growling loudly as he turned in a crouch to face her. She removed the dagger from her lips, clicking her tongue in disappointment.

"You're getting sloppy."

Keito hesitated a few seconds more before leaping forward again to continue the fight.

"This isn't looking good," Mitoki murmured. "Keito's not thinking straight."

"He can't," Hanyi agreed. "He's reacting only on instinct. That's when he gets particularly dangerous."

"Have you ever seen him lose control like this before?" Eclipse asked.

"Not in the tournament, but on cases, yes," Hanyi said. "When he was fighting for his life and it looked like he wasn't going to make it, he let his instincts take over."

"Must have worked for him, since he's lived this long despite so many wanting him dead," Eclipse noted.

"Keito's more cutthroat than you know," Hanyi murmured. "He's learned techniques from all the Old Blood Lords. He's run with bandits. He's been fighting for his life since it started. He's brutal when he's this reactive. I just hope he can keep enough sense of the situation so he doesn't become a danger to anyone in the stadium."

"Surely he wouldn't just attack at random," Tarrena whispered.

"I certainly hope so," Hanyi said.

The growling emanating from Keito was accompanied by the occasional snarl to keep his opponent back. He could feel himself becoming frantic. His body was screaming at him to either finish the fight quickly, or to lay down and quit. He knew he could not last much longer before he was in serious danger of fatigue-induced panic. His thoughts were wild, spinning in his head and causing a fog of confusion to settle into his mind.

He needed to finish the fight.

The movement of the female demon caught his attention. She leapt at him once again, clawing at him with one hand. He swiped her hand to the side, but her foot found his knee, kicking sharply while he was turned and sending him face-first into the ground, one hand trapped under his chest while the other was pinned by her knee.

She pressed the dagger to the back of his neck, letting him feel the bite of the blade.

"Ready to surrender?" she asked coldly, smiling, her heart thrumming against her ribs as she heard the amazed shouting of the audience. She could not help but feel proud that she could be the one to get a surrender from the famous Keito DeVero.

But something sharp and hot connected with the right of her chest, entering just below her collarbone and sending pain spiraling through her. She let out a choked cry, scrambling away from Keito, wondering how he had commanded his magic to spear through her

246

when his thoughts were so scattered and his hands were nowhere near her chest.

Without wasting a second, Keito flipped onto his back, sitting up and grabbing her hand, which was still clutching the dagger. Too fast for anyone to see, he turned her hand and stabbed her own dagger into her sternum.

Everyone fell into horrified silence.

Keito held her hand in both of his, the dagger buried deep into her chest. He stared at the handle, breathing hard, watching the blood seep through her shirt and run down her torso as she began gasping for breath.

One of her teammates screamed for a medic from their team box. The audience began whispering in fearful confusion, wondering if Keito had killed the other demon. Those in Team Dalton's team box could only stare, stunned.

Keito blinked rapidly, the noises beginning to swim through the fog in his head, the thick scent of blood so close bringing him back to the moment. His opponent shuddered, beginning to fall to her side as shock took over her system.

He grabbed her, carefully laying her on the ground and pulling the dagger from her chest. The moment the blade was free of her flesh, he pressed his hand hard into the wound, bright blue magic engulfing his hand as he used what little energy he could spare to heal the wound.

Her hands scraped at his arm, her breath escaping her in terrified pants.

"Keito...stop...you can't..."

But he persisted, the sweat beaded on his brow falling down his face as his skin started to pale. Blood began to fall onto her from Keito's own wounds. As she felt his magic mending her flesh, she started to worry for Keito's well-being.

"I surrender!" she called loudly, hoping Keito would stop draining his limited magic.

As Sammy nervously called the win to Team Dalton, she managed to push Keito's hand from her chest, trying to stand so she could assess how badly Keito was wounded. But once she sat up, she was hauled to her feet by one of her teammates, who snarled at Keito angrily.

"Stay the hell away from her!" he barked.

Keito stared up at him from his kneeling position, breathing hard, his pale and sweat-soaked face starting to worry everyone in the stadium as it was projected onto the screens around the ring.

"Team Keelan, do you need the medical team?" Sammy asked.

The female demon ran her hand over where the dagger had punctured her, finding only a small scrape that she could easily heal on her own. She shook her head, turning her attention back to Keito.

The older demon tried to get to his feet, but only stayed standing for a moment before he stumbled and fell to the dirt, sparking a new round of concerned whispers.

"Get the medical team!" the female demon called, rushing to Keito's side. Everyone from Team Dalton's team box, even Dalton, rushed into the ring. Hanyi reached Keito first, pressing his fingers to the demon's neck to find a pulse as he turned him onto his back.

"Is he alright?" Eclipse asked, falling to his knees next to his teammates.

"We need that medical team!" Hanyi yelled, seeing the gaping hole in Keito's chest before the others took note of the source of all the blood on the ground.

"He shot that magic through his own body?" Mitoki whispered, mortified at the thought that Keito would purposely cause so much damage to his own body.

"He must have been desperate to finish the match," Hanyi said. He turned his eyes to the female demon as the medical team rushed to load Keito onto the stretcher. "Are you alright?" She nodded silently, also stunned by what Keito had done.

Dalton was standing by Keito's head, watching the blood seeping from the wound in the demon's chest. The fear inside him was beginning to turn to a boiling rage threatening to eat him alive. He could not stop himself from feeling angry at Keito for pushing himself to the point of near-self-destruction. And as angry as he was at his teammate, he was angrier at himself for not stepping in and fighting before Keito had become so desperate.

He tried to follow the medical team as they carted Keito away on the stretcher, but Eclipse caught his arm.

"The match isn't over yet," he said. "If you want to forfeit the match and follow Keito, then that's fine. But he'll be really pissed he went through all that only for you to give up."

Dalton could not look at Eclipse. He was worried that if he did not plan each move, he would end up attacking his own teammate in his frustration. He took a deep breath, preparing himself to turn around, walk back to the team box, and wait for the next fight to start. He could not move or speak beyond those actions—there was no way for him to know which move would be the one to send him into a fury of his own.

He took measured steps back to the team box. Jikia waited for him to ascend the steps before opening her mouth to ask him what he planned to do. But the words died on her lips. He stopped in front of her, glaring down at her darkly, warning her not to speak.

Dalton stood near the door to the team box, leaning on the front wall, watching as the ring was cleaned and the short rest period ticked by. His teammates wanted to talk to Dalton, but they knew if they even asked him if he was alright, they were risking being on the receiving end of his anger.

Dalton's mind was clouded with dark, furious thoughts. His anger shifted from Keito to Yokouro, infuriated at the demon lord for the entire situation. Somewhere, he knew Yokouro was watching them, relishing in how difficult things had become for Team Dalton despite how little he had influenced the tournament. Dalton knew that Yokouro was quietly laughing to himself about how afraid Dalton was to use his power—no doubt the demon lord counted on Dalton's fear, as it would allow him to triumph in the end if Dalton was too afraid of his powers to properly use them.

While Dalton had always had a fear of his abilities, that day, the fear had been overwhelming—because he could feel the cold eyes of his mother boring into his back. She had been the one to plant the seeds of fear in him, and that day, her return had deepened those wounds. And Keito had paid the price. His fingers gripped the front of the team box even tighter, his anger towards Shannon swelling to the point of nearly suffocating him. His knuckles were turning white. His vision was tunneling. His ears were ringing. His arms were beginning to shake.

The rest of his team could only watch quietly as Dalton's shoulders became more and more rigid with each passing breath.

"May I have your attention please? We are ready to continue," Sammy announced. The speculative whispers silenced quickly, eager to see what Dalton would do. "Keito DeVero has been deemed unfit to fight as he is still unconscious. Dalton has the choice to forfeit, or to fight. He needs at least one more victory for his team to advance."

Dalton released the edge of the team box and entered the ring.

"I think we should have the medical team on standby," Eclipse whispered.

"I agree," Hanyi muttered. "Now it's time to worry whether or not *Dalton* can keep his rage under control."

Chapter Twenty-Four

There was no cheering in the stadium. Most of the audience was standing, staring with eyes wide and mouths agape at the ring. Those in Team Dalton's team box slowly stood as well, but they could not bring themselves to run to their team leader.

Dalton stood in the middle of the ring, breathing hard, flexing his bloodied fists as he stared down at the unconscious demon at his feet.

He had won the fight in less than three minutes. The next demon to step out and face him was confident up until the moment Sammy asked for conditions. Though neither of them had conditions, the demon could see that Dalton was barely containing himself from attacking the demon. The moment the announcer called the match to start, Dalton had lunged forward, his fists flying, the thick magic surrounding his arms feeling like knives whenever he made contact.

Even with the demon unconscious, the magic was still heavy in the air. Dalton's shoulders were rigid, and his eyes were still filled with dark fire.

"Uh...D-Dalton won..." Sammy murmured into her microphone. The sound of her voice over the speakers seemed to revive the audience. She cleared her throat as the murmuring filled the stands. "I mean, Guardian Teban has won the one-on-one match. The final member of Team Keelan has the option to fight or—"

"No, no," the last demon said, shaking his head quickly as he stepped out of his team box, moving slowly toward his unconscious teammate with his hands raised. "I surrender."

"With that final surrender, the winner of the first set of matches in Stadium H-2 is Team Dalton!"

Hesitant cheers greeted the ears of those stepping out of Team Dalton's team box. They approached Dalton slowly, watching as he retreated two steps from the unconscious demon to allow his teammate and the medical team to collect him, but his eyes still had not risen from his opponent.

"Dalton?" Tarrena asked, being the first to gather the courage to approach him and place her hand on his shoulder. "Are you alright?"

Dalton took a deep breath and turned to look at her. She removed her hand immediately, startled by his cold expression. His eyes passed briefly over the others, halting their steps. His eyes were still green, but they could see flecks of gold in the irises, nearly glowing as his magic pulsed rhythmically around him.

"What a waste of time," Dalton hissed, turning away from them, following the retreating medical team to Hall A. The other Guardians only had a moment to look at one another, silently debating whether to follow Dalton or leave him alone. They were sure to trail behind him at a distance, watching as he followed the team carrying the unconscious demon.

When Dalton stepped into the crowded medical room, lined with beds and nurses rushing to help the Guardians they still had in their care, he walked easily through the divisions between the beds, walking with purpose, as though he already knew which bed he wanted to find. Some of the nurses in the room turned to help him, but he ignored them and they backed away, reacting to the magic radiating from the human Guardian.

Dalton pushed aside one of the curtains, stepping up to the small bed where Keito remained unconscious, heavily bandaged, but otherwise only hooked up to a machine that monitored his magical activity, which seemed to be remaining relatively steady.

Jikia and the others found Dalton and slowly filed in around Keito's bed, looking him over. Jikia checked the readings on the machine before glancing over his bandaged wounds.

"Looks like he's alright," she said, holding her hand over the bandage near the center of Keito's chest, light blue magic surrounding her hand as she checked the wound. "They healed this wound entirely."

"Actually, he did most of that on his own," a nurse said, stepping to the trainer's side, startling everyone. "Demons have learned healing patterns," she explained. "Demons who have already healed from serious injuries throughout their lives actually heal faster than demons who have not yet had to heal from such wounds. Considering this is the famous Keito DeVero, I'm sure he's suffered more serious injuries than a hole in his chest before. By the time we got to healing him, his magic had already done most of the work."

"Do you have him sedated?" Hanyi asked.

"No. We gave him a very strong pain killer which has made him sleepy, but he should burn through that in a few hours."

"I thought you said it was dangerous for him to be asleep for a long time," Eclipse noted.

"Yes, but a few hours shouldn't be enough to make him lose himself like before," Hanyi said. "All the same, I'll keep an eye on him and make sure he wakes up before he falls too deeply into sleep."

"Can we take him home?" Jikia asked, briefly flicking her eyes to Dalton, who had not lifted his gaze from Keito the entire time they had been talking.

"We would prefer that he wake up in our care, but…" She sighed, looking over her shoulder. "It's been a very busy day here today. If you feel comfortable taking him now, you can. I'll just need you to sign some forms. Would you like a transport van for him?"

"Yes," Jikia said. She turned to the rest of the team. "Why don't you boys head back to the house and we'll ride with Keito in the medical van and meet you there?"

"I'll stay with him, too," Dalton said, his voice monotone and cold.

"It's alright, Dalton," Tarrena said. "He's in good hands. We'll meet you back at your house."

"I'll stay with him," he repeated. He had yet to lift his gaze.

The Guardians shared nervous looks, feeling tension they could not explain. Dalton seemed transfixed by the sleeping demon, like he could not let Keito out of his sight for even one second. His teammates did not know whether to respect Dalton's wishes or to break him away from Keito and try to get him to come back to himself.

"Someone has to drive the car back," Hanyi said, trying to keep his tone light. "I don't think Juki and Rutu would like us leaving their car—"

He stopped when Dalton extracted the keys from his pocket and held them to his side, waiting for someone to take them. Eclipse hesitantly took the keys. Jikia offered the concerned nurse a forced smile.

"I'll sign the necessary forms," she said, motioning for the nurse to lead her to the information desk. Eclipse walked around the bed to Tarrena.

"Maybe one of us should ride with you, too," he whispered to her. "I don't think Dalton's safe to be around at the moment."

"We'll be fine," she said with a soft smile. "Don't forget. We're dragons. We can handle ourselves just fine." She gently squeezed his arm. "Head back to the house. You might want to prepare Frieda and Theresa about how he's behaving. It'd be better to talk to them before we get to the house."

"She's right," Hanyi said, stepping up to the conversation. "Dalton isn't even acknowledging that we're talking about him. We need to warn Frieda and Theresa."

"Of course, but how do we break him out of this?"

Their eyes turned to Dalton, feeling helpless as they watched the team leader study Keito with unblinking eyes.

~/\~

Eclipse, Mitoki, and Hanyi tried to prepare Frieda and Theresa for Dalton's strange behavior, but they were still surprised at how distant and cold he acted. As the medical team carried the still-unconscious Keito to the guest room, Dalton followed like a hawk, his eyes remaining locked on the demon. He watched them carry Keito upstairs and transfer him to the bed, not even acknowledging the men as they left the house.

Frieda was hesitant to enter the guest room, holding Theresa's hand tightly, even though the young girl was loudly asking if everyone was alright and why Keito had so many injuries. Hanyi and Mitoki stood close to Dalton's family while Eclipse placed himself next to Dalton, ready to interfere if necessary. Jikia and Tarrena stood at the foot of the bed, unsure what to do for Dalton.

But Dalton remained staring at Keito, not even recognizing that there were others in the room.

"Dad?" Theresa asked quietly. "Dad? Is Uncle Keito going to be okay?"

Finally, Dalton lifted his gaze, his eyes briefly settling on Frieda and Theresa before dropping back to Keito.

Tears began to well in Theresa's eyes, sensing the cold aura from her father, terrifying her.

"Hey," Hanyi said quickly, crouching and taking her face in his hands, "it's alright. Keito is going to be just fine. We're just going to make sure he rests, okay?" He hugged her tightly. "You know what Keito would love when he wakes up? Some of those cookies you helped make up at the lake."

"Hanyi's right," Frieda said, seeing the plan to get Theresa's mind off of her father's frightening change in behavior. "Why don't we go make him a big batch of cookies for when he wakes up?"

As she started to leave the guest room, Hanyi placed a hand on her shoulder.

"I don't know what to do to help Dalton, but if you need us, you let us know. We're going to try and take care of him, but we're here for you, too."

She smiled, placing her hand on his.

"Thank you, Hanyi," she said, almost successful at keeping her worried tears at bay.

As Frieda and Theresa went downstairs, Hanyi returned to the guest room. Mitoki took a deep breath, leaning over to the wolf.

"This is getting scary," he whispered. "It's like Dalton's possessed, just staring at Keito while he sleeps."

"Maybe when Keito wakes up, Dalton will snap out of it," Hanyi suggested.

"You think so?"

"I have no idea," the wolf said honestly. He turned his gaze to Jikia and Tarrena. "How was the drive over here?" he asked vaguely.

Tarrena glanced at Dalton before answering. "Exactly like this," she said.

"Hanyi, maybe we should wake Keito up," Eclipse suggested, hoping that the demon would be able to snap Dalton out of his trance—or at least understand better what was causing Dalton to act so strangely.

With a hesitant nod, Hanyi approached the bed, placing a hand on Keito's arm and shaking him lightly.

"Keito?" he called. "Keito, wake up."

When the demon did not stir, Hanyi shook him a little harder, finally causing him to cringe and slowly blink his eyes open. He looked around the room, his expression becoming confused as he tried to recognize where he was and remember how he got there.

"We're...at the house?"

"We won the match," Mitoki said. "But you took it a little hard in the ring. You passed out after blasting a hold through your chest."

Keito's brow knitted together as he tried to remember the events of the tournament.

"I have vague recollection of that..." he muttered.

"How are you feeling?" Hanyi asked.

"A little groggy...tired...but otherwise, I'm alright." Keito tried to sit up, turning his head and finally catching sight of Dalton. He stopped, seeing the intensity in his team leader's expression and the flecks of gold in his green eyes. Dalton stared silently back at him, unmoving.

"Dalton?" Keito asked. "Are you alright?"

Dalton tilted his head, as though looking for something in Keito's expression.

"He's been like this since the last match," Eclipse said. "We don't know what's wrong with him. He hasn't stop staring at you."

Keito looked at the confirming nods from the others in the room before he sat upright and turned to face Dalton.

"Dalton," he started, "is there something you want to ask me?"

"Are you you?"

The sound of Dalton's voice startled everyone after his extended silence. While it sounded like Dalton, the monotone voice seemed foreign, not at all like the man they knew. Keito blinked at Dalton, also confused by the question.

"Yes," he answered slowly.

As though a switch had flicked in Dalton's mind, he turned away from the demon and left the guest room, turning down the hallway and disappearing from sight. Eclipse followed Dalton, worried he would frighten Frieda and Theresa more, but stopped when he saw Dalton go into the master bedroom. He pressed his ear to the door, listening carefully until he heard the shower running.

The members of Team Dalton took turns keeping watch over Dalton for the rest of the evening. Slowly, Dalton seemed to come back to himself. At first, he moved like a zombie, going through the motions of what he thought he should do. But as night rolled around, he started talking to the others in the house, though maintaining conversation was difficult, as he would zone out in the middle of sentences and then forget what they were discussing all together. By the time everyone sat down for dinner, he was acting almost like himself, though he was clearly exhausted, and excused himself to go to bed as soon as he had helped with the dishes.

Eclipse had gone to the backyard, sitting on the back patio quietly, trying to collect his thoughts and think around his own exhaustion. Tarrena stepped out to join him.

"We're going to be heading back to the hotel soon," she said, sitting in the chair next to him and looking briefly up at the night sky. "Now that Theresa's in bed, Mother's explaining what she can to Frieda, and we'll head out soon after that." She reached over and took Eclipse's hand. "Are you alright?"

He smiled thinly, squeezing his fingers around hers. "Just tired." He heaved a sigh. "The tournament felt different today."

"I think a lot of that had to do with Dalton," Tarrena agreed.

"What do you think is going on with him?" Eclipse asked. "Did he really just stare at Keito the entire drive home?"

She nodded. "The magic radiating off of him is dragon energy, just like last round when Vestera interfered."

"Did Vestera interfere today?"

"No," Tarrena said. "The dragon magic is coming from Dalton. Whatever his new powers are, they are connected to the dragons somehow."

"How do we find out more?" Eclipse asked. "Dalton seems to lose himself when these powers come to the surface. He's going to

255

need to know how to keep that from happening. Particularly since we're going to be fighting Yokouro, who now has celestial magic at his disposal."

"I don't know," Tarrena admitted. "It's difficult to explain, but the dragon magic that Dalton uses is old. It's more potent than my magic, or any magic of the dragons I know that are about my age." She shrugged. "I could always ask Vestera for information."

"Just call up the most powerful being in the known universe and ask him?" Eclipse scoffed.

"Why not?" Tarrena asked.

"Because it's *Vestera Hizoku*," Eclipse said, as though that was answer enough. She smiled at him.

"I keep forgetting that you haven't met him, yet," she said. "Vestera is very kind. He's always willing to help those who ask."

"Then why hasn't he come here to help us?" Eclipse questioned. "He cared enough to basically possess Dalton last round, and he cares enough to show up for two seconds to take Kawakara away, but otherwise, he hasn't been around to help us defeat Yokouro."

"I have a theory about that," Tarrena said.

"He's busy?" Eclipse guessed.

"Well, yes, but if Dalton's dragon magic is as volatile as it seems to be, being around Vestera could actually cause that magic to become more volatile," she explained. "All dragons are connected to Vestera. He's the leader of our clan, and the strongest living dragon, and as such, dragons instinctively respond to his presence. The dragon magic inside of Dalton could actually destroy him if he was not strong enough to be in Vestera's presence."

"Do you think Dalton is part dragon?" Eclipse asked.

"No," Tarrena said with a sad shake of her head. "It's not possible for a dragon to mate with a human." A heavy silence settled between them as Tarrena waited for Eclipse to react to the words. "I…suppose that is something we need to discuss."

Eclipse squeezed her hand again.

"I've never wanted children," he said. "So if you're worried about how I feel about that, I'm okay with it." He turned his attention fully to her. "Do you want children?"

"…I don't know. I never really thought about it," she said. "Having young is such an ordeal to dragons that I never thought it would happen for me anyway." She turned her gaze to her lap, her fingers tightening around Eclipse's. "Eclipse…I…"

When she did not continue, he pulled his chair closer to hers, wrapping an arm around her shoulders.

"Are you alright?"

She remained quiet, placing her head against his shoulder.

"What is it?"

"…I'm worried."

"About what?"

"Everything," she admitted with a nervous laugh. "The ordeal with the dragon clan, the decision to make Vestera have young…I think the dragons are preparing for an apocalypse. And I can't help but wonder if Dalton is a part of that."

"You sound awfully casual talking about an apocalypse," Eclipse said warily.

She giggled. "I don't know for sure if that's what's happening," she said. "But the fact that Dalton has any dragon magic to begin with is already very strange. And with everything going on with Yokouro…it just feels like this is leading up to something big. Not just a fight against a mass-murdering demon, but something that might alter the course of all five realms."

Eclipse sighed, resting his head on hers.

"I feel it, too."

Chapter Twenty-Five

"Are you going to pout for the rest of the day?"

"I am not pouting."

"Really? Because you look like you're pouting."

Rutu glared at Juki, not at all deterred by Juki's disguise spell, able to see through it with ease.

"I'm annoyed. That does not mean I'm pouting."

"Why are you annoyed?"

Juki stood from his seat, the six guards with the demon lords also getting to their feet, carefully maneuvering themselves in the narrow aisles of the airplane as the passengers behind them craned around the seats, trying to see if the "designated guests" on the flight were well-known celebrities.

"There are many reasons," Rutu groaned, following Juki off the plane. "Yokouro's been running us so ragged that the last time we slept was three days ago. Then he made us travel by motorcade, plane, and now by motorcade again, making a ten-second trip by dimension hopping into a seventeen-hour fiasco."

"Traveling has never agreed with you," Juki laughed lightly, leaving the jet way, Rutu stepping up to his side. "You have to admit, the plane is nicer than horseback."

"I prefer horseback," Rutu disagreed. "And I don't mind traveling, but there is no point in forcing us to take human transportation when we can dimension hop."

"It's for subtlety," Juki reminded him. "We—"

"Don't move!" a voice bellowed. People in the terminal screamed and retreated rapidly as over twenty black-clad men rushed forward in formation, pointing their guns at the lords and their bodyguards. The guards growled and started forward to protect their lords, though Rutu ordered them to still immediately. He sighed and looked at Juki, raising an eyebrow.

"*Subtlety?*" he repeated sarcastically.

"Demons, you have entered a human-inhabited realm in which you are not permitted." The commander's voice was a little weak, though he desperately tried to hide it. Rutu saw the slight shake in the hands of all members of the Demon Containment Unit as they aimed their guns. He knew that they were not in danger—even if they fired, Rutu could halt the bullets before they drew anywhere near. It was clear that the team had never faced powerful demons before, or they would not have bothered with the firearms.

"You will come with us quietly, where you will be detained until the higher lords of your realm can order your release," the commander continued.

"We have business in your neighboring city," Juki answered calmly. "We mean no harm to any humans. We only wish to pass through."

"You should have gone through the DPC and retrieved business passes and travel passes, then, which you did not show upon boarding your flight."

"You don't seem to understand who you are dealing with," Juki said with a quiet laugh.

"You do not match the description of any of the demons given permanent clearance for travel," the commander continued. "Either produce your travel papers or you will be detained."

"We have full clearance," Juki said gently.

The man hesitated. Rutu's ears picked up the static of a voice in the man's ear as he was instructed on what to say and do by someone who was watching the situation from the airport cameras.

"Then you should have your clearance cards," the commander said.

"We do," Juki said. "However, you immediately held us at gunpoint and we have not been able to show them."

"Reach for them slowly with your right hands and keep your left hands in the air where we can see them."

Rutu suppressed the urge to roll his eyes as he reached into his pocket, pulling out the laminated card as Juki extracted his own. Juki handed his card to Rutu, who took a step forward.

"No! No! Slide them toward us," the commander ordered sharply as the nervous and twitchy team took aim at the center of Rutu's chest. The guards around the Kage Lords were getting increasingly agitated, causing a few of the armed humans to train their guns on the growling guards. Juki had to, once again, order them to remain still.

Rutu crouched and slid the cards across the tile floor one at a time.

The commander of the unit stepped cautiously forward, never taking his eyes off the two demons as he gathered the cards. When he finally glanced down at the information printed on them, he saw the Dimension Protection Council seal and the words Permanent Demon Travel Exception above the names of all five realms. When he flipped the cards over, his eyes went wide behind his protective visor.

"If you have any disguise or cloaking spells in effect, dispel them now."

Juki snapped his fingers at his side. Spectators of the confrontation watched in amazement as the two demons grew taller, their faces changing as their eye colors morphed, their hair growing into long, intricate braids. Even the members of the Demon Containment Unit were startled by the transformation. The commander retreated a step, his entire body shaking.

"You're the Kage Lords," he whispered. The rest of the team straightened, their guns lowering as they looked rapidly between the two demons.

"That is correct," Juki affirmed.

"Lower your weapons!" the commander barked. The others in the squad quickly stood and lowered their guns, bowing their heads merely out of instinct, worried that they had offended or upset the two extremely powerful demons.

"I apologize, sirs," the commander said. "We were unaware that you were the ones traveling."

"We understand," Juki said. "You were only doing your duty. I applaud your commitment to keeping the people in your realm safe."

"Oh." The commander straightened, surprised by the praise. "T-Thank you, sir..." He cautiously stepped closer to the two lords and offered their clearance cards to them. "Do you have a car waiting for you?"

"We do."

"If you will permit us, part of regulation is to escort you to your car," the commander said, his voice shaking quite badly now that he was standing so close to the demon lords.

"Very well."

Juki did not need to snap his fingers again for the disguise spell to take effect, so the rapid change in appearance startled the commander as he backed away.

"Thank you, sirs."

Two members of the Demon Containment Unit fell into step beside their commander while the rest trailed behind the Kage Lords' guards, creating a very large group that had everyone in the airport watching as they passed. Several travelers even extracted their phones, trying to get pictures of the two surrounded by black-clad security, thinking they might be celebrities. A few even tried to follow the large group, desperate to see who was in the middle.

Three cars were at the curb waiting for the demon lords. The middle car had one guard posted at the back door, which he opened immediately upon seeing the group. The Demon Containment Unit filed to the side as the Kage Lords got into the back seat of the middle car, their guards walking to either of the other vehicles as the driver of the middle car closed the door and got into the driver's seat.

"What *morons*," Juki groaned, slumping back with a heavy sigh.

"Why did Yokouro think that this would be subtle?" Rutu asked as the driver started the engine and followed the lead car away from the curb.

"I think he just means that Vestera won't be able to track us as easily." Juki leaned his head back on the seat, rubbing his neck tiredly. "He can sense when we leave the realm by dimension hopping, so he probably thinks we're still in the Darkness Realm. With the clearance cards, he's not immediately notified that we're moving."

"What would it matter at this point if Vestera knew?" Rutu grumbled, pressing his forehead to the window and closing his eyes. "He's probably going to hear about all the ruckus at the airport. Why did Yokouro insist on public transportations? We should have just used our own planes."

"I called the pilots but they were on other charters. They couldn't get back in time," Juki said, his own eyes sliding shut.

"If we're not going to use the planes anymore, we should sell them," Rutu mused.

Juki only managed a small noise in response.

The drive was silent. When the driver glanced in the rearview mirror after an extended silence between the two demons, he saw that they had fallen asleep, Rutu shifting silently to place his head on Juki's shoulder, taking advantage of the two quiet hours to rest. The driver tried to avoid the rough parts of the road and take turns as slowly as possible, knowing the two demon lords were exhausted.

But as they pulled into the smaller city of Golden and drove into the industrial district full of warehouses, he tried to jostle them awake with his driving, clearing his throat a few times as they drew closer to the large warehouse on the edge of town. He even tried to put the car in park as loudly as he could, trying to make as much noise as possible as he got out of the car.

Still, the two demons did not wake.

He tapped his knuckles against the back door window, finally stirring Juki from sleep. When he saw Juki's eyes open, he opened the door.

"Forgive me for disturbing you, my lords," he said. "We're here."

Juki took a deep breath, pinching his eyes tight for a moment as Rutu lifted his head from his shoulder, struggling to wake. But the two stepped out of the vehicle and took a few deep breaths before turning to the back door of the warehouse where a short, fat man was wringing his hands together nervously, waiting for them to approach.

One of the Kage Lords' guards retrieved a duffel bag from the trunk, and four of the guards walked with their lords toward the man.

"Good afternoon," the fat man greeted, his voice breaking. "You must be the demon lords Juki and Rutu."

"We are," Juki affirmed. "Are you Samuel?"

"Sam," the man said, reaching forward with a nervous hand. "Forgive me, but you look nothing like the pictures I was sent."

"We have been asked by the leader of Demon Council to remain in disguise whenever in a human-inhabited realm, to keep a low profile," Juki explained.

"Oh, of course," Sam said quickly. "Please, come in, come in. Except, um, perhaps…would it be too much to ask that your guards remain out here? I would feel more at ease."

"No problem," Juki said, nodding once to the guards, who obediently retreated two steps.

"Thank you," the fat man said, visibly relaxing.

He opened the back door to the warehouse and led the two demon lords inside as Rutu grabbed the duffel bag. Sam tried not to be nervous, but when he had heard that two demons were interested in the decommissioned slaughterhouse, his imagination had run wild with possibilities as to why the demons were interested in purchasing the property. Being in their presence made his fears worse, not expecting the two to have such a potent energy around them.

The dark rooms and menacing equipment around them only amplified his anxieties as he showed them through the slaughterhouse, getting particularly nervous when he opened the doors to the killing floor. Sam had always considered himself to be very open-minded about demons, but he was starting to feel like the prey being stalked by two very dangerous predators.

"This slaughterhouse hasn't been used in twenty years," he said, walking slowly behind the demons as they looked around the killing floor. "It shut down after a bigger, newer one opened further out of the county. They thought it was better to keep the slaughterhouses further away from the city. No one has really taken an interest in this property, though. But as you can see, it's been thoroughly cleaned."

"Really?" Rutu asked, stopping above the drain grate in the middle of the floor. "Was it in use for a long time?"

"Only about seven years."

"I wonder why the smell of blood and meat still lingers so strongly..." Rutu murmured. Juki could not hide his grin at the rattled expression on Sam's face, but he did give Rutu a playful glare, silently telling his mate not to scare the fat man too badly. Rutu's response was a mischievous smirk.

After walking through the processing rooms, they came to the aging room, where hooks were placed on several tracks on the ceiling, tables scattered about the cold, dark room. Rutu stepped in first, looking around with a knowing glance that had Sam nearly shaking with concern about what the demons were planning. Juki followed him, grabbing one of the hanging hooks and pulling sharply, the chain snapping under his demon strength, causing the other chains on the track to shudder.

"That will have to be fixed," Rutu said over his shoulder. He could see behind Juki that Sam's face had drained of all color, sweat beading over his brow as he stared in terror at the two demons. Rutu raised his hand and flicked a nearby hook.

"*You know,*" he called Juki's attention, using the common Kage language and grinning when he saw the confused and horrified look on Sam's face, "*if I point at these hooks, and speak to you in this language, I bet we could make him incredibly nervous.*"

Juki laughed, walking closer and wrapping his hand around one of the hooks as he leaned closer to Rutu.

"*You're terrible.*"

"*Oh, come on,*" Rutu said, nodding over Juki's shoulder. "*Look how terrified he is.*"

Juki turned slowly, seeing that Sam was more nervous than ever, his hand reaching shakily for the door handle, prepared to run if the demons made one sudden move. Juki then turned back to Rutu, leaning even closer.

"*Try to behave yourself,*" he said with a tender smile.

"*I am behaving myself.*"

"I-Is...uh, is everything alright?" Sam asked, his voice cracking with nerves.

"Yes," Juki said, straightened and returning to Sam. "Sleep deprivation has gotten the best of him. Just ignore him."

The tour continued with Sam's heart beating so loud and fast that the demons could hear it laboring in his chest. He explained what every room in the facility had been used for, though it did nothing more than aggravate his nerves. The shared smiles and laughs of the two demon lords made him feel like he was showing his own murderers around their torturous playground.

"And that's pretty much everything," Sam said with a forced laugh. "Shall we go to the office, then? Discuss terms?"

"Before we do," Rutu started, his smile fading, "I must ask that you call your men out of the shadows. If you want us watched, then you best do it in plain sight. We feel more threatened with them sneaking around behind us."

Sam's eyes went wide. Juki did not think it was possible for the human to go paler until that moment. He choked on his next words.

"I-I'm sorry?"

"Your hired bodyguards," Rutu clarified. "Three demons and three humans, it feels like. Is that correct? Former Guardians?" Rutu turned his eyes to the rafters and the machines dotting the facility. "We do not mind if they want to guard you, but they better do it in our field of vision if they wish to continue living."

"I-I...I don't—"

"It's alright," Juki said, patting the man on the cheek. "You didn't know what to expect when we called you. But it has been increasingly aggravating having them sneak around behind us."

"I'm-I'm so, so sorry, sirs. I-I just..." Sam was shaking uncontrollably, feeling cold and clammy as he stared into Juki's vibrant eyes. "C-Come out!" he called to the six former Guardians he had hired.

Slowly, stunned at being spotted, the figures emerged. The demons were watching the two lords warily, unsure exactly who they were due to their disguises, but feeling very threatened by the intense energy surrounding them. The human Guardians also found themselves nervous, but they could not pinpoint why.

"Thank you," Juki said. "Now, let's go to your office and discuss terms of purchase."

The terrified man led the two demon lords to the old foreman's office, the six hired guards following cautiously. Juki and Rutu sat in the two chairs on the other side of the desk as the man sat behind it, nervously looking at the six stationed outside the door.

"I am so terribly sorry about that," he murmured. "I-I'm sure you understand that I was very nervous after receiving your call. Generally, law states that property cannot be sold to demons, only rented."

"We are aware," Juki said. "We have special clearance. We are allowed to purchase and own property in any realm."

"Then, if I may be so bold to ask…why are you interested in this property?"

"An associate of ours is interested in this building," Juki said simply.

"An a-associate?" Sam repeated nervously. "I-I hope you don't think I'm being too forward, but…I-I do know of your other title."

"As the Trade Masters?" Juki asked knowingly.

"Yes. So you can understand my concern that this building might be used for…some kind of trafficking. An outpost for your…*business*."

Juki chuckled. "You misunderstand. This is not for the Trade. We cannot use any property in the human realms to expand the influence of the Trade. That would be against our agreements with Vestera Hizoku."

"Oh," the man said. "But…if this is not for the Trade…"

"As I said, an associate is interested in this for personal use. A quiet place for him to work. We're purchasing this building for him. That allows us to keep a close eye on exactly what he's doing here."

"He? A-Another demon?"

"Yes."

"Do you mean…is this building going to be part of something illegal?" Sam asked, trying to strengthen his voice unsuccessfully. "Because I cannot sell it to you knowing that you have illegal intent."

"You needn't worry," Juki said. "This building will not be caught in the middle of any illegal activity." Juki nodded to Rutu, who grabbed the duffel and opened it. "Here is our offer," he said, as Rutu gathered several stacks of bound bills, setting them on the desk as Sam's eyes grew wider with each bundle of cash. "We will pay, upfront, in cash, the entire amount you have asked. We will also add five percent, something we hope will ease your mind about the use of this property."

Sam's quivering hands motioned to the money as he looked at Juki quizzically. Juki nodded. The human took one of the stacks and flipped through it slowly, his mouth falling open as he realized just how much money was sitting on the desk.

"This…all this in cash?" he whispered. Rutu placed the duffle bag on the table next to the extracted stacks, showing Sam the rest of the money. "But…this is such a large sum…"

"Money is trivial to us." Juki waved the statement away. "We are willing to pay what we have stated before. If this property is caught in any illegal activity and the transaction is traced back to you, you will tell any authorities that demons forced you to sign the building over and that you were not made privy to the future use. DPC Law D-9342, section three will allow you to be cleared of all possible charges if you find yourself in trouble because of this sale. You might want to write that down, just in case."

Sam could only stare at Juki, his mouth agape as his mind chewed over the information.

"Why would you tell me that?" he asked quietly.

"Because we want you to take the deal. And because we are very certain that this building will not be found hosting any illegal activities." Juki extended his hand across the desk. "Do you accept?"

Sam looked between the duffel bag and Juki's outstretched hand before nodding slowly and accepting the handshake.

Chapter Twenty-Six

The knocking was louder the second time and it finally stirred the two sleeping figures. One removed his forearm from his eyes as he blinked against the harsh, yellow glow of the bedside lamp. The other started to uncurl from the armchair in the corner, papers scattering to the floor as he cursed.

"That was a bad idea..." Rutu sighed, rolling the stiffness from his neck.

"I told you to come to bed," Juki said, standing.

"I was trying to get some work done," Rutu grumbled, lazily sliding the papers together before slapping them on the foot of the bed as Juki walked to the hotel room door. He looked through the peephole before groaning.

"Can we get at least three hours of sleep without being interrupted by something?" he said irritably as he opened the door.

"I didn't think you would be sleeping," Shannon quipped, pushing past Juki and looking around the small hotel room, smiling to herself at how uncomfortable the demon lords likely were in the cramped, dark quarters.

"What else would we be doing?" Juki said, closing the door, not sure if he had the strength to deal with Shannon's attitude.

"I'm sure I don't know," Shannon said suggestively, sitting on the bed and crossing her legs, being sure to hike up her short skirt. "Tell me, Lord Juki, what other things can two people do in a hotel room together?"

"Where is Acurala?" Rutu asked, looking between the door and Shannon. "I thought he was with you."

"Yokouro has him making preparations for the Guardians." She opened her purse and pulled out a large folder that had papers slipping out at odd angles. "He also asked me to deliver this."

Juki took the folder and opened it, glancing over the top sheet before closing it again and trying to hand it back to her.

"No."

"No?" she said with a startled laugh. "This is a direct order from Yokouro."

"I don't care," Juki said. "I refuse."

"He didn't give you the option to refuse," Shannon said. "He told me that, if you two pitched a fit, I was to remind you that you pledged yourselves to him."

Rutu took the folder from Juki to look over the information as Juki narrowed his eyes at the human woman.

"If he knew that we would refuse this order, he knows it's a bad idea. And I don't care if I've pledged my resources to him, I don't need to follow every order."

"Well, he is getting rather concerned," Shannon said, leaning back on her hands and giving Juki a confident smirk. "He's beginning to think you two are undermining every action he takes. You boys seem to be losing your touch. First, you let the demon Elder escape, then you lose track of his sister and her special little dagger, and now you're trying to make changes to his plan." She clicked her tongue against the roof of her mouth. "I think not following through with this order might be the final nail in your coffins."

"You think Yokouro will kill us?" Juki scoffed. "He wouldn't dare try."

"Then at least ease his suspicions," Shannon suggested. "Deal with those Guardians," she nodded to the folder Rutu was glancing through.

"He may be losing his trust in us," Rutu started, snapping the folder closed, "but he should trust us to tell him when something is a bad idea. And this," he lifted the folder, "is a very bad idea. It's going to bring a lot of scrutiny to the tournament from other Guardians and he can't afford that right now."

"Well he has to give you something to do," Shannon said. "Because he's putting Acurala in charge of Dalton and the others."

"Out of the question," Juki said sharply. Shannon's eyebrows rose.

"Oh?" She stood, walking slowly closer to Juki, her smile growing. "Interesting. You were just saying how exhausted you were and how you just wanted to get some sleep, but you refuse to let Acurala relieve you of some of your burden?"

"He cannot handle what Yokouro wants," Juki said. "He's been too volatile lately. If Yokouro wants this to work, it needs to be very precise."

"Acurala said he would be happy to do it," Shannon said. "And Yokouro feels more comfortable having someone who won't question or undermine his every move." She turned her eyes to Rutu. "What about you? You're supposed to know everything. Do you think Acurala can't handle it?"

"I know he can't," Rutu said strongly. "He is more likely to destroy Dalton or push him too far in the opposite direction. Acurala has no experience with this. So, go back to Yokouro and tell him that we will take over for Team Dalton, and Acurala can go back to the smaller tasks with you. We can't leave something like this to chance."

"Hmm…" Shannon pretended to ponder for a moment. "No, I think I'll follow Yokouro's orders on this. Unlike *some*, I am loyal."

"Congratulations," Rutu groaned. "Get out."

Shannon laughed, crossing her arms over her chest.

"A bit rude, *Lord* Rutu."

"It's not worth wasting my time trying to convince you of anything," Rutu said. "Yokouro has you wrapped so tight around his finger that nothing I say will even get through to you. So you go scurry back to his bed, and wait for him to praise what a good job you've done. Meanwhile, we'll be trying to keep your son alive, since Yokouro insists on moronic moves that are more likely to send the entire universe into chaos than achieve what he wishes. The only thing I will tell you to tell Yokouro is that, whatever damage is done, it is entirely on his head. I won't step in to save him."

"I've heard about your power, Rutu, but I don't have the same faith in your knowledge or abilities as everyone else." She stuck a manicured finger into the center of his chest, as if trying to pierce through him. "I'm a woman that has to see it to believe it."

"He told you to get out," Juki said darkly. "I suggest you do so."

"Happily. I don't need to be talked down to by Yokouro's disobedient lackeys." She brushed past Rutu, nearly bumping into him as she started toward the door. She put her hand on the handle before smiling over her shoulder at them. "By the way, you better take care of those Guardians before the next set of matches. Or Yokouro might ask Acurala to take over that job, as well."

She opened the door and strode confidently into the hall as Juki and Rutu sighed, turning to one another with tired and annoyed expressions.

~∧~

Dalton was both embarrassed and invigorated sneaking through the narrow hallways of Master Bowen's Guardian Training Center. He did not enjoy feeling as though he needed to peer around every corner like a thief, but he did not want to be seen by trainers or apprentices, as it had become difficult to avoid lengthy conversations with them once spotted. But he also felt a glimmer of child-like excitement at slinking around the hallways toward the back offices.

He found Master Bowen's office where it had always been. There was a sense of comfortable familiarity about the crowded, slightly-disheveled office of his former master. The bookshelves were still crowded with Guardian Code books, stacked in whatever way they could fit on the warping shelves. The desk was too large for the small room, and it was constantly covered in piles of papers and files that needed to be sorted. Dalton walked to the mismatched chairs on the opposite side of the desk, remembering how small he had felt sitting in those chairs as a child when he was being scolded for being out after hours, or trying a particularly daring and dangerous stunt performed by reckless boys in their youth.

But there was one memory he held of sitting in that chair, shying away from a red-faced woman as she pointed at him, trying to convince Master Bowen that Dalton was too dangerous to be around "normal" people.

He placed his hands on the back of one of the chairs, taking a deep, calming breath to combat the memory.

The sound of approaching footsteps caused Dalton to run to the door, pressing himself to the wall and flicking off the light just before the door opened.

A man walked into the office, stopping just in front of the open door, not even lifting his hand to the light switch.

"I know you're in here," he muttered. "Don't hide in the shadows."

Dalton remained still, scarcely breathing.

He let out a startled yelp when he was yanked by his arm away from the wall and flung to the ground.

"I told you, stay out of arm's length!" Master Bowen laughed, flicking on the lights and closing his office door. "It's a miracle you don't get hurt more on your cases."

"I was just testing you, old man," Dalton teased, getting to his feet to face his former master. Time had taken its toll on Master Bowen's face, but he was still sharp as ever. The grey hair and wrinkles around his blue eyes were a deceptive mask of infirmity that had everyone underestimating the elderly Guardian trainer.

"It's good to see you, Dalton," Master Bowen said with a warm smile, hugging Dalton briefly. "But if I may ask, why did you sneak into my office? I'm fairly certain they would have let you in through the front door."

Dalton smiled thinly, heaving a sigh.

"I need to talk to someone…I think you're the only one I can turn to."

"This must be about Andrew taking the oath," Master Bowen said knowingly, sitting heavily in his creaking desk chair as Dalton sat across from him. "Struggling to let him go?"

"No, it's not—I mean, yes, that's something that's bothering me. But it's not the main reason I came here today."

"I'm afraid I won't be of much help on your cases, Dalton. I'm not a Guardian. I'm just a trainer," Master Bowen said. "And I have been meaning to talk to you about Andrew. I want to know why you haven't had him take the oath, yet. He should have been sworn in as a Guardian six months ago."

Dalton's eyes went wide. "You really think he's ready?"

"I do."

"But I still have so much to teach him," Dalton said. "He's not ready for the job. He's still a child."

"He's had more training than you had when you took the oath," Master Bowen noted. "He will learn with his advisor, just as you did. The only way to adequately prepare him beyond what we provide here is for him to learn on the job."

"He's just a kid."

Master Bowen leaned back in his chair, offering a sympathetic smile.

"I know."

Dalton shook his head. "I guess...I don't really want Andrew to be a Guardian. It's what he's always wanted, and he's been an incredible student. But he could be so much more. He could become a member of Council, or a doctor. If he becomes a Guardian..."

"It's difficult to be on the other side looking back, isn't it?" Master Bowen said slowly.

"If he were to die...that would be on me."

"How so?"

"It would mean I didn't train him enough. That I didn't give him all the tools he needed to survive. How could I live with myself? He doesn't understand this job, not really. And I don't think that I can knowingly let him go into this life. I'm putting him in danger."

"Andrew has chosen this," Master Bowen said. "I know it can be difficult when you see a bright child choose a life of hardship and pain. But there are some destinies that cannot be derailed."

Dalton's brow furrowed at Master Bowen's choice of words.

"Destiny?"

The older man shrugged. "I didn't want *you* to be a Guardian. You were always too smart and too empathic for the job. But you were determined. You had to save as many people as you could."

Dalton scoffed. "I've killed more people than I've saved."

"You feel very deeply, Dalton," Master Bowen said. "I was worried that, as a Guardian, you would lose that empathy. But instead, it has grown deeper. It's one of your best qualities as a man. But I imagine it is one of the hardest parts of being a Guardian."

"What if...I *have* lost that empathy?" Dalton whispered.

"What do you mean?"

"I..." Dalton took a deep breath, closing his eyes. "I feel like I'm losing myself, Master." He dropped his head. "I feel like I'm losing my humanity. Half the time I don't understand what's going on in my own head. And my powers...they're growing. And they're hurting people again."

"You mean what happened at the tournament?" Master Bowen said with a knowing nod. "I told you before, Dalton. You can't ignore your powers forever. Eventually, they'll return to the surface."

"I can't let them, though," Dalton said sharply, fixing the older man with a dark glare. "I'm too dangerous to be around other people."

"No, Dalton, you're not."

"Am I even human?" Dalton choked.

"Yes," Master Bowen said strongly. He looked over Dalton's conflicted expression. "You've learned of Yasuain and Kuryaoin, then."

Dalton's eyes shot wide, not only at the mention of the dragons in his dreams, but also that Master Bowen knew the information.

"You *knew*?"

"I've known for a while."

"And you never thought to *tell me*?" Dalton gawked. "I *killed* another kid, and you *knew* it was because of some dragon magic I had inside me? But you never told me?"

"You were eight," Master Bowen said. "I'm not even sure *I* understand it, and you think I would have been able to explain it to a child?"

"That would have been better than trying to tell me that it was just self-defense and I had no reason to feel guilty."

"It *was* self-defense," Master Bowen said, leaning forward. "Dalton, he was going to shoot you. Your dragon magic defended you."

"He was going to shoot me because he knew I was too dangerous to live around people," Dalton mumbled, rubbing his face roughly as he hid his head in his hands.

"You're not some monster that needs to be locked away," Master Bowen insisted, walking to stand in front of Dalton. "You're a good man, Dalton. You're powerful. That doesn't make you evil."

"How did you keep that quiet?" Dalton whispered, slowly turning his eyes back to his master. "How did you keep his death quiet? I should have been kicked out of training. Did my grandfather pay you to keep me here?"

"No," Master Bowen said. "I actually never told your grandfather about that incident."

"Then how did you keep it quiet?"

"...I was offered money to pay off anyone who would raise a fuss," Master Bowen said honestly, though he could not meet Dalton's gaze. "They said that it was imperative that your training continued."

"They?"

"Two demons," Master Bowen said. "The Kage Lords."

Dalton's jaw dropped.

"Juki and Rutu...*paid* you to keep me here?"

"They were the ones who explained the spirit of the dragon Kuryaoin to me," Master Bowen said with a slow nod. "And they explained that it was more dangerous to leave you untrained than to pay off anyone who would raise a fuss trying to get you kicked out of the center."

Dalton ran a hand through his hair in frustration.

"The damn Kage Lords..." he groaned. "So my entire life hinged on them paying you."

"I'm sorry I didn't tell you earlier, about all of this," Master Bowen said. "I never felt that there was a good time to bring it up. You climbed the ranks so quickly and then you went into that very dark depression. Then Frieda, and Theresa, and...time just got away from me."

Dalton closed his eyes, a pained expression crossing his features.

"...I didn't recognize her."

"Who?"

"Theresa..." Dalton muttered. Frustrated tears began to pool at the corners of his eyes. "I didn't recognize my own daughter after the tournament. She was a stranger to me. Now she can't even look at me. She's afraid of me."

"Dalton..." Master Bowen's expression became concerned. "You mean, you haven't..."

"Haven't what?"

"You still haven't mastered Kuryaoin?"

"*Mastered*? I don't even entirely know what it is!" Dalton snapped, exasperated. "I'm slowly putting pieces together that it's a dragon, but I have no idea how I have dragon powers, or why I seem to just *check out* when these powers take hold. I have no control once they come to the surface, and it's getting harder and harder to keep this new magic in check. It feels like every time I try to use magic, I end up hurting someone."

Master Bowen leaned against the front of his desk, shaking his head.

"I'm sorry. I thought…your trainer should have found you and taught you."

"Jikia may be a dragon, but she doesn't understand what's happening to me, either."

"No, no, there's an entity. You haven't had any dream conversations with shadows? Or heard a voice when you were alone that explained any of this to you?"

Dalton's face turned pale.

"Tell me you're joking," he murmured. "I have been hearing a voice on occasion. It's come to me and…I suppose directed me on different paths."

"But nothing about the dragon Kuryaoin?"

"Only a little bit a few days ago," Dalton said. "Are you telling me I have some sort of…prophetic trainer?"

"No," Master Bowen said. "He's a spirit that has traveled through many planes of existence to learn about the dragons Kuryaoin and Yasuain. He was meant to explain this to you." He let out a long breath. "I'm so sorry, Dalton. If I had known you were still in the dark, I would come to explain what I knew."

Dalton let out a tired bark of laughter.

"I shouldn't even be surprised," he said. "I don't know anything. Everyone is keeping me in the dark. No one told me about Yokouro. No one told me about this dragon magic. No one is telling me anything." His eyes hardened into a dark glare. "But the moment this secrecy put my wife and daughter in danger, it went too far. I need to understand what's happening to me so I can keep them safe."

"Of course," Master Bowen said with a strong nod. "Again, I'm sorry, Dalton. I didn't know that things had progressed this way."

"Just tell me what you know, Master."

"Your bloodline is linked with the dragon spirit Kuryaoin," Master Bowen said. "You don't just have dragon magic inside of you, you have a dragon *spirit*. Yokouro's bloodline is linked with the dragon spirit Yasuain. These two dragons have been dueling for centuries. They're destined to fight until one is soundly defeated in a fair battle. And the outcome of that battle will decide the fate of humans in these realms."

"Decide the fate of humans?" Dalton repeated with wide eyes. "Are you saying that, if I lose, these dragons will wipe out humanity?"

"I don't know."

"Am I supposed to unleash this dragon spirit on Yokouro?" Dalton asked. "Is that how I defeat him?"

"I'm afraid it's not that simple," Master Bowen said. "The two dragon spirits fight from their vessels. Their bodies are long gone. Kuryaoin relies on you."

"This dragon spirit is a separate entity inside of me?" Dalton asked, unsuccessful at keeping the horror out of his voice.

"Yes," Master Bowen confirmed. "You weren't strong enough to handle Kuryaoin when you were a child. Your body had to grow stronger and your own powers had to mature before you would be able to handle sharing a consciousness with the dragon spirit. You were supposed to gradually have a meeting of minds as you matured, but something has kept that from happening."

"Then how do I have this meeting of minds with this dragon spirit? Will that help me keep control over these new powers?"

"I assume that will help you control the magic, yes," Master Bowen said. "But your fear of your powers has suppressed this dragon spirit. I think that is why you lose control when those powers come to the surface."

"How do I stop that from happening?" Dalton asked. "How do I come to an understanding with this dragon spirit?"

Master Bowen fell very silent, turning his eyes away from Dalton, avoiding answering.

"Master?"

He sighed heavily.

"My understanding is that there is a way to...*force* your mind to meet with Kuryaoin's. A means to force you to merge with him," he said hesitantly.

"How would I do that?" Dalton asked, worried that Master Bowen refused to meet his eyes.

"It would be a type of ritual torture," Master Bowen said quietly. "A physical and mental torment that would be designed to break you down to the point where you have no other means of survival than to accept Kuryaoin and incorporate him. Without your unconscious understanding, that dragon spirit will continue to be pushed away until it breaks to the surface and takes control, like it's done in the past."

"Is there some other way that doesn't involve *torture*?" Dalton asked sharply.

"I don't know," Master Bowen said. "Let me do some digging for you. I'll see if I can track down the entity who was supposed to explain this to you, and see if I can find more information about how to combine your powers with the dragon's. I'll be sure to let you know what I find."

Dalton did not tell anyone about his meeting with Master Bowen, and he was able to hide his anxiety relatively well. The following morning, he silently sipped his coffee as he tried not to let his imagination run away with possibilities of what ritual torture could possibly fuse him with the dragon powers within him. He was trying to think of ways he could meditate deeply enough to connect with the dragon spirit when he noticed that it was getting close to lunch time, and Hanyi still had not come out of his room. The other Guardians had joined Dalton for coffee and a walk around the neighborhood, but Keito had said that Hanyi was still sleeping and to leave him be.

But now Dalton was worried.

"Is he alright?" he asked Keito, glancing at the stairs after looking at his watch once more. "Should someone go check on him?"

"Just let him rest," Keito said.

"I'm just going to go make sure he's okay," Dalton said, moving toward the stairs.

"Dalton," Keito called, motioning him back to the living room, "the best thing you can do for him right now is leave him be."

"Is he sick?" Dalton had been so wrapped up in everything going on with his powers and the tournament that he had forgotten Hanyi's symptoms up at the lake. When he remembered what Keito said about the strain on Hanyi's mate bond with Xana, his heart fell. "Wait…is this the mate bond thing again? Is Xana okay?"

Keito let out a long sigh, dropping his head.

"Xana died early this morning," he murmured.

For several long moments, the Guardians were still, slowly digesting the words and their meaning. Dalton stepped back to the couch, sitting heavily as his eyes went distant.

"Why didn't you tell us earlier?" he whispered.

"He asked me not to," Keito said. "Hanyi is not the type to talk about his own problems. He'll hide them and bury them until they become too big for him to handle alone. He didn't want to tell you Xana was sick, and he doesn't want to upset you or make you worry now that she's gone."

"How can we not worry?" Mitoki asked. "His mate died. He should go home and be with his family."

Keito sighed. "I agree. But he won't go. I tried to tell him to leave, but he insisted he needed to be here to help us. I did my best to convince him, but he's stubborn as hell." The demon shook his head. "Hanyi is truly remarkable. He has a very complex string of loyalties and priorities that I have never been able to figure out. He says that fighting Yokouro takes priority over his personal matters. He asked for today to mourn, and said that he'll be back with us tomorrow."

"How can he just...decide like that?" Dalton asked.

"I'm sure it wasn't easy," Keito muttered. "Like I said, Hanyi's complicated. Honestly, I think it will cause him more pain if we fight him about his decision. If we tell him that the mission is not the priority, and keep telling him that over and over again, he's going to think something's wrong with him for not immediately deciding to go home."

Dalton cupped his hands over his nose and mouth and took a deep breath.

"I can't believe Xana is gone..." he whispered. "Is there anything we can do?"

Keito shook his head.

"For now, it's best to just leave Hanyi alone and let him mourn. Losing a mate is a very deep pain."

Dalton's stomach fell. "I'm sorry, Keito, I didn't mean to bring up painful memories..."

"I've had four decades to mourn the loss of my mate," Keito said. "But I remember the first few days. I did what Hanyi's doing. I locked myself away and let the pain consume me."

"What happened to Xana?" Eclipse asked quietly, his eyes low. "At the lake you said she was sick..."

"Hanyi said she was sick," Keito said. "And she was quite old, even for a Treneke wolf. It seems that the entire pack was expecting it for the past month or so."

Unable to think of anything he could say, Dalton excused himself from the living room, walking to the home office where his wife was answering her messages. He knocked lightly on the door and waited for her to call him inside.

"Hey," she greeted with a smile. "Are you guys heading out somewhere?"

"No," Dalton said, walking up to her chair and placing his hands on her shoulders. She looked up at him, smiling gently.

"What is it?"

"You know I love you, right?"

She placed a hand on his. "Of course I know that, Dalton," she said. "I love you, too."

He gently pulled her out of her chair, turning her so he could wrap his arms around her, cradling her head under his as he closed his eyes and listened to her breathing. Her arms went around his waist as she leaned into him.

"Are you alright?" she whispered.

"I just want to be here with you," he breathed, closing his eyes and relishing in her closeness, searing the feeling into his memory, never wanting to let her go.

~/\~

Keito had some regrets about telling the Guardians about Xana's passing. It made the day much darker, and all of them disappeared for a while. Mitoki called his fiancée and Eclipse called Tarrena while Dalton spent some time with his wife before Theresa came home.

Keito had spent his time in the backyard, watching the clouds pass over the treetops, thinking of his own lost mate, trying to remember her as she was before the Tournament Slaughter—before he saw her lifeless body. He could understand Hanyi's need to stay away for a while. He was not prepared to confront the reality.

Keito remained out of the guest room until everyone else had gone to sleep. Frieda had put aside a plate for Hanyi, which Keito took up to the room, but even as he set it down next to Hanyi, the wolf appeared disinterested. Hanyi had moved from the foot of the bed to the floor, curled up tight, his tail covering most of his face. Keito sat by Hanyi's head, leaning against the footboard, trying to think of anything to say that would ease Hanyi's pain.

The only thing he could think to do was place his hand on Hanyi's back and remain silent.

He did not know how long they sat in silence before Hanyi's voice came to him telepathically.

"*Are they worried about me?*"

"Of course they are," Keito murmured. "Are you upset I told them?"

"*No, I figured they would demand an explanation.*" Hanyi took a deep breath. "*It hurts. I feel the emptiness on the other side of the bond...I can't describe it...*"

"You don't have to," Keito assured.

"*I've been preparing myself all week...reaching out to her...she was trying to hold on until we could say a proper goodbye...*" Hanyi

278

let out a long sigh. *"I never planned on outliving her. I had every intention of dying as soon as my sons were old enough. I figured I was already on borrowed time. But I never thought…she would go before me…"*

"Why didn't you reach out to me and tell me you were feeling like that?" Keito whispered.

"I figured you had enough to deal with. My problems seemed pathetic compared to yours."

"They're not, Hanyi," Keito said. "And I'm sorry I ever made you feel that way."

"I feel sick for not rushing back home," Hanyi admitted. *"I know I should be with my children…but I want to stay here. I just…can't face it right now."* He let out a broken laugh. *"I remember I was so mad at you after Sadee's death. I was furious with you for locking yourself away for three damn years."* He closed his eyes. *"But right now, disappearing for three years sounds like a good idea."*

"You don't have to stay," Keito insisted. "If you want to leave, even if it's just to go off on your own and mourn, then go."

"I can't. Not with the tournament."

"Screw the tournament," Keito groaned.

"What about Yokouro?" Hanyi asked. *"What about those creepy people who keep spying on the house?"*

Keito turned quickly to Hanyi.

"What?"

"It was probably a really good thing I was in here all day," Hanyi said. *"I've seen about a dozen men pass by the house every other hour. A few have even been casing the house from the neighbor's roof."*

Keito immediately moved to the window, carefully parting the blinds to look over the neighbor's house. He remained completely still for several minutes, watching the silhouette of the rooftop for any signs of movement. He had begun to hold his breath in anticipation when he saw a shadowy lump move to scratch its nose, pressed against the neighbor's chimney.

"Apparently, I'm not paranoid," Keito whispered. "Something has felt off since the day we got back here."

Hanyi walked over to the window and tried to nose his way under the blind, but ended up whimpering in frustration when he could not get his head under the blinds completely. Keito fell to a crouch next to the wolf.

"Hanyi, if you want to go home, this might be your last time to do it. I have a bad feeling that Yokouro has been planning something big."

"I'm not going home, yet," Hanyi said. *"Xana is gone, but if I leave, and something happens here, I could never live with myself for not being here to help."*

Chapter Twenty-Seven

Dalton's eyes were bleary as he poured himself a cup of coffee the following morning. He walked back into the living room just as Eclipse and Mitoki were descending the stairs. Dalton returned to the kitchen and poured them coffee as well, only to return to the coffee maker a third time when Frieda joined them in the living room. He stubbornly sat down and refused to serve anyone else coffee, irritable from lack of sleep the previous night.

"Someone woke up on the wrong side of the bed," Mitoki noted.

"Someone didn't sleep more than two hours," Dalton corrected.

"Worried about Hanyi?" Mitoki deduced. Dalton nodded, smiling gently at Frieda when she took his hand.

"I just don't know what to say to him," Dalton muttered.

"You could start with good morning," a voice said at the top of the stairs. Everyone jumped, turning to see Hanyi walking down the staircase, his eyes surrounded by dark bags, but he was still smiling. "And is there more coffee?"

"I'll get you some," Dalton said quickly, standing.

"So much for not serving anyone else," Eclipse teased lightly.

Frieda set her mug down on the coffee table and walked to Hanyi with a sympathetic smile.

"Would it be alright if I gave you a hug?"

His smile widened. "I'll never turn down a hug." He wrapped his arms around her as she hugged him tightly.

"If you need anything, let me know."

"Thank you," Hanyi said mechanically as he broke away from the hug. He dropped his head as he pushed away the tears that had gathered on his bottom lashes. "Sorry…guess there are still some tears left."

"Here, Hanyi," Dalton said, handing him a mug of coffee. "Where's Keito?"

"Sleeping." Hanyi's grin turned mischievous. "I wore him out keeping him up all night."

The other Guardians looked at one another, not sure how to react to the joke.

Hanyi chuckled. "Sorry, humor is my coping mechanism."

"No, it's fine, it's just…" Dalton did not know how to complete the sentence.

"You're acting awkward around me," Hanyi noted, taking a sip of coffee. "There's no need to."

"But...Xana..."

"I know," Hanyi whispered, lowering his gaze again. "I'm sorry I didn't tell you sooner. I knew it was coming. She was very sick."

"Why don't you go home to your pack?" Eclipse asked gently.

"Because it won't bring her back," Hanyi said. "And...I don't think I can face everyone just yet. I'm still trying to process the reality of her passing." Hanyi lifted his coffee mug to his lips. "Plus, you will need me to protect you if Yokouro comes after you."

Smiling, Dalton nodded. "Okay. We're not going to press you about it," he said. "But you have to promise me that you won't hide stuff like that from us."

"Fair enough," the wolf agreed.

Half an hour later, there was a knock at the door. Frieda answered, trying not to show her worry that Shannon, who had been calling every day, might turn up at their door. But she relaxed when she saw Jikia and Tarrena on the front porch. As she welcomed the dragons inside, they both threw worried glances at Hanyi, having been told what happened, but startled by Hanyi's bright, cheerful greeting. They looked around the living room.

"Where's Theresa?" Jikia asked.

"At day camp."

"And Keito?"

"Sleeping," Hanyi answered.

"Will you wake him? There is something I need to tell all of you," Jikia said.

"Oh, that can only be good news..." Hanyi said sarcastically, ascending the stairs and returning a few minutes later with Keito. When the Guardians were all sat nervously in the living room, Jikia fixed them all with a stern look.

"There has been a lot of things going on outside of the ring this round of the tournament," she said. "We're not fighting tomorrow. We've been advanced automatically. The other teams were disqualified."

"What?!"

"Did the other teams call and drop out? Or were they injured in the first set?" Keito asked.

"I don't have all the details, but if I had to guess, I would say they were coerced out of the tournament. When I spoke with the Tournament Board and they told me about the advancement, they asked me if my team had been threatened or attacked. When I said no, they became indignant."

"Great," Hanyi groaned. "All the other teams get coerced out of the tournament, we remain untouched, and now it looks like the DPC has rigged it so that we win the tournament."

"Exactly," Jikia agreed.

"But, if Yokouro did this—which I'm assuming he did—why would he make it *easier* for us?" Eclipse asked. "I thought he liked seeing us fight in the tournament."

"Maybe he saw how difficult that first round was and didn't want to risk us being disqualified," Mitoki suggested.

"His silence this round of the tournament has me very concerned," Keito admitted. "I haven't heard of much activity back in the Demon Realm, so I know he's not distracted. He usually only goes this quiet when he's planning something big."

Dalton threw a quick glance around the room and then drew in a deep breath. "I think I have some idea of what he's planning."

"What do you think he's planning?" Hanyi asked.

"I think he's going to attack me...specifically me," he said. He lowered his eyes, rubbing his hands together nervously. "A few days ago, I went to speak with Master Bowen. I wanted to ask him what he knew about this new magic."

"Does he know something about dragon magic?" Jikia asked.

"No, he just...knows a lot about me," Dalton said. "I...I haven't told many people this, but when I was eight, and I was at Master Bowen's training center, I was bullied a lot because I was quite gifted...and as I continued my training, the other kids became afraid of me. Said that I was too powerful to be human. Thought I was a half-demon or some other non-human creature. And one night, a group of boys jumped me, and one of them had a gun." Dalton took a moment to collect himself before continuing. "I tried to run. They shot me. And I just blacked out. All I remember was seeing two of the boys on the ground and blood *everywhere*. Everyone was screaming. And the boy with the gun was dead...but there wasn't much left of him." He swallowed hard, trying to strengthen his voice. "Apparently, that was the work of a dragon spirit inside me. It reacted to my life being threatened back then. But now...it seems that those same powers are coming to the surface all the time."

"Like at the tournament?" Eclipse asked.

Dalton nodded slowly.

"What is the dragon spirit's name?" Jikia asked.

"Kuryaoin."

"I'm not familiar with the name," the older dragon said, shaking her head. "I should ask Vestera."

"Can we do that?" Dalton asked. "Because all Master Bowen could really tell me was that I was supposed to have a meeting of minds with this dragon, and that Yokouro might be able to force me to merge my powers with the dragon magic."

Everyone turned to Keito, hoping the demon had more answers. He lifted his hands and shook his head.

"I'm just as in the dark about this," he said quickly.

"How could Yokouro force you to merge powers with the dragon spirit?" Eclipse asked.

Dalton hesitated, turning to Frieda, who was pale on the couch next to him. He took her hand. "I don't want to scare you," he whispered.

"It's a little late for that," she tried to laugh.

"It would be a ritual of some kind. A very painful one," Dalton said, deciding not to use the exact words Master Bowen had used, not wanting to upset his wife further. "That makes me think that Yokouro's been so silent lately because he's planning that ritual. He said that he was training me, trying to get me to a certain point so that I can face him properly. I think this is the next step."

~/\~

Juki kicked the final bolt out of the machine and set it back on its feet. Looking it over, he tried to determine the best way to pick it up. Wrapping his hands around one corner, he tilted the machine to one side, slipping his hands under it and standing upright, straining only slightly against the weight.

Pivoting carefully to avoid hitting anything, his nose caught the scent of five people he desperately did not want to see. He groaned and turned again, still holding the machine. The five hooded figures were standing at the entryway to the back of the slaughterhouse, their leader laughing when Juki caught sight of them.

"Careful, old man. We wouldn't want you to throw out your back."

"Well, then, maybe you should carry it for me," Juki snarled, tossing the enormous hunk of metal toward them. They quickly retreated, tripping over each other, but the machine landed and tumbled only twice before coming to rest just in front of where they had been standing before.

"What the hell do you think you're doing?!" one of the women screeched at the demon lord.

"You said I was too old to carry it. You are all much younger than I," Juki laughed.

"Is there a reason you're destroying everything down there?" a voice called from one of the above offices. Everyone turned to Rutu, who was looking over the railing running alongside the warehouse wall.

"Oh, look, Juki," the leader sneered, "your pet is here."

Rutu rolled his eyes as Juki tried to suppress his snarl. Rutu descended the stairs to the main floor as the leader of the five looked between the two Kage Lords.

"That is correct, right? Since you're the leader of the clan, I assume you are Rutu's owner as well."

"Maybe, but you know what they say about the quiet ones," one of the other men taunted. "Juki could be the pet as soon as they're alone."

Juki's eyes narrowed.

"If you're going to talk down to me, at least have the decency not to hide when you do so," he growled, waving a hand in their direction, a burst of his magic knocking the hoods off their heads to reveal five very familiar faces.

"Nothing to say now?" Juki asked. "Why are you here, Jonathan?" he asked Elder Teban, who was standing at the front of the group of Elders. "Yokouro did not send for you and I remember explicitly telling you to stay the hell out of my way."

"You've overstepped your bounds," Elder Celeste snapped.

"We have bounds?" Rutu asked. "Funny, I thought we had clearance to do as we wished."

"We're talking about what you did with the Guardians in the tournament," Elder Ari said. "Council is having a fit and we don't know how to cover it up!"

"The Guardians are all still breathing, aren't they?" Juki asked.

"Yes," Elder Teban admitted reluctantly. "But they've all filed complaints that they were coerced out of the tournament. And with Team Dalton not being threatened at all, rumors are starting to spread about a DPC plot to have Team Dalton win the tournament."

"Then tell them the truth," Rutu said. "Tell them that a demon Old Blood Lord hired the Trade Masters to force the other teams out of the tournament in order to face Team Dalton in a battle that will decide the fate of humanity."

"That's *worse*," Elder Celeste snarled.

"Then perhaps you should just be content with the situation you have," Rutu said shortly.

"Juki, rein in your pet," Elder Teban snapped.

Rutu growled, taking a quick step forward, which made the Elders backpedal a few paces.

"That is *Lord* Juki to you, maggots," Rutu warned.

"Did Lord Yokouro ask you to take the Guardians out of the tournament in order to face Team Dalton, or did he see the trouble they encountered in the first set?" Elder Renard asked, placing a hand on Elder Teban's shoulder to keep him from retorting to Rutu's command.

"It's probably a combination," Juki admitted. "To be honest, we didn't ask for specifics. We merely followed our orders."

"You two are far too extreme," Elder Lunar growled. "Times have changed. Your methods are no longer acceptable."

"Really? Because they certainly are efficient," Rutu said with a dark smile, returning to Juki's side. "And I can assure you, we've adapted to the times. We've been in every period of human history. We know how to adjust."

"Then you should understand that this is particularly difficult for us to cover up," Elder Teban snapped. "No one trusts anyone in the DPC anymore. We've tried, but we can't just tell the council not to worry. We have to give them a reason to believe that everything is alright."

"Do you have any idea how many contacts we have in the DPC?" Juki asked, quirking an eyebrow. "You are not our only source of information. We know how the meetings have been going, and we know exactly how *little* you have been trying to contain the information."

The five fell silent, gawking at the Kage Lords.

"You've been *spying* on us?" Elder Lunar whispered in disbelief. Juki merely smiled in silent answer. "You two are menaces. You should be killed and ripped apart."

"Good luck with that," Juki laughed. "We didn't survive this long on luck."

"Your age is starting to show," Elder Teban said. "And with your power limiters on and the injuries you've been getting from your petty squabbles with your father, you might want to watch your back."

Juki smirked. "You have absolutely no concept of the amount of damage I could cause if I wanted, do you? I almost pity you. I may not be in my prime, and I may be injured, and I may have more power limiters on than I can count, but I could still destroy this entire realm with ease."

"Then why don't you, *Lord* Juki?" Elder Ari taunted.

"Where would be the fun in that?" Juki asked. "My pleasures in life are far more complex than Yokouro's. I don't want to destroy everything. I want to own it."

"Starting with the most powerful demon alive?" Elder Teban asked, nodding to Rutu. "Well, Rutu Kaneaka, the most powerful demon in history, reduced to being *owned* by the leader of the Kage Clan," the human Elder sneered. "How does it feel?"

Rutu smiled. "I like being owned. And if I wasn't mated to Juki, I would never have become the most powerful demon alive. Something for you to think about."

"Then your *owner* must have ordered you to go after those Guardians," Elder Lunar snarled. "Which means *you're* the person we need to punish," she completed, looking at Juki.

"You? Punish me?" Juki barked a laugh. "Don't be absurd."

"I could go to Vestera and explain to him what you did," Elder Teban challenged. "Then, I can make a motion to limit all contact you have within the DPC."

"Go right ahead," Juki said. "Go run to Vestera. See what he has to say. By the time you tell him anything, we will have already moved forward with Yokouro's plan. Unlike *some*, we actually get the job done."

Three of the Elders started forward, angry, their fists clenched, but Rutu extended his arm in front of Juki, glaring at the three approaching.

"Take one more step, and you will regret it."

"You won't kill us," Elder Ari chortled, even as the other two retreated, their eyes filled with fire, but knowing better than to stand against Rutu. "Yokouro ordered you to keep us alive."

"True," Rutu said. "But I can show you more pain than you ever imagined possible."

"Oh, right, your clan was known for torture, weren't they?" Elder Ari laughed hollowly. "Did they teach you some techniques? Were they teaching *babies* how to slice apart prisoners?"

Rutu's smile widened.

"My family may have been monsters, but give them some credit." Rutu's hand moved away from Juki, turning upward, his fingers flexing. "They waited until I was six before teaching me the art of torture."

Elder Ari let out a blood-curdling scream, falling to the ground as his left arm was yanked behind him, bending and twisting, bones snapping and mangling in midair as the others watched in terror. Elder Teban and Elder Celeste started forward, but halted once Rutu's eyes turned on them. Elder Ari fell to the side, his fingers popping and tangling, twisting into impossible angles.

Juki let out a dark chuckle.

"You should learn to respect your superiors."

Chapter Twenty-Eight

Keito was trying his best to hide his nerves, but he could feel something heavy in the air.

Once they learned that the tournament had been cancelled, Team Dalton and the two dragons had gone to the training center. They had every intention of using one of the empty training rooms to see if Dalton could control his new magic, but before they could start, Andrew, having heard where they were, entered the training room. None of the older Guardians had felt comfortable testing Dalton's volatile new powers around the younger man, so they spent two hours sparring with Andrew instead.

When the Guardian apprentice was called away for lunch, the Guardians had crowded into Master Bowen's office and asked him to explain everything he knew. Unfortunately, he did not know the specifics of the ritual that could force Dalton to merge with the dragon spirit, nor did he know how the fight between Yokouro and Dalton was supposed to happen in order for the fight to be "fair."

While all the Guardians were worried about what Yokouro could possibly be planning, Keito had the highest anxiety on the team.

The following morning, after a sleepless night, Keito took the opportunity of Hanyi taking a shower to try calling Vestera, but the dragon did not answer his call. After three failed attempts, Keito groaned in frustration, tapping his phone against the palm of his hand, staring out the window, trying not to shiver at the eyes he knew were watching the house.

He drew in a deep breath and lifted his phone once more, dialing another number.

When the phone buzzed twelve times without being answered, Keito knew Juki was ignoring him. He ended the call and, before he could think better of it, he called Rutu.

Still, there was no answer.

Since phone calls between demons were just telepathic connections, Keito knew that both the Kage Lords were aware he was trying to contact them, but they had purposely ignored him.

That only made Keito's anxiety grow.

He knew Yokouro better than most, and he had spent centuries learning Yokouro's patterns and tactics. But after hearing what Master Bowen knew about the connection between Yokouro and Dalton, Keito was worried he would not be able to predict what the demon lord was likely to do.

One more failed call to Vestera had Keito in a highly-agitated state.

"Do you really think they'll answer?"

Keito's head snapped around to look at Hanyi as the wolf left the bathroom, toweling his hair dry roughly.

"What?"

"Juki and Rutu? Do you really think they'll answer your call and just tell you what they're planning?"

"I was calling Vestera," Keito corrected with a groan, tossing his phone to the bed irritably.

"Oh, you mean, Mr. Don't-Act-Until-It's-Too-Late?" Hanyi quipped.

"Will you give him a break already?" Keito sighed. "He does the best he can. It makes sense that he can't come to help us yet if Dalton's got untapped dragon magic. Vestera's power could force Dalton's dragon spirit to the surface and kill him."

"You're always making excuses for him," Hanyi muttered. "We're on our own, Keito. Just like we've always been. Vestera didn't step in to save us before, and he's not going to do it now. Based on our history, I would put more faith in Juki or Rutu stepping in to help than Vestera."

Keito stood, pacing by the bed.

"I think this is about to get really bad, Hanyi," Keito said.

"You're working yourself up too much. Today, we'll tell Dalton about the people casing the house and we'll start preparing for an attack," Hanyi said.

Keito shook his head. "Do you remember when Yokouro captured us in the Realm of Light and held us in that warehouse for two weeks?"

"Hard to forget…" Hanyi grumbled, pulling on clean clothes and watching the anxious demon on the other side of the room. "You…don't think he's going to do something like that again, do you?"

"If he has to perform some sort of ritual to merge Dalton's powers before he can properly battle him…" Keito let out a long, shaky breath. "Hanyi, they're not ready for something like that."

Hanyi turned his eyes to the ground, nodding slowly.

"The first thing we need to do is secure the house, prepare for an attack, and keep an eye on Frieda and Theresa at all times," he said. He turned to leave the room, but stopped with his hand on the doorknob, slowly glancing over his shoulder at Keito. "You really have no idea what he's planning?"

Keito shook his head slowly.

"It's like he's disappeared entirely," the demon murmured.

Hanyi drew in a deep breath.

"I'm going to go talk to Frieda first," he said.

"Hanyi," Keito called his attention. "With the rest of this round cancelled, whatever Yokouro has planned might keep us here for a long time. If you want to return to your pack, you should."

Hanyi's expression remained stoic. He stared at the demon for a long moment before nodding shallowly.

"You're right. I should."

He left the room, leaving the door open as Keito sighed in exasperation at Hanyi's stubbornness. He snatched up his phone once again and pocketed it, wondering if he should try to call the demon lords again. He started to walk toward the open door when two figures stepped through the doorway, Mitoki lightly knocking.

"Hey, where's Hanyi?" he asked.

"He just went downstairs," Keito said, looking between Eclipse and Mitoki. "What's going on?"

"We've been talking, trying to figure out what's going on with Dalton," Eclipse said.

"Any luck making heads or tails of it?" Keito asked.

"Not exactly," Mitoki said. "But we thought about how Yokouro attacked Eclipse last round. How he knew that Eclipse didn't have control over his Antiquan Angel magic, and counted on him losing his focus during the fight. What if Yokouro wants to do the same with Dalton, but on a bigger scale? Outside the tournament?"

"You think Dalton's a danger to the public?" Keito asked.

"You didn't see him during that last fight," Eclipse muttered. "He beat the demon Guardian unconscious in under three minutes and then mentally checked out for the rest of the day. He stared at you for over an hour while you were unconscious. He would not leave your side." Eclipse shook his head. "We wondered if maybe that was because he sensed demon energy and was waiting for you to wake up and see if you were a threat before attacking you, too."

"Even with what you told me about Dalton's fight and his powers, he still doesn't have enough strength to defeat Yokouro," Keito said. "And even if Dalton loses himself with his powers, I don't think he'd be a danger to civilians."

"He doesn't want to train to find out, though," Eclipse insisted. "We offered to go with him to the training center again today, but he said he would rather go to the DPC compound and look up these dragon spirits in the archives. He's avoiding it. And we saw how avoiding his powers worked at the tournament."

Keito let out a heavy sigh.

"I'm going to tell you two, but please stay calm," he started. "I think Yokouro is going to attack us in the next few days. And I don't think it's safe for us to leave Frieda and Theresa unprotected."

"What makes you think he'll attack so soon?" Eclipse demanded.

"Men have been casing the house for the last few days," he said. "Who knows how long they've been doing it."

"What? When did you notice that?!" Mitoki gasped.

"Hanyi noticed a few days ago. We've been keeping an eye on them since," the demon said.

"We need to tell Dalton," Eclipse said, turning to leave the room when Keito grabbed his arm and pulled him back.

"I agree, but not this instant," Keito said.

"What? Why?"

"Because I'm worried about sending Dalton into a blind rage," Keito said. "You said it yourself, he doesn't really have a sense of these powers. And if he gets frightened enough, this dragon magic is going to come forward to protect him, which could spell disaster for a lot of people."

"So what are we supposed to do?" Mitoki asked.

"Hanyi is going to talk to Frieda, and I'm going to talk to Dalton," Keito explained. "Eclipse, why don't you call Jikia and Tarrena and tell them to come to the house. Mitoki, go around the house and make sure all the windows are locked. Maybe put an alarm warding on them to alert us if someone tries to break in."

The two younger Guardians nodded hesitantly, uncomfortable with keeping the information from Dalton, but understanding Keito's reasoning. The three left the room, Keito walking slowly downstairs, where Theresa was seated quietly on the couch, studying a puzzle she was putting together on the coffee table, still dressed in her pajamas with her hair sticking up at all angles.

"Good morning, monkey!" Keito laughed, startling her as he leaned over the back of the couch and hugged her, even spooking Rio, who was sleeping next to her. "How you this morning?"

"Good!" Theresa said with a broad grin, turning to kneel on the couch so she could hug Keito around the neck.

"Now that it's the weekend, you're stuck with us!" the demon chuckled.

"Can we go play outside on the swing set?" she asked with a wide grin.

"Maybe later. You need to go upstairs and get dressed and brush your hair and teeth first," he said. "And I have to make sure your dad doesn't already have something planned. Do you know where he is?"

"In the office," Theresa answered, pointing.

"Okay, why don't you run upstairs and get ready while I talk to him?"

She bounded off the couch, leaping up the stairs and rushing to her room as Keito slowly approached the open office door. Dalton was standing by the wall of books, thumbing through a volume of the Guardian Code, his eyes narrowed in concentration.

"Dalton?" he asked, startling the other Guardian. "What are you looking for?"

"I'm trying to find something that would grant me emergency access to the archives," Dalton said, turning another page and shaking his head. "Can you think of anything?"

"No, sorry," Keito said. "Are you alright?"

"I'm pretty far from alright," Dalton said, snapping the book shut and replacing it on the shelf.

"I wish I knew more about these dragon spirits, Dalton," Keito said. "I'm sorry that I don't."

"You know," Dalton started with a broken laugh, leaning against the shelves, "I've always known there was something wrong with me."

"There's nothing wrong with you."

"No?" Dalton challenged. "Then the dragon spirit I was born with wasn't the reason Yokouro attacked my family? It wasn't the reason my father was killed? It wasn't what scared my mother so much that she left me in the middle of the night? It wasn't what scared those boys at the training center into attacking me? It wasn't the reason I became top-ranked Guardian at such a young age, or the reason I was chosen for this tournament?" He let out a choked laugh. "I've always known. And yet I thought I could pretend I was normal. I thought I could have a family, a normal life, and now...I'm a danger to them."

"Dalton, I understand," Keito said strongly, walking into the room. "But you *can* have a family. You *do* have a family and they love you. And you have us, who are doing whatever we can to help you get through this. Just because you're powerful doesn't mean there's something wrong with you."

"Last night..." Dalton choked, "I woke up in the middle of the night...and I could have sworn those kids were standing around me again, ready to kill me. I almost got out of bed to defend myself, and then I remembered where I was...and who was next to me." He swallowed hard, letting out a shaky exhale. "What if I had hurt Frieda?"

"But you didn't," Keito insisted, stepping closer to Dalton, motioning his hand back to the door to close it in case anyone tried to eavesdrop. "The only way you're going to feel in control of this is to figure out what it is, and train to master it."

"How?" Dalton choked. "Am I supposed to let Yokouro torture me to the point where my only choice for survival is to accept the dragon magic? This isn't something I can just wake up and understand." He shook his head strongly. "I can feel Yokouro breathing down the back of my neck."

Keito hesitated. "...I don't know what to say to help, Dalton," he whispered.

"Tell me what Yokouro is going to do," Dalton said. "Tell me how to keep my family safe through this. Tell me how to not lose myself."

"I can't, I'm sorry. I don't know," Keito murmured.

"Hanyi, stop! Don't!" Frieda's voice yelled through the house. Dalton and Keito darted out of the office, following the voices to the living room, where Frieda was trying to pull her phone out of Hanyi's grasp. "Please, don't!"

"Hanyi, what are you doing?!" Mitoki gasped, rushing down the stairs, Eclipse close behind. Theresa also ran out of the room, eyes wide, terrified by her mother's cries.

"They have to know!" Hanyi insisted, yanking the phone back and pushing on her shoulder, gently, but insistently. Eclipse quickly turned to Theresa, forcing a weak smile.

"Hey, why don't you go to your room for a few minutes?" he said. "Let us talk for a little bit."

"No," Hanyi said, raising a finger sharply. "She needs to be in our sights at all times."

"Hanyi, what the hell are you doing?" Dalton growled, rushing to his wife's side, trying to shield her from the wolf. But Frieda rushed forward again, both her hands gripping Hanyi's arm as her eyes stared into his pleadingly.

"Please, don't," she whispered.

"Frieda, they need to know," Hanyi insisted. He extended the phone to Keito silently, who took it and glanced at the screen. Instantly, his eyes went wide as he scrolled through messages.

"Keito? What is it?" Eclipse asked.

The demon lifted his eyes, looking at the varying expression around him before his eyes settled on Dalton.

"Dalton, we need to start preparing for an attack."

"What kind of attack?" Dalton demanded, looking between his shaking wife and Keito. "Frieda, what the hell is he talking about?"

"I didn't think it was anything to worry about," Frieda said. "It seemed like a sick joke. I just ignored it. I get prank messages all the time."

"These aren't prank messages," Keito said. "This is a countdown. This is what Yokouro used to do to us." He turned the phone around to show Dalton the long list of messages, each with a single number, one message per day at exactly four-fourteen in the afternoon. He grabbed the phone, scrolling down the messages, seeing the numbers get smaller every day until he saw the message from the previous day, with the simple number two.

"Two? What? Two days until what?"

"Until he makes his move," Hanyi said. "Dalton, there are men casing the house. They've been doing it for a few days. Whatever Yokouro's planning—"

"Wait, you *knew*?!" Dalton barked. "Why the hell didn't you say anything?!"

"I'm saying something now," Hanyi said sharply. "Apparently, these started after Frieda was cornered coming home two months ago."

"You didn't tell me about that?" Dalton gasped, turning to Frieda.

"They didn't hurt me," she said quickly. "I was bringing in groceries when a few men tried to corner me around the car. I pulled out my knife and they ran."

"You carry a knife?" Mitoki said, startled.

"I stayed up the rest of the night with a gun in case they came back, but they didn't," Frieda said. "The next day, the text messages started. I didn't think it was a problem. I thought they were just prank texts, and I never saw those guys again..." Her voice became choked. "I'm sorry I didn't tell you. I didn't want to worry you further."

"Mom? Dad?" Theresa whispered, her voice shaking. "What's going on? Are we in danger?" When the eyes of the adults settled on her, their expressions terrified, the tears began to gather in her eyes.

Dalton turned to Hanyi, his eyes turning dark.

"Hanyi, you stay with Frieda and Theresa," he said. "Someone call Jikia and Tarrena. Tell them to get here."

"They're on their way," Eclipse assured.

"We're scouring this house from top to bottom until we're certain the house is secure, and then were going to hunt down these

294

men stalking my house," Dalton snapped. "We move together as a team. Our safety is in numbers."

"Dalton, I'm sorry..." Frieda whispered, stepping closer to him. He wrapped his arms around her, kissing her forehead as he held her.

"No, I'm sorry for putting you in danger like this," he said. He pulled away from her, taking her face in his hands, thumbing away a tear that escaped her eye. "You know where the guns are in this room?" She nodded. "Stay here with Theresa and Hanyi, and if anyone attacks, shoot them."

Swallowing hard, she nodded, motioning for Theresa to come down the stairs. She approached slowly, terrified at the nervous energy among the adults around her. Once she reached the bottom of the stairs, she rushed to her father, hugging him tightly. He lifted her onto his hip, kissing her forehead.

"Theresa," he whispered, "I need you to be really good today and just stay close to Mom, okay?"

"I'm scared..." she whimpered.

"I know," he said, his arms tightening around her. "Dad's scared, too. But I'm going to keep you safe. So I need you to stay with Mom and Uncle Hanyi, okay? We'll be back in a little bit."

It was difficult to pry Theresa's arms from Dalton's neck, but Frieda held their daughter close as they sat on the couch, trying to distract her with the puzzle while Hanyi stood nearby, nodding to Dalton. The four other Guardians went through each room of the house together, looking in vent grates for cameras and locking and warding windows, strengthening the protection Mitoki had already placed. They could find no cameras or microphones in the house, nor any sign that those watching the Teban home had tried to break in already. They scoured the attic and the basement, but still found no trace of an intruder.

Jikia and Tarrena were quickly filled in on what the Guardians knew and they, too, sat in the living room with Frieda and Theresa, protecting them while Dalton, Mitoki, Eclipse, and Keito went outside to find those spying on them.

At first, nothing seemed amiss. They did not spot anyone ducking behind bushes or fences, nor did they see any cars lurking on the street. When Keito mentioned seeing people on the roof of the neighbor's home, Dalton asked his neighbors if Keito could get a frisbee from their roof, which they agreed to, fascinated by watching Keito climb the side of their house.

As he approached the chimney, where he had seen someone watching Dalton's house, he was struck by several scents and auras.

He saw a collection of cigarette butts at the base of the chimney, and the energy around the roof was undoubtedly demon. That gave him pause. He had been certain that the men watching the house were *ubetin*, since he believed that Rutu would be the one performing whatever ritual was needed for Dalton to merge with the dragon spirit. But the sloppy scene and the demon energy told him that whoever had been watching the house was not working for the Trade Masters.

Dread filled his body.

Scanning the house from the same vantage point, he searched for anything out of the ordinary.

Focusing hard, he could see at the base of the window frames shallow etchings in the paint. One window had a crude letter D carved, while a T was carved two windows further down. On the window where he and Hanyi had watched the men, there was a K and an H etched into the paint.

Using a small disk of his magic to make it seem like he threw the "frisbee" back into Dalton's yard, Keito quickly descended to the ground, thanking the neighbors and hurrying the Guardians to the front of Dalton's house.

"What did you find?" Eclipse asked.

"Demons have been watching the house," Keito said. "There was demon energy up there, but I didn't see anyone watching now. I don't know if they know we're on to them, or if they've pulled back in preparation for attack. But, I'm fairly certain they plan to attack at night. They've marked the window frames with who is in each bedroom."

Ice filled their veins as the fear stabbed each of them.

"They wouldn't dare make a big scene in a crowded neighborhood like this," Eclipse said with a strong shake of his head. "I'm fairly certain the neighbors would either hear the sounds of torture, or notice a bunch of men breaking into the house."

Keito let out a long sigh.

"I don't think we can expect these demons to take the intelligent approach for this attack," he said. "Something tells me these demons are not as highly-trained as the ones we faced last round."

"What are you trying to say? That they might attack the house and make a scene?" Mitoki asked.

"It's possible."

Frieda's phone buzzed in Dalton's pocket. He pulled it out to see that, just like the previous messages, the next number had come through exactly on time.

One.

Dalton jumped awake when he realized he had fallen asleep, standing quickly from the couch, though he had to halt his steps instantly to avoid stepping on the sleeping Jikia.

Everyone was gathered in the living room, Frieda and Theresa nestled in the middle of the room with the Guardians asleep, facing each direction to be sure they could protect them no matter which direction they were attacked.

But Dalton did not want to sleep. He could not let himself become unguarded for an instant, certain that Yokouro was watching him very closely, waiting for the perfect opportunity to catch Dalton off-guard.

Keito was sitting by the front window, his head resting against the window frame as he peered out the small gap between the drapes and the wall. Dalton carefully maneuvered his way to the window, pulling over one of the dining room chairs and sitting across from Keito.

"You should get some sleep, Dalton," Keito whispered.

"I can't," he said. "What about you? If they do attack, I'm going to need you rested."

"I got a few hours last night. That's enough for me for now," Keito assured.

Dalton let out a long sigh, tentatively peeking around the drapes to the empty suburban street.

"Keito?" he started carefully, being sure to keep his eyes averted from the demon. "Do you think it would be better if I went and found Yokouro now?"

"What do you mean?" Keito asked.

"If Yokouro is going to attack us, it will be to perform this ritual on me, right?" he asked. "Because he needs me strong for this battle between the dragon spirits. So what if I just went to him and let him do it?"

"Are you out of your mind?"

"It would spare my family this fear," Dalton insisted. "And then we wouldn't be scrambling to try and figure out a way for me to master these powers before Yokouro manages to do whatever it is he's planning."

"Sleep deprivation is making you stupid, Dalton," Keito said with raised eyebrows. "You want to go to him and offer yourself up for torture?"

"I can't risk my family. I just can't," Dalton said. "Master Bowen said that it was a very precise ritual, and if done properly, it could happen relatively quickly. So I'm going to assume that Juki and Rutu are skilled enough to make it happen quickly."

Keito opened his mouth to speak, but hesitated. "That's why I'm worried," he said. "I don't think Rutu is going to be the one performing the ritual, which means this has the potential to go very, very wrong."

"Why do you think it won't be Rutu?"

"This whole thing with the house being cased, the countdown…it's too sloppy for Juki and Rutu. If they were going to do this, we wouldn't even know they had it planned until it was too late."

Dalton felt a fearful tremor radiate through his body.

"If you were in my shoes, what would you do?" he asked.

"I truly do not know," Keito admitted. "Dalton, I don't know that I would be able to handle what's sitting on your shoulders. And if I knew more about these dragon spirits, maybe I would be able to help more, but I'm just as worried as you."

"Do you think we can form a plan in one day?" Dalton asked warily. Keito smiled and shrugged a shoulder.

"Guardians tend to shine the most when under pressure," he said. "We'll do everything we can to keep you and your family safe, Dalton."

Dalton let out a long sigh, leaning his head against the window frame, waiting to spot movement through the narrow gap in the curtains.

Chapter Twenty-Nine

"Dalton! Dalton! Wake up!!" Mitoki's urgent voice called, shaking Dalton almost violently. The older man finally managed to force his eyes open, though the lights above him stabbed his retinas like a thousand burning suns.

"Dalton!"

"I'm awake!" he snapped, pulling himself to his hands and knees. It took him a few moments to realize he was face down on the carpet of his dining room. One hand raised to shield his eyes, he squinted at Mitoki's face. "What's going on?"

Keito groaned next to him, holding onto Hanyi's arm as he tried to stand, his fingers covering his eyes in an attempt to protect his pounding head.

The frantic energy in the living room brought Dalton fully to consciousness. He tried to get to his feet, but his muscles were uncoordinated and clumsy. Mitoki caught his arm to keep him from hitting his head on the dining table, but Dalton hardly noticed, thinking they were under attack.

"Where are they?" he demanded. "Did they get in?"

"They're not here," Jikia's voice said, her tone betraying her anxiety.

Dalton's senses were difficult to discern around his pounding headache. He did not understand why he was shivering until he was finally able to focus his eyes on the open windows around him.

Every window in the house was wide open, the morning breeze chilling them

"What the hell happened?"

Mitoki gently brushed off some fine, red powder that was covering Dalton's shoulders, arms, and back. "We think they put something in the ventilation system," he explained. "We all woke up with this red dust on us and all the windows open to air the place out."

"I thought we had all the windows warded," he said, angrily smacking off some of the dust he could see clinging to the fabric of his pants.

"They must have broken the warding," Mitoki said. "Not that any of us would have felt it while drugged."

Keito had to lean against the wall to keep himself upright, rubbing his eyes roughly as he tried to focus his vision. Dalton also managed to get to his feet, supporting himself on the dining table as he stood.

"Why did they knock us out and then leave us here?" Dalton asked, his heart knocking angrily on his ribs. Realization was tickling at the edge of his mind, but he refused to entertain his panicked thoughts until he knew exactly what had happened.

"They left this," Eclipse said quietly, extending a handwritten note in front of Dalton. He snatched the paper away, squinting as his eyes strained to discern the words.

"Dalton. I have made all the preparations necessary. You are expected to be in the city of Golden no earlier than eight p.m. Park in the back lot of the address below. The entire team is required to join you. I have taken something to ensure your cooperation."

His voice weakened as he read the last sentence.

Before his eyes left the paper, he knew what had happened.

Dropping the note, Dalton stumbled out of the dining room and frantically looked around the dust-covered living room. He met eyes with Tarrena and Jikia, his gaze then swooping around the room to count his grim-faced teammates.

"Frieda?" he called, moving toward the staircase and half-collapsing against the bannister. "Theresa?!"

Silence greeted him.

"No…" he whispered. "No, no, no, *no!*"

He spun around clumsily, stumbling toward the front door. Hanyi and Keito intercepted him.

"Dalton," Keito started, his tone even but firm, "take a deep breath. We have to comply by the rules exactly. We can't leave just—"

"He's taken my wife and my daughter and you want me to sit around and wait for his bullshit deadline?!" Dalton snapped, shoving Keito. "We're leaving now."

He took two more steps to the door, but Hanyi grabbed his arm, squeezing just hard enough to startle Dalton.

"No," he said. "The note says we can't be there any earlier than eight."

"Golden is a two-hour drive," Dalton snarled. "He's got plenty of time to run. I'm not going to sit here and *wait*."

"Dalton, please, listen to me—"

"Get out of my way, Hanyi!" Dalton barked, shoving the wolf away from him. "This isn't a damn *game*. This is my *family*!"

Keito grabbed Dalton's shoulders, pushing him back to keep him from reaching his car keys.

"If you go now, Yokouro will kill them," Keito warned darkly.

"I'll skin him before he has a chance," Dalton said, making another move for the keys.

"Dalton, *stop*!" Keito held his team leader back, keeping the keys out of reach. "You don't have the advantage. If you storm out of here now, your family is doomed."

"Why am I the only one who thinks that my family being kidnapped is a problem?!" Dalton bellowed. "*Yokouro DeVastes* has my family. My *daughter*. I won't let him live long enough to regret that decision."

"Enough, Dalton!" Keito said. "I know you're angry and scared. We all are. But you have to trust me. If you go now, he will kill them without hesitation, and the only thing you'll find when you get there are their bodies. Yokouro did the same thing with one of my teammates. And when we didn't listen to the rules, Jacob's family paid the price. I *will not* let you make the same mistake."

Dalton stared at Keito, his eyes growing darker with each labored breath. He shoved the demon back with more strength than a human should possess before turning and storming up the stairs. Keito rubbed the back of his head where he made impact with the front door, turning to Tarrena.

"Will you please watch him and make sure he doesn't do something stupid? Like climb out the window?"

She nodded silently, rushing after Dalton as Keito picked up the car keys and placed them in his pocket with a heavy sigh.

"This is bad..." he whispered.

"Yokouro did this to your team, too?" Mitoki asked. "Why did he target Jacob's family?"

"He was trying to get our attention, and at that time, most of us didn't have family to threaten," Keito explained. "So, he went after Jacob's father and two younger sisters."

"Do you think Yokouro will repeat the same pattern?" Eclipse asked. "Did he hide the family members somewhere? Was it some kind of trap?"

"It was a trap of sorts," Hanyi said. "He trapped Jacob's family members in a warehouse and had them killed just before we arrived to try and save them, since we didn't obey his rules. Then he held us there for two weeks..."

"Two weeks?!" Eclipse, Mitoki, and Jikia repeated, stunned. "What was he trying to do with you?"

The two older Guardians shared a silent look, debating how much detail to divulge.

"It was his way of pulling the rug out from under us," Hanyi finally said. "We had a plan to kill him, and after he had toyed with us for weeks about whether or not he was going to kill us or torture us, he revealed why our plan wouldn't work." The wolf shook his head, waving his hand in the air to change the subject. "That's not what's going to happen with Dalton, though. He's determined to merge Dalton with this dragon spirit. So he's luring us there to start that ritual."

Mitoki's face began to pale. He leaned against the dining table, lifting a hand to his mouth.

"Oh no…" he murmured. "I just had a terrible thought." He lifted his fearful eyes to the older Guardians. "What if we were wrong about the torture? What if the way to torture Dalton…is torturing his family?"

Even though he had nearly whispered the words, the question hit everyone like a knife to the chest.

"I don't think even the notorious Trade Masters would be able to torture a little girl like Theresa," Jikia said. She turned to Keito slowly, her eyes filled with uncertainty. "Right?"

The demon swallowed hard.

"…Rutu has tortured children before. Juki never would, but…Rutu has the ability to just…shut off."

Jikia's legs wobbled, bringing her to sit on the couch as the dizziness overwhelmed her.

"I feel sick…" She hid her face in her hands. "What if he actually kills them?" she whimpered. "Dalton would never forgive himself if—"

"We're not going to let that happen," Eclipse said strongly, kneeling in front of their trainer and taking her hands away from her face, fixing her with a determined stare. "If we have to follow some rules to keep Frieda and Theresa safe, then of course that's what we'll do. But once we're there, we'll gut Yokouro for this."

For three hours, the team remained in the main living area of the house, trying to clean up the dust and air out the house to keep their minds occupied. Rio had also been knocked unconscious, and was struggling to stand and move out of the Guardians' way as they paced nervously. Hanyi checked over the dog, sure that he would recover, though it was clear that the potent sedation had left Rio feeling unwell. Tarrena rejoined them, but stayed at the top of the stairs, listening to Dalton pace around the master bedroom.

After the fourth hour dragged by, Eclipse growled, no longer able to busy himself with cleaning the house.

"Damn that bastard," he snapped. "He made this confrontation so late because he wanted us to panic the entire damn day." He turned his eyes to Tarrena at the top of the stairs, heaving a deep sigh. "Dalton is going to be an uncontrollable wreck by the time we leave."

302

"Yokouro's trying to bring Dalton's power to the surface," Hanyi reminded them. "He wants Dalton in a heightened emotional state. This will certainly do the trick."

"We'll have to keep a very close eye on him," Mitoki chimed in. "He's likely to make a mistake just because of his agitation."

"I don't know that we'll be able to stop him," Keito said.

Jikia forced them to eat something so they would have some strength for whatever they were walking into, but they could not eat much before pushing the food away and anxiously waiting for the hours to pass.

By the time Dalton emerged from the master bedroom, everyone was a jumpy, nervous mess. He walked slowly down to the stairs, Tarrena watching him pass before she stood to follow, flinching from the powerful, sparking aura surrounding the Guardian. Dalton's eyes were dark, his face creased with purpose. He approached Keito, holding his hand out to the demon.

"It's a two-hour drive," he nearly growled.

Keito glanced at the clock before nodding slowly and placing the keys in Dalton's palm.

Jikia and Tarrena stayed behind, watching nervously as the Guardians stepped into the dusk air and climbed into the car.

Keito sat in the passenger's seat, programming the address on the note into the GPS as Dalton angrily reversed from the driveway.

He could not speak, grinding his teeth together as he drove, his fingers gripping the steering wheel so tight the leather groaned under the pressure. Several times, Keito had to remind Dalton that an upcoming light was red, since Dalton ran two in his desperation to get to his family. The freeway had little traffic on it, and once they turned onto the country highway leading them through the rural lands surrounding Kenburough, the roads were nearly deserted. Dalton was speeding, but occasionally slowed down when he made quick calculations in his head about when they would arrive if he continued at that speed.

Despite his rage nearly blinding him, he believed what Keito had said—they could not arrive before the designated time.

Golden was an industrial town, filled with warehouses and distribution centers, which meant there were more large trucks on the roads than cars as they drove through the city. The closer they drew to their destination, the more worried the Guardians became at not having a plan for saving Frieda and Theresa. Dalton's intense aura had kept them silent through the drive, but apart from knowing they were going to a warehouse, they did not have a plan. And no one dared try to discuss a plan with the aggravated Dalton.

Dark understanding was sitting in everyone's chest that things were going to get out of hand very quickly once they parked the car.

The car bumped over the curb into the back lot of one of the smaller warehouses in the area. Two yellowed lights were illuminated on either side of the back door, barely cutting through the darkness of the encroaching night, appearing like ominous beacons. Every movement Dalton made was filled with rage, from parking the car to slamming the door shut and storming toward the warehouse, the others of his team scrambling to catch up with him.

As Dalton tried the door knob, Mitoki and Eclipse both drew their guns, crowding in close behind Dalton to protect him. The door, however, was locked.

"Dalton," Keito whispered, "we need to take this slow and see what's in there. We can't just charge in—"

Dalton's fingers tightened on the handle, and a burst of magic created an explosion in the lock, startling those around Dalton and causing the door to violently slam open.

"Surely they didn't hear that..." Hanyi groaned, quickly following Dalton as he stormed into the warehouse.

There was a short, narrow hallway within that opened to a spacious warehouse, marked with the outlines of machines that had been bolted to the floor. Several pieces of equipment had been moved around the large space, providing strategic shields for the several dozen men and women in the warehouse that had been waiting for them.

Upon seeing them, Dalton also drew his gun and, without saying a word, began firing into the warehouse. Eclipse and Mitoki did the same, the shots echoing in the vastness of the space. But no bullets hit their targets. The magic surrounding the men and women distorted the paths of the bullets, causing them to fall harmlessly to the ground.

"Demons," Keito said just in time for Eclipse and Mitoki to drop their guns and ready their magic as the demons lunged at the Guardians. Hanyi shifted into his wolf form and launched at the closest demon, Keito also engaging in the fray as the humans prepared themselves. Eclipse and Mitoki wanted to keep a close eye on Dalton, but were soon overwhelmed by demons, only able to focus on keeping themselves safe.

Dalton acted as though he was possessed. Still holding his gun, he used the weapon to strike any demon he could in the face, his other arm emitting magic so powerful he could feel the demons' bones breaking whenever his fist made contact. Whenever a demon got in his line of sight, he easily put them on the ground. He was not thinking to clear the room of all the demons before continuing. He could sense where he needed to go, almost as though he had been in the warehouse before and knew which room held his wife and daughter.

Any demon he saw was just an obstacle in his way.

When the demons cleared away from him and focused their attention on the other four Guardians, Dalton did not think to check on his teammates. He moved immediately in the direction he instinctively knew to go. He felt the pull from deep in his chest, yanking him further into the warehouse.

His eyes focused on a door, tunneling around the handle as he picked up pace. By the time his hand came in contact with the cold handle, he could see nothing else around him.

Dalton threw open the door and ran inside, but was immediately overwhelmed by the ten demon guards that had been waiting for him. One tackled him to the dirty floor while the others tried to contain his flailing limbs. He kicked and punched, managing to knock several of them away before sharp, biting pain circled his wrists and yanked them together behind his back with enough force to send pins and needles up his arms. He could feel the magical binding digging into his skin, drawing blood. When the pressure from his back eased as the demons backed away from him, another sharp coil of magic wrapped around his legs, forcing them straight with the same sharp pain.

He rolled, fighting against the bindings until the moment he saw the two demons in front of him.

"Dalton," Yokouro greeted, crouching in front of him with a cold smile. "Right on time. Well done."

Dalton struggled harder against the bindings, managing to pull his arms apart briefly before they snapped back together.

"You sick son of a bitch!" he bellowed.

"Ooh, you mustn't use such foul language in front of the ladies," Yokouro scolded, turning over his shoulder to the other side of the room, where four remaining sections of a conveyor belt ran under a long line of hooks, glinting maliciously above the bound and gagged figures of Frieda and Theresa.

"I'll make you pay for this, Yokouro," Dalton growled.

"And how do you plan to do that?" Yokouro asked, standing once again as Acurala retreated, smirking triumphantly. "Dalton, you have to understand, I'm trying to *help* you. I cannot tell you the time it has taken to put this all together for you."

"Put what together?"

"The stage for your transformation," Yokouro said, spreading his arms wide.

Dalton's struggles began again when two demon guards hauled him to his knees, each keeping a firm hand on his shoulders as he was forced to face the Old Blood Lord.

"Well, Yokouro, I did underestimate you," Dalton snapped. "I thought you would be stupid enough to attack the house."

"Oh, the thought had crossed my mind," Yokouro said with a grin. "But there were too many people around, too many places to hide, and I don't think you have these convenient hooks anywhere in your home." Yokouro shrugged. "Or maybe you do."

"I know what you're planning," Dalton said darkly. "Ritual torture to fuse my powers with the dragon magic."

"You have been doing your research," Yokouro complimented. "But the ritual has already started, Dalton. It started the moment Vestera awoke your power two months ago. You've been fighting with yourself about your powers, plaguing yourself with stress-induced nightmares about what could happen if you lose control, recalling memories of that burned and bloodied child you murdered when you were only eight years old."

"Shut up!"

"There's no point in denying it," Yokouro tutted. "Those memories you blocked…they've been resurfacing, haven't they? You no longer see a corpse lying on the ground, you see the boy's arm snap, you see his body catch fire like dry tinder, and you see every oozing sore on his skin, hear his screaming—"

"Enough!" Dalton bellowed, his magic flaring high in rage. The bindings broke from his wrists and ankles and he leapt to his feet, much to the surprise of the two guards holding him down. He punched one in the face before tackling the other, stunning him just enough to round on Yokouro and launch forward.

Magic coiled around Dalton again, wrapping around his neck like the end of a whip and pulling him to the side, interrupting his path to Yokouro. Acurala lifted his hand, pulling the magic taught as Dalton choked, slicing his fingers open as he tried to pull the magic from his throat.

"Good," Yokouro complimented proudly. "This is what I was looking for. That blind emotional rage you had when you killed that child."

As Dalton's face began to go red from lacking oxygen, Acurala lowered his hand, the magic loosening just enough for Dalton to force air into his lungs, though the action made pain shoot through his jaw and neck.

"You're making beautiful progress, Dalton," Yokouro said, leaning over Dalton's face with a broad smile. "I went through a metamorphosis myself recently. And now that I have this new power, I'm able to see that dragon energy augmenting your magic, a dark, spiraling fire in your aura that is just waiting to consume you." He let out a long sigh. "It's much easier if you give in. Let it flood you, Dalton. Let it take control."

Still gasping, trying to gather the strength to break Acurala's magic around his neck, Dalton lifted his middle finger into Yokouro's face.

"Still so petulant," Yokouro chided. "Dalton, I've given you ample opportunity to incorporate Kuryaoin. I left you alone to stew, I made sure every team in the tournament had a demon so that your terrified human instincts would retreat and the dragon magic would come forward to protect you. I even made sure the second set was cancelled because I was certain that you were ready to pop, but you're still fighting so hard. I even reunited you with your dear mother, so that you would remember what it felt like before you locked away that power."

"Screw...you..." Dalton forced out around clenched teeth.

"That is what has led us to this night," Yokouro continued. "You leave me no choice, Dalton. If we want to fight this destined battle, you need to be stronger. I'm helping you. Yes, it will be agonizing, but that will focus your motivation and lead you to that battlefield with everything bared, ready to risk absolutely anything."

Dalton felt a chill run down his spine as his eyes turned to Frieda and Theresa, more worried than ever about what Yokouro planned to do to his family.

With a nod from Yokouro, Acurala loosened his hold on Dalton further, only to yank him to his feet and shove him back to his knees. The magic dissipated from his neck, but reappeared in an instant to bind his hands, this time in front of him. Before he could orient himself, Acurala pulled him up by his wrists and hooked the magical binding over one of the hooks in front of Frieda and Theresa. Dalton's toes barely scraped the floor as his shoulders strained and his wrists burned.

He tried to make eye contact with his crying wife and daughter, but before he could address them, Yokouro's hand yanked him around, the chain holding the hook jingling as he tried to keep his toes on the ground.

But he could not focus on the pain in his arms, nor the way his toes ran uselessly across the concrete floor. The moment Yokouro's hand made contact, fire raged inside his body. His internal organs felt as though they were pushing against his ribs as his rage surged forward, desperate to attack.

Yokouro removed his hand and retreated a step.

"Excellent," he said. "That is your dragon magic reacting to mine. They're desperate to tear each other apart. And your anger is fueling the fire."

Dalton was struggling to catch his breath, his eyes wide and frantic on the floor as he tried to comprehend what he had just felt. He wanted to turn back around to his family, to tell them that everything was going to be alright, but his head was still spinning. Even when the door opened once again for the demons to haul in the beaten and bound members of Team Dalton, he could not raise his eyes to look at them, unsure if his muscles would obey his command.

The demons, though beaten and bruised, hauled the chained members of Team Dalton to a row of hooks that would keep them away from Dalton, lifting each of them to dangle just off the floor by their wrists.

"There they are," Acurala announced with a smile. "Seems your teammates were giving my men quite the struggle."

"What the hell is all this?!" Keito snapped.

"You're just here as a spectator, mutt," Yokouro growled, turning away from Dalton to glare at the younger demon. "Because we all know that Dalton prefers to put on a strong façade. But tonight," he smirked at Dalton, "we're going to break that."

He nodded to Acurala again, walking to the far side of the room to sit on a discarded piece of machinery, watching casually as Acurala stepped up to Dalton.

"As you know, Dalton, what we plan for you tonight is ritual torture," he said. "But this has to be done quite delicately."

"Where the hell are Juki and Rutu?!" Keito demanded. "This has stupid written all over it! There is no way they would leave you to do this alone."

"I'm afraid my dear older brothers will not be joining us tonight," Acurala said. "They were exhausted. They're off getting some well-deserved rest. I can handle this just fine on my own."

"What are you going to do?" Dalton spat. "I've been trained to withstand torture."

"Oh, I know you have," Acurala agreed. With a flick of his fingers, Dalton spun on the chain, turning to face his terrified wife and child. "But the thing about torture is, anyone can make someone feel pain. But it takes an artist to truly torment someone."

"You're going to make them watch?" Dalton growled.

"No," Acurala said behind Dalton. "I'm going to make you watch."

Just as dread started to turn Dalton's stomach, the hot smell of sparking magic invaded his nostrils followed by several gasps and an ear-piercing crack.

Dalton flinched from the noise, but was instantly overwhelmed by agony searing across his back in a painfully precise, sizzling line. His back bowed and he let out a scream, confused and overwhelmed by pain.

Acurala clicked his tongue in disappointment.

"Oh, this just won't do, Dalton," he said. "One lance across your back and you scream? As my dear father would always say," another round of yells warned Dalton there was another slice of pain coming his way. The deafening crack split his ear drums, and another flash of blinding heat drew forth another pained cry, "*never voice your pain!*"

Dalton could not bite back the scream as a third slice ripped across his flesh. He could smell his own burning skin as the magic whipped his back, slicing through his clothes and flesh to sink deep into his nerves, causing pain to radiate into his bones. The fourth slice added to the intensity of heat under his skin. His own yells of agony drowned out the terrified cries of his family as they watched helplessly.

"Do you see how useless pain can be?" Acurala asked, leaning to Dalton's shoulder. "Here I am, inflicting pain, but you're not worried about your ability to endure it. That is what your training has taught you. You're familiarizing yourself with the pain, accepting it, and preparing for the next slice. But that is not how you properly torment someone."

Acurala backed away from Dalton, taking slow, deliberate steps around the conveyor belt to stand behind Frieda and Theresa. Even through the pain, Dalton could see what Acurala was planning.

"Torture has to be deeper than physical," Acurala explained. "And in your case, Dalton, we had the perfect opportunity to hit you where it hurts most."

"Do not touch them," Dalton growled darkly.

"Feel that pain in your back?" Acurala asked, lifting his hand and waving his fingers in the air, the dark purple magic arching around his hand like an electric whip. "How do you think they will bear up to it?"

The others of Team Dalton were yanking on their restraints, but even Keito's demon strength could not break the chains holding them. They screamed and bellowed at Acurala to stop, trying to use their own magic from a distance, but the fight before entering the room had drained much of their strength.

"Don't!" Dalton barked.

"It's very simple, Dalton. We want you to use your magic. If you want me to stop harming them, you'll find a way to stop me."

"No! No!!" Dalton bellowed, seeing Acurala draw his hand back as his magic extended to lash across Frieda. The room was filled with mortified cries as Acurala's hand snapped forward and the magic produced a resounding crack.

But Frieda's scream trailed off into a confused whimper as she turned to look at Acurala. She felt no sharp pain, and Theresa appeared unharmed as well. Acurala was still standing behind them, a disbelieving smile pulling at his lips as he watched Dalton grind his teeth together, breathing hard against the pain of a new slice across his back.

"That was fast..." Acurala said. "I wondered how much of this power you had tapped into in the tournament. Seems it's already bubbling just below the surface."

Dalton's eyes fluttered open, ignoring Acurala as he looked to his family.

"It's alright," he said breathlessly. "I won't let him hurt you."

"Shall we try again?" Acurala asked. He flicked his hand again and another whip crack sounded, but Dalton was the one who cried out in pain, his magic redirecting the attack from his family to him.

"I must say, Dalton, I am also impressed," Yokouro said from his seat. "I wonder how long you can keep that up."

Dalton flinched as he saw Acurala draw his hand back once more. Screaming surrounded him before his own cry joined in the noise. Acurala growled, shaking his head.

"Now I see why Father taught us to remain silent," he sneered, snapping his magic once more, hoping to catch Dalton off-guard, though the magic still sliced open Dalton's back, leaving Frieda and Theresa untouched. "How utterly irritating to be hearing screaming all the time."

Dalton closed his eyes when the next attack split his skin open but he bit his lip almost hard enough to draw blood, trying not to make a sound, though he failed to keep his agonized cry silent.

"Dalton, you'll need a higher pain tolerance if you plan to master this dragon magic," Acurala warned. "Otherwise the training will kill you before Yokouro has a chance to."

He cracked his energy yet again, the pain mounting as the strike hit two other lashes already on his back. He screamed, trying not to hear the way his teammates and family were also screaming with each blow.

"Come now, Dalton, this is a training exercise at this point. Never. Voice. Your. Pain!"

He punctuated each word with a short, sharp attack. Dalton only managed not to make a sound after the first word, yelping in pain with each successive slice.

When the enraged Acurala raised his hand to deliver another blow, Keito made his move.

The younger demon hauled his legs into the air, ignoring the snapping of magic as Dalton was, once again, sliced open. He contorted around the chain to wrap his legs over the track and slip his chained wrists off the hook. He then swung to the ground and sprinted toward Acurala.

"Acurala," Yokouro warned, though he appeared unbothered by Keito's escape.

Keito tackled Acurala to the ground, landing painfully on the dirty floor as he tried to scratch and bite at the older demon desperately. Eclipse followed Keito's example, releasing himself from the hook and helping Hanyi and Mitoki down once he twisted his wrists out of the chains, turning to use his magic against any of the demon guards coming to interfere. Frieda and Theresa started screaming again, but Dalton was too disoriented by pain and noise to immediately understand what was happening.

Rage strengthened the Guardians, making it easier for them to fight the demons, ignoring their wounds as adrenaline coursed in their veins. When Eclipse and Mitoki found an opportunity, they rushed to Dalton, easing him off the hook, though they were quickly pulled away from him by the demon guards, who were growling and swearing angrily. Hanyi stood guard by Dalton, launching with his teeth bared at any demon that drew too close. Keito continued to wrestle and scrape at Acurala, barely avoiding some extremely painful hits.

"Why do you always get in the way of everything, you pathetic mutt?!" Acurala bellowed, spinning Keito around so his face was pressed into the floor. Keito elbowed Acurala in the side just hard enough to startle him, which gave him the opportunity to lift his head and connect with Acurala's nose.

As the demons struggled to get the Guardians under control once more, Yokouro watched silently from his position, waiting to see what Dalton would do.

Still woozy and stumbling on shaking legs, Dalton clamored to Frieda and untied her, his clumsy fingers pulling the gag from her mouth before he hugged her tightly. Hanyi switched to his human form just long enough to untie Theresa, though he turned to fight off an approaching demon before he could remove the gag.

Frieda gathered Theresa in her arms and pulled her to the other side of the conveyor belt, ducking low to keep them shielded from the fight.

Dalton turned to join the scuffle, but one hit to his bleeding back from a demon put him on the ground with bolts of pain shooting behind his eyes. He nearly passed out, his eyes rolling in their sockets as he fought to remain conscious. When he was finally able to focus his eyes again, Keito was being dragged to the other Guardians, who were all pinned by the demon guards, breathing hard and struggling as much as possible with their waning strength.

Acurala rubbed the side of his face with a cringe, trying to ease the throbbing from his fight with Keito. Still rubbing his face, he turned to a demon stationed near another door further in the room, who rushed forward with two sheathed swords.

"Well, Dalton," Acurala started, taking both weapons. "I had hoped *you* would be the one to break your bindings and start a brawl, but at least I got some reaction out of you."

"Re-reaction?" Dalton stuttered. "You *bastard*! You were trying to torture my family!"

"No, Dalton, I was trying to torture *you*," Acurala corrected. He tossed one of the swords to the ground in front of Dalton. "And now that you can wield your new powers to protect your loved ones, let's see you use it to protect yourself." He unsheathed his own sword, tossing the scabbard to the side as he raised it with a challenging grin, motioning for the guard to release Dalton. "Pick it up."

"It's not a fair fight!" Mitoki yelled, trying to breathe around the weight of the demons pinning him to the floor. "He's a human! You're a demon!"

"When he fights Yokouro, it will be the same situation," Acurala said. "Pick up the sword, Dalton, and show me your power."

Dalton slowly brought himself to his hands and knees, his back radiating with bolts of pain as he moved. He tried to discreetly cast an eye around the room to find his family, catching a glimpse of them behind a leg of the conveyor belt.

He had to use the sword to help him to his feet, but he then quickly cast the scabbard away and shakily raised it toward Acurala. Taking a few deep breaths, he turned the sword toward the sitting Yokouro.

"I won't fight him," he growled. "*You're* the one who did this."

"Me?" Yokouro laughed. "I've been here the whole time. Acurala was the one who took your family and brought them here. These are all his men, not mine. I'm just an observer, and a catalyst to rile up that dragon magic within you."

"You and I are supposed to fight," Dalton snapped.

"This isn't the time for that," Yokouro said patiently. "You're not strong enough, yet. That's the whole point of tonight. If we fight now, and I kill you, I have to wait centuries before I can finish this ridiculous battle with these dragon spirits. I've been waiting nine thousand years, and I'm done waiting."

"I don't give a damn about the destiny or the dragons, I only care about killing you."

"Then tap into that dragon magic so you can actually stand a chance," Yokouro said with a condescending smile.

Dalton started forward, pushing his pain aside as he darted at Yokouro, sword raised. Acurala's demon speed allowed him to easily intercept Dalton, his blade clashing against Dalton's and throwing the human off-balance. Dalton stumbled to get his feet back under him, turning to guard against Acurala.

"Get out of my way," Dalton snarled.

"You'll have to go through me, first," Acurala said, placing his sword against Dalton's. "Just how badly do you want to kill him?"

Dalton attacked Acurala, spinning around him once before trying to attack Yokouro again. Acurala moved faster, defending Yokouro from attack in the blink of an eye. The younger demon lord did not seem at all worried about Dalton's attempts to attack him.

Dalton and Acurala clashed blades around the narrow room. Dalton would force the fight one direction when they got too close to the pinned Guardians or his hiding wife and daughter. When the fight got too close to Yokouro and Dalton would swing to attack the silver-haired demon, Acurala would take the fight in another direction.

The Guardians were doing their best to free themselves, but they were also distracted watching Dalton's every move. On occasion, Frieda would peek over the edge of the silver conveyer belt, trying to plan her escape. However, the small room left little possibilities for sneaking around, and it would be impossible to get past the demons unseen.

Dalton was rapidly tiring. He could feel his blood loss and the mounting pain made it difficult for him to move in certain ways, causing him to leave openings for Acurala to cut his flesh.

"Come on, Dalton, you're better than this." Acurala taunted. "You have magic. *Use* it. How else are you going to get through me to get to Yokouro? I'm not even breaking a sweat."

Acurala lunged forward, forcing Dalton to retreat. He backpedaled, barely fending off Acurala's attacks as they came faster and became more brutal. His fear was rising again, frantic to regain his footing against Acurala's relentless blows.

One of his feet connected with the foot of the conveyor belt, causing him to stumble and twist his body away from the rapidly approaching sword. The blade missed his chest, but sliced open the outer part of his leg.

Dalton let out a choked cry, nearly falling to the floor. But Acurala's hand tangled in his shirt and threw him haphazardly in the other direction, disorienting him and causing his pain to flare even higher when the open wound connected with the cold concrete.

Frieda and Theresa both let out terrified screams, drawing attention to their hiding spot.

"Will someone restrain those two?" Yokouro groaned irritably.

"Don't touch them!" Dalton bellowed, motioning one of his bloodied hands toward the guards who moved to obey the orders.

Magic far greater than Dalton could anticipate burst from his palm, sending a shockwave of sparking energy through the room, creating thin cuts along the skin of everyone it touched, including Frieda. The hooks along the track on the ceiling shuttered and fell with a cacophonous clatter when the chains holding them snapped as Dalton's magic radiated through the room.

"Bravo, Dalton!" Acurala laughed triumphantly. "That's what we've been waiting for!"

"I will not let you hurt them!" Dalton snarled, turning his hand in the air, his magic condensing around Acurala and slowly pulling him to his knees.

"That's it, Dalton. Let it consume you!" Acurala cackled. "Tear me apart! Get revenge for what I did to your family!"

Even though the pain was clouding his thoughts, Dalton managed to use his magic to pull Acurala toward him until he could tangle his fingers in the demon's shirt.

"I'm not going to let you manipulate me," he hissed angrily.

Acurala's smile made Dalton shiver.

"But it seems like you respond best to physical pain," Acurala noted. He lifted his sword. "So how about this?"

With crushing strength, Acurala brought the hilt of his sword down on Dalton's chest, shattering his collarbone and two ribs as

Dalton let out an agonized scream, falling away from the demon, his magic scattering with his broken concentration.

"Agh, we talked about this, Dalton," Acurala groaned, standing and prodding the edge of the sword against the still-bleeding leg wound. "A warrior should never voice his pain!" He dug the blade deeper into the wound, causing Dalton's body to shiver and shake as he resisted going into shock.

"Human bones break so easily..." Acurala sighed. "How pathetic. A dragon actually decided to bless his power to a worthless human bloodline, trying so desperately to prove that humanity is worth saving, when you can't even defend yourselves against the things that want you dead."

Dalton tried to fight the agony in his body, his vision blurring as he tried to focus on Acurala.

"Come on, Dalton, pull your pathetic self together," he tutted, tapping the broad side of the blade against the side of Dalton's face. "We're not finished here. If you don't start showing more progress, I'm either going to have to kill you, or go after your wife and child again."

Dalton tried to kick at Acurala's legs, but the demon lord stepped easily out of range.

"What a weakling."

Acurala lifted the sword, preparing to plunge it into Dalton's chest. The Guardians bellowed and fought against their captors. Frieda screamed, trying to cover Theresa's eyes.

Yokouro merely smirked and turned to the door.

The door opened with a resounding bang that startled everyone. The two gunshots punctuating the sound were just as unexpected. Acurala's shoulder was knocked back by the force of the two bullets, causing him to stumble as he turned his attention to the newcomer, ignoring the rapidly-healing wounds in his shoulder.

Dalton's were not the only wide-eyes in the room.

"*Andrew*?" he breathed in disbelief. "What the hell are you doing here?! How did you even get here?!"

The question was answered by the red-haired woman striding confidently into the room, her heeled shoes clicking on the cement floor. She walked to Yokouro, sitting next to him as she wrapped her arm around his neck and pecked a kiss on his jaw. His arm wrapped around her waist, pulling her even closer.

"Like I said, Dalton," Yokouro started, "I've been working very hard to set this all up for you."

The Guardians had suspected that Shannon's sudden reappearance had been connected to Yokouro, but seeing her smiling coldly at her son as though he deserved the pain he was in caused their anger and resentment to burn hotter than before.

Andrew did not seem at all surprised by the revelation that Shannon was working for Yokouro, which told those of Team Dalton that he had been coerced into coming to the warehouse and did not know the woman's identity. Dalton ignored the cold stare of his mother, getting to his knees.

"Andrew…just walk slowly over to me," Dalton said.

"Take one step, boy, and you will be dead before you hit the ground," Acurala warned.

Andrew dared not take his eyes off the demon, his gun poised for another shot, though he was certain it would do no good. Acurala cocked his head to the side, smiling.

"Do you fancy yourself as some sort of hero?" he asked, snorting with contempt. "Do you think your bullets will do anything more than annoy me? I'm more powerful than you could even imagine, kid."

"Leave him out of this," Dalton snarled, his magic flaring once again, reacting to his desperation to get Acurala's attention off his apprentice. "If you harm him, I will rip you limb from limb."

The lights in the room began to flicker. The temperature rose several degrees.

Acurala turned over his shoulder to Dalton.

"That's better…"

Andrew fired two more shots at the demon's chest before Acurala lifted his hand and closed his fist, causing the gun to buckle in the young man's hands. Andrew dropped the useless weapon and rushed forward, his own magic sparking around his fists as he tried to punch the demon.

"Andrew! Stop!" Dalton ordered sharply. What remained of the chains on the ceiling rattled, the lights pulsing and flittering as Dalton's magic grew thicker in the confined space.

Yokouro let out a soft groan, wincing as he rubbed at his chest, his own dragon magic reacting violently to Dalton's. Shannon worriedly placed her hand on his chest.

"Maybe we should leave," she suggested.

"Yes, I think that might be best," he agreed, worried that if Dalton came into his power at that moment, he would be unable to contain the dragon energy clawing at his ribs.

No one noticed Yokouro and Shannon leaving, too focused on getting Andrew away from Acurala.

Acurala delivered a hard punch to Andrew's chest, forcing the young man back, though he recovered remarkably fast, breathing hard as he waited for the demon to attack him.

"Andrew! Don't fight him! You can't win!" Dalton barked.

"Aw, let the kid fight if he wants to play hero," Acurala chided. "Besides, he seems to be working quite nicely to get you in the correct frame of mind. I've tried threatening your loved ones, threatening physical harm, causing physical agony, and threatening your own life, but you're still keeping that dragon energy tightly locked away from your consciousness. This is the next thing we're going to try, threatening your student."

"You're saying that this ritual torture is trial and error?!" Mitoki gasped.

"A little," Acurala admitted. "You must understand, I'm not trained in this like Rutu. I can't weed into someone's mind and create torturous illusions. So the plan had to change when I took the lead. My plan is to slowly walk you further and further into desperation until you finally accept this power of yours and use it to stop the torment. We will try everything we have to until it finally works, so Dalton, it's in everyone's best interest if you just let go of whatever is holding you back."

Dalton could feel his fear spiraling out of control, bringing him to a darker and darker frame of mind. He was becoming angrier and angrier, his rage blinding him to Yokouro's absence. But there was still the lingering fear that if he tapped into those powers, they would overwhelm him, and lead him to harming his loved ones.

He watched in terror as Acurala turned his attention back to Andrew, and the sickening feeling only grew worse when Dalton watched Andrew dart to the fallen sword, snatching it up to defend himself against Acurala.

"Acurala! You're going too far! You're going to kill all of us if you keep this up!" Keito bellowed.

"Someone gag the mutt," the demon lord ordered.

The moment Keito opened his mouth to retort, a demon guard shoved a length of chain between his teeth, holding it tight behind his head.

Eclipse turned to Dalton, trying to lift his head from the cement.

"Dalton, don't be afraid of this," he told him. "We'll be fine. And we'll protect your family. But you're the only one who can end this."

Dalton could feel his vision tunneling. The pain radiating through him and the panic he felt at how out of control the situation

317

had become were nearly enough to make his eyes close. He knew the feeling, understood that he was moments away from blacking out and letting his powers take control of his actions.

But the distant sobs of Theresa forced his eyes back open.

He could not risk it.

"What's it going to be, Dalton?" Acurala asked. Dalton turned his conflicted gaze to the demon, unable to move as he stared at his cold expression. "Seems like we still have work to do."

Acurala lifted his sword and went after Andrew, who blocked as best he could, though he had never sparred with a demon seriously before, and he was startled by Acurala's brute strength. He stumbled away, losing his focus and breaking his form. The Guardians began screaming at Acurala, struggling against their captors, hoping they could find a way to interfere with the fight before Andrew was seriously harmed.

Dalton tried to stand, but his leg refused to hold his weight and his arm was hanging uselessly at his side as the pain in his chest made him see stars. He tried to move closer to the fight, his magic radiating from him without form, reacting to his pain and panic, though he could not think clearly enough to direct it.

Andrew turned when he had found his feet and rather than defend against Acurala, he pushed forward, attacking aggressively as Acurala parried every swipe of the blade. Dalton watched each step, each slice, each minor injury, and felt his stomach turning sickly as he watched the smile on Acurala's face widen.

Dalton's anger was growing stronger, threatening to burn his insides as he watched the fight.

Acurala deflected another attack from Andrew, turning in a quick circle to spin his blade around and grip the hilt tight as he punched Andrew in the abdomen. As the young man dropped the sword and curled around the demon's fist, Acurala's other hand grabbed his shoulder and kicked the back of his legs. Andrew fell to his knees, gasping for breath.

Acurala brought the hilt of his sword down on top of Andrew's skull with a sickening crunch before grabbing his hair and yanking his head back to slide the blade across his throat.

The Guardians shouted nonsensically. Frieda screamed, hiding the crying Theresa's face in her chest as she turned away.

Dalton's entire world stopped spinning the moment the blade hit Andrew's neck. In that split moment, he was certain he could reverse time, dart forward, and kill Acurala before he had a chance to finish the cut. Fire raged through his veins, clouding his vision and forcing a dark growl out of his throat.

But in the next second, Acurala had finished the cut and the world moved even faster than before. Blood tumbled down Andrew's chest as a surprised expression overtook his face. The blade did not stop moving, tilting and skewering Andrew's chest in a swift motion.

Dalton was unsure if the sword was now sheathed in Andrew's chest, or his own. But he felt no warm blood trickling down his abdomen. He only saw the rivulet of blood that stained Andrew's clothes.

The painful fire in his body halted, but did not leave. Dalton's brain took in what happened next, but he could not react to it. He felt trapped in his own body, in consciousness, and in time. His eyes followed Andrew as the boy slumped to the floor, dead. Then Dalton's head fell forward, and his own body fell to the side, limp.

"Dalton!" Hanyi yelled.

"Not to worry, he's not dead," Acurala said, producing a cloth from his pocket and wiping the blood from his blade. "Seems that did the trick. He'll come to, soon." He nodded to the two nearest guards in the room. "Keep him upright."

The two black-clad demons pulled Dalton off the floor, holding him on his knees while they kept his arms spread wide. The two guards looked at one another, surprised that Dalton had not reacted at all to the jarring of his injured shoulder.

Acurala also hesitated when he noticed the lack of reaction.

"Oh? Are you stuck?" he asked. He crouched in front of Dalton, trying to peer into his eyes. "Really? Even that didn't work? Your aura is so constricted now."

He sighed dejectedly, studying his sword as he stood.

"I think your dragon magic has put you into a protective coma," he mused. "Maybe I just need to cause a little more pain."

He placed the tip of the sword against Dalton's unbroken clavicle.

"Sir!"

Acurala spun round just in time to grab the thin pipe Frieda tried to swing at his head.

"You really thought you could sneak up on me?" he jibed, his wrist twisting as he bent the pipe easily. Frieda was glaring defiantly, despite the tears streaming down her cheeks. With a dark laugh, Acurala shoved Frieda to the ground, turning on her as the Guardians struggled once again.

"Glad to see you're not completely useless," he laughed. "I guess you're volunteering now." He pointed his blade at her, stalking forward as she tried to crawl backward. "This should get his attention."

Adrenaline coursing through her, Frieda kicked the blade to the side, ignoring the way it sliced into her leg. At the same moment, her arm swung out with the pipe and struck Acurala across the face with a crunching sound.

"My lord!" several of the guards gasped, rushing forward. He held up his hand to them before gingerly pressing his fingers into the blood that spilled down his face.

"Impressive," he said darkly. "You actually managed to hit me." He licked the blood off his fingers. "You know I can't let that slide." He turned over his shoulder. "Get the girl."

"No!" Frieda screamed, trying to get to her feet as Acurala kicked her back to the ground. "Run, Theresa!"

The young girl ran from her hiding spot, slipping under the machine in front of her to avoid the grasping hands of a demon as she sprinted for the door. The guard caught her and pulled her into his arms even as she screamed and kicked, flailing wildly. The other demons were straining to keep the Guardians down as they fought to help Theresa and Frieda.

Dalton had still not moved.

Acurala turned to Theresa, pointing his sword at her, which stilled her struggles immediately.

"You're pretty feisty, too," he noted with a sick smile on his face.

Frieda scrambled to her feet and ran at the demon guard restraining her daughter, slamming into him with her entire body and bringing all three of them to the ground. She pried Theresa from the demon's grip and started for the door, but Acurala leapt in their way, his sword extended in front of him, forcing them to retreat as his smile grew unnaturally wide.

"I had no plans to hurt the women, but don't think I won't. My job is to get Dalton and the dragon magic into one consciousness, and if that means I have to spill your blood as well, be assured that I will do so."

Acurala's eyes fell to Theresa, who was hiding behind her mother as they crawled backwards, shaking and crying in terror.

"Why don't we start with the little one?"

He grabbed Frieda by her hair and yanked her to the side as she screamed. He then turned his sword to Theresa.

A hand wrapped around Acurala's wrist and twisted it angrily, another arm locking around his chest as he was pulled backward.

"Enough, Acurala!" Juki snapped, pulling his struggling brother back as the sword clattered to the ground. Rutu ran around the brothers to Andrew's pale figure, kneeling next to the body.

An overwhelming wave of relief washed through the Guardians at the sight of the Kage Lords.

"Get the hell off me, Juki!" Acurala bellowed, trying to free himself from his older brother's grip. He turned in his brother's hold and lifted his free arm, bringing his elbow down on Juki's right shoulder. With a hiss of pain, Juki released Acurala, who rounded immediately on Frieda and Theresa once more.

But Juki moved faster, wrapping one hand around the back of Acurala's neck and turning him to the side, his foot connecting with the back of Acurala's knees, forcing him to the ground.

"Damn it, Juki, stay the hell out of this! I have it under control!"

"You're completely out of control!" Juki barked.

Acurala ducked out of Juki's grip leaping up and rounding on his older brother.

"Do not get in my way, Juki," he growled. "I am doing what needs to be done, and if you oppose me, I will take you down."

"You do not want me as an opponent, Acurala," Juki warned. "Stand down, *now*."

"No."

He leapt at Juki, but before he could close the space between them, he let out an agonized groan, his body crumpling to the floor as pain descended on every inch of his body. When he was flat on the ground, Juki shook his head.

"Don't make me hurt you more."

"You won't hurt me more than that," Acurala sneered, slowly standing, trying not to show how wobbly his legs had become. "And I am sick of you ordering me around like you know everything about everyone. I am following my orders. You were the ones who decided this plan was too messy for you." Acurala's magic began to spark around him as he glared at Juki. "But I'm not afraid to get my hands dirty."

"If you insist on challenging me, Acurala, I will not show you mercy just because you are my little brother," Juki warned.

"I'd like to see you try."

Juki moved faster than even Acurala could comprehend, wrapping a hand around Acurala's neck before spinning him, holding him tight as they faced Frieda and Theresa.

"Take a good look at them," Juki snarled.

"They're just humans."

"Shut your mouth and *look*," Juki said. "Look at their faces. Look into their eyes." His grip tightened around Acurala's neck. "If you wanted to know what our father saw when he plunged that sword into our baby sister's chest, *this* is it."

Acurala stilled, his mouth open to respond to Juki, though the words remained lodged in his throat.

"Do you remember Miu?"

"Of course I remember her!" Acurala snapped.

"Then how could you do the same to this little girl?" Juki growled.

Acurala's eyes fell on the sobbing Theresa, who was hugging her mother so tightly her knuckles were turning white, her entire frame shaking with terror as she stared at Acurala. Frieda's arms were trembling around Theresa, her eyes filled with a mixture of terror and rage as she watched Acurala look between her and her daughter.

"Can you say you had everything under control now?" Juki hissed.

Before Acurala could respond, a crushing weight fell on his bones. He slipped from Juki's hold, doubling over as he choked, fighting for air against the pain that nearly crippled him. He went to his hands and knees, struggling against Juki's power with every ounce of strength he possessed.

Juki leaned down to him.

"I never thought I would see the day where you became our father," he said. "And if you *ever* pull stupid shit like this again," he leaned even closer to Acurala's ear, "I *will* end you."

When Juki straightened, Acurala let out a loud gasp, barely keeping his face from hitting the concrete as the pressure released suddenly, siphoning away any remaining strength he had.

"Get out, Acurala," Juki ordered.

His eyes low and his frame quivering, Acurala stumbled out the open door behind Juki.

Rutu stood, casting his eyes to the guards around the room.

"Release them," he commanded.

In the following instant, the Guardians leapt to their feet, running to Frieda and Theresa. Hanyi crouched, wrapping his arms protectively around them.

"We're here, it's okay now..." he murmured.

"Where the hell were you?!" Keito bellowed at Juki. "Things got out of hand a long time ago!"

"We got here as soon as we realized," Juki defended, though his dark glare warned Keito not to question further.

"Talking of which," Rutu said, glaring at each guard he met eyes with, "someone better explain exactly what happened tonight before I start removing heads." His eyes passed over the bowing guards again. "No one?" When no other demon lifted their head, Rutu pointed at one guard, his magic latching into the front of his shirt as he was dragged toward the infuriated Rutu. The Old Blood Lord placed his hand over the demon's forehead, staring into his wide eyes for three seconds before pushing him away.

The guard fell to his knees, pressing his forehead into the concrete at Rutu's feet.

"All of you, on your knees," Juki ordered.

The guards obeyed immediately.

"You are lucky we don't execute each and every one of you right now," he said sharply. "It seems you have forgotten who you truly serve. And if we were not in the Human Realm where we must maintain some form of discretion, know that you would all die agonizing deaths. You *knew* that Yokouro and Acurala were deceiving us, and none of you bothered to tell your Old Blood Lords that we had been tricked. Instead, you aided them in keeping us in the dark. That is an unpardonable offense."

"Please, my lords," one woman whispered, inching forward on her knees before pressing her head to the concrete. "Yokouro ordered us—"

"Yokouro does not own you!" Juki bellowed. "You serve *us*. Not him."

"Your true punishment will be dealt with when we return home," Rutu added. "If any of you wish to continue breathing, you will obey our orders now." He pointed to two of the guards near the back door. "Find Acurala and be sure you keep him in your sight at all times. Escort him home and keep him there." He motioned to a collection of five kneeling guards. "Go to the palace, retrieve our medical supplies and bring them here immediately. Also inform the household and advisors of the situation." He pushed his foot against the head of the guard at his feet. "And you, retrieve ten Amboria candles and bring them here."

"M-my lord...we do not have any at the palace," he stuttered. "Only Lord Vestera—" His protest was cut short by Rutu stepping harder on his head, pushing him into the concrete.

"Was that order in any way unclear?"

"N-no, my lord."

When Rutu removed his foot, the guard scrambled away.

"You two," Rutu said, pointing to another two terrified guards. "I want you to send a warning to Yokouro, that if he dares to show his face in this realm, no amount of deep magic will put him back together after what I do to him."

"Yes, Lord Rutu," they mumbled quickly, leaving the room on trembling legs.

"The rest of you, start cleaning up the mess you've made," Juki added, turning with Rutu to approach the Guardians surrounding the Teban family.

"Rutu," Mitoki asked, nodding worriedly to Andrew's body. "Is there anything you can do?"

"I'm afraid not," Rutu said. "His soul has already departed. Resurrecting him now would be too damaging."

"Rutu," Juki called, stepping around Frieda and Theresa to kneel next to Dalton. Rutu rushed to the human Guardian, who was still kneeling despite the fact that the guards had released him.

Juki took Dalton's shoulders to lay him on the ground, but released him immediately when he felt the weakness in Dalton's right shoulder.

"His clavicle is shattered," he noted. "Likely a few ribs, as well."

"This leg wound is more serious than the broken bones," Rutu added, pressing his hand against the bleeding gash. He helped Juki guide Dalton to the ground.

"Dad?" Theresa whimpered, finally catching sight of Dalton as her fear slowly abated. "Dad!" she screamed, trying to pry herself out of her mother's arms. "Dad! Wake up!"

"Theresa, it's okay, it's okay…" Hanyi said, stopping the girl from approaching Dalton as Frieda's eyes also rested on him. She had fallen into a state of shock, unable to move. Mitoki and Eclipse stayed by her while Keito hugged Theresa tightly.

"Why won't he wake up?!" Theresa screamed into Keito's chest.

Rutu held his palm over the gash in Dalton's leg, blue healing magic stretching from his hand and gently floating toward Dalton. The streams of energy brushed off Dalton's wound, disappearing into the air. Rutu hesitated before trying again.

"Come on, Dalton," he whispered. "You have to let me help you."

"I don't think that will work," Juki said, studying Dalton's vacant expression. "I think he's too deep."

Rutu leaned over Dalton's face, pressing two fingers into his neck before resting a hand over his half-opened eyes. He sighed heavily, shaking his head.

"He's too far away," he whispered. "That dragon magic is going to keep me from healing him."

"What do you mean?" Eclipse asked, unable to keep the concern from shaking his voice.

"It means we have to do this the hard way," Juki said, extracting a small pouch from one of his inner robe pockets and tossing it across Dalton's body to Rutu. As Rutu reached into the pouch and pulled out a pinch of grey powder, rubbing it between his palms as it dropped into the bloodied flesh of Dalton's leg, Juki tore Dalton's collar, allowing him to examine the rapidly-swelling shoulder.

"You can't heal him at all?" Juki asked as Rutu tore the sleeve from Dalton's jacket to wrap around the leg wound. The younger demon lord shook his head. "How are we going to deal with this, then?" He motioned to the shattered collarbone.

Rutu sighed as he contemplated his options.

"I might have to use an acclimation spell and reconstruct it internally. But that will take several hours. I would rather treat all the bleeding wounds first."

"He also has lashes across his back," Keito said quickly. Rutu turned over his shoulder.

"You should have mentioned that before we put him on the floor."

Juki propped him up, Rutu holding him upright to allow his mate to study the wounds.

"This is not a good place to treat him," Juki mused, glancing around them. "I think we need to get everyone home and cleaned up. But dimension hopping with him in this state could be dangerous."

"We would have to drive," Rutu agreed. "But it's about two hours to Dalton's house, so we need to stop this bleeding as well before we move him."

Rutu passed the pouch back to Juki, who placed the powder over Dalton's bleeding back while Rutu studied everyone else in the room, finally resting on the body of the Guardian trainee.

Juki briefly left the room as Rutu maneuvered Dalton onto his left side. He then walked to the group in the middle of the room.

"We're going to wait here until the guards show up with some medical supplies. Then we're going to drive back to Dalton's house. We'll take Dalton in one car, but someone will need to drive Dalton's car back."

The Guardians nodded silently, unable to voice the numerous emotions racing through them.

Rutu crouched in front of Frieda, though she instinctively flinched from him.

"I wish there was a way to apologize for what happened tonight," he said softly. "This should never have happened, and I apologize for not realizing what was happening sooner. But I want you to know that we're going to do everything in our power to set things right."

Frieda could only nod nervously in response.

"I think it would be best if you were to ride in the car with the other Guardians. We'll take care of Dalton, but I am worried about overstimulating Theresa," he continued, motioning to the girl who was shivering in Keito's arms. "Is that alright with you?"

"A-aren't you…the enemy?"

"Not right now," Rutu said. "I know you have no reason to trust us, but I assure you, we only have the best intentions in mind for you and your family right now. I'm going to make sure you get Dalton back. You can trust me."

"How?" she choked.

"You can trust him," Keito seconded. Eclipse and Hanyi looked at Mitoki and then each other before nodding.

"He's right," Hanyi agreed. "He's probably the only one who can really help right now."

Juki returned to the room, holding up a plastic tarpaulin. "This was the best I could find," he said. Rutu groaned.

"That's an infection waiting to happen." Rutu stood, slipping the robe from his shoulders. "We'll use that to cover the seat in the car. We'll put this around Dalton."

"Quite the expensive wound dressing," Juki said, his eyebrows going high as he took the robe. "Keito," Juki called, jerking his head for the younger demon to follow him. Keito passed Theresa to her mother before joining Juki and Rutu by Dalton, helping to prop him up and wrap the robe around his back.

Eclipse's eyes fell on Andrew's body and he cleared his throat.

"I'm going to call Guardian Forensics," he muttered. "It will take them some time to get here, but we need to get Andrew's body moved and prepped for services."

"That would be greatly appreciated," Juki said. "We'll have a few of the guards here to lead them to him, but I would rather not stick around too long. We're going to need to treat Dalton as soon as possible."

"Why not take him to a hospital?" Mitoki asked.

"We can do a much better job of treating him than any hospital," Juki said. "He'll heal faster if we do the job ourselves. Once we get him back to the house, we'll take care of him."

Chapter Thirty

"This guy drives like a race car driver," Eclipse noted as they drove along the final turns into Dalton's neighborhood, following the black van.

"Which one of them is driving?" Mitoki asked from the passenger's seat.

Frieda had calmed considerably. Theresa had fallen asleep in her mother's arms with Hanyi pressed into her side in wolf form, providing as much comfort as he could. Frieda had not spoken during the entire drive, her eyes tired and distant out the window as she tried to fight the numbness threatening to take over in response to the traumatic evening.

The van stopped on the curb while Eclipse parked in the driveway. The Guardians scrambled out, eager to help Dalton in any way they could. Hanyi helped Frieda extract the sleeping Theresa from the car as Eclipse and Mitoki walked toward the van.

Juki got out of the passenger's seat, shaking his head.

"You are *damn* lucky," he groaned, glancing sideways at Rutu.

"I told you we had enough fuel," Rutu retorted, tossing the keys over the hood of the van to Juki as he approached. The older demon gave him an exasperated look.

"We rolled in on fumes," he said. "We would have been fine if you stopped gunning it like we were in one of your sports cars," Juki continued to tease as he opened the side door of the van.

"You love it when I drive fast," Rutu snorted. "It's the perfect catalyst for your road rage."

Juki and Keito gathered Dalton's unconscious body as Rutu grabbed the medical bags on the floor and the glass orb providing fluids to Dalton. Frieda was trudging up the porch steps when the front door flew open to reveal a very flustered and worried Jikia and Tarrena. Tarrena let out a long sigh of relief and threw her arms around Frieda.

"Thank goodness you're back safely," she whispered. As she broke the hug, her eyes took in Hanyi carrying the sleeping Theresa and Juki and Rutu approaching the house behind him, Juki carrying Dalton.

"What happened?" she gasped.

"We'll explain later," Hanyi said. "It's been a hell of a night."

He walked into the house and moved to the stairs to put Theresa to bed when Rutu's voice stopped him.

"Hanyi," the younger Kage Lord called, also stepping into the house. "We need to check her for injuries. Take her to the master bedroom."

The wolf obeyed quietly, stopping at the top of the stairs and waiting for Frieda to lead the rest of the way to the master bedroom. Jikia and Tarrena trailed behind the group worriedly, their faces going pale as they took in Dalton's state. At seeing the two powerful demons, Rio let out a terrified whimper and scampered to a hiding place, overwhelmed by the energy radiating from Juki and Rutu.

"Frieda, is it alright to treat him in the master bedroom?" Juki asked. "Or would you rather we treat him somewhere else?"

"The bedroom's fine," she said, turning down the upstairs hallway and opening the door for them.

Hanyi gently set Theresa in one of the large armchairs in the corner as everyone else filed in behind Juki and Rutu. Rutu pulled the bed covers down, turning to Frieda once more.

"I'm sorry to bother you again, but do you have any old towels? Ones that you can part with?"

She nodded wordlessly, stepping back into the hallway as Rutu moved the pillows out of the way and motioned Keito to bring the medical bags to him. Frieda returned with the towels, which Rutu took once he passed the glass orb for Keito to hold. He spread the towels over the bed and then helped maneuver Dalton onto them.

The others gathered on the other side of the bed, watching silently, feeling helpless.

Rolling two towels to prop up Dalton's torso, Juki removed the bloodied robe, setting it aside before he glanced up at Frieda's pained expression. She had stationed herself at the foot of the bed, her eyes locked on Dalton and the deep wounds she could see on his body.

"Frieda," he called to her. She jumped, startled at the sudden address. "I know that this is overwhelming. But we will help Dalton. He will be alright."

"He hasn't moved..." Frieda breathed, her gaze turning back to Dalton. "Even when he was in pain...he didn't move." She closed her eyes against new tears threatening to fall. "Someone tell me what the hell happened tonight..."

"We will answer all of your questions as soon as we've tended to Dalton," Juki said. "You have my word."

She hesitated, but eventually nodded, her jaw clenched tight.

"Just promise us you won't break out the liquor," Rutu added with a smile. She shook her head, a thin smile pulling at the corners of her mouth.

Rutu returned to Juki's side, helping him clean the powder out of Dalton's wounds, allowing the blood to flow freely once more. Working in sync with one another without exchanging words, Juki and Rutu began methodically treating Dalton's injuries, stitching together deeper gashes before wrapping the cleaned and treated wounds with bright gauze.

The Guardians also remained silent, sharing concerned glances with one another as they watched the treatment. Jikia and Tarrena were slowly inching closer, whispering to one another about the various powders and herbs the demons used. With a smile, Rutu explained the ingredients they were using, agreeing to sell them some since several of the herbs were exceptionally rare.

When the dragons said they did not want to diminish the Kage Lords' supply, Juki explained that they owned part of a shipping company that went to an island in the Demon Realm where they obtained most of the rare herbs, so they were rarely in short supply.

The Guardians were unsure why they were still surprised to hear about Juki and Rutu's connections.

"How did you learn to do all of this?" Tarrena asked the two demons. "I would think as princes, you would have learned politics more than medicine."

Juki shrugged. "We both relinquished our royal titles when we were young, and then we fought our way back to the top. Most of our knowledge came from necessity. We had many instances where learning improvised medical techniques was a matter of life or death."

"In fact," Rutu added, lifting one of the large leafs they were wrapping in the gauze around Dalton's wounds, "we were the ones to discover the healing properties of this herb. During one of my particularly stupid moments on that island, I was attacked and badly wounded. We used these to camouflage ourselves until we were safe again, and realized that most of my wounds had healed very quickly. After some tests, we found out this plant was the reason. Therefore, we found a way to capitalize it."

"You two are unbelievable," Eclipse grumbled. "Is there anything you aren't involved in?"

"I'm not sure," Juki said with a mysterious laugh. "I've lost track of everything we've done in the last several million years."

The Trade Masters continued their work on Dalton, being sure all injuries were properly treated. When they were certain they had stopped all his bleeding, Rutu began grinding a concoction of leaves and seeds in a bowl. Juki walked around the bed toward the others in the master bedroom.

"While Rutu's preparing that, I'll treat any other injuries you have."

Juki started with the human Guardians, healing minor injuries with healing magic and then checking for more severe damage internally from their struggles. Since most of the Guardians had relatively minor injuries, he moved easily through the room, finally stopping in front of the sleeping Theresa. He reached forward to heal the girl, but stopped, his hand hovering in the air.

"Rutu?" he said, turning to his mate. "I don't want to hurt her."

"Oh, right," Rutu said, setting the bowl aside and walking to Theresa, understanding what Juki meant. While the Guardians were trying to find a way to ask Juki what he was talking about, the older Kage Lord slowly approached the nervous Frieda.

"Do you mind if I heal your injuries, Frieda?" he asked.

"Why would you hurt my daughter?"

"I would never hurt your daughter," Juki said.

"Then why did you just say that?" she demanded, nodding toward Rutu and Theresa. Juki hesitated.

"It's nothing to be concerned about," he said. "Rutu just has more control over his powers than I do."

"What does that mean?" she growled, flinching away when Juki reached a hand out to her.

"Now is probably not the best time to discuss this," Juki said. "You're already overwhelmed."

"And you think ignoring it is going to make me feel better?" she snapped. "What did you mean you didn't want to hurt her?"

"I meant that if I used my magic to heal her, it could cause her pain," he said. "I don't have the same control as Rutu, which means your daughter could latch onto my magic and prematurely awaken her own gifts."

"Her *what*?"

"Your daughter is magically gifted, just like her father," Juki elaborated. "She has a dormant power. It's not a dragon or some other spirit, it's just raw magical energy," he said quickly when he saw Frieda's horrified expression. "She's too young to be opening that flood gate. In about a year, she'll probably start showing signs of her abilities. But right now, my power level could overwhelm her and force her powers to mature too quickly. Rutu has the ability to temper his powers and keep her safe. That's why I asked him to heal her."

Frieda retreated until her back was pressed to the wall, covering her face and curling forward, trying to bite back her tears.

"I am sorry. I did not want to overwhelm you further," Juki murmured, gently taking her shoulder and guiding her to sit against the wall. "Keito, get her some water."

The younger demon left without hesitation.

Juki pulled out a handkerchief, pushing it into her hands as she shook and cried quietly. After a few minutes of everyone awkwardly watching Dalton's wife break down, Keito returned with a glass of water. Juki took the glass and wrapped one arm around Frieda, helping her stand.

"Let's go to the other room," he coaxed.

Juki guided Frieda from the room, nodding once to his mate over his shoulder. When the door closed, everyone turned to Rutu.

"He's going to make sure she drinks some water and then gets some rest," he explained. "She's in no state to be dealing with this."

"Yeah, but you're just going to disappear later, right?" Mitoki asked. "She's still going to be overwhelmed and confused when she wakes up."

"No," Rutu said, resting two fingers against Theresa's neck and closing his eyes, psychically searching her for injuries. "We'll remain here until Dalton is healed and conscious. We might have to slip away for a few hours here and there. We do have a territory and business to run. But we will see that this gets righted." With a soft sigh, he stood, finding and healing the minor injuries Theresa had obtained.

"Why didn't you just do this ritual in the first place?" Keito asked.

"Yokouro doesn't trust us anymore," Rutu said. "And he openly deceived us about when he was planning to go through with this. Had we known that this was his plan, we would have interfered much sooner." He turned his attention to Hanyi. "Hanyi, she seems comfortable around you. Will you please take her to her room and put her to bed?"

The wolf nodded, stepping forward to collect the sleeping girl. Rutu caught his arm, his eyes turning sympathetic.

"I'm sure this isn't the appropriate moment, but I want to extend my condolences about your mate," he said gently.

Hanyi straightened, staring suspiciously at the demon lord.

"How did you..."

"I can sense the broken mate bond in your aura," Rutu noted. "I am truly sorry for your loss. Thank you for saying here and helping, despite everything."

Hanyi lowered his gaze, unsure how to respond. With a quiet "thank you" he gathered Theresa in his arms and left the room. Rutu returned to the bowl he had left, stirring in some oil before carefully pouring the concoction into Dalton's mouth, drawing the bowl back repeatedly as he did to ensure Dalton did not choke. The Guardians were too tired to ask what Rutu was doing. Once Rutu had given Dalton the mixture, he extracted some tissue-wrapped candles from his bag and used magic to light three of them on the bedside table.

Jikia and Tarrena straightened, lifting their noses in the air once the candles were lit.

"Amboria blossom?" Jikia asked. "How did you get those?"

Rutu smiled. "One of my good friends is a dragon," he teased. "This will soothe the dragon magic within Dalton without suppressing it. It should calm Dalton down a little." Rutu rolled up one of Dalton's eyelids, peering briefly into his eye before turning back to the others. "Reconstructing Dalton's bones will take a substantial amount of time," he said. "There is no reason for the rest of you to exhaust yourselves further by staying up. You are more than welcome to get some sleep. We'll be here in the morning."

"No, we'll stay up," Mitoki said, uncomfortable with the thought of sleeping when Juki and Rutu were treating Dalton's substantial injuries. When the others agreed, Rutu merely shrugged, cleaning some of the supplies from the bedspread and replacing them in the bag.

"Do you think he'll recover from this?" Eclipse murmured.

"He will survive, and he will wake up," Rutu said confidently. "But it will certainly take time for him to heal from the psychological damage inflicted."

"But he's merged with the dragon spirit, right?" Keito asked.

"No, not yet."

"Even after all that?" Eclipse asked incredulously.

"This is a very delicate process, and unfortunately, it was done very poorly. Acurala and Yokouro took things too far and pushed him past the ideal state for incorporating the dragon magic. Thankfully, Dalton's psyche didn't break completely. But now we have to wait for the dragon magic to calm, and Dalton's mental state to strengthen so the magic can merge properly. That's why Kuryaoin put him in the coma. We can't force things now. The dragon magic will keep him in the coma to keep him safe from outside influence until Dalton is in control of it."

"So we have no way of knowing when he'll wake up?" Mitoki asked.

"No," Rutu agreed, closing the medical bag and placing it on the floor. "But we're going to do everything we can to facilitate the merging of powers," he motioned to the candles. "Otherwise, we just have to watch and wait."

The bedroom door opened as Juki reentered.

"She's asleep," he told them. He glanced over the remaining Guardians in the room. "Everyone healed?"

As they nodded, Rutu walked to his mate and placed a hand on his right shoulder.

"You're not," he noted. Juki flinched away immediately, backing away from Rutu.

"That's my bad shoulder," he snapped.

"And it's swollen. Come here." Rutu put his hand on Juki's shoulder once more, his palm emanating with blue magic as he healed the swelling. The older demon rolled his shoulder a few times as he nodded to Dalton.

"Is he ready?"

Rutu returned to Dalton's side, sitting on the bed and pressing a finger to Dalton's neck.

"Almost," he said.

"How are you going to reconstruct his bones?" Jikia asked, stepping closer, interested in the new healing techniques.

"Once he calms and that brew takes effect, I should be able to manipulate a small amount of healing energy from within his body. His defenses are so high that his body won't allow for outside help, but once my magic starts getting in his bloodstream from that concoction, I should be able to telekinetically move the bone fragments back into place and then heal them."

"How do you even know how to do that?" Eclipse hissed, his eyes wide.

Rutu's only response was a mysterious grin.

"May I observe?" Jikia asked.

"Of course," Rutu said.

Hanyi returned to the master bedroom around the time Rutu knew he could start healing Dalton's broken bones. He made an incision over Dalton's ribcage, slipping two fingers into the cut while Juki placed a clean towel against the open parts of the wound to dam the bleeding. Rutu's other hand rested over Dalton's unbroken clavicle as he bent his head and closed his eyes.

For several long, silent minutes, the exhausted Guardians could not see anything different about the purple and red blotchy skin of their team leader's shoulder. As more time passed, they though they thought the fading dark colors in Dalton's skin were hallucinations from tiredness mixed with desperation to see progress. But when part of Dalton's skin ballooned up into the position of the collarbone, they gasped in surprise.

"That's incredible," Jikia whispered.

"I can't handle watching this when I'm this tired," Eclipse grumbled, rubbing his eyes. "I'm going to get some sleep."

"Please do," Rutu said, opening his eyes to look at the progress he was making. "The damage is a little worse than I anticipated, so this will probably take the better part of four hours."

Keito looked torn when Mitoki and Hanyi followed Eclipse out of the room. Keito walked closer to Jikia and Tarrena, temporarily breaking their focus on Rutu's work.

"Are you two staying here?"

"Yes," Jikia said. "I want to learn how to do this."

Rutu nodded to the two fingers he had under Dalton's skin.

"Place your hand on mine so you can feel how I do this."

She did so, her eyes beaming with intrigue. Keito sighed heavily.

"Alright, fine. I'm going downstairs to rest."

Chapter Thirty-One

A gentle tapping on his shoulder caused Hanyi to jump awake, startled. When he saw the pale face of Theresa in front of him, he sat up immediately from the couch, shifting into his human form.

"Theresa, you're awake." He pulled her onto the couch with him, wrapping her in his arms. "How are you feeling?"

"Okay..." she muttered, winding her arms around Hanyi as tight as she could. "Is my dad okay?"

"Yes," Hanyi said. "He just needs to rest."

"Who were those men?"

"...they're here to help us," he said gently. He did not want Theresa to be afraid of Juki and Rutu, despite the danger they posed to the Guardians. Hanyi knew better than to outright trust the Kage Lords, but he knew they would keep their word to help Dalton and his family, which meant Theresa had no reason to fear the powerful demons.

He turned his eyes to the clock on the wall, seeing it was nearing seven in the morning. Frieda had fallen asleep in the guest room Keito and Hanyi had been occupying, but Keito was no longer in the living room. Hanyi's ears picked up several sounds of movement through the house, telling him that everyone was already awake and shuffling around their rooms.

"Where is everyone else?" Theresa asked, noticing Hanyi looking around the living room.

"I'm not sure," he said. "I'll go find them."

"No!" Theresa gasped, tightening her grip around him when he tried to move. "Don't leave me!"

"Okay, okay," Hanyi cooed, his arms going around her once more. "It's alright. I'm here."

His heart broke for Theresa. He could only imagine how traumatized Theresa was after the ordeal the previous day. He was certain Frieda would also be in a high state of anxiety. And until Dalton's condition improved, he was worried the two would struggle to control their residual fear.

Carrying Theresa, Hanyi went upstairs, pressing his ear to the door of the master bedroom first. When he heard nothing within, he opened the door a crack and peered inside, closing it when he saw Dalton's solitary figure in the room.

"Is Dad in there?" Theresa whispered.

"Yes, he's sleeping," Hanyi whispered back. "Let's let him rest."

"Where's Mom?"

Approaching the door of the smaller guest room, he listened for any sounds within, hearing the shower running.

"She's taking a shower," he answered. "We'll meet her downstairs when she's done."

He turned to the door across the hall as it opened and Eclipse and Mitoki stepped out of the other guest room.

"Morning," Eclipse greeted. He placed a hand on Theresa's back. "How are you feeling, kiddo?"

"Okay…" she said, reaching out for a hug. Eclipse took Theresa out of Hanyi's arms, hugging her tightly.

"Where is everyone?" Mitoki asked Hanyi.

"Frieda is taking a shower. Dalton's sleeping," Hanyi answered. "I'm assuming neither of you have seen the demons this morning."

Both humans shook their heads, wondering if they could discuss what had occurred the previous day with Theresa around. Eclipse moved some of her bed-mussed hair from her face.

"Are you hungry?" he asked.

She shook her head, looking around the hallway. "Where's Uncle Keito?"

"How come you don't call any of us Uncle?" Eclipse play-pouted.

"Sorry, Uncle Eclipse," she giggled, hugging him tightly once more.

"Thank you." Eclipse looked at Hanyi. "What about Jikia and Tarrena?"

"I don't know," the wolf answered. "I didn't hear or see them downstairs."

"What about…*them*?" Mitoki asked, briefly flicking his eyes to Theresa. "Did they leave?"

"They said they wouldn't," Hanyi said with a heavy sigh. "Amazingly, I actually believe them."

"…yeah, I do, too," Mitoki admitted. Eclipse groaned and rolled his eyes.

"As much as I hate to say it, I believe them, too."

"Do we just leave this in their hands, then?" Mitoki asked. "They seemed to understand what needed to be done."

"Do we have any other choice?" Eclipse said.

"Are you talking about the men who saved us?" Theresa asked, looking curiously among the three Guardians. "Where are they?"

"We should probably track them down," Hanyi declared, leading them downstairs and listening to the rest of the house with his head cocked. Hearing nothing, he followed Keito's scent to the door leading to the backyard. When the Guardians stepped onto the patio, they found a very peculiar sight on the swing set.

Keito was seated at the bottom of the plastic slide, against which Rutu was leaning. Juki sat on one of the swings with two unfamiliar demons standing in front of him. All five demons turned when they heard the Guardians step out of the house.

"Uncle Keito!" Theresa called, scrambling to get out of Eclipse's arms. He set her on the ground, but kept a firm hold of her hand to keep her from running to the demons as they cautiously approached.

"Who are the humans?" the unknown male demon asked, scanning them.

"They're none of your concern," Juki said darkly.

"When can we reschedule Lord and Lady Orthean?" the female demon said, grabbing Juki's attention.

"We'll have to move that meeting to the next cycle. I don't have time between then and now."

"And Lady Trewne?"

Juki turned over his shoulder to Rutu.

"I know she makes you uncomfortable…"

"That's a gross understatement," Rutu grumbled.

"Please, just handle that meeting for me," Juki said, exasperated.

"She's far too forward," Rutu said, raising an eyebrow. "You want to put me alone in a room with her? My virtue will be compromised."

"Well, I would be happy to meet with her, but then you'll have to meet with Lord Clotin for me," Juki said, a smile pulling at the corners of his lips.

Rutu groaned in frustration, shaking his head.

"Fine," Rutu groaned. "I'll meet with Lady Trewne."

"Thank you, Lord Rutu," the female demon said with a deep bow of her head.

Juki chuckled lightly at the pained look on Rutu's face before turning back to the two demons in front of him.

"Is that all?"

"Yes," the woman said, holding out an envelope to Juki. "Pyrneatt asked me to give this to you, but that is all."

Juki took the envelope and nodded to the two demons.

"You are dismissed."

The two demons bowed their heads, retreated three steps, and then disappeared with a crack of displaced air. Juki stood, nodding to the Guardians.

"Sorry about that," he said. "We had to reschedule some business meetings." He passed the envelope to Rutu, who opened it and read over the letter. "I'm surprised to see you awake already."

"Where are Jikia and Tarrena?" Eclipse asked, slowly walking closer to Juki and Rutu now that the unknown demons were gone.

"They went shopping," Juki answered. "They figured Frieda was in no state to be shopping or cooking." Juki turned his attention to Theresa, who was staring at him nervously from behind Eclipse's leg. "How are you feeling, Theresa?"

She did not immediately answer, instinctively understanding just how much power Juki possessed. She nervously bit her nail, not sure if she should answer him. Seeing her apprehension, Juki crouched and smiled gently.

"I know, I look scary," he said. "But I'm not going to hurt you."

Cautiously, still biting her nails, she stepped away from Eclipse. Juki did not move, allowing her to approach.

"T-Thank you for saving us."

Juki's smile widened. "Are you alright?" he asked. "Nothing hurts? No injuries?" She shook her head. Juki looked at Rutu. "Did you have to heal much for her?"

"Minimal bruising and swelling, a few scrapes," Rutu answered, pocketing the letter.

When Juki turned back, Theresa jumped, having been studying him intently, her wide, curious eyes roving over him.

"What?" he asked softly.

"You have long hair…" she mumbled. Juki grabbed the end of one of his braids and tickled her nose with it.

"I do."

"Why?"

"Because I am a very high-ranked demon lord," he answered. "Old Blood Lords like me and Rutu have to keep our hair long. It's a sign of our authority."

"Really?" Eclipse and Mitoki asked simultaneously.

"The standard only applies to Old Blood Lords, now," Rutu elaborated. "A very long time ago, it applied to any demon with status. The longer the demon's hair, the higher their status." Rutu sighed heavily. "If it wasn't for tradition, I would cut it off. It's more of a hassle than you realize."

"You have a lot of earrings," Theresa noted, reaching out to Juki's ear. The demon turned his face, allowing her to touch the power limiters. The Guardians also got their first good look at the sheer number of piercings Juki wore.

"Why do you wear so many external power limiters?" Eclipse asked. "Wouldn't it be easier to add more internal limiters? They're more powerful."

"It's his fault," Juki said with a laugh, motioning to Rutu. The other demon nodded with a knowing grin.

"We've been together for so long that our auras have merged completely. Because of that, we have daily changes to our powers that most do not. We need to be able to put on and take off limiters as necessary. We already have twenty-nine internal power limiters, but the seventeen or so external ones make it easier to fine tune things based on day-to-day need."

"Together?" Theresa asked, taking advantage of the Guardians' stunned silence. "Are you two married?"

"In a sense," Juki answered.

"Do you have kids?"

"We do. Three of them."

"How old are they?" Theresa asked excitedly.

"Oh..." Juki said slowly, thinking. He turned to Rutu, both of them pondering the number. "Our oldest is four-thousand, seven-hundred, and thirty-two," he answered carefully, trying to think of the exact number.

"Demons live that long?!" Theresa gasped. Juki nodded. "Do you have boys or girls?"

"Two girls and one boy."

"Still freaks me out..." Eclipse said with a shudder. Rutu laughed from where he stood.

"You're not alone."

"Can I give you hug?" Theresa asked Juki nervously, turning her eyes to the ground. The older demon smiled and extended his arms. She rushed forward excitedly, wrapping her arms around his neck. "Thank you for saving us," she said again.

"You're welcome, Theresa," Juki murmured, gently patting her on the back. "You are a very brave girl. Don't you ever forget that." When she pulled away from the hug, he pointed over at Rutu. "But you know, Rutu did most of the work. Why don't you go give him a hug?"

Theresa ran to Rutu, her arms wide. The other demon lord picked her up and gave her a hug, setting her on his hip.

"They're so much fun when they're this young," Rutu said, patting Theresa's back gently as she squeezed her arms around his neck. He smiled at Juki. "Sure you don't want another one?"

"Hey," Juki said with a teasing grin, "we've had this conversation. The answer is *no*."

"I think you already have your hands full," Keito laughed, finally standing from his seat on the slide. "The three you have are practically your clones, stubbornness and all."

"True," Juki admitted. "They can be a handful."

"Keito, why are you out here?" Hanyi asked, suddenly realizing how strange it was for Keito to be involved in the meeting Juki and Rutu were having.

"Now that you mention it…" Eclipse said, also coming to the same conclusion. "Why *are* you out here with them?"

Keito retreated a step.

"Why are you glaring at me like that?" he asked.

"I'm curious about that myself," Juki said, his eyes turning sharp as he looked among the other Guardians. "Is he not allowed to speak with us? Because I might have a few things to say about that."

"Juki…" Keito murmured, shaking his head.

"You two are making this look much worse than it is," Rutu laughed brokenly, still holding Theresa on his hip. "We asked him to join us because we were speaking with Vestera and, as an honorary member of Demon Council, Keito had to know what Vestera's orders were regarding the situation with Dalton."

"What do you mean?" Theresa asked worriedly as Rutu set her back on her feet.

"Well, your dad is sick. We're here to make sure he feels better, and Keito was helping us decide how best to treat your father," Rutu said with a reassuring smile.

"Why couldn't you just say that?" Mitoki asked Keito.

"I didn't really get a chance to explain myself before you got all suspicious," Keito said.

"Do you not trust Keito?" Juki asked, perplexed.

"It's not that…" Mitoki grumbled.

"It's just…with you two…" Eclipse shook his head, trying to find the words to explain. "We know that he lived with you two for several years, and since you work with Yokouro and everything…"

Juki's surprised gaze turned to Keito.

"You told them you lived with us?"

"No, they found out on their own," Keito said reluctantly.

"And you think that means you cannot trust him?" Juki asked the others. "I can assure you that Keito did not *want* to live with us. He tried to run at every opportunity. But he was stuck with us until I said he could leave."

"I thought you two were friends," Mitoki said, confused.

Juki barked a laugh. "No offense to Keito, but we're too many social levels apart to be considered friends. Of course, I have his best interest at heart, and I did teach him a lot while he was living in my home."

"You don't get all the credit," Rutu grumbled.

"In any case," Juki said, deciding to ignore Rutu, "Keito and I have a complicated history, but I'm not going to command him to turn against you. Not that he would listen even if I did." Juki smiled knowingly at Keito who nodded sheepishly.

The back door opening halted further questions from the humans as Frieda stepped into the backyard. Her face was pale, accenting the dark bags under her eyes. Her feet dragged as she approached, trying to smile in greeting. The Guardians shared a worried look as Juki turned to Rutu.

"Rutu..."

"I know," Rutu said with a nod.

Theresa ran for her mother, throwing her arms around her in a tight hug. Frieda held her daughter close for several long moments before walking the final distance to the Guardians and the demon lords.

"Good morning," she greeted tiredly, holding Theresa's hand as she stopped to look among the group. "What is everyone doing out here?"

"We were playing on the swing set," Juki said with a chuckle. "Then the Guardians caught us and we've been awkwardly trying to explain ourselves."

Frieda laughed, even though she knew he was lying.

"I wasn't sure you would stay..." she murmured.

"We promised you we would," Rutu said. "We won't go anywhere until Dalton is back on his feet."

"Well, possibly with one exception," Juki said. "We will probably have to slip away for a few hours tonight, but we'll be back as soon as we can."

"Oh?" Frieda asked, worried. "Are we keeping you from something important? I'm sorry..."

"It's alright, we want to help," Juki reassured. "We've rescheduled all major meetings for the next few weeks. But I'm afraid to cancel on my daughter. She'll hunt me down."

"Your daughter?" Frieda repeated, surprised, looking between the two Kage Lords. "I thought you two..."

"We are," Juki confirmed. "Rutu is also the biological father of our children. And yes, that is possible with the type of power we possess."

"What's going on with your daughter?" Hanyi asked.

"Our oldest, Kree, is going to be officially mated soon," Juki said. "Tonight there is a scheduled ceremony where he must ask for her hand in front of us and the Kage Court so that we can give him consideration for becoming part of the royal family."

"It's really just for ceremony," Rutu added. "We've already given our blessing, of course. Well, *I* have." Rutu raised an eyebrow at his mate. The Guardians laughed at the pained expression that crossed Juki's face.

"I've given my blessing…" he mumbled.

"In that exact same tone," Rutu teased.

"Having trouble letting go of your princess?" Keito quipped.

"It's not that easy," Juki lamented. "It's not that I don't like her mate, and of course I trust him, but it's difficult to see her getting ready to start her own family. I keep thinking she's too young. It seemed like only yesterday she was the same age as Theresa." He turned to the young girl. "Stay that age as long as you can."

Theresa laughed and nodded quickly.

"Frieda," Rutu started, "can I persuade you to drink some water? Or maybe some tea?"

She nodded. "I would love some tea."

"Shall we go back inside?" Juki suggested. When Frieda nodded again and motioned everyone toward the door, they filed inside. Frieda placed a hand on Juki's arm to stop him.

"How is he?"

"He's alright," Juki assured, patting her hand. "We only left him two hours ago. Things are looking good."

Rutu busied himself in the kitchen making tea for everyone as the Guardians greeted Frieda gently and hugged her as they gathered in the living room. Frieda sat heavily in one of the arm chairs, pulling Theresa onto her lap, closing her eyes as she kissed her daughter's head.

Juki stood next to the chair, offering Frieda a small smile.

"How are you feeling?" he asked.

She sighed heavily. "Horrible," she admitted. "Which is a little better than yesterday."

"You are handling this far better than I could have imagined," he said.

"I don't know if I'm handling it at all…" she grumbled. "Will you please explain what is happening to my husband?"

"Yeah, could you explain it to all of us?" Eclipse said.

Juki hesitated. "I will tell you what I know, but to be perfectly honest, even I don't know all the details," he said. "I'll answer any questions I can, but you might have to reserve some for Vestera."

"Fair enough. As long as we get some information," Eclipse agreed.

"I don't know how much you know of the realms before they were connected four thousand years ago," Juki started. "But the dragon regime had a system for keeping watch over the development of human civilizations across most of the universe. Some systems were left without guidance, others were heavily monitored with dragons acting like dictators over humanity. In this collective of realms, the dragons watched from a distance, occasionally stepping in to guide humanity in certain directions. But because there are far more humans than dragons, civilizations were assigned to dragons to monitor. But, of course, as the human population grew and advances were made, most dragons were seen as threats and killed. This was in a time where magic was also seen as a taboo practice among humans.

"During this time, two dragons, the brothers Yasuain and Kuryaoin, oversaw two different groups of humans in what is now known as the Realm of Light," Juki continued. "Yasuain saw the attack on dragons as humans reaching a dangerous point in their evolution, and he took it upon himself to destroy the humans under his charge."

"Did he have that authority?" Mitoki asked. "I would think Vestera would stop him."

"Vestera may be extremely powerful, but he is not omniscient," Juki said. "He did not know about the attack until it was too late. And the method of attack left many of the surrounding countries in such a state of chaos that wars plagued that region for nearly two centuries. This led to other Watcher dragons wondering if they needed to annihilate their own human populations. It created an enormous amount of tension among the dragon clan. Yasuain was put on trial for trying to incite a rebellion against Vestera and for creating so much chaos among the humans. I don't know the specifics, but Yasuain's brother challenged him to a duel that would prove if humans were more evil than good."

"How would a battle between two dragons do that?" Hanyi asked.

"The two dragons had a spell cast upon them that connected them to all the humans under their charge," Juki explained. "Their magic was fed by the deeds of humans. Yasuain is strengthened by every malicious act humans commit against one another, from fits of blind rage to wars between countries. Kuryaoin, who believed humans were worth protecting, is empowered by the goodness in humanity and the kind deeds done in service of their fellow man."

"Then how did Dalton and Yokouro get wrapped up in all this?" Eclipse prompted.

"As with all duels, a second had to be chosen," Juki said. "If the spell was not satisfied by the time one of the two brothers died, the spirit of that dragon, as well as the power gained from the acts of humanity, would pass to the chosen second. Yasuain killed his brother in an unfair fight, which passed Kuryaoin's spirit to Dalton's ancestor—his chosen second. And it has passed through generations of Dalton's family down to him."

"That does explain why Dalton's father was such a powerful human..." Keito murmured.

"The dragon passed on through his mother," Juki corrected. The older Kage Lord cringed. "I guess we're going to have to explain her involvement, as well."

"Later," Eclipse said, waving the question away. "Does this mean that only the Realm of Light will suffer the effects of this duel?"

"No," Juki said. "Even before the realms connected, Kuryaoin was connected to the humans of this realm and Yasuain was connected to the humans of the Realm of Light. But with thousands of years of these realms being connected, all humans in this collective will be subject to the outcome of this duel."

"Then Yasuain chose *demons* as his second," Hanyi deduced. "Then how is a fair duel possible? Dalton doesn't stand a chance against Yokouro."

"Not without the help of Kuryaoin," Rutu agreed, returning to the living room with a tray filled with mugs. He set it on the coffee table, picking up one mug and offering it to Frieda as Theresa hopped down to get the smaller mug of hot chocolate Rutu had made for her. "Kuryaoin is fueled by thousands of years of humanity's decisions. If he meets Yokouro in battle, once he's trained and mastered the dragon magic, and the dragon spirits fight with all their power bared, then the spell will be satisfied upon the defeat of one of the dragons."

"And this has been going on since before the realms connected?" Mitoki gawked. "What has taken Yokouro so long to finish this duel?"

"None of us understood the dragon magic inside Yokouro," Juki said. "He was a very powerful, and very angry young demon. When he performed certain dragon spells, we assumed he had found

344

a spell scroll somewhere and learned on his own. We had no idea that he was holding this dragon spirit."

"And when there was a host strong enough to hold Kuryaoin," Rutu added, "Yokouro would become obsessed with ending their life. He had a sense for it, and he would hunt down Kuryaoin's new host and kill him. He said the mere existence of the other host was too painful to bear, as though everything inside him was clawing at his chest, trying to rip him apart from the inside. We didn't learn the specifics of this duel until shortly after Dalton was born. That is why Yokouro's intent on making sure this duel happens. He wants this spell to be satisfied and broken."

"That's why he did all that to Dalton yesterday?" Frieda asked.

Juki and Rutu shared a quick, worried glance, before Rutu spoke.

"Yokouro tried to do what he could to prepare Dalton for the battle," he said. "But, clearly, it did not go as well as he hoped. Dalton is now strong enough to host Kuryaoin, but he wasn't born that strong. His powers had to mature and his body had to grow before he could handle the magic of the dragon spirit. His Guardian training did most of the work already, but that incident at age eight when the young boy was killed had Dalton too afraid to let those powers come to the surface. He has kept them repressed most of his life, and he built a barrier between his consciousness and Kuryaoin in response to the trauma of killing that boy."

"There is a separate entity inside my husband?" Frieda whispered, sipping on the tea, her eyes distant.

"…that is very difficult to answer definitively," Juki said slowly. "I suppose, at the moment, yes. But Kuryaoin is not a voice that Dalton hears in his head. It's a very old dragon spirit that has latched itself onto Dalton's magic. Once Dalton combines his power with the dragon magic, the spirit will be an extension of Dalton's powers, one that he can command just as he does his own magic. But Dalton has been sure to keep that power at bay, which means that the magic acts as an entity that will protect its host if endangered."

Frieda sipped her tea again, her eyes still lost in the space before her.

"Is any of this making sense?" Juki asked.

"A little…" she said. "But I don't like it at all." She turned over her shoulder to fix Juki with an anxious stare. "When he wakes up…will you have to do the…ritual?"

"No," Rutu answered, causing her head to spin toward him. "The ritual failed. Even if we tried it now, it wouldn't work. At this point, Kuryaoin's power is keeping Dalton safe by keeping him in this coma. Dalton will wake up only when he accepts the dragon power and can command it to release him."

Frieda's mouth opened, her lips quivering as the words sunk deeply into her skull.

"He could stay like this for months…" she whimpered.

"He won't," Rutu said with a reassuring smile and shake of his head. "The candles are keeping the dragon magic in an active state, which is keeping them both awake. We just have to wait for the two powers to negotiate and integrate. Dalton was already making progress by the time we finished treating him last night."

"And…*when* he wakes up?" Frieda asked. "Will he just…be more powerful?"

"Yes," Juki said. "And he will need training as soon as possible. Dragon magic is nothing like human magic."

"And training will be enough to get him strong enough to fight Yokouro on equal ground?" Mitoki asked skeptically.

"It will depend on his trainer," Juki said. "If he started training under us the moment he wakes, we might be able to get him to Yokouro's level in about four months. As it is, we can't train him." Juki drew in a deep breath. "My suggestion? Go to Vestera as soon as possible as a team and train with him. He knows more about this duel than anyone, and he knows how best to train all of you for fighting Yokouro."

"Are we allowed to fight Yokouro alongside Dalton?" Hanyi asked.

"I believe so, but check with Vestera," Juki said.

Frieda had gotten through half of her tea when she rested the mug on her leg and closed her eyes tiredly.

"Then…everything Yokouro said, about finding Shannon, and rigging the tournament…that's all true?" she murmured.

Juki nodded. "He was trying to bring Dalton back to the same heightened state of anxiety he experienced as a child, before the incident with the other child at the training center. Shannon was the first part of that."

"And she…she wanted to hurt Dalton? She wanted him dead?" she choked. "I don't understand how a mother could be so cruel…"

Juki's eyebrows rose. "She's very easily influenced, and she certainly harbored a lot of hatred towards Dalton that Yokouro fed into. Yokouro knew just how to charm her into working for him."

"Then they're…" Hanyi lifted his eyebrows, trying to motion with his hands. Rutu shrugged.

"For now," he said. "Yokouro is not good at maintaining relationships. He'll tire of her."

"And then what? He'll kill her? Is that what happened to his mate?" Eclipse growled. Both Kage Lords blinked in surprise.

"You know about Marrina?" Juki asked. "But no, Yokouro did not kill his mate. He loved her very dearly, so I don't suggest you bring her up around him, unless you want him to tear you limb from limb."

"But he'll kill Shannon?" Eclipse pressed.

"He won't kill her as long as she's useful to him," Juki said. "If we had had our way, she would not have been involved at all. But Yokouro took control of the ritual, and had Acurala trying magic and techniques he was not prepared to use. I apologize for my younger brother's abhorrent behavior. I tried to tell Yokouro that he was not ready, but Yokouro doesn't trust us very much anymore."

"Why do you serve him at all?" Mitoki asked in disbelief. "You two are the most powerful demons in the realm, right? You're far more powerful than him. Why do you listen to his orders?"

"That's our own business," Juki evaded. "But had we been involved more last night, I assure you, the young man would not have been killed."

The Guardians flinched at the thought of Andrew, unable to stop the flashing image in their heads of the blood cascading down his chest as he died. Theresa's eyes began to well with tears, her voice choking as she looked around the room.

"Is Andrew...really dead?"

Keito tenderly took the mostly-empty cup from her hands and pulled her into a hug, silently answering her question. She buried her head in his chest, crying at the realization of Andrew's passing. Frieda also dropped her head and pressed her fingers into her eyes to dam her tears.

Rutu crouched next to Frieda's chair, tapping her arm. "Will you please try and finish that tea?" he asked softly. "I'm worried you'll get dehydrated."

She mechanically lifted the cup to her lips, sipping again.

Rutu let out a long sigh as he stood, meeting eyes with Juki. No words passed between them, but the Guardians were startled to see the silent conversation occurring. They could speak volumes with a single look, sharing their concerns about Frieda on a deep, silent level. The depth of the look was evidence of just how long Juki and Rutu had been together, and the Guardians felt as though they were witnessing a very private moment between the two, having to turn away from the profound understandings underlying the glance.

Juki nodded minutely to Rutu, before looking over his shoulder at the front door.

"Jikia and Tarrena will be back in about a minute. All of you should eat something," he said, stepping closer to Frieda's seat and putting a hand on her shoulder. "Promise me you will try and finish an entire meal." She nodded slowly, but the distant look in her eyes made them wonder if she understood what was being asked of her, or if her mind had turned numb as she struggled to comprehend the new complexities of her life.

Chapter Thirty-Two

The Kage Lords did not eat with everyone else. They did not even sit at the table when offered. They politely declined and slipped upstairs to check on Dalton. Keito smiled and shrugged at the questioning glances the others gave him.

"They're *very* old-fashioned," he laughed. "They are acutely aware of the fact that they are guests. They don't feel comfortable accepting most hospitalities that humans offer. They will not sit while in the house. They won't accept any food you offer them, either. To them, it's good manners." Keito smirked. "I'll bet you anything that, when they come back after the ceremony tonight, they won't even walk into the house unless you invite them in again."

Frieda was not the only one having difficulty finishing the late breakfast. The Guardians found their own appetites lacking, picking at the food, their stomachs twisted in worry over Dalton's condition. Theresa managed to finish most of her food, as did Jikia, but much of the food was left untouched as a pensive silence gripped the dining room.

Juki and Rutu returned as Keito was standing to take his half-full plate into the kitchen. Juki peered over Frieda's shoulder at her plate before reaching into his pocket and pulling out a small, silver container of pills. He opened it and offered two to Frieda.

"What are these?" she asked.

"Basic painkillers. Something to take the edge off," he said, his hand unwavering in front of her. She plucked the pills out of his palm, taking them with a blank stare.

"How is Dalton?" Hanyi asked.

"He's responding well to the herbs and treatments. And his aura is slowly starting to stabilize, which is a very good sign," Juki answered.

Rutu leaned over Theresa's shoulder with a soft smile. "Are you finished?" he asked, motioning to the plate. When she nodded, he grabbed the plate before moving to ask Mitoki if he was finished.

"You don't need to do that," Tarrena said quickly, standing to take the plates from the demon lord.

"It's alright. I'll help," Rutu said. "You two prepared breakfast. I will clean."

"No, really, I'll do it," Tarrena insisted. "You're a lord. You shouldn't be doing dishes."

"My title doesn't exclude me from anything," Rutu said. "Besides, I used to work in the Kage Clan kitchens. Doing dishes was my main job as a servant."

"Servant?" Tarrena repeated, startled.

"It's best to let him do it," Juki said with a grin. "He's incredibly stubborn."

"Who said I was doing them alone?" Rutu asked mischievously. Juki shot him a playful glare before taking Frieda's plate from the table.

Jikia and Tarrena still helped the Old Blood Lords with the dishes while the Guardians returned to the living room with Theresa and Frieda, keeping a close eye on the two, most worried about Frieda's blank staring.

When Juki and Rutu had finished with the dishes, they agreed to take everyone upstairs to check on Dalton. While the Guardians tried not to be disturbed by the pale, bandaged appearance of their team leader, Theresa was lingering around the bed, clearly distressed to see her father in such a state, despite the brave face she was trying to show. Frieda held her hand in comfort, but everyone could see the powerful emotions playing over her features as well.

The Guardians were worried that Frieda was reaching her breaking point.

Juki and Rutu tried to explain the way Dalton was healing, but their overwhelmed minds could not take in the information. The Kage Lords slowly stopped explaining, tending to Dalton in almost complete silence under the various watchful eyes in the room.

The silence was broken by the ringing of the doorbell.

"Are you expecting someone?" Keito asked, turning to the Trade Masters. Rutu sighed, pursing his lips as he turned to Juki.

"Do you want to stay?" he asked.

The older demon's expression became pensive.

"It seems that Elder Teban has come to see for himself what happened to his grandson," he explained. "Would you like us to leave before—"

"No!" Frieda gasped almost desperately. The Guardians were startled by her adamant response. She lowered her head sheepishly. "Please don't leave any more than you absolutely have to…"

"Okay," Juki said gently. "We'll stay."

The doorbell rang again, followed by insistent knocking, bringing everyone out of the master bedroom and to the front door. Frieda moved to answer the door while the Guardians shared worried looks, unsure how Elder Teban would react to Dalton's condition—as well as the close proximity of the Kage Lords.

Frieda had barely opened the door before Elder Teban burst in and hugged her.

"Frieda, I'm so sorry," he whispered, pulling away and taking her by the shoulders. "When I heard about what happened to Andrew, I just…" He shook his head, at a loss for words. "What about Dalton? Does he…" The older man trailed off as he scanned the faces in the room, his gaze finally settling on the two demon lords.

"You two…" he gasped. "What are you…" He looked rapidly between the Guardians and the Kage Lords. "Anyone care to explain what is going on here?"

"Grandpapa…" Theresa choked, wrapping her arms around his waist tightly. He placed one hand on her back, but his eyes never left the demons in the room.

"You two are in the same house as my grandson and great-grand daughter?" he growled, glaring.

"Elder," Frieda started, "Without them, Dalton would be dead…"

"They're not trustworthy, Frieda," Elder Teban hissed.

"So far, I think they've proven otherwise," Keito quipped. Elder Teban pointed angrily at the demon Guardian.

"I don't want to hear a word from *you*," he snapped. "You're always on their side."

"I don't believe this has anything to do with sides, Jonathan," Juki said.

"You both are too self-serving for this to be out of the goodness of your hearts," Elder Teban sneered, contempt dripping from every word. "Whatever you did for Dalton, I'm sure it comes at a price."

"It does," Juki agreed shortly. "We don't have the most open schedule in existence, you know."

"Not cost to *you*."

"Elder Teban," Mitoki said, stepping forward to divert his attention. "I understand that it is difficult to trust them. We all understand. But they really have been helping Dalton. Without them, Dalton, Frieda, and Theresa would all be dead."

Confused and mortified, Elder Teban turned to Frieda.

"What?"

"We were attacked…kidnapped. They intervened…" she choked, her voice trembling as the memories of that night threatened to bubble to the surface.

The older man turned back to Juki and Rutu, his eyes cold and dark.

"Don't think I'm going to *thank* you," he growled.

"Elder!" Frieda gasped.

"There is no need to defend us, Frieda," Rutu said. "Jonathan has a long history with us. His hatred goes back far further than today."

"Then, Rutu, you wouldn't mind leaving while I speak with my family and the Guardians."

"You will show him the proper respect and address him by title," Juki ordered, his voice dark.

"What respect? He's just your attack dog, isn't he?"

"Shall I turn him loose on you?" Juki threatened. Rutu smirked coldly at the Elder, which caused him to visibly shudder.

"I don't see what is wrong with me asking you to leave. This is my family, and I have a right to speak with them in private," Elder Teban said. "Besides, you are out-of-realm demons. I have rank over you as long as you're in the Human Realm."

"Really?" Juki asked skeptically. "I thought that applied to all demons other than Old Blood Lords." He raised an eyebrow. "I think that was in the DPC Interrealmal Code, Dimension of Demons, section two...what subsection?" Juki asked Rutu, though it was clear he already knew the answer.

"Subsection one," Rutu completed.

Elder Teban's face was turning purple with rage.

"How dare you?"

"This is very telling indeed, Jonathan," Juki said. "Your behavior speaks for itself. You care more about not losing face in front of the demons you hate than asking about your grandson's condition. I guess when you leave an orphan to his own devices when he's seven in order to pursue your own political agenda, it would stand to reason that your reputation is more important to you than your family."

"I want you both out of this house."

"Only Frieda can ask us to leave," Rutu said.

Elder Teban turned to her, placing his hand on her shoulder once again.

"Frida, please, try to understand. These demons are *dangerous*. I would feel more comfortable talking to you and the Guardians if they were not in the room."

Frieda hesitated, debating with herself as she slowly turned to the two demons. "I suppose you already know everything he wants to discuss with us," she muttered.

"Probably," Juki agreed.

Nodding reluctantly, Frieda heaved a sigh. "I'm sorry, but could you two maybe step out for ten minutes?" she asked.

"Of course," Juki obliged, walking over and placing a gentle hand on her shoulder. "Just call us if you need us. We'll be in the yard."

"Don't touch her," Elder Teban snapped, grabbing Juki's wrist. An angry growl rumbled from Rutu's chest, which caused Keito to instinctively growl, tensing in preparation for a fight. Juki stared at Elder Teban, waiting for him to remove his hand. Once he did, Juki nodded once to Frieda and went toward the back door, Rutu close behind.

"I don't appreciate the way you treated them," Frieda said, turning back to Elder Teban.

"Do you have any idea who those two demons are?" he hissed.

"Only what the boys have told me," she said, motioning to the Guardians. "But those two demons saved my life. They saved Theresa's life. And Dalton's."

"They're *dangerous*."

"But they are guests in my home," Frieda said strongly.

"I did not mean to upset you," Elder Teban said, raising a hand. "I just want someone to explain what happened without them looming over us. They might have told you to lie."

"They have been nothing but helpful," Frieda snapped. "That tournament you and the others reinstated has brought out a complete psychopath. Those two actually know what the hell is going on, which is more than I can say for you and the rest of Council. Maybe you should have figured out exactly what was happening before you threw your own grandson against a mass-murdering demon that hosts an ancient dragon spirit."

"A what?"

"Your grandson and Yokouro are supposed to fight to the death with the help of two dragon spirits that could bring about the end of humanity," Frieda snarled. "But, by all means, start a tournament so that your best fighters are too busy fighting one another to be efficient at their jobs!"

"How can you say—"

"My husband is lying up there in a coma!" Frieda interrupted. "My daughter was almost *killed*! And I don't know how I'm even supposed to start to handle that. So having you come here and tell me that the only two who have made any sense in the last few days are not welcome in *my* house makes me more than a little upset."

"Frieda…" Elder Teban started cautiously, taking her shoulders once again. "You've been through a lot. I understand."

"No, you don't!" Frieda yelled, shaking his hands away. "You don't know how I feel. And to be honest, I could kill you for pitting

Dalton against this demon without even thinking about what it would do to me and his daughter, or what it could mean for everyone who depends on Dalton to keep them safe. He's the best Guardian in the branch, and you offered him up like bait!"

Her voice broke and she sniffed back her tears, covering her nose and mouth with one hand as she tried to collect herself. She took a deep breath.

"So why don't you do what you've always done?" she growled. "Leave Dalton to find a way to survive. Get the hell out of my house."

She turned on her heel, yanking open the front door, where the Elder's security detail was patiently waiting.

"Frieda, I—"

"Go!" she barked.

For a few seconds, Elder Teban could only stare at the others in the house. Theresa was worried, her eyes wide in confusion, but every other face in the room was drawn and dark. Even though the Guardians felt some obligation to the Elder, Frieda's words radiated through them, igniting their own rage at being offered up as bait for Yokouro.

Elder Teban left without a word and Frieda slammed the door behind him.

~∧~

Juki and Rutu left later in the afternoon, saying they would be gone only for a few hours. They asked the Guardians to keep careful watch over Frieda, hoping they could convince her to drink more water and eat a full meal.

After they left, everyone fell into helpless silence. They would periodically glance up the stairs, wondering if they should go see Dalton, but they remained in the living room, lost in private thought. Tarrena and Jikia tried to bring coffee and water to the Guardians, but no one was particularly interested in either. Theresa, bored with the silence and overwhelmed with the tension in the house, fell asleep in one of the chairs, leading Hanyi to take her to her room.

Frieda continued to glance at the clock, as though counting down the minutes until Juki and Rutu returned.

After sighing heavily for the umpteenth time, she shook her head.

"Why are they helping us?" she murmured.

The Guardians shared a look before shaking their heads and shrugging.

"I think only they can answer that question," Keito said. "Things went very wrong the other night. They might just want to help because they know it's the right thing to do."

"They are the two most powerful demons in existence?" she asked. Keito nodded slowly. "And they serve Yokouro?"

"Apparently, not very faithfully," Keito chuckled brokenly. "But, yes."

"Why hasn't Yokouro tried to attack Dalton again?" Frieda asked. "Dalton's helpless up there. You would think he would at least want to see if his moronic ritual worked."

"Even Yokouro isn't stupid enough to come near Rutu right now. Rutu will likely tear him to shreds if he sets foot anywhere near this house," Keito said. "He's fuming right now."

"He doesn't appear to be too angry," Eclipse noted.

"If you watch carefully, you'll see how often he's chewing the inside of his lower lip," Keito said, one side of his mouth quirking into a smirk. "Juki told me that if I ever saw Rutu doing that, I should run like hell."

"Rutu's..." Frieda stopped, her eyes turning to the ground as she searched for the words. "Something's...off about him."

"How do you mean?" Mitoki asked.

"I don't know. I can just sense it..." Frieda muttered. "I know he's powerful, but there's something *more* there. It's like Dalton. I knew there was something more to him." She sighed and rubbed her forehead tiredly. "I guess that something was a dragon spirit..." She shook her head. "But whatever Rutu has, it's far bigger than a dragon spirit."

Keito sighed. "When Rutu's power is off-balance, or when he loses control, you would be amazed at the destruction he can cause," the demon said quietly. "I've only seen one of his mild fits, and it was a long time ago, but he brought about the most violent storm I have ever seen in my life. He uprooted trees, completely killed every living plant around him..."

"That could have been the storm," Eclipse tried to suggest.

"In five seconds flat?" Keito challenged with a raised eyebrow.

"I think that's why he understands how to help Dalton," Frieda continued, ignoring the conversation. She lifted her eyes to Keito, her gaze pleading. "He's going to bring Dalton back, right?"

Keito's smile was a little shaky. "He promised he would."

Frieda ate a little more at dinner, but pushed away her meal in favor of coffee to keep her exhausted eyes open. Theresa and the others began putting a puzzle together, though no one could really focus on the pieces, feeling as though they should be doing something to help Dalton.

As the time for Juki and Rutu's return passed, Frieda became more and more anxious, eventually standing and pacing the room, wringing her hands together in front of her as she watched the minutes tick by.

Nearly an hour after the demon lords were supposed to return, there was a knock at the door. Frieda sprang forward to answer it, finding Juki and Rutu on the porch, dressed in extremely lavish robes. Keito raised an eyebrow.

"You didn't change?"

"The ceremony took longer than expected," Juki said. "We didn't want to worry you, so we came right back." He turned to Frieda and offered a gentle smile. "How are you feeling, Frieda?"

"I think the nausea is normal at this point..." she said with a quiet laugh. "Please, come in," she motioned them inside.

"Did you eat?" Juki asked as he stepped over the threshold.

"Yes."

"Good. Have you been drinking water?"

"Coffee."

Juki made a face. "Will you drink a glass of water while we check up on Dalton?" he asked, nodding to Keito, who went to retrieve the glass.

"You're really focusing on my health," she noted suspiciously.

"*You* should be focused on your health," Juki chuckled. "Have you been up to see him?"

"...a few hours ago," she admitted, her eyes falling to her feet. "He doesn't look very good..."

Juki placed a hand on her shoulder, giving it a comforting squeeze before going upstairs to check on Dalton. Once again, everyone trailed behind, collecting in the master bedroom to watch Juki and Rutu clean wounds and change bandages. Frieda sat in one of the reading chairs, her eyes glassy and distant. Theresa was hugging close to Keito's leg, curious about what was happening, but too nervous to step forward.

Once all physical wounds had been redressed, Rutu rolled one of Dalton's eyelids open, before placing his hand over the human's eyes, his own eyes closing as the energy in the room began to grow heavy and spark from the demon's magic. Keito was about to take Frieda and Theresa from the room, as the magic was getting to be too heavy for them to keep their eyes open, when Rutu sighed and stood straight, reigning in his powers again.

"Is...everything alright?" Frieda barely managed to choke out.

"He's making progress," Rutu said carefully. "But he's still fighting Kuryaoin's powers. This fear he has is very deeply rooted."

"Is this dragon spirit...going to kill him?" Frieda whispered. "If he doesn't...accept it? Will it kill him?"

"No," Rutu said. "Dalton will remain in this state until he has accepted the dragon magic as an extension of his own. How long that takes is entirely up to Dalton."

"...he could be stuck like this for a very long time," Frieda breathed, tears gathering in her eyes. "And even if he does wake up...Yokouro might just kill him, like he almost did tonight..."

"Mom?" Theresa asked, worried about the pain and tension she heard in her mother's voice. Keito wrapped his arm around her to keep her close, worriedly watching Frieda as she curled forward in the reading chair in the corner, holding her abdomen, tears beginning to fall. Juki crouched in front of her.

"I don't know how much of this I can take..." she choked. "I can't live with this shadow over my head."

Juki placed a hand on her knee, his gaze compassionate and understanding as her body began to shake.

"Every damn day I have to wonder if he's going to come home, but I always...thought about how good he was at his job. How strong he was...and now...now he's lying there...and I don't even know if he's going to wake up." She sobbed heavily, hiding her face in her hands. "I can't do this..."

After several long moments, Juki tenderly pulled Frieda's hands away from her face.

"That's because you love him," he said. "You can't bear the thought that this burden is looming over him. You want to help him, to take some of the weight off his shoulders. It's very difficult to be in love with someone who holds such a fate. That feeling of being powerless is torture. I understand how painful that is." He dropped his head to catch her tear-filled gaze. "But you have to put your faith in him. He will do everything in his power to protect you, and that alone is enough to keep him strong and bring him back home to you."

Frieda curled forward again, shaking her head as she tried to bite back her sobs.

"Look at me," Juki whispered, waiting for her to straighten and meet his gaze. "He's not going to leave you."

She broke down, curling forward as Juki held her hands in his, offering silent support as she cried.

"Nothing...is going to be the same..." she whimpered.

"That might be so, but that does not mean things are going to be horrible." Juki pushed her upright once more. "Your family is going to change soon, anyway."

She tried to blink the tears away, staring at him in confusion. He rested his hand on her abdomen.

"You didn't know, yet?"

Her hands flew to press into her stomach, her breath hitching as her eyes shot wide. The others in the room rapidly looked at one another, stunned.

"I'm..." Frieda stared, wide-eyed, at Juki.

"I guess this wasn't planned," Juki chuckled lightly. "You probably thought you were merely stressed, but I can tell that you're about five weeks..."

"But...I don't...how do you *know*?"

"There is a distinct change in aura and scent when a woman is with child," Juki explained. "Demons just happen to be very sensitive to it."

"I didn't sense it," Keito muttered under his breath.

"You don't have as much experience as we do," Juki told him. He turned back to Frieda. "Why do you think we've been pestering you so much about your health?" He chuckled, pushing her hair away from her face. "Are you alright?"

"...y-yes...I'm just...surprised..." Frieda's hands remained pressed over her abdomen, shaking slightly. "I didn't even think...but after everything—"

"You are an extremely strong woman. The baby is fine," Juki said, lifting a hand to stop her worried questions. "And this baby is going to bring you and Dalton closer, and your family will become even stronger. And that is how I know Dalton will wake up, and always come back to you."

"Mom?" Theresa whispered, her smile growing wider and wider as she started to understand what Juki had said. "You...you're gonna have a baby?"

"I...suppose I am," Frieda said, new tears in her eyes. She motioned Theresa over, hugging her. "You're going to be a big sister."

Theresa giggled in delight, hugging her mother tightly as Juki backed away.

"She's really pregnant?" Mitoki asked.

He nodded. "That's why we've been trying to get her to eat and drink more water. I would do more to help, but I'm sure she has a regular physician she would rather see."

"Do you know if it's a boy or a girl?!" Theresa gasped, whipping around to look at Juki. The older demon crouched again.

"Don't you want it to be a surprise?" he asked with a grin. "Do you want a little brother? Or a little sister?"

Theresa looked thoughtful.

"A little brother!" she declared.

"Why's that?" Juki laughed.

"So I can tell him what to do and boss him around!" Theresa laughed loudly, breaking the tension in the air and bringing broad smiles to the faces around her.

"That sounds familiar," Rutu said.

"We should tell Dad!" Theresa gasped, bounding out of her mother's arms and jumping up on the bed next to Dalton. "Dad! Mom's gonna have a baby!"

"Theresa—"

"It's alright," Juki assured as Frieda stood to retrieve her daughter. "She won't hurt him. It will help if she talks to him."

"Talking while he's unconscious actually helps?" Frieda asked skeptically.

"It will likely bring him around faster," Rutu agreed. "You should talk to him. Hold his hand. Tell him about the baby. Your voice and touch can help him navigate his way back."

Frieda hesitated, her eyes scanning Dalton's pale, still features. She took a few nervous steps closer, her heart thumping against her ribs as Theresa excitedly spoke.

"I want a little brother! Can you make sure it's a boy?"

Frieda's legs were shaking as she rounded the other side of the bed, tears blurring her vision as she approached her husband. Juki turned to the Guardians and silently nodded to the door, asking them to leave the Teban family in privacy. They quietly filed out, Jikia and Tarrena throwing worried glances back at Frieda as they closed the door behind them. Rutu slowly approached Frieda, smiling tenderly when she turned to look at him.

"It's okay to take his hand," he said.

"I-I don't know what to say to him," she said, trying to strengthen her voice.

"Just talk to him," Rutu said. "Tell him about the baby."

"But he can't actually hear me," Frieda whispered.

"Yes, he can," Theresa defended from Dalton's other side. "He's been listening to us this whole time."

Frieda stared at her daughter, dumbfounded, her brain trying to recall that her daughter was already tuning in to her developing powers, able to sense that Dalton could hear and understand them even in his coma. Seeing the terrified expression, Juki nodded to Rutu before sitting next to Theresa on the bed.

"Theresa, I want you to try something," he said, tapping the back of her hand. "Hold your dad's hand...now close your eyes..."

Frieda's breathing picked up pace as an overwhelmed panic invaded her chest. But the moment she turned to ask Juki what he was teaching Theresa, Rutu's hand fell on her shoulder, diverting her attention.

"It's okay to be afraid and confused," he said.

"I just can't talk to him right now."

"Why not?"

"Because..." She swallowed hard. "I can't...let him hear the fear in my voice."

"Why not?" Rutu repeated.

"I need to be strong for him."

"Frieda, showing and acknowledging your fear doesn't make you weak. You don't need to put up a front. He knows you're afraid. On a subconscious level, you already know what the other is feeling." His fingers wrapped around her hand, his thumb rolling her wedding ring on her finger. "When you exchanged rings, you formed a bond, just like a mate bond. Just like how I can feel what Juki feels, you can feel Dalton's emotions right now." His fingers tightened around her hand slightly. "What is he feeling?"

Frieda's tear-stained face turned toward Dalton.

"Fear..." she choked.

Rutu nodded. "He's just as afraid as you are. But that doesn't mean that you cannot be afraid together. It's better to just admit it and find a way through this time together. You don't have to be strong for him, or pretend you're not afraid. Just be here with him as you are, and let him be here with you as he is."

The tears returned once again, but the tension seemed to seep out of her shoulders as the words sank into her mind. She stood and turned to Rutu, wrapping her arms tightly around him and crying into his chest. She could feel his power radiating from him, and even though she could instinctively feel how dangerous the demon was, she felt safe with his power surrounding her, grounding her in the moment as the overwhelming emotions hummed along her already-raw nerves.

She finally pulled away, trying to wipe the tears from her face with her sleeves before Rutu offered her a handkerchief.

"I'm sorry..." she murmured, embarrassed.

"You have nothing to apologize for," Rutu said.

"I can't tell you how grateful I am that you two have been helping us for the past few days," she said. "I can't imagine how we could have coped if you weren't here." She hugged Rutu again, sighing heavily as she leaned against him. After a few seconds, she pulled away quickly, laughing in embarrassment. "I'm sorry I keep hugging you."

"Again, you have nothing to apologize for," Rutu said with a grin.

"But your mate is right there," she said, nodding to Juki, who laughed lightly.

"I'm not worried," he teased. "He's never shown an interest in women, and I don't think he's about to start now."

She dabbed away some stray tears on her cheeks. "You both have been so supportive. I know that things between you and the Guardians are quite complicated, but I'm so thankful you're here. Is there anything I can do to repay you?"

"Will you take better care of yourself?" Juki asked with high eyebrows. "You're not going to be healthy enough for that baby if you don't start eating more."

She smiled, nodding.

"Mom…" Theresa said quietly, opening her eyes and looking at Frieda in wonder, "Dad is…I-I felt him following me."

"What do you mean, sweetheart?" Frieda whispered.

"I…I don't know," she said, releasing her father's hand as her smile widened. "I just…*felt* him take my hand, and we started walking…" She giggled. "He's coming back!"

Frieda turned to Juki for an explanation.

"It's always easier for younger children to tap into their powers," he said, standing from his seat next to Theresa and nodding to Dalton. "Just take his hand. He's looking for his path back to you."

Slowly, Frieda sat on the bed next to Dalton, her hands taking his and squeezing, lifting his hand to kiss his fingers lovingly, smiling around the few remaining tears that escaped her eyes.

"I'm here, Dalton," she whispered.

Chapter Thirty-Three

Noise surrounded him, rushing into his ears like water, encasing him in a sound that seemed to move and heave like the ocean. The movement became its own cacophony, tossing Dalton around like a ragdoll, disorienting and confusing him. He had no sense of his body, of his limbs, of his breath, or even of his thoughts. He was only aware of movement and noise, rushing around him, but never carrying him in any particular direction.

Occasionally, the movement would slow and calm, and when Dalton became aware of the lack of noise and movement, a pull in his belly caused memories to flood through him, of blood rushing down a young man's chest, of a blade glinting in dim, yellow light, of fear gripping his body so tightly he was paralyzed.

And in an instant, the movement would begin again.

Time had no meaning. Pain held no sway. Emotions were a fleeting glimmer. There was too much around him to conceptualize it. He was merely prey to the tumultuous movement and brain-rattling noise.

But after a while, he noticed that the calm spells were longer than before. The noise was slowly untangling from a battery of sounds to a melodious wave that wrapped around him, smooth, like the scales of a snake. And the barrage of movement seemed to stumble into a pattern, similar to a steady breath, or thumping heartbeat.

It was not until there was a warm glint tickling the edges of his consciousness that a framework to the movement snapped into focus. He could not see anything around him, but he felt himself within a space that was spiraling around him, winding tightly as it circled him over and over again. He could feel the soft ridges of scales, the sharp focus of vision that came with non-human eyes, and the deep growl that was created from millions of voices. If he focused on any particular note of that melody, he was filled with a glow of understanding, the image of someone helping a struggling family, of communities coming together to rebuild after a tragedy, the deep appreciation of someone who had just received a kind word when they so desperately needed it…they melded together into the growl of the coiling, dark dragon that surrounded Dalton, waiting for him to move, ready to coil itself tighter, until it sank into his skin and permeated into his veins.

But even as his mind put the pieces of that framework into place, he was focused on a warmth he could sense nearby. He tried to understand how it fit into the framework, knowing that the way it drew his focus meant it was the most important part of his growing understanding.

It was warm. Comforting. Beckoning him closer.

His hand came into sharp focus for the first time since he had found himself tossed about in the sea of bellowing noise. He felt five fingers gently close around his hand, and a familiar sense of home moved up his arms, bringing his nerves to life as he came to feel his arm, his shoulder, his neck, his chest, and the rest of his physical being. There was a dull ache in remembering how he fit into his body, but the warmth of the hand holding his urged him closer, pushing away the discomfort and the fear as he felt the scales surrounding him brush against his skin, sinking deeper and deeper the closer he drew to that comfortable, loving warmth.

~/\~

Frieda showed just how stubborn and brave she could be when everyone was turning in for the night. Once Theresa had been tucked in and the adults began to feel the exhaustion settling into their bones, Frieda looked among her guests.

"Jikia, Tarrena, you're welcome to stay here for the night," Frieda said.

"You can take the guest room," Keito offered. "Hanyi and I can sleep down here. Hanyi generally sleeps on the floor anyway and I'm comfortable on the couch."

"No, we can sleep down here," Tarrena said. "I'm sure you're exhausted."

"I would feel better if you took the room," the demon insisted,

"What about you, Frieda?" Eclipse asked. Frieda pursed her lips, glancing over her shoulder at the top of the stairs.

"I thought I would stay with Dalton tonight," she murmured. "Unless you two advise otherwise," she quickly whirled back to look at Juki and Rutu.

"No, I think that would be good," Juki agreed.

"What about you two?" Frieda asked.

"We're fine, Frieda," Juki said.

"No, you've been helping us for the past two days. You even went all the way to the Demon Realm for a ceremony and then came back. When was the last time either of you slept?"

"It wasn't that long ago," he said. "I promise, we're fine. You should all get some sleep."

"Will you at least sit down somewhere?" Frieda laughed, looking between them incredulously.

"Thank you, Frieda, but we wouldn't want to impose."

"It's not an imposition," she said with a chuckle. "You are allowed to make yourselves comfortable."

"We are comfortable," Juki said.

"Then sit down somewhere," she laughed. "And I'm not asking."

Juki blinked, his jaw dropping a little as he let out a short bark of laughter.

"Oh? You're not?"

"No," she said. "I don't know what kind of customs you have in the Demon Realm, but you are in the Human Realm, and you are in my home. I feel very uncomfortable with you standing all the time. I want you to sit down and relax a little."

Juki and Rutu both smiled.

"It's been quite a while since we've been ordered to do something."

"I'm sure it has been," Frieda said, grinning. "But you are in my house, so you should do as I ask."

Rutu turned to Juki, nodding to the nearest empty chair.

"You first, my lord."

"That's not fair," Juki groaned, shooting Rutu an exasperated look.

"I'm offering the seat to my Old Blood Lord. I'm just being polite," Rutu said with a mischievous glint in his eyes. He motioned to the couch. "I'll sit here."

"After I sit?"

"After you sit."

With a sigh of defeat, Juki approached Frieda, holding his hand out, palm up. When she gave him her hand, he kissed the back of it.

"You are very gracious, Frieda."

"Thank you," she said before glaring playfully. "Now, go sit down."

Juki obeyed, though with everyone now watching him so carefully, he was even more uncomfortable doing so. Once he was seated, Rutu took the seat on the nearest couch as Frieda nodded triumphantly.

"Thank you."

"Everyone should get some sleep," Rutu said, casting his eyes to everyone in the room. "We'll still be here in the morning."

As promised, Juki and Rutu were there in the morning, in the same positions they had sat the previous night. When Jikia and

Tarrena walked downstairs, Keito was quick to motion them quiet, pointing at the two demon lords. Juki's head was propped on his hand, sleeping in the chair he had occupied the previous night. Rutu was on the far side of the sofa, arms crossed to cushion his head as he slept against the arm of the couch.

Frieda appeared downstairs shortly after and was just as surprised to see the two demon lords asleep. She leaned close to whisper to Keito, hoping not to wake them.

"When did they fall asleep?"

"Before Hanyi and I," Keito answered, also trying to stay as quiet as he could. "They were asleep before we even turned the lights off."

Frieda's worried eyes traveled back to the demon lords.

"I feel guilty asking them to stay..."

"They told us they wanted to help. There is no reason to feel guilty," Keito said. "Just don't get close to them. Their defenses are sharp as hell. They'll attack anything that moves too close."

Once everyone, apart from Theresa, had gathered downstairs, they tried to decide how best to wake the demon lords. Frieda was torn, constantly throwing looks back at the two older demons, worried that Theresa would wake and wander too close to them, not understanding the danger.

"I want them to sleep if they're so exhausted, but..." A wobbly smile came to her lips. "Dalton's color was much better this morning. I want them to check on him."

"His color was better?" Hanyi repeated, a smile breaking over his face. "That's a very good sign."

Keito sighed, glancing over his shoulder into the living room.

"I'd rather let them sleep, too..." Keito murmured. "That might have been why they were so unwilling to sit last night. They thought they would fall asleep."

"Maybe we should just go wake Theresa up now and be sure to keep her away from them," Mitoki suggested.

"No, we should wake them," Keito said begrudgingly. "Who knows when they last slept. They could stay asleep for the entire day if we leave them. We should have them check on Dalton sooner rather than later."

"Okay, but how do we wake them up?" Hanyi asked.

Keito motioned for them to remain in the archway between the dining room and living room as he stepped slowly across the hardwood to the back of the opposing couch.

"Juki?" he called, barely raising his voice above normal volume. The demon lord did not stir. "Rutu?" he said, slightly louder. The two remained still. Keito drummed his fingers along the back of the other couch before ducking into the kitchen and grabbing an apple. Standing at what he hoped was a safe distance, he gently tossed the apple across the room toward Rutu.

Moving faster than the humans could comprehend, Rutu's hand flew into the air to grab the apple, his claws piercing the fruit as it split in his grip. He sat up in an instant, eyes scanning the room. The startled humans just stared at him, waiting for him to remember where he was before they relaxed.

Rutu's eyes went to the apple in his hand, slowly unclenching his fingers around the pieces of fruit. With a sighing laugh, he stood.

"Sorry, we didn't mean to fall asleep," Rutu said as the others slowly entered the living room. "You should have just yelled at us."

"I tried," Keito said. "You were out cold."

"So you decided to lob an apple at me?" Rutu asked, rolling the stiffness out of his neck.

"I didn't *lob* it. It was underhand."

Rutu's eyes fell on Juki, who still slept despite the noise around him. Rutu's face fell as he let out a long sigh, looking over his mate. The others could not help but worry about Juki's continued slumber, as well.

"Is he alright?" Frieda asked worriedly.

"He's alright," Rutu murmured. "He's just exhausted."

"I-I'm so sorry...I should have realized..." Frieda cleared her throat. "You don't have to continue to stay here. I'm sure you have so much else going on..."

Rutu smiled, raising a hand to stop her from apologizing further.

"We want to help," he said. "And, believe me, this is a respite from what we have to deal with at home. He's been worn down for several months now. That has nothing to do with you."

"Should we let him sleep?" Mitoki asked, unable to hide his surprise that Juki still had not woken. Rutu fell quiet, looking over his mate with a torn expression.

"You know, Rutu, if you two become too exhausted, it becomes dangerous for others to be around you," Keito said. "You need to keep your energies balanced, and you can't do that if you're this tired."

"We have a few extra power limiters on right now. No one here is in danger," Rutu assured. He took a few slow steps toward Juki, standing next to him and placing a hand on his shoulder. "Juki," he called. Juki's eyes tightened almost imperceptibly, but he did not wake. Rutu leaned to his ear, unable to hide his grin. "Juki. Kree is here. You're late for the ceremony. She's about to break down the door."

The older Kage Lord groaned, flinching as though the words had struck him.

"That's not funny..." he grumbled.

"I think she scares you," Rutu teased with a laugh. Juki cracked an eye open.

"A little," he admitted. He drew in a deep breath, standing as he pinched his eyes tight and rolled his neck.

"I apologize. I did not intend to fall asleep."

"You needed the rest," Tarrena said.

"How did Dalton look this morning?" Juki asked Frieda.

"I think he looked better."

"Really? Let's go check on him."

The entourage made their way up the stairs to the master bedroom, filing in yet again. When Juki and Rutu stepped into the room, they both let their shoulders drop and smiled.

"Much better," Rutu said, walking to Dalton's side. The other Guardians crowded around the bed, eager to see Dalton's improving condition. He did have better color in his face, but the bandages and bruises still gave him the appearance of being quite ill.

Rutu placed his hand over Dalton's eyes and, once again, closed his own, his magic filling the room, sparking over the skin of everyone present. While the Guardians were worried that Rutu would say Dalton was still struggling to accept the dragon magic, Rutu's face slowly broke into a smile and he nodded.

"I can feel that change from here," Juki agreed.

"What change?" Eclipse asked.

"He's becoming more active," Rutu answered, removing his hand from the human's eyes as he straightened. "He's in the process of incorporating that energy now. Think of it as though he's been confined to a small space, but he's realizing that if he pushes on the walls a little, they start to stretch and break. He's pushing those boundaries now, trying to break to the surface."

"You mean he's about to wake up?"

"He's getting quite close," Rutu confirmed. Juki straightened, turning to Frieda.

"Why don't you bring Theresa in here? Let's see if we can help him find his way to the surface."

She scurried away to get her daughter, her heart filled with hope.

"Juki, can I ask you something?" Mitoki said, causing the two Kage Lords to turn to him. "I know we all appreciate what you've been doing for us these last few days, but…you're not going to be able to help us after this, are you?"

Juki pursed his lips and shook his head.

"I'm afraid not," he said. "At least not for a while. Yokouro isn't the only one we must answer to. After he heard what happened to Dalton, Vestera has ordered us to see him for punishment."

"When did you talk to Vestera about that?" Keito asked.

"Yesterday. Needless to say, he is not at all pleased at the approach Yokouro chose to take. But I take responsibility for Acurala, so I will take the blame for how poorly the situation was handled."

"Why?" Hanyi asked. "I know Acurala is your brother, but he was the one who screwed up, not you."

"I should have kept a better eye on him," Juki said. "I knew he would be unable to properly execute something so delicate. And he has an enormous amount of rage from what our father did to us when we were younger. When that anger takes hold of him, very little can stop him."

"But it still wasn't your fault," Hanyi insisted.

"It's alright," Juki said. "Believe it or not, Vestera and I are friends. He'll scold me, probably hit me over the head a few times with a scroll, which is something he likes to do, and then he'll tell us we can't travel to the human-inhabited realms for a few months. So, I might not be able to help you from here on, but once Dalton gains better control of his new powers, Vestera will be able to help you whenever you need."

Frieda returned to the bedroom with a sleepy-eyed Theresa.

"Good morning, Theresa," Juki greeted. "I was hoping you could do something for me."

She nodded, rubbing her sleep-swollen face.

"Do you remember what we tried yesterday?" he asked, helping Theresa climb onto the bed. She nodded again, her eyes still mostly-closed.

"Does she need to be awake?" Eclipse chuckled.

"It actually works better if she's half-asleep. Her mind is quieter." Juki guided Theresa's hand to Dalton's, being sure her pointer finger rested against the inside of Dalton's wrist. "Take a deep breath and close your eyes," he instructed calmly. "Do you feel his pulse? Follow it."

Rutu straightened, turning to Dalton.

"That was an immediate reaction," he muttered.

"What does that mean?" Tarrena asked.

"That it might not take much for him to wake up," Rutu said.

Theresa's face broke into a huge grin and she gasped, breaking her concentration as she turned to Juki.

"He's coming back!" she announced happily. Juki laughed as she threw her arms around his neck and hugged him.

"Very well done, Theresa," he complimented.

"Her concentration's broken," Rutu said with a laugh, reaching over to press his fingers to the side of Dalton's neck, but his hand immediately recoiled. "It might not be such a good idea for me to be his anchor. I felt his dragon magic flinch." He looked at Frieda. "Frieda, would you please kiss him?"

"What?" Frieda asked, blinking in surprise at the request.

"Since Theresa's concentration broke, we need something to anchor him to the waking world, and since you don't know how to do an energy guide, a kiss is the most efficient way to bring him back to the surface."

"Rutu, were you going to kiss him just now?" Hanyi asked nervously.

"Try it, and I'll punch you."

Every eye in the room turned to Dalton, who was blinking his eyes slowly, trying to focus his vision. Frieda let out a choked sob, her hands going to her face as her knees threatened to give out in relief. Dalton turned his head toward Rutu.

"You better not have tried to kiss me, Rutu..." he growled, though his voice was dry and broke as he spoke.

"Don't worry, I wouldn't have allowed it," Juki laughed.

Dalton turned his eyes to the crying Frieda next to Rutu, but as he reached a shaky hand toward her, Theresa bounded to his other side and kissed him on the cheek.

"There! I kissed you!"

He wrapped his other arm around his daughter, his eyes closing, his breathing slightly labored as his senses began to return to him. With a gentle tap on her arm from Rutu, Frieda rushed forward and threw her arms around Dalton's neck. He cringed at the strength of the hug, but wiggled his arm out from under her, wrapping it around her shoulders, holding her as tightly as he could. She cried into the crook of his neck, holding onto him as though worried he would disappear if she released him for even a moment.

When she found the strength to pull away, she still kept a firm hold on his hand, using her other hand to furiously wipe her tears away.

Dalton finally caught sight of everyone else standing awkwardly on the other side of the room, trying not to intrude on the moment.

369

"Oh…it's a full house," he chuckled weakly.

"We were worried we were going to lose you," Keito said.

"Looks like I'm harder to kill than I thought." Dalton turned his tired eyes to Juki and Rutu again. "I have to admit, though, I've had prettier nurses in the past."

"I'm sure," Juki agreed. "But I'm certain you haven't had any nurses who could reconstruct a collarbone and ribs from the shattered bone fragments," he said, nodding his head to Rutu.

"You would be correct," Dalton said. He turned back to his wife, squeezing her hand and offering a reassuring smile. "I'm so sorry…for everything."

"Stop," she said. "You're here. That's all that matters."

She hugged him once again as Dalton let out a long sigh.

"I…feel different…" he muttered.

"I'm sure you do," Rutu said. "You just completed a very complex magical incorporation. The exhaustion and sensory sensitivity will take a few days to fade. And after that, you'll need to start training how to properly use these new powers."

"Well," Juki interrupted, "maybe wait until you've healed a little first. Let us clean your wounds and change your bandages, and then we can discuss the training."

Dalton was an extremely stubborn patient.

Juki and Rutu were constantly pushing him back to keep him still as they changed his bandages and checked him over once more, but he was restless. He outright refused when they told him to walk with crutches or a cane until completely healed, which led to both demon lords trying to explain to Dalton's petulant expression that they were trying to save him from long-term damage.

He eventually gave in when Frieda assured the Kage Lords that she would be certain he followed their instructions.

Once they were done with their examination, Juki and Rutu explained the dragon spirits to Dalton, the rest of the team also gathered in the bedroom, listening intently to be sure they had not missed anything. Dalton's eyes were glazing over a bit by the time they had finished explaining, but they told him that he was always welcome to contact them if he had any questions. And while Juki gave him a phone number to call, everyone knew it would be too weird for any of them to just *call* the Kage Lords.

Dalton managed to shower, change his clothes, and limp his way down to the dinner table that night, which allowed Juki and Rutu to fully clean up their supplies from the master bedroom while everyone ate.

Later in the night, Dalton was helped back up the stairs to the bedroom, where Juki was closing the lids of two pill bottles.

"Good, just in time," he said.

Dalton sat on the foot of the bed as Juki handed him one of the bottles. "Two of these once a day, with food, for the next two weeks," he said. "And if your pain gets unmanageable, take one of these," he handed over the second bottle. "But they are very potent, so try not to take them too often, or they might burn your organs."

Dalton hesitantly took the second bottle. "Thank you."

"Also," the older Kage Lord reached into his pocket and extracted a coin, holding it out to Dalton. The Guardian stared at it for a few moments before looking back up at the demon lord.

"What's this?"

"It's a dragon power limiter," Juki explained. "Courtesy of Vestera. He said that, when you felt ready, you should seek a trainer and they will help you use this properly."

The coin felt cold in Dalton's fingers as he took it from Juki. His eyes traced the intricate engravings on the surface, where he could have sworn the symbols were slowly moving, following set paths along the surface of the coin in constant motion.

His hand suddenly felt very heavy, and his shoulders dropped.

"Is everything alright?" Juki asked, seeing the darker expression on his face.

"Am I...uh, is it going to be safe for me to be here? While I don't know how to use this?" he lifted the coin.

"I don't think there's cause for concern," Juki assured. "Just try not to let your fear get the best of you. Your fear will stress those new powers and it could cause the dragon magic to react in a defensive way."

Dalton's body tensed, his eyes falling to the bedspread. Juki glanced over Dalton briefly before turning to Rutu and nodding once. Rutu took a step forward and extended a hand to Dalton.

"Give me your hand."

"Why?" Dalton asked.

Rutu gave him an exasperated look. "There's something I must ask you concerning our future together," he joked. He chuckled and crooked his fingers twice. "I'll strengthen your internal power limiters. That should give you a little peace of mind."

Dalton placed his hand in Rutu's, but when the demon's fingers closed, a sharp spark shot up Dalton's arm, causing him to pull away quickly with an exclamation of pain. The sharp needle of pain spread through his shoulder and into his chest, radiating through his entire body within seconds.

"What the hell was that?"

"Think of it like a booster shot," Rutu explained. "It's not a permanent strengthening spell, but it should last you about two months, which is more than enough time to find a trainer."

"Can you strengthen them permanently?" Dalton asked hopefully.

"I could stress the spell too much and it might break them," Rutu said, shaking his head.

Juki nodded again. "I think that's everything. New bandages, medications, power limiter..." He turned to Rutu. "Anything else?"

When Rutu shook his head, Juki turned to Frieda.

"We'll get out of your hair, then."

"Thank you both for everything you've done..." Frieda said sincerely, reaching out to take Juki's hand as he approached. "I don't know what we would have done without you."

"We did the easy part," Juki said with a laugh as he held her hand in both of his. "Now you're the one that has to deal with him as a patient."

"Rutu!"

Dalton's sudden address startled the demons, Rutu turning quickly to look at him. "Could...could I ask you something?"

Dalton had not lifted his head, staring at his feet as he spoke, his entire frame tense. Rutu turned to Juki, sharing a short, silent conversation with his mate. The older Kage Lord turned to the others in the room and ushered them out, giving Frieda a reassuring smile as they stepped into the hallway.

When the bedroom door was shut, Rutu turned fully to face Dalton, waiting for him to speak before he approached.

"I-I'm sorry..." Dalton said. "I guess I just...I need..."

"You don't need to apologize."

"I just...I figured, from everything I've heard about you...you could answer something for me."

Rutu smiled thinly. "Has Keito been telling stories about me?" He slowly walked toward Dalton, standing in front of him. "What do you want to ask?"

"...why me?" Dalton murmured, finally lifting his gaze to the demon. "I know it sounds stupid, but...this prophecy, the dragon spirit, this destiny with Yokouro involving all the humans in the realms...I'm just so confused. Does the entire universe really hinge on my fight with Yokouro?"

Rutu's silent and stoic expression made Dalton's heart race, terrified that he was going to confirm Dalton's fears. Instead, Rutu smiled.

"That's a pretty self-centered thing to say, isn't it?"

Dalton blinked, stunned by the answer. Rutu sighed heavily, his eyes falling to the ground.

"No, Dalton. The entire universe does not hinge on your battle with Yokouro. The universe is far bigger and more complex than that. It does not all rest on your shoulders."

"Then why does this have to happen at all?"

"Because that is just the way it is," Rutu said with a shrug. "Destinies are created through a very complex string of events and coincidences. Eventually, circumstances build to the point where a destiny like yours is created to resolve the imbalance. I know it might not feel like it, but your destiny is a very simple one. You fight Yokouro with everything you have, and you win or lose. That's the extent of it."

"But what happens to me will affect all humans," Dalton hissed, his voice weak. "My fight with Yokouro will change *everything*."

"Maybe, but maybe not," Rutu said. "The prophecy of Yasuain and Kuryaoin is quite small in the grand scheme of the universe."

"I just wish I had a clear understanding of what was going to happen," Dalton said. "Isn't there supposed to be some sort of scroll? Or magical tome to tell me about all this?"

Rutu laughed. "As someone who has read the scroll containing the prophecy of these dragon spirits, I can assure you, it would not give you any greater understanding."

"Wait, there *is* a scroll?" Dalton gawked. "I was half-joking."

"Most prophecies are written," Rutu said. "But they're not particularly reliable. There is a reason they are always so vague. The Balance changes constantly."

"Then why write them down at all?"

"Because even though things change, everything occurs in cycles," the demon explained. "If something doesn't line up at a given point in time for the prophecy to play out, then that prophecy applies to the next cycle. Four thousand years ago, just before these realms were connected, the Balance was in prime position for this prophecy to be fulfilled."

"What?" Dalton gasped, his eyes going wide.

"Your ancestor held Kuryaoin four thousand years ago," Rutu elaborated. "But Yokouro cheated in the duel, so the destiny was not fulfilled. And now, it passes to you."

"Was that what caused the realms to collide and what made Vestera place the seal?"

"It was a factor," Rutu admitted. "But there were many more variables that led to these realms coming together. This destiny that you bear now is the start to a greater series of events. Last time, when the realms came together, times were difficult, but as you can see, there is still a human race. Not everything is black and white."

"Then it was just...*time* for this to happen again?"

"Yes."

"That's extremely unfair."

Rutu barked a quiet laugh. "The Balance doesn't discriminate."

Dalton inhaled deeply, looking imploringly at Rutu.

"You're ridiculously powerful, and you seem to know everything, so...you know how this is all going to end, right?"

"I'm afraid I don't," Rutu said gently. "As an oracle, I can only make my best guess."

"What is your best guess?"

"I should think that would be obvious," he said. "After all, I did just spend these last few days making sure that you rallied back stronger than before. I could have stood back and left you to your own devices, but I didn't."

"But I assume you gain something out of this," Dalton muttered. "I know you won't tell me what, but you have to have some other reason for wanting to help me."

"It would benefit me greatly if you won."

"So, if I win, the Balance, or whatever, gets put back in order and everything's alright again?"

"No," Rutu said with a shake of his head. "But, if I told you what is going to happen in the future, regardless of the outcome of your battle with Yokouro, you would probably rip your wounds open again."

"That bad?"

The demon lord hesitated. "Dalton, this may sound harsh, but you are only in this life for a very short time. There is no need to worry about the distant future. Only worry about your life, about being there for your children, and teaching them everything you can. Regardless of anything you do, or anything *I* do, the Balance will right itself in the end. We're all powerless to stop it. It's just the way the universe works."

"I guess you've seen enough to understand things in a way I don't..."

"I've seen quite a lot," he agreed. "And I've seen humans make the same mistakes over and over again. So worried about the distant future they forget to live in the present moment. I would like to see you break at least part of that cycle. Work yourself up about this fight with Yokouro if it's going to help you win. Think about the distant future of your grandchildren and great-grandchildren if that gives you the strength to defeat him. But don't let yourself become obsessed with righting every wrong in the universe, because you will never be able to do it."

"But I should do *something* to at least try and build a better distant future."

"You *are*," Rutu said. "You are doing your part, Dalton. And no one is asking you to do more than that."

"I'm just supposed to focus on Yokouro and then…sit back?"

"Focus on Yokouro, and then *live*," Rutu corrected. "You can continue to help people as a Guardian, or whatever you want to do, as long as you don't forget to live your life and live in the moment. Your time is so finite that you think you have to achieve all these grand things, but the greatest thing you can achieve is to live a good, full life."

Dalton lowered his head, nodding somberly.

"I'll let you in on a secret, Dalton," Rutu said, causing the human to lift his head. "There are a few creatures powerful enough to *shift* things in certain directions to keep the Balance steady and allow life to flourish as it has. All those creatures have been around for millions of years and have seen more than you could ever imagine. But still, they are trying to keep everything in order to allow the human race to grow and thrive."

Rutu smiled mysteriously. "We're on your side. I promise."

Chapter Thirty-Four

Dalton insisted on driving with the Guardians to the portals while the Guardians, Jikia, and Tarrena tried to convince Dalton to stay home and rest. They had been putting off going home for over a week, but finally felt that it was time they left the Teban family so they could get accustomed to the many changes coming their way. They tried to leave as quietly as possible, but Dalton was stubborn about joining them to the Kenburough portal building. He even went to sit in the large van they had taken to the lake, waiting for them until they begrudgingly climbed in. They did, however, manage to convince Dalton that Frieda should drive, since Dalton's leg was still heavily bandaged and the painkillers Juki had given him were "extremely effective," according to a slightly-loopy Dalton.

Dalton did his best to act like his old self, but there were moments when everyone could see that he was struggling to understand his new magic. He tried to explain to them how he was able to see connections between people as though events were happening simultaneously, using the example of looking at Eclipse and seeing his perspective about how the rest of the team reacted to the injury that had blinded him in the previous round. But no matter how he explained it, no one could quite grasp what he was experiencing.

The intensity of Dalton's powers was never more apparent than at the funeral services for Andrew.

There were only a few people present at the service, as Andrew's connections did not extend far outside of Master Bowen's Guardian Training Center. The already dark day had only been soured further by Dalton's fight to get Andrew's name placed on the plaques of Honorable Deaths in the halls of the Guardian Branch. He had been insisting that Andrew had died with all the honors of a Guardian, but his grandfather had shut down the idea, claiming that they could not honor his name without disclosing that he was the first confirmed Guardian to die at Yokouro's hand, which would send the entire branch into an uproar.

The anger Dalton held in his frame through the service permeated through the entire room, causing everyone to clench their fists and grind their teeth without understanding why their sadness was overwhelmed by anger. It was not until Andrew's simple casket was wheeled from the room for cremation and they stepped into the hallway that they noticed how much easier it was to breathe. It did not take them long to figure out that Dalton's emotional distress had triggered his new powers to choke the air out of the room.

The Guardians were struggling with leaving their team leader, knowing that Dalton had an enormous amount of training to do, which would leave his wife and daughter alone a majority of the time. Even though Dalton had lined up a therapist who specialized in working with the families of Guardians, they were hesitant to leave without being certain that Frieda and Theresa were going to be alright.

But eventually, they found themselves outside of the portal building, grabbing their bags from the back of the van as Theresa tearfully hugged all of them, demanding they visit as soon as possible, not caring who in the parking lot saw her tearful goodbye.

Frieda was holding back her own tears as she hugged and thanked each of the Guardians. She was sad to see them go, but she knew that she had to turn the focus on her family and learn how to live with Dalton's new magic while preparing for the new baby. The others of Team Dalton hugged her tightly, thanking her for everything, and telling her that she could call any of them to put Dalton back in his place if he proved to be too stubborn of a patient.

Grumbling irritably about his cane, Dalton limped alongside his teammates to the lobby of the portal building, gathering the team in the corner of the room so he could say goodbye.

"I want to thank all of you, for everything," he said sincerely. "I know that we're still in the thick of all this, but...I don't know what I would have done, what my family would have done, if you weren't here supporting us."

"We're a team," Eclipse said, giving Dalton a quick, one-arm hug. "But take care of yourself because, I swear, if we hear from Frieda that you've been a horrible patient, one of us will show up to give you some new bruises."

Jikia and Tarrena hugged Dalton a little longer, wishing him well and congratulating him on his new baby.

"You two are amazing," he said with a smile. "I really appreciate everything you did for Frieda while I was...incapacitated."

"We did very little, in reality," Jikia said.

"Juki and Rutu did most of the work," Tarrena agreed. "You should mail them a thank-you note."

"Sure," Dalton chuckled. "I'll send them a thank-you text."

"You could," Keito said with a shrug. "They gave you their number."

Dalton rolled his eyes. "I'm not going to do that. Are you crazy? I'm not just going to start texting Juki and Rutu. That's too weird." He drew in a deep breath, looking sheepishly to the ground as his fingers tightened on his cane. "I…don't really know how else to say this, so I'll just say it. I owe you an apology, Keito."

"For what?" the demon asked, confused.

"For jumping down your throat so much when it came to Juki and Rutu," he elaborated. Eclipse also let out a sigh.

"Yeah…we just didn't really understand how you could trust someone who worked for Yokouro," Eclipse grumbled. "I'm not saying I entirely trust them now, or anything, but…we shouldn't have attacked you because we didn't understand."

"No need to apologize," Keito assured with a shake of his head. "Honestly, I'm glad that you're now just as confused as I am when it comes to them."

"It is a small comfort to know that, if things get really bad, they're willing to step in and help," Mitoki agreed. "Because we would have been screwed without them."

"Did they tell you how to find a trainer?" Hanyi asked.

"No, that was one thing they were not at all helpful with," Dalton groaned. "All Rutu said is that I'll likely meet him very soon, whatever that means." He turned to Jikia. "When do you want us all to meet up at your house?"

"Let me check the dates for the next round, and I'll let you know," the older dragon said. "I want a few extra days with you before the fourth round. We're switching from five-on-five fights to one-on-one, so you'll need to brush up on some techniques." She narrowed her eyes playfully at Dalton. "But you listen here. Don't you dare push yourself to train. You wait until you are healed enough to start something that rigorous. Don't cause yourself permanent damage."

"I won't," Dalton assured. "In fact, I plan on taking Frieda car shopping today while Theresa's at soccer practice."

"Remember," Hanyi said, lifting a finger with a mischievous glint in his eyes. "It's Juki's money. Spend all of it and get an awesome car."

Dalton was about to joke with Hanyi, but stopped, remembering that his teammate was returning home to grieve his own loss, something he had not brought up since Dalton had woken. The wolf saw the change in Dalton's expression and his face fell.

"What?"

"Just…if you need anything, or even just need to talk, call me, okay?" he said.

Hanyi took a deep breath, raising his hand again to stop Dalton from continuing. "No. There have been enough tears among this group these past weeks," he said strongly. "Thank you, Dalton, but I'll be fine. And I don't want you focused on anyone other than yourself and your family."

"Okay," Dalton murmured, offering a consoling smile to Hanyi. "But call me if you need me."

Hanyi was the one to rush the rest of the goodbyes, claiming that Dalton needed to get off his feet and rest. They filed toward the portals to the Middle Dimension, fighting against the crowds as they started their journeys home. Dalton watched them until he lost sight of them among the bustling travelers. He then limped his way back to the van, kissing his wife and hugging his daughter.

"Let's go home."

~/\~

Early the next morning, Dalton took a taxi into the city, leaving a note for his family that he was going to the local Guardian Branch office to file some paperwork.

Instead, the cab dropped him off in front of Master Bowen's training center. He stumbled his way out of the vehicle, leaning on his cane as he looked over the large structure, trying to keep his heart from shattering once again as memories of Andrew flooded into his brain. He had done everything in his power not to think about the young man's death in front of his family and teammates, but too often since he had woken had he replayed the moment Acurala's sword dragged across Andrew's neck before plunging into his chest.

Nearly nine years prior, he had been called in to assist on a case that had gone very badly. A cult in a nearby small town had been practicing dark magic, and had been under the observation of four other Guardians, but the first raid of the compound had ended the lives of two Guardians, and severely wounded a third. The cult had vanished, and Dalton had been called in to assist in finding their new location, since the remaining Guardian was worried the cult had disappeared into the large city of Kenburough.

With Dalton's help, a new group of Guardians had raided the new stronghold of the cult, finding most of the missing families dead and mutilated. Once the property had been secured and the cult eliminated, Dalton had followed the sounds of choking to a woman barely clinging to life. She had pointed weakly at a pile of five mutilated bodies, which had Dalton scrambling to get emergency crews in to help any survivors, yelling over his shoulder as he checked the corpses the woman had indicated.

In the middle, covered in blood that was not his own and shaking in terror, Dalton had found Andrew, barely six years old. He had gathered the young boy in his arms and rushed to the woman on the floor, but once she saw her son was safe, she had smiled, thanked Dalton, and breathed her last.

Since that moment, Dalton had felt responsible for Andrew. He looked at Andrew as a son. Dalton was in his early twenties at the time, and had yet to be instated as the top-ranked Guardian, which afforded him more time to check in with Andrew as he healed from his trauma and threw himself into training to be a Guardian. The two had become very close, even as Dalton had met and married Frieda. Andrew had even been at Dalton's wedding.

He had become an extension to the Teban family—a son and Theresa's older brother.

But as Dalton stared at the large building, it felt empty to him, knowing he would not find Andrew within, eager to show off what he had learned that week.

It took Dalton a few minutes to build up the courage to walk inside. The moment he stepped through the security doors beyond the front desk, he heard the sounds of a general defense class in one of the smaller rooms off the main hallway. He peered in the partially-open door, watching the six-year-old trainees practicing their stances for defending against attack.

Continuing down the hall, Dalton passed the classrooms where general classes were taught, allowing Guardians to get an education certificate that equated to a high school diploma. But Dalton always remembered those classes as the ones where he caught up on lost sleep. Judging from the number of heads down on desks as he passed, he figured several of the pre-teens were sleeping through the history lecture.

The familiar halls were easy for him to navigate, though he hurried past the large dome where older trainees were practicing magic. The double doors were open to the domed room, allowing the trainees to spot Dalton and pause what they were doing. They did not approach him, but they watched him with concern as he hurried past and walked into the administrative offices at the back of the training center.

He knocked lightly on a very familiar door and heard the man within call him in a moment later. Master Bowen was seated at his desk, setting down the papers Dalton had drawn his attention from as the Guardian entered the office, closing the door slowly behind him.

"Dalton..."

"I can't keep doing this," he murmured.

"Doing what?" Master Bowen asked, unable to stop his eyes from roving over Dalton's noticeable injuries.

"My entire life, I've felt that there was something wrong with me," Dalton said. "Needless to say, these past months dealing with Yokouro has not helped in the slightest. I know we didn't have a chance to really talk at Andrew's services, but I'm assuming you know what happened to me."

"Yes," Master Bowen confirmed. "You've merged with Kuryaoin's magic."

"But that's not the end of it," Dalton said, sitting heavily in one of the chairs in front of Master Bowen's desk. "Yes, I came out of this alive, but...I need to be assured I will soundly defeat Yokouro. I won't miss out on Theresa's life. And I don't want my next child to come into the world without a father. I want to be there for them. I want them to grow up happy, and safe. I want to grow old with my wife. I want to meet my grandchildren. But I can't do any of that if Yokouro wins this fight. And I can't win against Yokouro as I am now."

Master Bowen leaned back in his seat.

"You're ready to train to master this magic?" he asked. "You're not just saying that?"

"I need to master this," Dalton said strongly.

"What brought about this change of heart?"

"Believe it or not, Rutu."

"Which one is that?"

"The quiet one that sort of looms behind the dark-haired one," Dalton elaborated. "He told me that, no matter what I do, eventually some sort of cataclysmic event will take place. At first I was pissed at him for telling me that...but then I realized that if I win the fight with Yokouro, then that time is long in the future. I'll be long dead and maybe there will be new advancements in humanity by that point to help curb any destruction.

"But if I lose to Yokouro because I was afraid of this magic, as I always have been, then I'll be bringing about that destruction even sooner. But Rutu said that it's not the end of the universe. I'm just another piece in a greater plan and if I do my part to remove Yokouro, that plan will remain in place." He shrugged. "I don't know...it took some of the pressure off. Seeing Juki and Rutu really put things into perspective for me."

"Put things in perspective for me, too, when I met them," Master Bowen agreed, raising his eyebrows. "It made me realize how powerless I really was."

"Exactly," Dalton said. "I don't have the power to radically shift the direction of the universe, even if I have this new dragon magic at my disposal. I only have the power to make it stay as it is. And I like the way things are. I'll like it even more when Yokouro is dead for good."

"I'm very happy to hear that, Dalton," Master Bowen said, standing to walk around his desk. "I know I've said it often, but I think you might actually hear it this time," he laughed. "I'm very proud of you."

"Thank you, Master."

Master Bowen leaned against his desk, crossing his arms.

"I think you're already doing better than you realize when it comes to these new powers," he said. "Why did you come see me today?"

Dalton hesitated before responding.

"I'm...not sure. I just felt compelled to come here and tell you in person. Why?"

"Because I was actually going to visit you today and tell you that your trainer was poking around here looking for you."

"My trainer?" Dalton repeated. "You mean the voice that's been stalking me?"

The older man laughed lightly. "Yes, I suppose that is all you know about him as of now," he admitted. "He told me that Yokouro recently had a power spike of his own, and when he acquired his new power, his first target was your trainer, trying to eliminate those who could help you properly master your new magic. So he had to go into hiding and find a way to get some help from Vestera to keep him hidden from Yokouro."

"Then...he's here somewhere?" Dalton asked.

"He is probably..." There was a soft knock on the office door. Dalton spun around in his chair to look as Master Bowen's smile widened. "Right there. Come in!"

The door creaked open as Dalton pulled himself to his feet, leaning on his cane, feeling oddly apprehensive about meeting his new trainer—someone he had only ever known to be a voice on the edge of his consciousness.

The man who entered was dressed entirely in black, fabric covering his nose and mouth and a hood covering his head, leaving only his green eyes exposed. He was broad, the clothing accenting the muscles of his frame, though he moved very quietly for his size.

He closed the door behind him, never breaking eye contact with Dalton.

"Hello, Dalton," he said. The voice was exactly the same as Dalton remembered from previous encounters, but there was something about the energy the man exuded that made Dalton wonder if he had known the man all his life.

"I'm still not sure how I feel about all this..." Dalton said, studying the trainer cautiously. "You haven't really been around to teach me about this dragon magic stuff so far."

"I would have been there from the moment you had that dream at the cabin," the man said, taking slow steps closer, worried about startling Dalton. "But once Yokouro took the throne of Antiquan, he tried to hunt me down. I have some protection charms from Vestera now, and he was kind enough to give me my body back, temporarily, of course, as once I have finished helping you as much as I am able, I must pass on to the next life."

Dalton had forgotten that the voice had told him that he had been murdered by Yokouro many years previous.

Something was stirring in Dalton's chest, his new magic reaching out with curiosity, searching the man for any familiarity.

"I know you..." Dalton murmured. "You're...familiar."

Though his green eyes showed how nervous he felt doing so, the figure removed the hood from his brown hair and pulled down the fabric covering the rest of his face. Dalton's head went light as he gripped his cane for support, his blood running cold.

Dalton could hardly believe his eyes. The man before him was more than familiar. He had seen his face every day for years in the picture frame on his mother's bedside table—a face that bore a striking resemblance to his own.

His father, William Teban, was standing before him.

"I understand you're finally ready to train," he said. "We better get started."

To Be Continued...

~In~
Dimension Guardian: Realm of Light
Imbalance

More Works by K.J. Amidon | Kyra Anderson

The Dimension Guardian Series:

The Realm of Beasts – The Guardian Tournament
The Realm of Darkness – Blind Ambitions
The Realm of Humans – Fate
The Realm of Light – Imbalance
The Realm of Demons – Scars in Time
The Realm of Exile – Continuum

The Roadside Paradise Series:

Into Oblivion
Wander the Lost
Until Dawn Breaks
Hiding from Sight
For Fools
Challenge Gods

Inside

(Written as Kyra Anderson)
Inside – Pt. 1
Inside – Pt. 2
Inside – Pt. 3
Inside – Alternate Pt. 3
Inside the Commission: Tales from Within
Inside Special Expanded Edition

The Significant

(Written as Kyra Anderson)

The Significant Expanded Story:

(Written as Kyra Anderson)
The Degenerates
The Deserted

The Faith Series:

(Written as Kyra Anderson)
The Faith
The Sacred

The Coalition Series:

(Written as Kyra Anderson)
Forged Under Fire
The Rising Tide
With Banners Raised